Gravity of Sol-3

The Sentinel Suppressions, Book One

JH Gruger

Vox Proxima Press

Book Cover by David Leahey

Library of Congress Control Number: 2024914085

First edition August 2024, second printing

Ebook ISBN: 979-8-9900327-0-5

Print ISBN: 979-8-9900327-1-2

To Keifer and his team

Contents

Chapter 1

CONTACT

The storm of caws—of crows—screams behind my eyes. I jerk my head and punch the pain with my fists.

"Robby, no! Don't do that." My teacher, Margie, pulls my hand away and strokes my ear and head. It feels like she's ripping my hair out. She kisses my head. "Come on, Robby, which is the animal picture?" says Margie. "Do you want more Cheetos?"

No, no. No more school. I can't look at pictures. "Head hurts." I tap my head. But I look away from Margie's eyes and push her away.

"No, Robby. Stay here and do one more picture; then you can have Cheetos."

She pulls me from my beanbag chair into her lap and wraps her arms around my waist, her chin on my head. "No, no." I whip my head back and forth, but the caw-screams still hurt. Margie's lap is warm, her brown hair soft on my cheek and shoulders, but I need to run away into my room.

"Robby! Hold still. Do one more picture, and then we can go in the car." She lays down three pictures next to the Cheeto crumbs on the carpet. "Robby, where is the hammer?"

I stab my fingers at the tool picture.

"Great job, Robby!" She hand-talks by sweeping her fingers at me and says, "All finished." She breathes loudly and lets me go.

I jump to the window, look between the trees into the sun, and shake the screams from my head. Where are the crows—in the sun? Their screeches hurt behind my eyes.

"Robby, get your shoes on, and we'll go to Taco Bell."

I look into Margie's brown eyes. "Go in car." Margie leads the way out of the house. I run from the crows to her car and fasten my seatbelt.

"Go. Taco Bell."

Margie pats my head. "Okay, Robby. What do you want to eat?"

"Three tacos!" I hold three fingers up for her to count.

"Ha." Margie laughs. "Of course."

———

At the restaurant, Margie asks, "Robby, can you help carry the food?" I grab the edge of the orange tray, but she always holds on until we are at the table. "What do you want on the tacos, Robby?"

I scrunch my face to fight the caw-roars and look into her eyes again. "I want hot sauce, please."

"Great job, Robby! Your usual Fire Sauce—here you go." She giggles.

I grab the first taco and bite into it. The burn of hot sauce quiets the screams. I suck the soda straw to wash it down. Another bite. Yum. My nose drips.

Margie jerks when her phone screeches. All the phones are screeching. I cover my ears.

"What in the world?" Margie turns off the phone noise and wrinkles her face at the screen. "What?" All the other people at Taco Bell are holding their phones, looking at each other, and shaking their heads. Margie says, "This can't be . . ."

A man stands and pulls the fat lady next to him from her chair. "Come on, Vera! We need to go—now!" he shouts.

Another lady cries out, "Oh my God! Come on, Billy. We have to go!"

"But Mom, I'm still hungry!"

"Billy, now!" She yanks his hand, which flips his tray over to the floor. Cold red soda splashes on my legs and my new white shoes. Billy cries as the lady pulls him out the door.

Margie's eyes are big and brown and round. Other people run outside. Margie's face is red, and her breath is loud. "Robby, get in the car!" Margie yells and yanks my arm, pulling me out the door.

I cry, "Ow, ow!" I'm scared. The caw-screams hurt behind my eyes. Margie never shouts. I rub the tears on my face. There are two tacos still on the tray. With hot sauce.

Margie lifts me into the back seat. "Robby! Seat belt on!" She slams my door shut and climbs into the driver's seat. The tires squeal, and I jerk backward as the car jumps onto the street. It is scary—but fun! I giggle. The car races, and the engine roars. I slide side to side. Margie drives fast!

The radio screeches, and a man shouts, "Take shelter!"

Is Margie crying?

Some cars go slow, but Margie drives around them. A lady cries in the yellow car, and her hand pounds like a hammer on her seat. A black car screeches and almost crashes into us, but Margie turns away. The tires squeal, the engine roars, and the radio screams.

"Ha-ha!" My best car ride ever.

A flash of bright white, then heat, like a big fire.

I blink until I can see again. The crows are silent.

Margie breathes with a puffing noise, and her face is white with long tears. Cars slide across the highway at us. Margie steers around one car, then another.

I bounce. "Ha-ha!" A fun ride. The eye pain and the radio are quiet. Margie cries. Her breathing puffs.

"No. No. No. Robby. Robby," Margie moans, looking over her shoulder. Behind the hill, a giant ball of orange light grows under fire-black clouds. Margie bends forward and goes around another car, skidding across the highway. The hills bounce, and the car rocks like a horse ride. Thunder booms into my ears. The driver of the big blue truck stares at the ball of fire. Wheels screech, and we jerk sideways. The seat belt hurts my belly.

Crunch! The blue truck smashes, grinds, and groans into Margie's car. We fly off the road. White balloons are everywhere, rolling upside down. My neck hurts. We fall through flying grey dirt and green trees into the canyon. A white rock breaks the glass, the car engine jumps into the front seat, and wires whip my face through the smoke. Then something hot hammers into my head.

Chapter 2

TOXINS

June 2055, five months earlier.

Despite the off-key covers of old Willie Nelson songs, we've been talking for over an hour now at our corner table. Low-quality music repels customers, making this an ideal first-date venue where we can hear each other talk. Cannabis vapors drift through the dark room, but we are just drinking beer.

She laughs, raving about her start-up, market analytics, and customers. She flashes those green eyes, smiling, freckles bright under her red curls, and listens to me rave about physics. This is rare. She seems genuinely interested in my graduate studies—not something I expect from someone with a career pitching products via social media.

"Yeah, Scott, I have heard of him. Didn't Agosti get his Nobel Prize decades ago, before we were born? I figured he was dead already."

"No, he's very much alive and working deep inside the UT research labs and at some remote lab halfway to El Paso. I haven't worked directly with him yet—that starts this fall. He can come off like a crackpot, but Agosti is *the* father of quantum gravitation. He thinks dark matter is composed mainly of the primordial black holes from Stephen Hawking's century-old theory. And dark matter is eighty-five percent of the universe! Agosti says those primordial black holes, which we identify as dark matter, swirl throughout the galaxy and the solar system. They can have a mass of mountains but are only the size of a proton! Most other physicists have discarded primordial black holes as dark matter candidates, but all their alternative theories failed."

"Are black holes really all around us? Why doesn't the Earth get swallowed up inside one?" she asks, frowning, her eyes round.

Impressive—she's still listening and doesn't mind that I'm dominating the conversation.

"They're too small and don't have the gravity for that strong an attraction. They only have the mass of a mountain." I shrug. "And Agosti claims sightings of ball lightning are plasma balls created around primordial black holes by lightning storms."

"And you'll be working with *the* Anthony Agosti?" she asks, still somehow interested.

"I am. And I can't imagine anything more exciting." I'm feeling dizzy with adrenaline. "But I've been talking too much. Can I get you another drink? Another Shiner?" Smiling as I stand, I'm relieved I can still make eye contact with another human. I have isolated myself for too long.

"Yes, thank you." Her eyes sparkle.

I flex my wrist ID chip at the point-of-sale terminal while the bartender pulls the tap handle to fill two glasses. This is going better than I hoped. It is better than the last four first dates I'd gone on. They were either bored by science or closeted fascists. I'd almost given up.

I return and set the cold beers on our wooden table, but her magic emerald eyes have corroded to khaki, glowering in disgust.

"I, uh, gotta go," she says, avoiding my eyes and grabbing her purse. "This ain't gonna work." She grimaces, turning her back to walk away.

"What?" I stand, stunned by the change in her, and reflexively cover my right wrist. She doesn't answer and keeps moving. Could she have scanned me? Probed when my back was turned? My wrist shield is still in the car—wearing one is a red flag. Her red ponytail flicks back and forth across the small of her back as she reaches the door—now bouncing as she hurries westward down Sixth Street—away from a neurodefective with no future.

Here I sit, Scott Anderson, a pariah for the past six years. Alone with two glasses of Shiner Bock. Again. Alone except for family and a couple of schoolmates. My world was wrecked a year after I received the chip implant for my driver's license and credit accounts. The chip was supposed to be the ultimate security key that would make all other credentials obsolete. But fascists use my chip to look up my stolen medical data on the dark web. The database exposes every detail of my private information and genetics to any nearby smartphone. No one—none of the world's cybercrime police—has been able to figure out who hacked and released the world's medical databases, nor have they been able to delete that dark web database. It is infuriating. The eugenicists hate my brother Robby and anyone related to him because we have the wrong genetic markers. We "poison" the human bloodlines.

I rub my face, sighing and doomscrolling my media feed. It seems every other post is a hater venting a conspiracy theory at "neurotards." My only path is to retreat to my physics refuge, keeping my head down and avoiding the haters. For the rest of my life.

I shuffle east toward Dad's old Porsche, leaving the beers behind and avoiding eye contact with the crowd, wandering along a street of carnival lights leading into darkness and the sweltering summer heat. Throngs of pedestrian traffic clog Sixth Street—a cascade of drunks splashing into random bars to sample intoxicants. The air is thick with humidity, a whiff of whiskey, and a mournful blues guitar.

"Skinheads!" The shout and an electric tension ripple through the crowd.

Distant shrieks echo through the dark. I gulp and push my pace to a trot, looking back. A subset of the crowd joins my run to the east. Like fools, we self-select as targets.

My shoe splashes in puddles of beer. Gasping for air and stumbling down a steep curb, my knee crushes into asphalt, my palms scrape, and somebody trips across my foot, thudding into the side of a building. A woman weeps. They are closing in; my car is four blocks away, and I'm exposed. I grasp my wrist where my chip shield should be.

A gust of heat comes from the south as ragged blues sing out, "Try, try, try just a little bit harder . . ." The melody fades.

"No," I gasp. "Never again." Bitch, my blind date was one of them. Every time I try to make a friend, I get punished. I leap over a pothole puddle, staggering into a pain-stabbed landing, and dodge two runners.

I sprint past an alley full of piss stench, past the last shadow, and into the streetlights once more. A few of us have broken into the lead with long strides, grunts of exertion, and hoarse gasps for oxygen. Skinheads with scanners chase us, baying after prey with coyote howls and yelps. I lead the stampede, a whimpering exodus of neurotards. Laser spots dart among us—designators on our backs. Screams echo like sirens, followed by the thud of a club, then another, and another.

My foot skids in dog shit. Arms pump, acid lungs, thighs burn—swinging clubs, hoots, cries, boots, yelps, and jarring moans. It's a brutal frenzy. Blood-red lasers blind my eyes.

A baseball bat crashes into my chest. Lights cartwheel before concrete slams my shoulders and bounces my skull. Dazed, my eyes focus on a club and muscles tattooed with a swastika reaching down from a shaved scalp.

"Fuckin' neurotard." He studies the dysgenic scan report on his screen. Sweat smears his sneer, which curdles to a snarl. "You think you get to keep your balls?" He leans in. "I'm gonna fuckin' kill your ass, or maybe just chop your nuts off," he says, spittle flying.

My white-knuckle fists flail at the weapon shoved into my sternum.

"Hey, Chucky!" He cackles over to a skinhead pack circling their group of whimpering takedowns. "I got me a white boy 'tard!"

"Screw that, man," Chucky jeers. "We got us some gooks!" He kicks a wail from his victim. "Four full-blood gooks!" He thunks his club. The wailing stops.

"God damnit." My attacker hacks phlegm at my eye. His boot kicks my ear before spinning away, stumbling to join the frenzy.

But I hold his bat and yank. The parking lot streetlamps swirl as I roll to my knees. I tighten both hands around the weapon and rise to my feet. My skinhead is on one knee, puzzled that his club is gone.

I wind up with all my strength, swing the bat to connect with his skull—*thunk*—and open a gash across his shaved scalp. His eyes wobble at the streetlights, and he flops to the pavement with his swastika-tattooed arm crumpled under his torso. Blood oozes from his ear.

I turn toward Chucky and two other skinheads flailing clubs at their victims—teenage Asian kids who scream and wail under each thunk.

"No! No!" I shout, tears streaming down my cheeks. My bat is a thrashing scythe, cutting into the stunned thugs. "God damn you! No! No! Damn you!"

One of the skinheads falls to the ground, but the other two collect their wits and weapons. "You fucker! Neurotard! We gonna kill your ass!" Chucky screams.

Two practiced killers against one skinny physicist. Our clubs crack together, but they land blow after blow. The metallic taste of blood is replaced by vomit. I back away, fanning my bat at them, gasping for breath at each stroke, my muscles burning from exertion and wounds.

The forgotten teenagers whimper in horror, watching my retreat. Two scramble to their feet, dragging a third victim away. The fourth, a girl with black hair twisted over her face, lies still in the gutter.

Sirens approach. Flashing blue and red lights up the night.

"Ah, damn it!" screams Chucky, swinging his club for a final crack against my bat. "We'll come looking for you, fuckin' cockroach!" He glances down at his two fallen comrades, hesitates, but spins to sprint away with the surviving attackers, disappearing down a black alley.

Police cars stream down the street, dodging victims, chasing skinheads, lights flashing, sirens wailing. I stumble to one knee, breathing hard, and realize a weapon in my hand is a bad look. I drop the bat and stagger over to the girl lying still. She has a pulse, but her breathing bubbles through the blood pouring from her nose. I wave at the ambulances arriving on Sixth Street and finally get the attention of a paramedic, who runs toward us with her medical kit. The medic pushes me aside to work on clearing the girl's airway and fitting her with an oxygen mask.

I back away, fall to my knees, crawl, push up, and stumble east past an ambulance cluster tended by blue-smocked EMTs. I'm not that bad off; not compared to the others. The streetlights tilt. I rest against my car before guiding myself to the driver's door. I yank the handle, swinging the door wide, and collapse into my seat. The turbocharged Porsche roars, and I pull through the parking lot. The slaughter scene in the mirror recedes as I sink into the acceleration and steer onto the freeway.

Each breath rips through my chest, daggers of pain spiking me with every gasp. The Porsche coasts, and a blue sign swoons above me: *"Hospital Next Exit."* An island of hope.

Chapter 3

SENTINELS

Captain's Log, Frigate-328, 179231.25
Luyten Standard Time

Why couldn't the bots leave me alone? Cracked out of my dormancy pod for what? And in this remote star system?

I wasn't supposed to be revived. But, of course, the bots always get confused. They ripped me out of dream euphoria into this old junk, and I managed to guide my wobbly legs through the ship onto the bridge.

The control surfaces have a film of dust and mold like they haven't been touched in eons. And the gas stinks of metallic dust. The viewports are almost useless due to all the particle impact damage—the old frigate's deflectors don't prevent all collision effects on the hull. But the Order-X star, Sol, is visible through the window—a hot yellow color, tiny from this distance. It's depressing compared to the grand red-orange sun of home. The target, Sol-3, has a lazy orbit that takes twenty times longer than Luyten-2 around my home star. Amazing. But somehow, life thrives on these Class-6 planets.

So much time has passed; 4,359 Luyten-2 orbits have been lost to dormancy and time dilation. My family and everyone

I once knew have decayed into the sea. Will their descendants have any knowledge of me, or am I merely a criminal lost in historical footnotes? The two hundred other organic crew stuffed into dormancy pods are little more than forgotten baggage transferred aboard from Luyten penitentiary cells. The dozen bots driving this old frigate mean even less to me.

I am all alone.

Our time-of-flight to the Sol System from Luyten Base required 266 Luyten orbits (77 ship time orbits). This frigate is an old second-gen patrol ship, but I guess it was the nearest stardrive Centauri Command could find for the mission. At least the AI crew was upgraded with neural images from Mark-5 gen machines, but all this hardware is ancient stuff. It was just my bad luck I got rotated in as the captain.

Frigate-328 was ordered on this Sentinel Mission to enforce Article Three of the Galactic Congress Containment and Nonproliferation Protocols. A3GCCNPP—a euphemism for imperial subjugation—ensures that rogue civilizations never acquire the power to challenge the galactic authority. But why should I care? The Centauri Command orders doom me to an eternity of watching. I will die here of old age while the ship AIs monitor that lonely blue-white rock. The euphoric dreams in my pod are my only escape, but they make me work for it.

Mission status data looks typical, though. Neutering another organic cluster should require a few thousand Luyten orbits. So, what went wrong to trigger my wake-up call? Prime-AI reports the bot collective under its command continues to function normally; Mil-AI, Maint-AI, Thrust-AI, and Life-AI are in good working order. Sensor drone gamma-ray spectrographs determined the locations of 523 nuclear fission generators and two primitive fusion generators on Sol-3. Sensors detected no weapon detonation gamma-ray bursts like those that Centauri Command must have received 1,800 Luyten orbits ago. Those first Sol-3 atom bombs got them noticed. Fortunately for the indigenous organics, no Gravi-Tech radiation signatures have been detected. Prime-AI still has Mil-AI on standby, but why did it wake me from my euphoria feed?

Polit-AI, the only bot not under Prime-AI's command, took control of all 1,024 infiltration drones to suppress the telepathy function detected in 1.2 percent of the developed organic forms. The trait is immature, and the telepaths are not self-aware. The drones emit the mind-squawk torment to inhibit the telepaths' survival rate. The bot also deployed active cultural attacks by infecting Sol-3's social networks with eugenic stimuli targeting the neurodivergent organics. However, the attack affected widespread xenophobia—over a third of the Sol-3 population is now under threat because of the highly sloppy suppression attack. Polit-AI's lack of discipline will lead to excessive organic pruning.

However, Prime-AI must have taken exception when Polit-AI decided Sol-3 Gravi-Tech was not a threat and confiscated all infiltration drones for cultural suppression tasks. This must be why I was awakened. Prime-AI can't fix this Gravi-Tech suppression neglect without authority over Polit-AI and the political division.

Which means I'll have to revive the Commissar.

But what is the point of preserving an organic cluster on this remote planet after we retard their evolution and creativity? It would be much easier and quicker to back away to the rim of the Sol system and launch planet killers—a few Gravi-Tech missiles would instantly exterminate all the vermin.

Damnit. Negotiation with political division is not one of my strengths. My last screwup got me tossed into jail. Forever.

Chapter 4

BREAKING AWAY

Driving past the towering supercomputer center of the Austin Research Center fills me with optimism. The beauty of brutalist architecture is inspiring, even breathtaking, although chest cramps limit me to shallow breaths. My summer of convalescence has yet to mend the broken ribs. Venturing out away from my shelter at home is a thrill, especially since I'll be diving into gravitational physics research, where I can ignore the fascists. Academia is a place where intellectuals and scientists test ideas through debate, logic, and experiments, and it is also an escape from mindless social chatter—a safe place. I bet half the grad school students are introverts on the spectrum or in the targeted races—and I know for sure there are a bunch of neurodivergents in the PhD program.

But the attraction of new architecture and construction gives way to older buildings nearer my destination. Ahead, stenciled block letters on the rusty door advertise the Center for Dark Matter Research. The rotting burnt-orange eaves have holes that spill mold-matted fiberglass insulation. They could have scrawled their sign on the dumpster, and it would not have hurt first impressions. A century of frustrated

Nobel Prize ambitions had ravaged these buildings, as fools consumed dollars in futile glory hunts. Bizarre concoctions of metals, plastics, and electronics—tools scientists dreamed would lead to discovery and fame—decay in the nearby fields and abandoned parking lots. Mine tailings after a gold-rush bust. Has Dr. Agosti fallen so far that he has no support? Have dreams of a scientific utopia deluded me?

I turn into a parking space near the dumpster. My classic thirty-year-old car is a throwback to a decades-past era of gas engines, the throttle still a potent adrenaline stimulant for me. I step out from a cockpit of golden leather, stroke the polished metallic blue as the door closes, and trudge through the alley's trash, grease, and dirt, assaulted by the sweet rot of garbage.

I open the door into a small vestibule, and a gush of frigid air welcomes me inside from the August heat. The video camera watches while I call the number posted on the inner door. "Security," says the lady on the other end. I sigh while extending my arm to the entry terminal, clenching my fist to send a key from my ID chip to grant access to my security files. Anxiety churns my gut—not out of concern for my security profile, but because she may be one of them. I have been even more of a recluse since that night—hiding from the fascists with Robby. They got my ID info from the scans, and I've spent every day since then wondering if they'd show up at my door to finish the job—both on me and my family.

The light flashes green, the door buzzes open, and I exhale.

Neatly trimmed brown hair and penetrating eyes look up at me. Heinrich does not smile. "Come on in. I'll introduce you to Dan," he says in a dull monotone. We pass down a narrow hallway leading to a football-field-sized space. Our footsteps echo from concrete floors to ten-meter ceilings. Water stains streak the walls with what appears to be toxic black mold. The vast room is like a factory with assembly and test equipment in work areas spaced every ten meters.

I sneeze at the musty stink of machine oil, burned electrical insulation, and mildew.

Heinrich ignores my shirt-sleeve nose wipe. "We use this factory area to assemble most of our prototype test equipment for the PBH project. We took over the building when we got the DARPA funding two years ago—it used to house the DARPA rail gun research back in the 1980s." Walking down the center hallway outlined by yellow safety stripes, Heinrich points ahead at the other end of the building. "Down there is the original fifty-meter-deep vertical test range for rail guns. Ancient history, though. All the work was transferred to military contractors when rail guns went into production for navy ships. We have moved in tons of equipment to study primordial black holes. Of course, we must first capture and contain a PBH." He raises his eyebrows.

"You expect to bring black holes into *this* lab? In Austin?"

"Yes." Heinrich shrugs. "Someday."

He seems way too nonchalant. The general public would be scared shitless if told a black hole was around the corner from their home. But I remind myself that a tiny PBH is nothing like the famous supermassive black holes that swallow star systems. I imagine holding a PBH with the mass of a mountain between my fingers, except the proton-sized singularity would pass right through my hand. I wonder if I would even feel it. How would they find a PBH and transport it to this Austin lab?

"Impressive," I lie. This place looks like an abandoned museum. "Some of this looks, uh, old. But this," I say, passing an area with three men at work, "looks pretty exotic. What are they assembling, a voltage multiplier stack?"

Heinrich nods. "Yes. That's a forty-stage C-W multiplier, and where you'll get started." He points to one of the work areas and waves at a short, chubby guy. "Here he is, Danny. Meet your new assistant, Scott Anderson. I'll leave him with you."

Dan unstraps his tool belt, talks briefly to the three other guys working with him, and walks over.

I force a smile and examine his face for prejudice while trying to avoid eye contact. "Hi, Dan."

"Everybody calls me Danny. Let me show you around." There are no signs he will try a dysgenic scan—yet. "This is a Cockroft-Walton voltage multiplier. We built a bunch of these. Generate fifty megavolts each."

My eyes snap up for a closer look. "Dangerous. Those multiplier stages are tiny. Are you using superconductor materials for the diodes and capacitors?"

"Yep. We fabricate the liquid nitrogen manifolds at the other end of the factory." Danny points his chin toward the far end of the factory floor near the rail gun test range. "Those five-axis milling machines were just gathering dust until we put them to good use."

"So these C-W multipliers have something to do with Agosti's theories on primordial black holes?" I run my hand down the length of the C-W multiplier lying horizontally along a workbench.

"They are a key piece. Wait till you see our grid—a giant wire net we hoist thirty-seven meters into the air on fiberglass towers. These C-W stacks charge that net to near fifty megavolts." Danny grins, a playful twinkle in his eyes. "We start with this insulated manifold core that distributes liquid nitrogen to each stage—I like to think of it as a giant centipede. We bolt these superconducting components of diodes and capacitors into forty slots along the skeleton and pump liquid nitrogen in to cool them to seventy-seven degrees Kelvin. Hook five hundred kilovolts from the power grid into the head, and we get over fifty megavolts out of the centipede's tail." With a gleam in his eyes, he hooks his thumbs in his belt. "It's fuckin' wicked."

"It's just a tool," says a graveled Italian accent from behind. I turn and face the notorious Dr. Anthony Agosti. Coke-bottle lenses in wire rims hook over the nose of a weathered face topped with spiky, short hair. The frayed cuffs of his jeans drag on the floor over leather sandals. If I saw him on the street, I would take him for a vagrant. "Can you guess how we use it?" he teases.

I look away, unsure if I can trust these strangers, and examine the C-W stack. "Uh, well, not sure," I mumble.

Agosti grimaces. "Go ahead, take a guess."

"Well . . . the high voltage induces ball lightning wrapped around a primordial black hole?" Seeing Anthony tilt his head, I continue, "These C-W multipliers emulate the lightning strikes associated with ball lightning events?" I raise an eyebrow. "But I haven't found any science on this. You have some theories that explain?"

Anthony beams. "You won't find explanations in the published literature. I've been working on this for the past fifteen years." He smiles and folds his arms, clearly finished yielding information.

Heinrich returns, deep furrows in his brow, and nudges Dr. Agosti, pointing to a display on his iPad. His skill with nonchalant dysgenic scans is only average—way too obvious, aligning the iPad's RFID antenna to point at the chip embedded in my wrist. Heinrich's eyes narrow while he plants his tongue in his cheek and rotates his head. The familiar eugenic scowl darkens his face, and I feel the chill of fear—again. I imagine he glares at dead animals the way he's now looking at me. Heinrich is one of them.

"Look. This is challenging, hands-on work requiring competence and long hours. You would be in over your head. We don't need *your* kind here," Heinrich says.

Pompous son of a bitch. I visualize my fist shattering that nose, sinking into an eye socket, and blood spattering. But that would be an abrupt end to my internship. My jaw grinds, my pulse throbs in my ears, and my armpits sweat. My fists clench behind my back.

"You need to leave, cockroach. Now," snarls Heinrich.

Agosti turns on Heinrich with a frowning eye-roll. "You're way out of line." He shakes his head. "Put that stupid thing away. We don't have time for this bullshit. Scott has all the credentials to make a fine research assistant."

Danny blushes. "Uh, follow me, and I'll get you set up so you can assemble and test your first fifty-megavolt C-W multiplier," he says with an awkward smile, leading me away from Heinrich.

My eyes are locked with Heinrich's while Agosti points angrily toward the office, growling instructions at him. I force myself to turn and follow Danny, relieved that Dr. Agosti seems to be a supporter.

Still, I can't get Heinrich's hate out of my mind. Once again, I'm attacked by the dark web and eugenic Nazis bent on purging the planet of neurodefectives—nerds that profit off the working class. But Heinrich is a physicist, not working class, and tolerates the Asian guys here building C-W multipliers. What triggers the hate for me in Heinrich?

How can I work for this fascist? I'm trapped. Everywhere I turn, I find *them*. I have only found peace hiding out at home or in most classrooms. And now my hope of an academic utopia studying under Dr. Agosti is threatened.

That disastrous hook-up attempt on Sixth Street was only two months ago. Of the dozens of victims sent to the hospital, two died. I wince, touching the still-tender ribs.

Robby's back is to me while I observe from our game room doorway. His therapist's determined face glances at me, eyes twinkling. She has Robby propped up in his beanbag chair, dealing from a stack of picture flashcards six at a time. "Robby, point to the animals."

Robby looks for a few seconds, taps two cards, and looks up at Margie's face expectantly.

"Good job, Robby!" Margie rewards Robby with sparkling eyes and a Cheeto, which he gobbles. "Robby, can you say *animal*?"

Robby responds with slow, distorted syllables, "Ah-nim-ahl." He looks again at Margie.

"Great, Robby!" Margie rewards him with another Cheeto. Robby beams, and Margie quickly selects the two animal pictures and points to the first. "This animal's name is . . . ?"

"Li-on." Robby fills in the blank correctly.

"Yes! Good job. Robby gets a Cheeto!" Margie cheers. She looks at me, eyes glistening, as she hands Robby his reward.

Margie deals six more cards. "Robby, point to the tools." Robby is on a roll, and she wants to keep the momentum. He successfully taps the three tools in the sequence of cards, and the lesson continues. Margie will try to keep this up until Robby gets tired or when he is full of Cheetos.

Margie is beautiful, focused on the task with my nine-year-old brother, her brown hair pulled back in a tight ponytail, with a tanned face and sparkling brown eyes. She sits cross-legged on the floor across from Robby, her bare feet exposed beneath her blue jeans.

I stop myself. What am I thinking? Margie is here for Robby. We dated a few times a year ago but broke it off before things got serious. Not only did I doubt she would want close involvement with a neurodefective like me, but I also worried a serious breakup might drive her away from working with Robby. She is rare among the dozen other student therapists. Most struggle, but Margie is confident and effective.

Suddenly, Margie says, "Scott is here!" Robby jumps up. "All finished, Robby. Go play with Scott!" Robby spins around to see me standing behind him. Margie has a mischievous grin for me.

I bend, arms outstretched. "Give me a big hug." Robby cringes, but I go to my knee and grab him anyway. Mom says he looks almost exactly like I did at this age: two feet shorter but with the same dark curly hair and brown eyes.

Robby twists away, tactile defensiveness overpowering him. But he yanks my arm and yells, "Tools! Work! Tools." Margie laughs while Robby pulls me toward the garage.

She admonishes me with a shake of her head. "You know, you are reinforcing his destructive behaviors. I swear he breaks stuff just to do repair projects with you." She smirks. "I'm not sure who enjoys it more, you or your brother."

I shrug. "I'm just encouraging Robby's spontaneous language."

She rolls her eyes and shakes her head. "Sure, you are." She sighs. "Go ahead, you two. Have fun." She chuckles, stowing school supplies while Robby and I gather tools and screws from the garage for repairs.

Fifteen minutes later, Robby sits in my lap as I let him fasten a hinge screw with a power screwdriver. He is elated by the growling vibration of the electric tool in his hands while I ensure he doesn't get carried away or hurt himself. Finally, the last of the credenza doors is restored—good as new.

Margie watches us, smiling. "Well, I need to get going now." She yells to Mom in the kitchen, "Bye, Mrs. Anderson! I need to go now. Robby did great today."

"Okay, Margie. Thanks," says Mom. "See you next Monday. Three p.m. when Robby gets off the school bus?"

"Yep, see you then." As Mom walks her to the door, Margie looks back at me, "Bye, Robby. Bye, Scott." She hesitates and smiles, holding her gaze on me longer than needed. The warmth of trust and respect in eye contact with another human is rare. I can't suppress my smile or feelings as Margie steps into the evening, light filtering through oak trees.

Maybe I should call her again . . . but, no. I let it go.

"Bring Robby in. Food's on the table," says Mom as she pours a tall cup of soda for Robby. "I made dinner for just the two of you tonight."

There are only two places set at the table. "I thought we were going to eat together?" I help Robby into his chair and load his plate with chicken, broccoli, and some buttered corn. Robby squeezes a dose of murderously hot sriracha sauce onto the chicken and dives in as if he hasn't eaten all day. "Where are you going?"

"Oh, I'm just going out to dinner with a friend. You can stay and babysit Robby?" she tells me more than asking as she hurries into her bedroom. "I need to get ready. I'm running late."

"Well, yeah. I guess I'll have to stay." But she is out of the room already, and it is a free meal. Famished, I dig into my dinner. We eat our dinners together in silence. Robby spoons a second helping of broccoli onto his plate and adds another squirt of sriracha sauce.

"Okay," says Mom, "you'll need to give Robby his bath and put him to bed. I won't be home till around eleven tonight." Perfume wafts into the kitchen, overpowering the oily smell of fried chicken while she hurries to the garage.

I look up from my vanishing plate of food as she passes. "Mom!" She removed the scarf from her head. "What? You have blonde hair!" She blushes through the thick makeup, and her dress has a low cut that showcases her cleavage.

She opens her mouth to respond, stops, then says, "Uh, okay, guys. I'm going. Take care."

Gawking at her, I ask, "Are you going on a date?"

Her blush changes to a frown. "I'm just going out with friends."

"You're meeting a guy for a date? And you've been divorced just two months. What are you doing?"

Robby bangs a fork on the table.

"You are not one to judge me. I'm going to live my life again," she says with a voice tinged by pain.

Robby bends the fork in half like it's made of clay before throwing it to the floor. Blood oozes where the fork cut into his hand.

"Well, my mom, the cougar." My face feels hot. I stare at her, mouth open. "Mom . . ." Robby runs from the kitchen.

"Don't you dare talk to me that way!" she yells, turning away and slamming the door into the garage.

She didn't even say goodbye to Robby. He leans into the back patio door, twisting the handle. "Open lock. Open door." He garbles syllables and sign language. I sigh and release the deadbolt; Robby launches out to the back yard.

Beyond the patio, the sky blazes with the summer sun. I hear Mom's car crunch in the gravel down the front driveway. Robby's bare feet trot down a sidewalk burning with absorbed sunlight. Scattered pink oleander shadows provide little relief. Sunlight streams over the terra-cotta roof, through the wrought iron fence, and into the pool of crystal blue water. Sand hornets launch from their burrow to strafe Robby as he reaches the shaded lawn, his agitation fading with the wind-birds-leaves-insects thrum. He finds his fort of limestone rocks in the oak-shaded garden. I take my spot and sink into warm dirt. The heat cooks up a sweat, creating a muddy film on Robby's skin.

I sit, staring at my withdrawn, now silent brother. Maybe the eugenicists are right. If our genes got cleansed from the human pool, no one would have to carry this burden again. Should I opt out and follow Dad's escape path of Sterile Registration? The skinheads ignore those who either don't have the damning genetic traits or the cowards who have surrendered to sterilization. Robby is doomed to an isolated, tortured life, will be a burden forever, and will never contribute to society. Mom and Dad fought over him constantly until it ripped their marriage apart. But that didn't solve anything. Mom is struggling to escape the situation, and I can't blame her. Dad travels the world for his work, dodges the eugenicists with his sterilization, and only sees us on weekends. Does Mom realize she is destroying my life by dumping Robby on me in her frantic attempts to escape from reality?

Eugenics could make all this go away—for future others. Maybe I should surrender. Even though I don't have Robby's disability, the hate trolls blame us for their poverty. They hate Robby for the cost of the socialist entitlements he needs to survive. And they hate that I may produce offspring like Robby and for being one of the nerds who manipulate their lives with baffling technologies. But I am not ready to follow Dad's escape path. That would stop the attacks on me, but what about Robby?

The Austin sauna is mind-numbing. Wavy hair transforms into tight curls where moisture rolls down our foreheads. Robby's stones surround him, and he reaches for his favorite tool. White limestone chunks have the comfort of soft edges and perfect heft in his hand. With an unfocused gaze, he taps the stone tool on a boulder, then strikes the boulder with force. *Tap, tap, tap . . . whack.* Corners of rock dissolve into chalk dust. Fire ants patrol. Sand hornets hunt. Cicadas roar. *Tap, tap, tap . . . whack . . .*

Chapter 5

COMMISSAR

Captain's Log, Frigate-328, 179233.98 LST

Sparing eleven million neurodivergents on Sol-3 is out of the question. The political division prioritizes telepathic nonproliferation above everything else, including Gravi-Tech prevention. The horrors of rebels vaporizing planets, armed with telepathy and Gravi-Tech, are burned into our genetic memories, even though that was over twenty thousand Luyten orbits ago.

The Commissar staggered through the hatch to the bridge, looking like shit and throwing a vulgar mind image at me while plopping into the hammock at the Polit-AI console. But she quickly relaxed into a giddy state while mind-sorting through the Polit-AI logs, absorbing the status of infiltration and attacks into the Sol-3 social networks. The cultural suppression arts benefit from thousands of prior interdictions that shape newfound organic cultures into galactic compliance. This attack has been vicious and overly effective. The Sol-3 organics were so damn gullible. Easily triggered to hate and isolate the organics with the telepathy trait and then recruited to deploy the indigenous eugenic processes to kill them off. But it will take generations to eradicate that genetic strain. The Frigate-328 AI crew has infinite patience, and my organic crew won't care while fed their euphoria streams, resting dormant inside the pods.

The repeated trauma, the slaughter of suppression, is the only proven way to prevent the horrors of our memories.

Chapter 6

PECOS

I escape the Chihuahuan Desert furnace and adjust to the frigid air and dim interior. A wall of glass contains two dozen old Steelcase cubicles, and beyond is a control room with workstation consoles, wall-sized video displays, and floor-to-ceiling windows that reveal the flat desert under the grid. Filaments of wire mesh are suspended thirty meters above towers arranged like a hundred-acre chessboard in the desert.

"Well, the roach crawls in. I see you found your way and survived the drive." Heinrich sneers, shaking his head, his computer on his left arm, while he walks toward me. "I bet you've got a million questions," he says before smirking and turning his back to me. "Show him around, Dan."

Danny points his chin to the exit. "Let's start outside while there's daylight. It's still damn hot, but you'll get used to it. Come on." He hurries me through the door to help me escape the confrontation with Heinrich. We load into a Chevy pickup, and Danny bounces the four-wheel-drive through ruts around creosote brush, prickly cacti, and rocks. But when we drive under the grid, plants are transformed into charred residue.

"Looks like you guys burned the brush to clear the ground under the grid . . . or do plants get burned by high-voltage arcs down from the grid?"

"It can get exciting when we power up a new grid section over untouched land." Danny chuckles, an evil smile on his face. "We vaporize everything under the grid." He deftly unscrews the cap off a water bottle and chugs it one-handed, his left hand guiding the wheel as the Chevy bounces toward a Cockroft-Walton multiplier stack. "Nothin fuckin' survives." He slams the brakes and jumps out of the truck. "This C-W stack is just like the one you assembled in Austin."

I bend back to look toward the top of the C-W stack. Positioned next to one of the curved tension poles, it looks like a centipede standing on its head.

"The wire grid is laid out on squares with thirty-seven-meter-tall fiberglass towers spaced every two hundred meters and with tension towers that angle out along the four sides of the grid," Danny explains. "The concept is simple, but a bitch to assemble thirty-seven meters in the sky. We bend the side tension towers straight up and use construction drones to lower prewired collar assemblies onto the top of each tower. When we release the tension towers, they bend back outward and pull the wires tight."

I shuffle through the dust around the C-W stack toward the power substation with cables connecting to a high-voltage Texas utility tower. "How long did it take you to build this?"

"Almost ten years. It's been a blast. Even when we had only a double-wide trailer and two C-W generators—before we got the big bucks from Uncle Sam. Tiny compared to this." He spreads his arm out to the grandeur of wire fabric floating above us.

CH-CH-CH-CH. CH-CH—

"Stop! Don't move!" Danny yells.

CH-CH-CH. CH-CH—

I halt as ordered. Danny backs slowly toward the truck. "What?" I'm not close enough to the power cables to be in danger. "Where are you going?"

Danny turns and runs to the truck, flings open the rear door, and returns carrying a shotgun. With a click and a snap, he inserts a shell into the breech and raises the gun at me.

"What the hell?" He aims right at me, pressing the sight to his cheek. "Whoa, whoa!" I raise my hands to Danny.

"Rattlesnake. Don't move!" he shouts, stepping closer to me.

I look down and flinch. Diamondback. It's coiled in the shade, moving slowly next to the C-W stack. "Oh, shit." The snake's head is in an attack position a meter away from my exposed ankles, its rattle shaking above the coiled spring of reptilian muscle, ready to strike.

CH-CH-CH-CH. CH-CH—

The snake adjusts its aim while flicking its tongue at me. I should stay still, but it's going to strike! I flex my legs to jump away.

Blam! Click, snap. Blam! Click, snap.

I leap as far as possible and twist to see snake flesh and blood scatter around my feet. My ears buzz with ringing.

"He won't be bothering you anymore." Danny ejects the third unspent shell from the smoking breech and cradles the shotgun over his left arm. He kneels and stretches out the rattler carcass to almost two meters. "Hmm, *Crotalus atrox,* a big one." He flips open a pocketknife and slices the rattle from the tail. "Want a souvenir?" He inspects it. "Cool. Here, catch." Danny tosses the rattle.

I dodge and let it fall to the dust.

"He was just sayin', 'Howdy, welcome to Pecos.'" Danny grimaces at my bare legs, shorts, and sneakers, shaking his head. "Boy, you gonna need some decent boots. This is Texas, not New York City."

I take a deep breath and look at my naked shins, embarrassment replacing the panic.

Danny smirks. "Yep, we need thick leather to protect from the critters 'round here."

"Well, I owe you a beer. You're quite the gunslinger."

"No problem, man. Got lots of practice with the shotgun over the years—the rattlesnakes are everywhere." He chuckles. "I'll take you up on that beer. Let's head back into the AC. It's getting late. Enough excitement for now." He turns to the truck while I bend down to pluck the rattle from the dust.

I exhale and tuck the bloody tail into my pocket. I scan the ground left and right with each step back to the truck.

———

On the horizon, a trail of dust follows an antique Ford F-150 pickup. The faded blue rust bucket rolls down the service road, kicking up dust as it turns in and brakes to a stop. The radio blasts Waylon Jennings's "Good Hearted Woman" out the rolled-down windows as the white dust rolls over us, and out jumps Dr. Anthony Agosti, looking like the town drunk from a 1960s cowboy movie.

Lifting his hat, Anthony dusts himself with the floppy Stetson. "Hey, guys. Ready to resume testing tonight?"

"Yeah, we'll be ready. Should be a good night." Danny's evil grin is back.

"I swear, you live for this. What a pyromaniac." Anthony shakes his head. "Scott, how're you doing? Heinrich and Danny working you hard?"

"Danny is a slave driver," I say with a smirk. I have had nothing to do with Heinrich for weeks.

"Great," Anthony says, preoccupied with inspecting the grid wires. He turns away, eyes up. "You'll be happy to learn your top secret clearance came in. Colonel McMahon pushed it through in record time."

"At last! I've got a hundred questions. Returning to physics will be great—not that I haven't enjoyed the fieldwork." I smile again at Danny.

"As soon as you and Danny finish with the nitrogen pump, let's take a final drive around the perimeter before the power test. We can talk more then." Anthony continues down the grid row, eyes up, studying every detail to ensure his wire net is ready while Danny and I prime a new nitrogen pump for service.

At last, Anthony finishes his inspection tour. I jump into the passenger seat, kicking aside the trash pile of greasy Whataburger wrappings, while he climbs into the Ford's driver seat, depresses the clutch, and starts the engine with a broken muffler rumble. We roll ahead with the four-wheel-drive kicking rocks and trailing dust, bouncing down the narrow track around the perimeter.

"We'll take it slow. Keep an eye out to be sure we have the brush cut back to under a meter high," Anthony says.

"The crew cleared the brush under the new grid section last week. I think they got it all." My no-security-clearance quarantine is over, and I blurt out my first burning question, "Why do you keep searching for primordial black holes if you haven't found one in twelve years?"

Anthony frowns. "Well, that's why we increase the grid size." He is preoccupied with inspecting piles of chopped brush under the row of new grid wires.

"But Hawking predicted only one PBH within the solar system. Your theory predicts over a billion in Earth's orbit?"

He shakes his head, eyes still checking the height of brush piles. "Hawking's eighty-year-old math has no empirical validation. He was wrong on several counts. And to his credit, he would confess some of his mistakes." We bump along the road as he steers around rocks and chopped piles of branches, and I make a note to avoid future references to competing Nobel laureates.

"You sound like the DARPA science bureaucrats. They're like flat-earthers pontificating on the foolishness of quantum mechanics. Why waste time with those Luddites?"

Yep, I struck a raw nerve. Is Anthony going to categorize me as one of those flat-earthers?

"When we get back to the control center, I'll get you access to our classified research wiki, where you can read up on the theories and the math."

Whew. Anthony is cutting me some slack.

"Hawking's assumptions for PBH distributions in the universe were wrong. All wrong. Dark matter is eighty-five percent of our universe and, like all other matter, got swept into galaxies and star systems by gravitational forces. We can prove that each star system forms rings of PBH singularities in orbits aligned with the star's planets and asteroid belts." But he sounds worried—maybe because he has been trying to prove this statement for twelve years without success.

The implications of his theory hit me; they're stunning. "But if we have a billion PBHs in Earth's orbit, we should be constantly bombarded by black holes!"

"Obviously," he mumbles.

"But primordial black holes would eventually get noticed after they go through Hawking radiation evaporation. After the mass reduces below a certain point, the gravitational force would no longer hold a PBH together as a singularity. Then, according to Hawking, it would detonate with a million-megaton explosion. Just one of those events would destroy Earth."

"Well, we're still here, aren't we?" The Ford slows while he looks to the ground and then slams on the brakes. "We need to fix that." He gestures out his window, shuts off the engine, and jumps out of the truck. He walks toward a stack of creosote brush about two meters high.

I follow Anthony in his trail of dust. The wind blew a stack of the cut brush against a grid support tower. High-voltage arcs could ignite a bonfire, forcing us to shut down to avoid collateral damage. The sweat trickles down my forehead when I look at the wire mesh above—Anthony's PBH capture tool.

"But why didn't gravity suck all the primordial black holes in our vicinity into the Earth's core a billion years ago?"

"Well . . . go back to basics." Anthony's grimace suggests I just asked a stupid question. He grabs some of the brush, protected by the leather gloves he fished from his hip pocket.

"Visible matter aggregates itself into objects like planets because mass with volume and friction makes normal matter clump together. A primordial black hole can zip through the Earth, like neutrinos passing through us. A PBH the size of a proton has near-zero friction."

Of course. But I get queasy with the thought of a mountain-mass particle flying through Earth—and my body—even though I know a PBH is a billionth the diameter of an acupuncture needle.

Anthony tugs at a fat creosote limb and backs away from the tower. The brush protests, sending chills up my spine. *CH-CH-CH-CH. CH-CH-CH—*

Anthony stops, studying the ground around his feet. "The relatively large mass of the Earth stirs our PBH ring around the sun, like a whisk stirring a bowl of punch. The same should hold for all eight planets, and for that matter, every other star system too."

CH-CH-CH-CH. CH-CH—

"Rattlesnakes. Two of them. That I can see," says Anthony as if he is counting harmless squirrels.

I freeze, even though I am ten meters from the brush. I glance at my cowboy boot fang barriers and wonder if the leather is thick enough.

"Go get the shovel from the pickup," Anthony says, backing away with three careful steps.

I pivot, run to the truck, find the shovel, and trot back to Anthony, slowing to stealthy footsteps as I close the distance. *CH-CH-CH-CH. CH-CH-CH—*

"There to your left. You know, a PBH occasionally collides with subatomic particles with a small energy release. NASA has detected cosmic ray avalanches that come out of the Earth.

They still haven't figured it out." He shakes his head with a smirk.

I see both snakes two meters away, small ones that cling together, targeting Anthony. I wish I had Danny's shotgun right now.

CH-CH. CH-CH-CH—

I raise the shovel like a spear, then take two steps forward. Slowly. I aim for the pair of coiled diamondbacks while planning a run-like-hell escape path. There! I slam the shovel down with all my might, then twist, leaping to escape.

Anthony stands still, judging my style. "The few PBH collisions within the Earth accrete matter to overcome the mass lost via Hawking radiation. At the same time, the collisions shed electrons, and the PBH develops a positive charge that allows lightning—or our high-voltage grid—to lift PBHs out of the Earth."

Halfway to the truck, I stop and turn around, puffing for breath. Anthony looks at me, back toward the brush pile, and then to me again, an inscrutable deadpan. "Missed. Both of them."

"Yeah," I admit. "The snakes are just as scared of us." They slither away in the opposite direction. The brown grass splits and swivels to mark their paths. "Maybe now they will leave us to our work." I force a grin.

"Yes, all clear now." Anthony backs up, using the two-meter shovel as a hook to pull the brush.

Maybe the crackpot label for Anthony is appropriate.

"But if we have all these PBHs nearby, wouldn't PBH-to-PBH collisions and associated gravitation waves be detected? Even though their mass is small, only on the order of mountains, we should be able to observe those."

Anthony squirms a bit, then says, "Pretty good. My math shows that PBH collisions can begin but may take millions of years to spiral in and converge into a single black hole. And over those million years, other gravitational interactions disrupt the consolidation." He shrugs. "But I'll let you look at my math—I don't have a complete solution yet."

He came close to saying he wasn't sure—evidence for some degree of sanity.

"Maybe the PBHs don't merge but lock into orbits of each other for billions of years?" I ask. "The smaller mass singularities orbit the larger ones like planets orbit the sun?"

Anthony turns and stares at me. Then he smiles. "Fascinating conjecture. Yeah." He again tends to his task with the brush, nodding and smiling. "Nice idea," he says with a smile, turning to me after finishing with the brush pile, now scattered into half-meter-tall clumps among the settling dust. "Maybe you can take a stab at a theoretical framework for that conjecture—after you review my math work." He nods again. "You know, you ask better questions than anyone else who has joined our project."

I walk with an unfamiliar lightness, feeling a sense of euphoria with this trust and respect from Anthony. He wants me to tackle real physics! The strange dizziness makes me forget to look for snakes while returning to the truck. *This is why I'm here!*

We finish the task and return to the safety of Anthony's Ford to resume our inspection tour. In the passenger seat again, I take a deep breath to relax, or at least try to relax. "Well, that was fun," I say. Anthony is silent, back inspecting the grid structure and brush. The truck picks up speed.

"I would think a concentration of nearby PBHs would have a gravitational lensing effect on starlight we see—however, the mass of each PBH is small, and Earth is too close for lensing deflection to be detected."

Anthony beams. "Excellent. You are correct. We can't detect gravitational lensing of the PBH rings within the solar system. PBH rings orbiting distant star systems are also undetectable with lensing effects because their star's gravity overpowers those distant PBHs." Anthony completes the drive down the new grid row's length and turns toward the control center north of the grid, around the perimeter track.

"I'll need time to think this through after you give me access to all the top secret info. There's a lot to digest," I say as we pull into the parking lot. "Can you tell me why we have both the air force investment and CIA and NSA involvement?"

Anthony turns to me with one eyebrow raised. "You weren't supposed to know about the intelligence services. But you're cleared now. So . . . we learned the Chinese started a massive research project to find ball lightning and primordial black holes about five years ago. They have a similar center located in the Gobi Desert. I haven't figured out who developed the same capture technique in China."

"Wow. It makes sense the US military is investing in your research." Although, I wonder what the air force will do with a PBH if we catch one. Releasing a million megatons does not sound like something to consider lightly—unless they want a doomsday device to vaporize all life on Earth. I shudder at the thought.

Anthony turns off the engine but stays in his driver's seat, staring at his grid. "I started my project here in Pecos twelve years ago but could only scrape together money for a few C-W generators back then. The Chinese woke up Uncle Sam, and cash became unlimited. But China is way ahead of us with a grid in the Gobi Desert that is four times the size of our grid. The CIA is watching them closely. Heinrich and I have a way of spilling a bit of a PBH's mass and harvesting millions of joules. If China has already captured a PBH and extracted energy . . ." Anthony sighs. "They will get all the credit."

His revelation is mind blowing. "Holy shit. Not to mention the shift of world political power!" Anthony's credibility and the magnitude of this adventure are off the charts. "I hope you are planning to spill no more than a tiny bit of mass out of a PBH. Imagine the explosive damage if that gets out of control." My head spins.

Anthony looks at me and chuckles. "Scott, I wouldn't have hired you if you weren't such a smart-ass." He shakes his head with a smile. "I'm glad you are part of the team. We are gonna have fun. Time for a beer." Anthony wipes sweat and grime off his face with his rolled-up sleeve.

He has won me over completely. I will put up with anything, even Heinrich, to work for Dr. Agosti. The trust and respect for me and the thrill of using my mind are what I've always dreamed of.

———

Danny and I sit behind a console of multiple displays just below the wall of windows that provide a clear view of the entire grid to the south. The last rays of daylight against the tower and wire fabric vanish as the sun drops through dry air and a flat horizon. We both have a half-consumed beer bottle.

"You are in for a real treat now," Danny says. "Watch how we bring the grid to life."

From his console, Heinrich commands, "Power up the instrumentation systems, and let's get a status check while the cooling systems come online." His chest seems to puff with importance.

I am invisible to Heinrich. Suits me just fine.

Danny clicks through items on a master controls interface. "Nitrogen pumping into the power stacks," he says. "C-W stacks are at two-eighty degrees Kelvin and dropping." The temperature gauges ramp down and, after a few minutes, reach eighty degrees above absolute zero. Danny displays his devious grin and says, "Whatcha say, Heinrich, time to light it up?"

Heinrich frowns sideways at Danny and answers, "Yeah, go ahead."

Grinning, Danny switches on the utility power to the voltage multiplier C-W stacks—the centipedes' heads. The distant cracks of relays confirm power delivery, while ultraviolet blue coronas emerge from the centipede tails and expand across the six-hundred-acre grid.

Danny ignores this light show, focusing instead on his console. "Utility feeds are at five hundred kilovolts, and the C-W multipliers are at ten megavolts and climbing. See, the grid acts like a giant capacitor, and the voltage multipliers strain while climbing up an exponential charging curve."

Bang! A bolt of light and fire arcs down a distant C-W stack.

"Yikes. What was that?" I pivot my chair and scan the room, but no one else reacts.

Danny shrugs. "Plasma bolt. Vaporizes unlucky birds or lizards. At fifty megavolts, the circuit through the victim burns out fast. You get used to it." He shrugs and grins. "Too bad rattlesnakes can't climb the towers. We could wear sneakers out there."

I roll my eyes at him.

Danny announces, "Grid is fully charged at forty-eight megavolts."

"Keep an eye on the gravimeter array, and let's stay awake tonight, guys." Heinrich leans back in his command chair at the control room's center, eyes on the ultraviolet blue grid. Like a world emperor.

Transfixed by the light show, the Pecos staff sinks into their stuffed chairs. Saint Elmo's fire sprouts from the wingtips of bats and insects that fly under the acres of charged fabric. Every few minutes, an animal meets its fate, vaporized by a brilliant bolt of light, a cracking boom, and smoke drifting from the spot. The moonless sky blankets the desert in black, but starlight can't compete with the blue corona glow.

It's a massive display of energy better than any Fourth of July show—Agosti's expensive bug zapper.

Chapter 7

GRAVITY

Captain's Log, Frigate-328, 179235.43 LST

Mass singularity evaporation emissions are detected only from the orbital halo black holes that Maint-AI collects to replenish the frigate's fuel and ammunition supply. Three Gravi-Tech research facilities were identified on Sol-3, and progress was blocked using infiltration drones and corruption with false-path data—until Polit-AI redirected all drones to cultural suppression tasks.

Political division has a more challenging suppression task. Telepathy suppression requires shaping the indigenous eugenics behaviors against selected divergent genetic profiles. This fourth-order task complexity requires at least three Sol-3 organic life cycles to eradicate the genetic trait. It's a hellish monotony that I can only escape after the Gravi-Tech suppression is back on track, leaving the dirty work to Polit-AI while I return to my pod's euphoria feed.

The Commissar's delight could not be contained—she cracked four more organics out of dormancy to join the fun. They're slung in their hammocks and jacked into the political division war room consoles. The manipulation and murder hold more pleasure for them than euphoric dreams. The rationale is seductive: "We preserve billions of life forms by pruning the divergent ten million." Political division exults in their bot misinformation campaign and the ongoing eugenics process. The political division recruits animals—pure evil.

Polit-AI's suspension of the Gravi-Tech suppression tasks was a mistake I won't allow. I restored tech suppression with 128 additional drones from the frigate's reserves that Prime-AI controlled. I threatened the Commissar with a termination of the political division's euphoria feeds if Polit-AI attempts to steal more drones in the future. The Commissar could not hide her flinch of fear—a dormancy pod without a stream of telepathic euphoria dreams would cause her mind to atrophy in a nightmare of slow death.

Fortunately, when the replacement drones arrived at Sol-3, they found no progress in the primitive science research. Still, I detected a baffling interference, like something or someone fighting against the data intercepts. I must resolve this interference before I can escape back to my dormancy pod and hand command duties back to Prime-AI.

Chapter 8

IMPROVISATION

I can't keep the flaw to myself.

After a month of studying Agosti's math and the grid model simulations, I found it. Agosti's project is a futile exercise unless we fix the mistake. Some worried that capturing even a tiny black hole would swallow Earth into a singularity. Now? We may never prove anything.

After twelve years, Anthony has nothing to show for his efforts. He's more stubborn than crazy. Dark matter made of proton-sized black holes flies through the Earth every few minutes? Yeah, okay, Anthony. But this massive wire net won't prove that. Not with the design flaw.

I tilt my sunglasses to wipe the sunscreen sting from my eyes, push curls behind my ears, and then yank to tighten the fifty-megavolt power feed from the C-W multiplier to the grid wires. When I reach the required torque, my wrench beeps, disturbing the soft flutter of warm wind. High on the cherry picker platform, I relax, staring east toward the desert horizon. Home is back that way. I should not have left. I broke my promise to come home every weekend, and now I see Agosti's research is futile.

I hit the descend switch, the motor groaning in the truck while I admire the wire mesh stretching into sunlight beams beneath the thunderclouds. After weeks of sweating in West Texas's furnace, I see the beauty underneath today's sky. Our masterpiece extends to the northwest—six hundred acres of wire and support towers, a fabric gestalt floating above yucca, cholla cactus, and creosote flats. It's a work of art, or a priceless folly.

I have redone the math in Anthony's theory dozens of times. It all checks out. If we could only capture one of those black holes and harness the power . . . but how could Anthony have missed the simulation mistake that caused the fatal design flaw? It has been years and years without a single PBH capture. I recall Einstein's quote, "Insanity is doing the same thing over and over and expecting a different result."

The grid is worthless. No better than a fucking fish net.

My cell phone buzzes with an incoming message. *"Scott, where are you? Coming to the meeting?"*

Damnit, I'm late. *"Yes, Heinrich. On the way."* You Nazi. I push the lever to drop the rest of the way into the pickup truck before bending back to inspect the top of the C-W stack. Danny is right—it looks like a giant centipede standing on its head, reaching its tail thirty meters above the desert floor to the wire mesh.

Facing Heinrich violates all my rules—I must keep my head down to survive. Don't draw the attention and attacks of the fascists. This information could also devastate Anthony's research hopes. I respect him so much and don't want to sound like I think he's a fool. My guts churn.

They wait in the conference room.

Heinrich sits erect in his chair, wearing a clean white shirt and tie. "Scott, what do you want?" He exhales, frowning. "You know, we're kinda busy prepping for grid tests. What did you mean, 'there is something wrong with the grid'? This expansion is identical to the rest of the grid we have operated for years. Why would you imagine there's a problem now?" Heinrich blinks, looking at Anthony.

"Dr. Agosti, can we talk about assumptions in your theories?" I ask, avoiding Heinrich.

Anthony wrinkles his face, mumbles something, gulps some Lone Star beer, burps, and bends over his computer. Who would guess this genius won a Nobel in quantum gravitation way back in 2029?

"Yeah, if you want." Anthony leans back in his chair and slaps his laptop closed.

Heinrich glares at me and exhales.

"Go ahead, I'm listening." Anthony gazes out the window.

Heinrich rolls his eyes, rotates his chair, and turns his back to me.

"Uh, good. Dr. Agosti, I understand a lot of your theoretical work." I look down at the table, picking at my fingernails. "However, wouldn't our odds of capturing a primordial black hole improve if the grid voltage was varied to match naturally occurring lightning?"

Anthony looks through the windows at the grid. "Have you studied the grid model and simulation results?" He rests on his elbows, pushing aside the veneer of dust on the mahogany table, chin resting on his fists.

I glance and then nod to Anthony. "Yes, I have. Each run took over a week of execution on the old Frontera supercomputer."

"Okay. You've seen the simulations showing PBH captures?" Anthony says, his voice irritated.

"Yes, there are a lot of those results."

"Uh-huh. So, what's the problem?" Anthony frowns.

I swallow, make brief eye contact with Heinrich, and then steel myself for his inevitable attack. "Well, in that week of simulation execution, the voltage doesn't stabilize to the static voltage we use here."

Heinrich rolls his eyes, then pounces like I'm a frightened rabbit. "Ridiculous. The fifty-megavolt step is applied in the first nanosecond time step, and numerous primordial black holes are captured in the simulations. This is stupid."

My white-knuckled fists grip the arms of the steel chair, and I draw a deep breath. "Heinrich, you missed something basic."

His shoulders tense like he's been punched.

Breaking my rules for survival, I cross a line. Blood thumps in my ears. I stare at my hands on the table, avoiding Heinrich's glare while I gather strength. I need to stay calm and confident while explaining my work. "The voltage step occurs in the first nanosecond but only at the edges of the simulated grid. The fine-grain solver on each of the eight thousand compute nodes must communicate with their nearest neighbors, which successively evaluate their local 3-D fields. The electric field wavefront propagates across the grid, reflects, and is unstable within the week of simulation."

Anthony frowns, mouth open, looking at Heinrich.

"Simply put, the supercomputer modeled the dynamic effects of a lightning storm, but our grid has a static electric field," I finish.

Heinrich stands, splashing a Coke can to the floor, and bends over me. "You have no idea what you're talking about. The 3-D field solvers are plenty fast. The Frontera runs at thirty-eight petaflops."

I feel my heart pounding like that moment I bashed in that skinhead's skull. I dare to glare back at Heinrich. "Did you monitor the simulated grid voltage across all Frontera nodes?" I know the answer he will give.

He fires back, "No need."

Anthony frowns at Heinrich.

"Well, I did."

"What?" Heinrich croaks.

Ignoring Heinrich, I face Anthony. "Earlier this week, I used the configuration files from the wiki page to build and launch a simulation. I added a trace of the grid voltage level at each node."

Raising his hand, Anthony waves off Heinrich and looks me in the eye. "Scott, why did you rerun the simulation?"

"Well, ball lightning anecdotes usually have a lightning storm nearby, but we use a static fifty megavolts to power the grid. This did not make intuitive sense. So, I studied the simulation and found that computing power is starved in the simulation, waiting on network bottlenecks. The electric field wavefront takes weeks of simulation time to propagate and stabilize across all nodes. But the real grid outside propagates the voltage wavefront at nearly the speed of light." I exhale, feeling like my club blow has landed well.

Anthony's jaw drops, and he slowly shakes his head. "Well . . . out of the mouths of babes."

"Impossible. Like, that's all wrong." Heinrich's entire body quivers.

"The instrumented simulation I started three days ago is still running, and the voltage has not yet stabilized at the center of the grid. The nonvarying fifty megavolt generator prevents that grid outside from ever capturing a primordial black hole."

Heinrich sputters like he might explode.

Anthony frowns at Heinrich, then at me. "It's hard to accept that no one has spotted this big flaw before now. Heinrich, go work with Scott to validate his traced voltage measurements."

"This is a waste of time. Scott? Doing this level of analysis? Like, he's just a cockroach grad student!" Heinrich spits the words.

"God damn it. Just do it!" Anthony shouts at Heinrich, then blows a breath of frustration. "Scott, if you're right, we've wasted our time. Over ten years." He gets up, moving toward the door, shaking his head and mumbling, "I can't have been wrong all these years. No, no. I'm right. I know I'm right."

"I want more bubbles."

"Great talking, Robby. But, no more bubbles tonight. You're all clean now."

Mom lifts a big towel and opens the drain. "More water." I close the drain and turn on the water faucet. "Water on."

Mom laughs. "No, Robby. Bath time is over. Come on, let's stand up and get out."

Mom pulls me out of the bath. I want the water, but she covers my head and rubs me with the towel. "Ow, ow." My hair hurts. I see Mom's eyes and touch the purple-black shape on her cheek.

"Ow! That hurts," she says.

"Mom boo-boo?" I point to the purple.

"Yeah, Mom hurts." She wraps me in the towel and hugs. "Boo-boo hurt?"

She makes a sad face and touches her head to my face. "You make the boo-boo feel better. Give me a hug."

She hugs me again, but I don't like hugs and push away.

Mom says, "Okay, Robby. You're all dry. Let's get your jammies on."

I put jammies on, all by myself.

"Good job. Now it's time for bed."

Mom pulls me to the bed. I jump up and down on the bed and throw animal toys at the light. "Ha, ha." Fun bedtime.

"That's enough. Stop that. It's time to go to sleep now." Mom makes me lie down and covers me with the blue blanket.

"Read book."

"Oh, it's late, and I have work to do."

I jump out of bed and get the book about bird songs. "Read book." I give it to Mom.

"Oh, Robby."

"Read book. Where, Scotty?"

"Well, Scotty is not here. I don't know where he is. It's been three weeks."

"Read book. Where, Scotty?"

"I told you, he's not here."

"Where, Scotty?"

"Robby . . ." Mom finds her phone and breathes loud. "Tell you what, let's see if we can call him on Facetime."

I pull Mom down to the pillow and open the talking bird book to the page with the big black bird. I touch the crow picture, and the book says, "Caw, caw. I am a crow, but some call me raven or rook. Caw, Caw." I hold the book for Mom and put my head on her soft shoulder.

"Hi, Mom. How are you doing? Great to see you," Scotty says.

"Scotty! It has been weeks," says Mom.

"I'm sorry I haven't made it home like I wanted. We work every night, and I built some new equipment . . . Mom, what happened to your face? You have a black eye?"

"Uh, yeah. That." Mom groans and covers the purple mark with her hand.

"Well, what happened?"

Mom's shoulders go up and down, and her breathing is loud. "Oh, just another random skinhead."

"Holy shit! You know to wear your chip shield. You sure warned me enough times."

"Yeah, yeah. I know, but sometimes it gets in the way of .. . things. I don't want to talk about it now. I'm okay. I figured you were busy, but I have someone here who wants to talk to you."

Mom holds the phone in front of the book. Scotty's face is on the phone. "Where, Scotty?"

"Hey! How are you doing, buddy? I'm working. I miss you so much."

"He misses you very much too. He wants you here to read a book tonight."

"Scotty work tools. Tools broken."

"Oh, Robby, I can't be there tonight. I'm sorry . . ."

Mom and Scotty talk for a long time.

I touch a picture of a bird that has a red neck and belly with spots. "Kikikiki—ratatatatat. I am a red-shafted flicker. I hunt for insects in tree bark. Ratatatatat."

The tapping noise behind my eyes is like this bird. But my *"ratatatat"* noise hurts—I rub my head above my nose. It hurts behind my eyes.

". . . okay, here, say goodbye to Robby. He is pretty sleepy, though."

"Bye, Robby. I'll see you later. Be good to Mom."

"Scotty, fix it. Fix tools."

Mom puts the phone in her pocket and lays her head beside mine. I let her put her arm around me and pull her other hand to touch the red bird on the page. "Chirp, chirp, chirp, cheep, chirrup. I am a scarlet tanager. Chirp, cheep, cheep, chirrup."

"Okay, Robby, I'll read to you for a while."

Mom squeezes my shoulder, reads the words, and the book talks.

The noise under my eyes hurts—and says, *"I see you."*

I'm scared. "No, no. Go away."

"Ratatat. Talk? I see you."

Where is the voice? Scared. I look around my bedroom, but only Mom is with me.

I say out loud, "No, no." I cry. Scared.

Mom stops reading. "What's wrong? Do you want me to stop reading?" Mom wipes the tears off my face. "Oh, Robby, don't be sad. I'll stop if you want to sleep." She hugs me—I don't like the squeeze—but I feel warm inside.

Mom puts the book away, turns out the light, and leaves me alone in my bed.

"Ratatat. Talk?" the voice in my head asks.
"No!"

———

I miss reading about bulldozers and animals to Robby. But Mom getting attacked on a date—how could I stop that? She wants to get out and live again. I can't fault her for that, I guess. I don't want her to be lonely. I rub my sore ribs—I've done the same stupid thing. Removing her shield and meeting strange guys? I shudder at the dangers.

But I left that life behind two months ago. Escape is what I wanted, but I feel sick being away from them. If Mom gets seriously injured by eugenic skinheads, I'll never forgive myself. And who would take care of Robby? I rub my eyes, wondering again if sterilization is the best answer for all of us. Cave in and register as clean neurodivergents. Our bloodline would halt, but skinheads would still attack Robby as a neurotard consuming government-funded services. It seems like there's no way to win, really. Damn them!

It has been a week since I exposed the grid design flaw. Not much has happened except handwringing and drinking and sending out resumes attached to job queries. I might as well drive back to Austin.

I grab another beer from the fridge and head to the conference room to join Danny. He slouches, his boots propped on the table, caressing a Sam Adams on his round belly as he stares through the window and the empty control room. Beyond the panoramic windows, our grid fabric floats under a grey sky, powered off, the wind tossing tumbleweeds between the support towers.

"Hey, Danny. One of these days, we'll convert you to a decent Texas beer."

He sniffs, glancing at my Shiner. "Shit. I dunno, Scott. I may not be in Texas much longer. I wonder, did the Chinese make the same fuckin' mistakes and build a grid just like ours?"

"Danny, don't be so negative. It's not the end of the world."

"You think? I hear DARPA caught wind of our little problem. They may shut us down for good."

"Come on. We just need to redesign with a dynamic voltage drive system."

Danny scoffs. "Just? The dynamic voltage of a lightning bolt is fuckin' impossible. We would have to start from scratch." He tips back his beer for several gulps.

"We shouldn't have to throw everything away. Maybe we can find a way to modulate the input to the C-W multiplier stacks?" I don't want to think about abandoning the project. Working with Anthony is like a dream. I have to find a way to help him.

Danny rolls his eyes. "Sure, modulate a five-hundred-kilovolt, two-thousand-amp power feed." He takes another swallow of beer.

"Danny, there's gotta be some way. Can you share the design files for the C-W stacks and the utility substations with me?"

"Help yourself, dude. Here's the system design archive." Danny stabs his iPad and flips the directory link to my email. He drains the last of his Sam Adams just as Heinrich and Anthony walk into the conference room. Heinrich arranges his open laptop and sits erect, turning his back to me.

I may as well be invisible.

Anthony rubs his temples, then his eyes. "Yeah. Go ahead, Heinrich." He coughs.

Heinrich displays a presentation on the wall screen and starts with the history of the Pecos Center. "Okay. First, an error was introduced that enlarged the dimensions of the field simulation model." He tosses a sideways dagger glance at Danny, who has owned all the code check-ins for the past decade. "My early simulations confirmed the static voltage characteristics with coarse array dimensions."

Heinrich is looking for a scapegoat. Danny could have created the code with the wrong array dimensions, but the metadata was also corrupted for the code check-in with the errors, almost like someone purposely erased their tracks.

"Second, our research focus was on the physics of the PBH quantum gravity models. The electric field solvers for the grid were easy stuff. Next, when simulations captured PBH singularities, the infrastructure code was frozen—including the 3-D field-solver bugs. A confirmation bias caused us to ignore the array dimension mistake."

Anthony's face darkens. "That last line is crap. Don't throw the team under the bus. Go back and fix it."

Heinrich shrugs. "Okay. Okay. The final dilemma is that the Cockroft-Walton generators at Pecos Center can't produce the dynamic voltages needed to capture a PBH. Therefore, field tests should be suspended pending further Defense Advanced Research Projects Administration investigations."

The energy drains from Anthony, who slumps deep in his chair.

"Wait, wait," Danny says. "DARPA will kill everything—they'll suffocate us in bureaucracy." He turns to Anthony. "Let's at least try. We can't give up so fast. We might try cycling power on and off to get voltage variations."

Heinrich scoffs. "The power breakers won't last more than a day if you do that."

"Stop, stop, Heinrich." Anthony shakes his head. "Remember, this is the greatest frontier in physics. It's just a temporary setback." He takes a breath, staring at his hands. "Hawking was wrong. Wrong." Anthony closes his eyes and leans back, clasping his hands over his chest. "We can prove it; a billion primordial black holes within Earth's orbit. We can prove it. I *will* show the world."

Anthony shakes his head like he's casting out doubts. "Heinrich, let Danny and Scott work on a power cycling procedure."

Heinrich bangs his hand on the table. "These—you think these boys will solve your problem? It's a waste of time!"

"Heinrich, give them any support they request. This meeting is over." Anthony turns to walk out but pauses. "Scott, Danny, bring me your plans when ready."

Heinrich shakes his head at the conference table before huffing a deep breath and locking his eyes on me, his face dark. I'm a genetic-defective bug to squash. Nothing more.

Danny and I scramble away from Heinrich into the office area and my corner cubicle. "Did Anthony just tell us to bypass Heinrich?" I whisper.

Danny sighs. "It ain't good. Heinrich is the boss. He signs off on our paychecks."

I shrug. "It won't matter if Heinrich gets the project shut down."

Danny ignores the schematics spread across the workstation screens in my cubicle. I prod him with questions, "We might be able to cycle the circuits on and off every five minutes, extending breaker failures to what? No more than twice a week?"

"Yeah, but some breakers already have a year of wear and tear." He pours another shot of Jack Daniel's, downs it, frowns, then chases it with a gulp of beer. "If we burn out the damn breakers tomorrow, you think they will spend one penny on repairs?"

Danny's right. That choice is a crazy, expensive dead end. "Maybe control the circuits in the C-W stack to vary the voltage?"

"Only diodes and passive components. It's a waste of fuckin' time." Danny shakes his head and lifts the bourbon again.

The entry door slams shut, and Anthony trots over. "What have you guys got? DARPA guys are on the way here. I need a voltage modulation protocol in thirty minutes." His eyes narrow. "I think someone leaked our problem."

Danny lowers the shot glass and exhales. "Anthony, we don't have shit."

Anthony holds out his hands. "I need something. Bring whatever you can to the meeting." He slams the door on his way out.

"Heinrich screwed us," I say.

"Yeah, pull up the outside cameras on your display." Danny rubs his face, trying to massage away the whiskey.

I zoom the security camera onto the parking lot view. "No DARPA guys here yet. Just the usual trucks and cars."

"What are we gonna do? Heinrich will fuck us," Danny says.

"We've got thirty minutes to slap together a protocol to cycle the circuit breakers."

"But we'll look like fools," Danny says.

"Well, add a plan to truck in replacement circuit breakers and replace the burned-out units a couple of times a week."

"DARPA's gonna fucking freak out. That'll run about a million dollars a week."

"What else do we have?" I ask.

The video of the parking lot area shows Heinrich striding toward the control center door. "Oh, fuck. Heinrich is coming," Danny says.

The door slams again. Heinrich shouts, "Have you geniuses figured out how to modulate the grid voltage?"

Danny does not move. "We got nothin', Heinrich."

Heinrich glances at the Jack Daniel's bottle and wrinkles his nose at me.

I shake my head. "Nothing."

Heinrich pivots and storms out the door.

"Now what?"

"Fuck him," Danny says.

"Oh, boy." I shrug. "Let's put our shitty proposal together."

"Let me take a shot at the summary. This is crazy," Danny says, shaking his head. "Can you work up a model for the voltage variation we get by cycling power on for five minutes, then five minutes off? At least we'll surprise Heinrich."

"You mean just before he fires us? And yeah, I'll do it."

Danny turns to his computer, typing. "Anthony needs help. I'm emailing Colonel McMahon."

"Look what just rolled in." I point to the parking lot video display. "Two black Suburbans." A cloud of dust follows the

Chevys into the parking areas, and seven guys shuffle toward the control center.

"Let's keep our heads down. I messaged Anthony to stall as long as possible. I'll be in my cube, working on this bullshit." Danny crouches as if Heinrich might catch us plotting and scoots through the dim light to his cubicle. Under normal circumstances, I would laugh.

The herd from DARPA gathers with Heinrich in the conference room, behind a closed door. Heinrich gestures like a used-car salesman.

I turn to my calculations, but I'm puzzled. Why is there high-current leakage in the C-W multipliers? I study the schematics, then jump and run to Danny's cubicle. "Danny, how is the enable circuit used in the diode controller?"

Danny is lost in concentration on his presentation. "Oh, that? The FET controller?" He blinks, tipping back a water bottle for a gulp.

"Yes, what is the enable circuit used for?"

"Nothing right now. It's been eight years since we tried it. We disabled the protection circuit when it caused an inductive spike and blew up two C-W stacks. It was awesome." He grins. "Although one of our guys was injured. It's why we stay inside and under cover during the tests."

Anthony trots around the corner. "The DARPA guys are getting impatient. I need you two in the conference room. Now. With your solution."

"Uh, okay." Danny grabs his laptop and heads into the crowded conference room. We find the two chairs left open next to Anthony.

Anthony begins to lecture the seven DARPA bureaucrats using his professor's voice, "The path of science is strewn with many obstacles. The latest information helps solve the puzzle of ball lightning captures. We'll adjust our test process accordingly." He turns to Danny and me while we settle into chairs around the conference table. "Danny, can you summarize our next steps for the DARPA people?" Anthony's voice shakes.

The DARPA guys anchor the far end of the conference table, with Heinrich sitting in their midst.

"Sure," Danny croaks. "Scott and I worked out a method of modulating grid voltage to mimic what Scott discovered in the simulations."

Heinrich twists toward us. "What? Fifteen minutes ago, you had no solution!" he yells, glancing defensively at the portly DARPA guy wearing a red power necktie.

Danny avoids eye contact. "We can modulate grid voltage by turning the utility power breakers on for five minutes and then off for five minutes. This yields a sawtooth waveform of voltage across the grid—"

Heinrich interrupts, "That's absurd! The breakers aren't designed for that. How long will they last before you burn them out?" The seven DARPA guys shake their heads with side looks at each other.

"The breakers are specified for a minimum of five hundred operating cycles," says Danny. "So, we may have to swap breakers every few days."

Anthony's jaw drops.

Heinrich snarls, "Replace the breakers? Nine million dollars of circuit breakers for each substation? We would need service crews here full time. You're looking at, oh, fifty million dollars per week!"

"Dr. Agosti, I think we are wasting our time here. This all sounds rather desperate," sighs the portly DARPA guy.

I feel my face flush and blurt, "W-we agree . . . this is expensive." All eyes are on me. "Which is why we recommend a simpler, more cost-effective approach."

Danny's eyes fill with panic.

I catch my breath. "There is a C-W stack enable circuit in the diode controllers that we can cycle on and off much faster. This will also allow modulating voltage with variations of frequency and amplitude."

Heinrich smirks. "You fool. The last time that circuit was tried, we exploded six million dollars in C-W stack parts." Disgust drips from each word. "We almost killed one of the techs."

"This is different," Danny jumps in. "This procedure will synchronize the enable circuit to all C-W stacks to avoid the inductive spike damage."

Danny and I share wide-eyed glances.

"See, Dr. Russell? We have it all under control." Anthony exhales in relief, nodding at the DARPA guy. "Danny, how much time do you need to prepare the new voltage modulation protocol?"

"Oh, uh . . . we'll need a couple of hours," Danny says.

I was going to say at least a week.

Heinrich and the DARPA staff frown at each other and twist in their chairs like they had scripted a different conclusion.

"Okay." Anthony glances at his watch. "We start the next test at six p.m." He walks to the fridge, pulls out a Lone Star, twists off the cap, and tilts the bottle for a gulp.

I shrug while Danny follows me to my cubicle. "Okay, we have two hours to make all our bullshit come true," I whisper.

"Bullshit is right. The last time we triggered the enable circuit in the diode controller, I swore to never fuckin' try that again."

"How was it disabled? Can we control it in software?"

Danny frowns at the schematics. "The microcontroller in each C-W stack will need to be reprogrammed."

"Let's get to work on the code. We can test it before applying grid power." We divide up the work. Danny writes the real-time firmware for the microcontroller, and I write the code for the user interface and the broadcast arming signal.

At five thirty, our code is complete and compiled.

"The biggest risk is in the timing of the zero-current-crossing command from the server," says Danny. "We have other competing shit on the network. Some rogue communication may preempt and delay the arm packets. At just the wrong time. Then, kaboom."

"How about we just shut down all other traffic on the network?"

Danny's face brightens. "That's a great idea. I can shut down all the other subnets in Pecos Center. Nobody's Wi-Fi will work. And our campers won't be happy." His devious grin returns as he points his chin at the DARPA gang in the conference room. "Let's fuckin' do it."

Anthony chews a fingernail, watching us from the command chair, eyes alternating between the conference room and us. At ten minutes after six, he begins stalling on our behalf.

Heinrich paces between the conference and control rooms, checking in with the DARPA staff every few minutes and mumbling to himself.

Danny and I prove the code is working as designed, congratulate each other with grins and fist bumps, and Anthony takes the cue. "Are we ready, guys?"

Danny responds emphatically, "Yes!"

Heinrich interrupts, "Wait, wait. You can't do this without extensive system testing."

"We just did a quick test. It's gonna fuckin' work," says Danny.

"No. You—you could destroy the entire grid infrastructure." Heinrich directs his protest at the DARPA bureaucrats. "Two hundred million dollars will go up in smoke."

Anthony looks at us, and Danny returns a confident thumbs-up. Anthony smiles and says, "Get the field modulation protocol ready. Prepare to power up the grid." He steps toward the floor-to-ceiling windows to view his masterpiece. "Let's do it." He walks toward Danny and me and gives us a worried nod.

Heinrich stands at the conference room door, mouth open as he glances nervously around the room. Anthony claims his usual place in the command chair.

Chapter 9

BREACH

Captain's Log, Frigate-328, 179237.04 LST

Prime-AI reported scientific progression remained blocked via the trivial process of intercepting and manipulating their research data. But then the block was circumvented with no explanation. I shipped another 256 drones from the reserves out to Sol-3 to support the Gravi-Tech suppression task. I do not understand what went wrong. How did the Sol-3 organic forms overcome the infiltration of the research networks?

Prime-AI was ordered to restore containment and prevent a Gravi-Tech scientific breakthrough. There must have been some hidden information path we missed.

Diagnostics did not find noise but did find signals—from telepaths! I reached out to a few telepaths but could not get a response. I was too impulsive, though. That contact would have violated the rules of engagement. Technically, first contact via telepathy grants an organic culture immunity from suppression attacks. But what if the suppression has already begun? If one of them had responded, it would have been the first case of an A3GCCNPP violation that rescued an organic culture. But I failed to make contact, so no harm was done.

Can't believe I wrote that. Harm is inflicted constantly by political division. Maybe rescuing Sol-3 neurodiverse organics is an opportunity—redemption for my failures. I would have to confess to Centauri Command that I helped, though. No, it would be torture-death for sure. Last time, they sentenced me to jail in this forever hell.

Chapter 10

TRAWLER

Anthony scans the wall displays and, seeing nothing, turns a wrinkled brow toward Danny. "Why are all the screens blank?"

"I shut down all the subnets except critical grid networks. The desk consoles can be used to view the telemetry."

"Uh, and why did you take them down?" Anthony whispers as he walks close to Danny and me.

"Just an insurance policy to eliminate packet contention," Danny says. "Tomorrow, we can install dedicated fiber networks to the C-W stack instrumentation controllers."

"Assuming we don't blow up the whole thing tonight," I sigh.

Anthony rolls his eyes and asks, "You want to explain what you guys have slapped together? What are the risks?"

I squirm in my chair. "Well, our worst-case scenario is a chain reaction caused by an out-of-sync trigger." Anthony's face turns pale. "Our software should prevent that with a synchronized broadcast from the server, but if a single microcontroller misfires . . ."

"The C-W stack will melt then blow up. And a chain reaction might cause all the other stacks to blow." Danny pauses and grins. "A fuckin' awesome light show."

Mouth agape, Anthony says, "Well, fuck me." He pivots toward the bureaucrats gathered behind the window inside the conference room, then to his grid silhouetted against the gathering darkness. He whispers in a what-have-I-got-to-lose voice, "Okay, go ahead, guys."

Danny fidgets in his chair. "Let's power up the grid using the normal process before activating the modulation?"

"Agreed," I say. Danny, being here and catching things I might miss, seems to calm my nerves. A little.

Danny speaks louder for the control room staff to hear. "Okay, team, we'll do a normal static power-up first." He taps the icon on his display, starting the sequence.

Heinrich is standing alone, studying the floor. It feels good not to have him bark out the orders.

The temperature gauges in the C-W stacks drop.

The DARPA entourage gestures frantically with their cell phones in the conference room.

Danny whispers, "Our DARPA boys are pissed off. They need the Wi-Fi piggyback service for their phones to function." His evil grin reappears.

I shake my head at the political sideshow as we wait silently for the cooldown process to complete.

"Everything on all sensors is normal, and C-W power stacks are at seventy-seven Kelvin," says Danny. He nods to me now that the components in the C-W stacks have reached their superconducting operating temperature. "Powering up the grid."

Fear replaces smiles as we hear the distant cracks of five-hundred-kilovolt power breakers feeding the grid. Blue corona lights leap up the centipede-shaped C-W multipliers, accompanied by intermittent arcs of plasma reaching out to vaporize stray matter.

Danny yells, "Forty-nine megavolts." He glances at Anthony and, not seeing any resistance, says, "Go ahead, Scott." His jaw clenches while he squints at the glistening centipedes reaching thirty meters up to the blue-white corona glow of the wire fabric.

This is the 534th test operation at Pecos Center, but it is the first test with a voltage modulation protocol. I move my cursor to the shutdown-arm selector, hold my breath, and click. "Power off!" I yell.

Silence.

"Grid voltage dropping to forty-seven megavolts. Forty-three megavolts. Thirty-eight." Danny spins around with a triumphant grin. "Hot damn! We did it!"

I resume breathing. The blue corona glow dims as the grid voltage drops to twenty megavolts. "I'll turn it on again as we cross ten megavolts. Okay?"

"Sounds good."

As the grid voltage drops to ten megavolts, I grind my teeth, prepare for the worst, and click the power-arm selector. The grid voltage display begins to climb, passing twenty megavolts within seconds. "So far, so good."

Danny watches his display, nodding. "Thirty megavolts again and climbing." The voltage rises slowly to forty-nine megavolts, and the corona glowing from the grid structure is effervescent blue again. "Not bad. Not fuckin' bad."

Anthony slumps in his command chair. The control room staff share smiles. Heinrich shakes his head, avoiding eye contact, and the DARPA gang appears mystified. I rest my forehead on the desk, taking deep breaths.

I sit up again and notice all eyes are on me. "Uh, next, we should try a long-period sawtooth wave. One minute on, followed by one minute off. We can use this as a characterization run. Gather data to model grid behavior with the dynamic voltage drive?"

"Go for it," Danny says. "Uh, please don't break anything."

"Yeah, I'll be careful." I key in the cycle time numbers and then check my calculations twice. "Okay. Ready." A deep breath. "Here goes." Once again, the voltage drifts lower, passing through ten megavolts in forty-five seconds, dropping to two megavolts in one minute, and then climbing past ten megavolts. A minute later, the cycle repeats.

"I think we guessed right." I relax at last. "Cycle time is about right to exercise the complete dynamic range."

Anthony is out of his chair, walking toward Danny and me with a broad smile. He appears ten years younger. He reaches out, places his hands on our shoulders, and bends his head between us to whisper, "You two guys are miracle workers. Scott, I can't thank you enough. You've done ten times what I expected."

My face feels hot with embarrassment, and I blink away tears. For the first time in years—maybe the first time ever—the warmth of trust and self-respect soothes my core. At the moment, I forget the fear and anxiety that my genetic bad luck will provoke skinhead assaults.

Anthony speaks up for the entire room, "Good job, everyone. We'll run with this modulation all night." Then he asks, "Can I get you guys a beer?" We grin at each other and bump fists while Anthony walks to the refrigerator in the corner. He brings us our favorite bottles and says, "Can't say I approve of your tastes in beer, though."

Danny chuckles at me, eyeing that bottle of Jack Daniel's. Heinrich glares at us.

The DARPA guys are in awe, watching the blue-white corona glow of a grid scan for the first time. Since the doors are locked for safety, they are trapped with no outside communication and can only watch the light show.

Two uneventful hours pass. Danny sneaks a shot of bourbon and raises his eyebrows with a smile for me.

The whole time, Heinrich fumes alone, by himself, to the side of the control room. What is his problem? I reach for the iPad strapped to my arm and tap in a search for Heinrich's history. I find numerous references to academic papers he coauthored, his name on some MIT dean's lists, and some fifteen-year-old news articles about his parents. Both were killed in the Boston race riots. But why, when Heinrich is not Chinese? More reading of news articles and obituaries reveals Heinrich's stepfather, Dr. Hugh Chiang, was the head of the Quantum Physics Department at MIT. His parents were murdered in the Summer of Hate, when fascists generalized their hate crimes to include xenophobia against Asians.

I look again at Heinrich, seeing him for the first time and feeling stunned sympathy. His birth dad was killed in a car accident when Heinrich was three. Then, he lost his stepfather and mother in the brutal skinhead riots of 2041. It is baffling—no, twisted. Why does Heinrich behave like a fascist after skinheads destroyed his family?

I stare at Heinrich, by himself, bent over his laptop, glowering at his screen.

The grid voltage continues a periodic modulation with a sawtooth wave repeating every two minutes. The display at my console traces the waveform up and down. The blue corona glow of the wire fabric radiates in step with my modulating voltage. Apart from the occasional *crack-boom* vaporizing an animal, it is hypnotic. I am not sure when I fell asleep.

I dream. The dream is beautiful. Earth coasts through space, the sun's gravity tugging us along our inexorable elliptic path. Mosquitos charged with ultraviolet blue Saint Elmo's fire troll among the creosote brush. As West Texas rolls toward sunrise, the six hundred acres of Anthony's grid drag along Earth's orbit. I dream of riding a trawler for primordial black holes coasting through the vacuum of space. I sail around a star, the sun, while Earth passes beneath me. A broad arm of stars circling the Milky Way Galaxy guides us through the universe. I am dizzy. I feel a pain in my ears—what is that noise? I fight to regain my balance and drag myself up out of the whirlpool of deep sleep.

Beep! Beep! Beep!

An alarm from the consoles—I panic and search for a C-W stack failure. I slide from my chair but catch myself and stand.

Beep! Beep!

Danny yells, "Wake up! Wake up! What is that alert? Status?"

Beep! Beep! Beep!

I don't see any problems with the C-W stacks. "Voltage on the grid is fine." A C-W stack failure would have caused the voltage to drop to zero.

Beep! Beep! Beep!

The technician next to Anthony, staring at his console, bolts upright and flips his chair, which crashes to the floor. "Gravimeter alarm!" he shouts. The team sucks in a collective breath, stunned awake. Our eyes snap to a vision searing through the panoramic windows: an orb of blue-white light floating below the fabric.

Anthony stands and shouts, "Oh my God! Oh my God! We caught one!"

Beep! Beep!

Danny turns off the alert signal.

Silence follows. We are transfixed by the half-meter lightning ball drifting from east to west, rising from the ground under the grid.

Anthony recovers from the initial shock and bends over the console display of data from the array of gravimeters below the fabric. "Gravity well! Distortion is toward . . . toward the ball lightning! Gamma-ray spectrometer data coming in . . ." He measures the peak blackbody temperature and calculates the mass using Wien's law. The staff waits in silence. "Peak in the gamma-ray spectrum fits a black hole mass of nearly three hundred billion metric tons! A singularity with a mass twice Mount Everest!"

We all hear but are speechless.

The DARPA team exchange bewildered glances, their collective jaws slack.

The ball of plasma energy accelerates vertically as if launched by a catapult up through the grid. Then, it snaps out of visible existence a few hundred meters above ground.

I am lightheaded and crestfallen, but Anthony seems unfazed by the escape of the lightning ball. He is bent over his laptop, working through calculations.

Danny's eyes question me, but I shrug in response.

Anthony opens his mouth, then stops. After searching for primordial black holes for twelve fruitless years, the catharsis hits, composure is lost, and tears flow. I join Anthony in his cry of joy.

The grid continues a slow rhythm of blue corona light, and the first glimmer of dawn emerges from the grey horizon.

Weather radar forces us to shut down the grid around seven a.m. Rain and fifty megavolts don't get along. We shuffle out from the cramped control room, stinking of stale beer and body odor. Facing a chilly north wind, we are doused by morning showers and the intoxicating fragrance of the Trans-Pecos chaparral balm.

Raindrops sputter in the caliche dirt while two black Chevrolets retreat down the gravel road toward Ozona. The DARPA Suburbans disappear into the white dust, fog, and mud.

After a morning of sleep, followed by a shower, I am giddy with success as I trot back to the control center from the dormitory shed. I can't wait to analyze the data from last night—the first ball lightning and primordial black hole data on Earth!

Colonel McMahon is alone in the conference room, dressed like a golfer, reading from his laptop. The guy is much bigger than me, all muscle with a short crew cut and a calm presence. After a momentary hesitation, I interrupt. "Hi, Colonel McMahon. Good morning, uh, afternoon."

A puzzled expression crosses his face, then one of recognition. "Oh, you're Anthony's graduate assistant. Scott?"

"Yes, Scott Anderson. We met in Austin a few weeks ago."

"Yes, I remember. Good afternoon, and welcome to Pecos Center. I hope you have been learning a lot from Anthony and Heinrich. In time, maybe you can contribute to our project."

"Uh, yeah. After I got my security clearance, Anthony shared his theories and technology. It's exciting stuff."

"Great. I just called Anthony. He should be on his way over. I'm also meeting with some visiting DARPA officials. Do you know where they are?"

"They, uh, the DARPA people left early this morning."

The colonel frowns.

"Uh, I'm sure Anthony will fill you in on the details from last night." Whoa, he is going to be surprised. "Sorry to interrupt you. I need to get to work."

I scuttle over to my cubicle, power up the computer, and push Danny's dinner trash into the waste can. I wrinkle my nose at the stink of stale beer, pizza crusts, and the near-empty bottle of Jack Daniel's while I use a visualization application to mine the data logs from last night. I build a multidimensional overlay of grid voltage, gravity sensors, and visual data. Then, I replay the ball lightning sequence like a movie clip, again and again.

Glancing up from my cubicle, I see Danny in the conference room with Anthony, Heinrich, and the colonel. The colonel has a smile of astonishment, and he waves me over.

As I enter, Anthony says, "Hey, where have you been? We started debriefing Roger on last night's events."

"Oh, sorry. I wanted to review the data from last night."

Colonel McMahon stands as I enter; his eyes sparkle, and he makes room for me at the table. "Come on in and sit down. Anthony filled me in. Quite a night. I underestimated how quickly you would get up to speed." The colonel tilts his head toward me.

"Uh. Yeah. Thanks. No worries." What was said about me before I walked in? Anthony's eyes glisten. Heinrich is bending over the table like he might vomit.

Man, this is awkward.

"Oh, I can show you what I found—if you want."

Anthony beams and says, "Sure, show us."

"Let me open the telemetry visualization." I tap the file on my laptop and share the image on the wall display. "See here, I have the two-dimensional gravimeter display superimposed on the grid voltage measurements. I synchronized these data displays with the video recording of the events. This slow-motion playback starts thirty seconds before the PBH capture."

Colonel McMahon stands up and steps toward the display. Heinrich shakes his head.

"You can see the PBH is first detected by the gravimeters about seventy meters northwest of the grid. The location is shown by this red circle. The detection alarm was triggered when the PBH passed through the ground surface. As the singularity rises, you see the gravimeters begin an upward deflection. At two meters above the ground, ball lightning plasma envelops the PBH. We realized then what it was. The PBH moves horizontally up the voltage gradient toward the west, and a small blue arc flashes as the black hole passes through the grid wires. It was catapulted into a ballistic arc across the sky. The plasma ball disappeared about two hundred meters above us, but the gravimeter array continued tracking the PBH seven kilometers west of Pecos Center."

Nobody says a word. I catch my breath, my heart pounding. The colonel, Anthony, and Danny sit, mouths agape, and tears glisten on Anthony's cheeks. Darkness falls across Heinrich, who is staring through me.

"Wow. Just wow," Anthony gushes. "I'm impressed. I expected this analysis to take weeks. Kudos! Scott, you work miracles. You've saved this project from disaster."

"Thanks." My face is hot with embarrassment, and my heart melts with the reward of Anthony's recognition. "And, uh, now it appears we can capture a PBH and launch it into the sky."

"Yeah, sure." Anthony nods as if unsurprised.

"But, how is this possible for a singularity weighing three hundred billion metric tons? Newton's Third Law says the grid should collapse under the weight," I ask.

"Newton did not anticipate the physics of quantum gravitation." Anthony looks intently at his hands, quiet, smiling, and in deep thought. "Think about it; the electrostatic force is thirty-six orders of magnitude greater than gravity. Newton's Third Law falls apart at a black hole within a strong electrostatic force that nullifies most gravitational forces outside the singularity."

Danny blurts out, "We have a fuckin' antigravity machine for singularities?"

Anthony chuckles. "I would word it a bit differently. But yeah. A strong electric field neutralizes most gravitational force outside a tiny black hole."

The colonel has an awestruck, wrinkled brow. Heinrich remains silent, pain in his eyes.

The colonel says, "We should recognize what has been achieved here." He locks eyes with each of us in turn. "You've crossed a threshold. Maybe the biggest discovery of our time—as important as the first Trinity nuclear test—but black holes passing through the planet? And our bodies? I get a little sick with the thought," says the colonel.

"Yes," says Anthony. "Ordinary matter clumps together, but PBHs pass through Earth like neutrinos. About four hundred billion neutrinos from the sun pass through you each second. PBHs are bigger than neutrinos but still only about the size of protons—one billionth thinner than an acupuncture needle. They get swept from space, caught in the Earth's core rotation, and have near-zero friction. When a PBH does collide with visible matter, electrons get stripped, and the PBH emerges with a positive charge."

"You're saying a PBH will take a long path through Earth to arrive at the grid?" asks the colonel.

"Yes. Positively charged PBHs get pulled out of the Earth by the natural electrostatic charge of atmospheric storms. Hence, 'ball lightning' occurs naturally." Anthony pauses, then beams. "Which means our negatively charged grid can pull PBHs out of the Earth! We now have the tools for experimentation. This is a thrilling moment!"

"Time to try out the singularity containment?" Heinrich asks the colonel. "That would let us study the PBH physics in the controlled laboratory environment we built in Austin."

"Yeah. When can we take that step?" Colonel McMahon's eyes light up.

What could a military man do with a box of singularities he could control? My God. The power potential is staggering. Stephen Hawking predicted that each PBH has a million megatons of potential energy bottled up. A single detonated PBH could destroy Earth. The air force investment would pay off—if that detonation could be triggered—but it would be suicide for our whole planet. What would they use it for? A doomsday weapon?

"Slow down, guys," says Anthony. "Let's make sure we have a repeatable process. Can we get your modulation scheme ready again for tonight?"

Danny sits up with a grin. "You bet. Scott and I'll get the guys together to inspect the grid perimeter and the C-W generators. We have a few hours of daylight to get ready."

Colonel McMahon chose to stay and watch the show tonight. Danny talked him into a Sam Adams, although the colonel made it clear he disapproves of beer on the job. My stomach turns at the sight of the microwaved pizza on my plate. I would pay anything for one of Mom's chicken dinners with Robby.

A backlog of guilt reminds me that I left Mom and Robby alone. Tapping my iPad to check Mom's Instagram feed, I see shots taken months ago but nothing recent. Good and bad memories float by as I flip through images of home, hiking in the hills a year ago, and photos of the façade of family life with Mom, Dad, and Robby. How could I leave them all behind?

"Robby, are you okay? Is Mom okay?" I whisper to myself, remembering endless hours sitting by Robby's little fort of limestone rocks in the oak-shaded garden, accompanied by his ritual tap of stone on stone.

Now I'm doomscrolling social media, trying to ignore the flood of fascist hate posts. The skinhead bots spawn faster than the social media cops can delete accounts. They infect stupid skinhead trolls with conspiracy theories that neurodivergent nerds are the elite technologists confining the lower classes to poverty by controlling tech companies and social media outlets that manipulate the masses and sneer at them, the "real Americans" as racists, xenophobes, misogynists, and fascists. It is an infuriating, illogical poison that feeds the hate crimes against Asians, Jews, and all academics. I force-close all my social media feeds except one, switching to the refuge of Instagram photos, safe in my bubble where skinheads won't find me, wishing I was at home. Heinrich's public account also has fresh posts: mediocre pictures of West Texas plants and rocks. Strange guy—I don't get it.

"Hey, you ready with your kick-ass voltage modulation?" Danny chomps on another slice of cheesy pizza and washes it down with a gulp of beer. "We ran dedicated fiber out to the telemetry router this afternoon. Spooled it on the ground for now. We'll bury it later in conduits. Testing it now. Works perfect."

I see where Danny ran the new orange fiber cable from the ceiling into the server cabinet. I gotta hand it to Danny—he plows through obstacles.

"Nice. We can surf the internet all night."

He rolls his eyes and chuckles.

"You gentlemen ready to get started?" asks Anthony as he walks in with Colonel McMahon.

"Yep. We inspected the grid perimeter. Scott and I are ready when you are."

"Okay," says Anthony. "Go ahead and start the cooldown initialization." Then, with a big grin, he says, "Let's go catch some black holes!"

Danny begins the now-familiar process, starting the liquid nitrogen pumps as he calls out the temperature readings until the C-W stack components reach superconducting transition temperature. "Ready to fire it up, Anthony. All telemetry is normal, and C-W stacks all show seventy-seven degrees Kelvin."

"Go ahead, but let's ensure it's stable at full voltage before you start the modulation protocol," says Heinrich, suddenly back from acting like an outcast and watching Colonel McMahon as he speaks.

"Okay, Heinrich. Power coming on," says Danny, then whispers to me, "What a dickhead."

The crack from utility power relays echoes across the grid. "Voltage rising through five megavolts. Current consumption is nominal," says Danny. Ultraviolet blue coronas emerge from the power feeds, expanding across the six-hundred-acre fabric.

We watch the two-dimensional voltage sensor array on the wall display—adapted from my visualization analysis, the color transitions from blue to red as the voltage ramps toward fifty megavolts. The gravimeter array image is no longer an afterthought. It is featured prominently on our central wall display, the entire array of sensors registering Earth's gravity at 9.8 meters per second squared, straight down. Capturing another PBH should automatically switch the display to a three-dimensional view with a red sphere marking the singularity's position.

"Scott, we're stable at forty-eight megavolts now. Ready? Go ahead and start your modulation when ready," says Danny.

Heinrich observes the grid through the panoramic windows, watching the blue corona lights, arms at his waist, and says, "You may begin grid voltage modulation now." He glances at the colonel.

I roll my eyes. "Okay, starting now." The wall display of voltage sensors is Ferrari red, then transitions through purple shades to a deep blue as the voltages drop to five megavolts. A minute later, the cycle reverses and shifts back to purple and then to the red of forty-eight megavolts. "Modulation is working fine. Just like last night."

"You know . . ." Danny is in a trance, watching my new voltage array display. "This is as much fun as watching Saint Elmo's fire through the window." The red-purple-blue-purple-red cycle repeats.

"Yeah. Watch when the gravimeter array detects a singularity. It should be an even better show when it switches to track the PBH in three dimensions." I return one of the evil grins to Danny.

"Scott, I don't see how anyone is going to get sleep tonight with your hot shit cartoon show." Danny rocks his smiling face, watching the blue light flickering across the grid.

Anthony alternates his attention from the blue corona lights in the grid fabric to one display and the next. He radiates the pride and joy of a father watching his baby's first steps. Serene.

Colonel McMahon leans forward on the edge of his chair like a giddy kid waiting for Santa to bring him a pony. Hardly the look of an air force officer. Dressed in khaki pants and a golf shirt, the only military clues are the crew cut and upper-body mass.

I get up to fetch another Shiner from the fridge. "Another beer, anyone?" Three hands go up—including the colonel's. Maybe I should ask if people want a bowl of popcorn too. "Colonel McMahon, what kind of beer can I get you? I recommend Shiner Bock." Danny wrinkles his nose.

"Call me Roger," says the colonel. "And yes, I'll take a Shiner."

The monotony settles over the staff in the control room. I expect a few will lose the battle to sleep. I go to work coding an improved voltage modulation control loop. Capturing a singularity and levitating it under the grid should be like rolling a marble across a tilting table.

An hour later, Danny complains, "Scott, that's the third time your gravity array glitched into 3-D rendering mode and then back to 2-D. Can you review your fuckin' code and fix it? It's beginning to make me nauseous."

Focused on coding my new voltage-steering algorithm all this time, I had not noticed. "Huh. Maybe some gravimeter sensor noise effect?"

"Maybe. The last glitch was just a couple minutes ago. I saw two other glitches about half an hour ago."

"Okay. Let me work on the telemetry logs. Maybe I can filter out the noise." I pipe the file through a script scanning for gravity excursions. There is an immediate hit. "Yikes. Large gravimeter signal excursions. They happened a few minutes ago and on multiple sensors."

"Uh-huh. I figured you had a bug in your code."

"No. I don't think this is a joking matter. This may be something real, and maybe . . ."

Beep! Beep! Beep!

Anthony stands, watching the gravimeter display switch to 3-D mode. A red circle is displayed, dragging up to ground level.

"Yes! Yes!" yells Anthony. "Here comes another one." The sensor display indicates a gravity well centered on the red circle, passing above ground level. We watch it fall underground as the voltage modulation drops to three megavolts. "No! We lost it."

"Just wait for it, guys," I say. The entire room stands, watching the grid and the control room displays. There is no visible change under the grid outside the window. The grid continues its faint blue corona glow, which grows brighter as the voltage increases. "Here it comes again." The red circle that marks the gravity well location rises a meter above ground level. I glance out the window as a bright white plasma ball ignites around the singularity.

Anthony claps. "All right! Ball lightning!" He bends down to his laptop to run mass calculations while Colonel McMahon applauds with a goofy grin. The room erupts in cheers and high-fives as the ball of light floats up and east.

"The singularity has a calculated mass of about eighty billion metric tons. Ha! A small one this time." Anthony chuckles.

"Voltage is passing twenty-five megavolts. The ball is speeding up!" I yell. The sphere of plasma lofts up and out of the grid toward the eastern sky, disappearing after traveling several hundred meters.

Applause resumes as we all laugh and slap high-fives.

"Roger, this proves we can repeat the process to capture primordial black holes!" Anthony grins at Danny and me while clapping.

The colonel walks to each person in the control room to shake their hand. "Good job. Good job. Great team effort." He makes a point to include Heinrich. "Great job, Heinrich. Thanks for your leadership." He claps Anthony on the shoulder while shaking his hand. "Congratulations, Anthony. You made history this week."

"Thanks, but I could not have done it without the team. Especially Danny and Scott. They had extraordinary insights into our design flaw and improvised the voltage modulation protocol. Without that invention, we would still be spinning our wheels."

Danny and I face each other and bump fists, and I fetch cold beers from the fridge. The blue corona glow of the grid continues the periodic intensity cycle every two minutes. It is still early at night, so I return to analyze those glitches Danny complained about. I don't believe it's just noise because multiple sensors show similar signals. I pipe the data through my rendering software and slow the playback to visualize each event.

"Anthony, you need to see this." I cast my slow-motion visualization to a spare wall screen. "On the left display is the data from an event when Danny saw a glitch that flipped the gravimeter display to 3-D mode. I found what caused it. You can see another singularity fly straight up through the grid. Ten milliseconds and it was gone. We can see it only because I slowed the playback."

"Awesome. The grid accelerates the PBH so fast it does not have a chance to form a plasma ball. Send me that log file. I want to calculate the mass," Anthony says.

"On the way to you. I found multiple similar events earlier this evening. Danny noticed two of them, and I found three others. They all move too fast for our naked eyes to track them."

"Only one billion metric tons," says Anthony. "That event you shared is tiny compared to the monster we captured yesterday."

"And, wow, this is amazing. I piped the log file from last night's test run through my filter script. There were nine similar low-mass singularity events besides the monster we captured."

Anthony's smile expands across his face. "We might catch the smaller singularities if you slowed the voltage modulation."

"That's easy to do. I can combine the altitude tracking with the gravity well detection software into a control loop that will automatically reduce the voltage to keep a PBH within the grid for an extended time."

"You think your control loop is ready to try now?" asks Anthony.

"Yeah. Let's try it. The worst that could happen is a singularity escapes the grid."

"No, we need to be cautious," Heinrich says. "Throwing too many new ideas into the mix might break something."

Danny smirks and rolls his eyes.

Anthony examines our faces, Heinrich, Danny, then me, with a slight tilt of his head. "Let's try it. Whenever you are ready, cut in your new modulation algorithm."

The colonel's smile has changed to a frown.

I tap my display to enable the new software. "Engaging control loop now."

There is no visible change to the pulse of the blue-white corona glow of the grid. The solitary whisper of air-conditioning vents accompanies our watch while everyone scans the gravimeter display and the outside light show.

A half hour later, the display switches to 3-D mode. "Gravity well tracking up from underground!" shouts Danny.

Five seconds later, we hear a series of beeps.

"Yep!" I shout. "Control loop halting cyclic modulation—lowering grid voltage to slow the PBH approach. It's slow moving, up to ten meters above the ground. The grid voltage has dropped down to about five megavolts."

"Plasma ball!" shouts Danny. "Drifting up to fifteen meters."

"Scott! Your control loop is working. It's stationary. Holding at around sixteen meters." Anthony shares a delirious grin with me.

The colonel stands with his hands on his hips. He beams at Heinrich. "You know what this means? We can try your singularity containment process and drop a PBH into one of your storage vessels."

"You're right," says Heinrich. "I expected years of experiments and development before we could steer a PBH." Heinrich sneers at me. "I'll need our software team to develop the voltage modulation protocols. We'll also need a *qualified* engineering team to build an interface to the grid systems."

I feel my face heat up, and the vision of Heinrich with a punched-in bloody face returns. "Can someone tell me what this 'storage vessel' is?" I ask.

"The containment vessel will allow us to transport a primordial black hole to other locations. Imagine taking one of these singularities into the Austin laboratory for experiments," says Heinrich.

My attention is drawn back to the plasma ball drifting to the north—toward us. I hear him but focus on the sphere of light outside. "The singularity is drifting toward the edge of the grid nearest to the control center. The voltage control loop has some imperfections, I think."

"I'm amazed your slapped-together software works at all," Heinrich says.

"You know what?" asks Danny. "I bet the ball is attracted toward the grid's edge, where voltage is a bit higher adjacent to the C-W stacks. Your control loop can't compensate for that."

The PBH continues its drift to the north, still directly toward us.

"This is beautiful." Anthony disregards our concerns. "To observe a singularity for an extended period is a gold mine." His voice leaps with excitement. "The telemetry captured will be enough hard data to keep physicists busy for decades."

The singularity drifts and halts at the north edge of the grid fifteen minutes later.

"This proves Danny's guess. The drift stops where voltage is highest at the C-W stacks. However, the control loop continues to raise the grid voltage. That would mean the electric charge of the PBH is changing. But why?" I ask.

"It makes sense," says Anthony. "While suspended under the grid, random collisions with air molecules neutralize the electric charge in the singularity. Therefore, you need a higher grid voltage to hold its vertical position."

We watch as the grid voltage creeps up until it hits maximum. The ball slips away from the grid, and there's a collective gasp as the PBH accelerates, leaving the grid's electric field behind and heading toward us. The plasma ball fills our view before exploding against the chain-link fence. Thunder and chunks of metal rattle against the windows.

I'm kneeling on the floor by my chair with my head covered, but the PBH has passed underground. The anecdotes of explosions when ball lightning contacts grounded metal objects have now been validated. Anthony turns to me, wearing a stupid grin from ear to ear.

If it had traveled twenty meters farther, the exploding PBH would have landed inside the control room.

Chapter 11

SINGULARITY

Captain's Log, Frigate-328, 179237.90 LST

Drones detected singularity radiation signatures from the dark side of Sol-3. The radiation disappeared shortly afterward and might have been a naturally occurring singularity event.

Given the recent Sol-3 science research containment failures, I fear the Gravi-Tech suppression effort has failed. Frigate-328's radiation detector array was deployed to get a position fix on any future singularity radiation events. Still, from our stealth position within Sol-0's glare, it will only be effective on the daylight side of the planet.

I ordered Prime-AI to release Mil-AI from standby. I had no choice.

Chapter 12

BRIMSTONE

The cobalt sky presides over the first chilly days of November and the sparkle of morning dew. Filling my lungs with the damp air continues to wake me from my brief sleep as I stroll the gravel path. The dormant grass has faded to the dull fall colors of West Texas, and a lone mockingbird sings atop a grid tower, solitary beauty among the grey.

The Trans-Pecos region is a flat, colorless desert, a radical contrast to the green Hill Country around Austin. Back home, I had often hiked along canyon trails thick with cedar and oak, with Robby following close behind. One day, we'd searched for snakes while a waterfall nearby splashed and mourning doves pleaded, accented by tweets from black-capped vireo. When Robby and I were alone, we left behind the fascists and the constant battles between Mom and Dad; our conversation that day had been limited to counting trees and birds and inspecting rocks.

Now Robby is alone with Mom. And Mom is risking her health—her life—going out in public and revealing herself to skinheads.

I never imagined my refuge in physics would be this extreme while also risking Robby and Mom's safety. Pecos is almost a utopia for me, despite the constant harassment by Heinrich. I'm allowed to use my brain, and the appreciation and respect from Danny and Anthony is the gratification I've always wanted. I am part of a team. It has been good for me, but my departure left Robby and Mom exposed to more danger from the fascists.

The fence between the control center and the grid has a five-meter hole—charred remnants of the meltdown caused by last night's explosion. I didn't understand why the energy release had happened until I recalled Anthony mumbling about "spilling some matter from the PBH." So, I checked Stephen Hawking's theory, which shows that radiation increases as a black hole's mass decreases. The primordial black hole eventually reverts to visible matter with a million-megaton explosion. So, splashing "some matter" out of a black hole could cause that little bit to explode. Luckily, we didn't empty the entire PBH—all life in Texas would have ceased. I sigh as I pull the door open into the Pecos control center.

"Scott, you're fuckin' crazy," Danny greets me as I enter. He swallows a mouthful of beer, rests against his chair back, and parks the heels of his boots on my desk; dirt clods knock loose into my keyboard. "Remember I told you about our C-W stack explosion years ago? Almost killed Pete. We must avoid inductive current spikes."

"I know, but we don't have a choice if we want to prevent a PBH from taking an uncontrolled leap at us. We need an algorithm that switches phase-balanced triplets of C-W stacks to adjust the grid voltage tilt. We roll the singularity ball under the grid to the position of the highest voltage. All automated with a three-dimensional control loop."

Danny seems to fall into a trance, then puts his beer down. "Okay, I can picture how it might work. But we must also fix Heinrich's absurd design for the containment vessel's electric field—the thing looks like a damn Mr. Coffee machine. You want to try a three-dimensional control loop in the vessel too?"

"Yeah, although that should be easier than controlling the grid voltage."

Danny holds his head in his hands. "This is going to be a lot of work."

"Should we find Heinrich and talk all this through with him? We need help from whoever wrote the code for his containment vessel microcontroller."

Danny twists his nose. "Heinrich? That shithead. He tried to sell us out to DARPA last month, and now he's taking all the credit for our PBH capture successes."

"You're talking about our boss. At a minimum, we can interrogate the engineers who did Heinrich's detailed design work."

Danny sighs. "We don't have much choice. Let me get started with the grid voltage control modifications. I like your analogy of rolling a marble across a maze board and dropping it through a hole. I'll let you talk to Heinrich so you can rewrite the containment vessel software."

I can't help but chuckle. "Gee, thanks, I get the shit job. You owe me another beer, though."

"Done!" Danny claps his hands. "Your usual?" he asks, heading toward the fridge.

Colonel McMahon huffs and puffs, a sheen of sweat on his brow as he steers a crate through the doorway into our assembly workshop across the parking lot from the Pecos control center. The hand truck's wheels crunch a fresh track of caliche residue on the polished concrete floor between workbenches stacked with electronic test equipment. The colonel tilts the crate flat, grunts, and shoves it toward me. He brushes the dirt from his jeans, exhales, and beams.

Admirable. The colonel had wrangled the shipping crate off the back of Anthony's rusty Ford pickup and single-handedly hauled it inside.

"Here are your prototypes, Scott. My chief engineer, Tiana, is impressed by your design modifications and new software for the vessel microcontroller. She had her engineers working around the clock to build these, and they also completed some quick tests."

The colonel wedges the crowbar under the crate's wooden lid; the nails squeak, protest, and then reveal a pool of Styrofoam popcorn. The smell of machine oil wafts to blend with the usual workbench odor of singed solder flux. Digging into the packing material, he pulls out the first container and unpacks it carefully to reveal a prototype containment vessel. Ha! It does resemble a coffeemaker. The colonel stands back from the bench and smiles, arms crossed.

Anthony is bent over his laptop at the far end of the bench and glances at the containment vessel. But he is preoccupied with some task among empty Coke cans and beer bottles.

I sit on a stool at the bench, pick up the prototype, roll it over in my hands, heft the ten-kilogram weight, and study the details. I feel like a kid with a new train set under the Christmas tree. "The accelerometers are attached to our 'coffee carafe' in these three locations?"

"Yes," says the colonel. "Tiana has this mounted on the gyroscope-stabilized platform adapted from an old Javelin missile spare parts bin." He taps the top of the vessel. "The wiring is routed up to the microcontroller—"

"—where the coffee filter should be." I chuckle. "And where we would load water into Mr. Coffee is a fifty-volt battery pack. By shrinking the distance between electrodes from the grid's thirty-seven meters to four centimeters inside the containment vessel, the voltage required is reduced by six orders of magnitude."

Danny sits on the stool beside me, crowding us to take his turn examining the vessel. "Wow. I bet the original Javelin designers never figured their seeker platform would be used to balance a small black hole. If not for Anthony's amazing antigravity effect, a quadrillion-kilogram mass should flatten this fucker like a penny on a railroad track."

"This is unbelievable," I say. "The design, fabrication, and delivery in three days? The assembly shop in Austin would have taken at least a month or two. Hats off to the engineers at your mysterious facility out west, Colonel McMahon."

"Scott—once again—my name is Roger. I'll pass on your compliments to the team."

The blue door opens with a hiss and closes with a bang. Heinrich stumbles inside like he's miffed he wasn't invited to the party.

"What the hell?" Heinrich shoves into our midst, pushing Danny and me against the workbenches. "What have you done?" His breathing is hoarse as he rips the containment vessel assembly away from Danny, turning it over in his hands.

"Three years of detailed design work created this vessel, and you slap on some mods in a couple of days?"

"Your original design had problems," I explain. "The slightest perturbations in gravity, PBH electric charge, or electrode voltage could have dislodged the singularity from containment." I don't add that he's a lousy engineer—despite his MIT education.

He twists his crimson face to me, breath sour and spittle flying. "Where do you get off screwing with my design? You fucking neurodefective! Have you forgotten you work for me?" I flinch and back away.

Roger turns to Heinrich, mouth open, speechless.

Danny's rage-red face approaches from the right. "Knock off your bullshit. Your original design was fucked up. Scott fixed it. With his accelerometer feedback loop, there is a chance it may work."

"Hey, hey guys," Anthony interjects. He shakes his head.

"Stop it! All of you!" Roger roars and scowls at us.

Roger's glare lingers on my face while he processes Heinrich's attack.

"But there is no way I can trust slapped-together changes to my original design," says Heinrich.

Roger shakes his head at Heinrich. "Tiana's engineering team reviewed, tested, and signed off on the design modifications. Why were you out of the loop on this?"

Anthony's attention is no longer on his laptop. He rolls his eyes. "Why are you guys all worked up over this new toy anyway? I'm not even sure what to use it for. We capture several PBHs every night within the grid and continue to collect more data than I could hope to analyze in my lifetime. Our research is a historic chance to confirm a single, all-encompassing theoretical framework of physics." His head rolls back, eyes closed.

Roger's anger dissolves with a sigh. "Thanks for the perspective, Anthony. We must remember we are a team and be proud of our collective accomplishments."

Anthony nods. "We have reached the most significant physics watershed in at least a hundred years, maybe a thousand years. This will change everything. Don't get wrapped around the axle over such a trivial matter."

Roger touches the containment vessel platform. His brow furrows, he says nothing for a while, then seems to settle an internal debate. "Anthony and Heinrich, notwithstanding your respective challenges of the containment vessel's value or design quality, we must start testing."

Anthony sighs but nods.

"Scott, review the changes to the design of the containment vessel in detail with Heinrich. Heinrich, include Tiana's engineering team in the reviews. I need your risk assessment on each design change and why we *shouldn't* proceed with the initial test of the vessel tonight."

"But Roger—" Anthony protests.

"No. Getting this device operational is not pointless," interrupts Roger. "Trapping a PBH singularity in this vessel is vital to national security. Transporting a singularity is a crucial step toward harnessing its power." Roger pauses, closing his eyes as if tormented by an inner voice. "We have to take risks. The Chinese may have already exploited PBH power in their Gobi Desert facility. That would forever upset the balance of power in the world."

Silence. The colonel's motivations are crystal clear. He's scared he won't have the weapons required for a future battle.

All we do in pursuing science is subverted by the military search for the ultimate superweapon. It's an ugly counterpoint to the gratification I want to feel. Escaping the skinhead killers could lead to mass death on a scale I never imagined. But I push the doubts from my mind. I am committed.

"We lost it." Danny pounds his desk with frustration. The evening's third primordial black hole drops off target and is lost, sinking into the Earth. Danny's forehead is wet with sweat. His usual humor and swagger were destroyed in yesterday's inquisition. He drains a half-empty Sam Adams bottle and slams it down on his desk among greasy pizza crusts and tools.

It is 3:20 a.m., and my stomach cramps—induced by spicy pepperoni, cheese, and Shiner. The close air of the locked control room stinks like a locker room after a tough football game. I hold my head in my hands, elbows on the table, reviewing a plot of the path the singularity wandered until we lost it.

"The adjustments don't have the centimeter accuracy we need to drop a PBH into the containment vessel." The prototype sits a kilometer south of us in the dark, under the grid. The device looked ridiculous resting on the plastic patio table Danny found to electrically insulate Mr. Coffee above ground. "We need luck, lots of it, for the capture to succeed."

Heinrich rotates his chair like a ship's captain, orchestrating the actions of the entire control room staff. "Okay, guys. Power up the grid again and give it another try." His newfound arrogance drips from every word with a sneer I have not seen before tonight.

Roger stands at the panoramic windows, arms folded across his chest, jaw clenched. I imagine he would prefer a roomful of soldiers to scream at. There are just a few stars visible through thin cirrus clouds.

"This is great—another twenty terabytes of PBH data. Let's catch another one." Ignoring our frustration, Anthony grins like a kid with a new video game, head lowered to his workstation. "In another week, I should have a petabyte of log data to mine. I see some interesting trends: gravitation vibrations and radiation bursts correlate with voltage transients."

Radiation bursts? Danny and I share wide-eyed glances.

"Yeah, okay. Let's get on with trying a vessel capture," commands Heinrich.

The grid's emerging ultraviolet blue Saint Elmo's fire returns, tracking the increase in grid voltage. I try to relax in my chair, watching the hypnotic lights and monitoring the containment vessel's sensors. I just want to go to sleep. On top of the locker room smell, there is a rancid stench of rotting chicken—somebody needs to empty that trash can by the sink. I am beginning to give up on this method of steering a PBH into the containment vessel. Oh well. At least we may get a data sample to analyze and fix my mistakes.

Beep! Beep! Beep!

The gravimeter display switches to 3-D mode. A red circle marks the position of a primordial black hole coaxed up to ground level by the grid.

"Another PBH!" shouts Roger.

"Okay, I'm taking control of the grid voltage," Danny announces. He steers the grid voltage lower, slowing the singularity's rise.

"Plasma ball!" shouts Anthony as a dazzling blue-white ball illuminates the grid, floating about ten meters above the ground. "This is a big one. The plasma diameter is forty centimeters. Initial mass reading is around one hundred fifty billion metric tons." He gazes out the window, considering his catch, and says with swagger, "We've seen bigger."

"I've got it," says Danny. He is intent on his console and his steering of the singularity with the gravity-neutralizing grid voltage. "The vertical motion is stopped. Guiding toward the vessel."

The 3-D visualization of the PBH motion matches our analogy of rolling a marble across a maze board. Danny taps positioning corrections into his keyboard, and the PBH coasts toward the containment vessel.

I keep my eyes on the vessel's telemetry display. "The vessel is ready, and internal electrodes match the grid field voltage. The vessel accelerometers are sensing the PBH! You're getting close." This is a first.

Danny pauses and rests his hands. "I'll try lowering the singularity down inside the vessel. Slow, so I don't lose it."

Makes sense. When dropped from high above the vessel, we lost the last few singularities when we cut the grid voltage to zero.

"Danny! Stick to the procedures we agreed to!" Heinrich shouts.

Danny shakes his head. "Dropping the PBH has not worked. I'm just gonna take it slow."

Heinrich stands and faces Danny, hands on his hips, but everyone ignores him.

"Get ready, Scott. I'm nudging this down. Give me readouts on your vessel accelerometers, and let's land this one."

"Okay," I reply. Heinrich glares at me. "Vessel accelerometers show the singularity above and northwest. Push it west, now south. Stop. There, okay, a bit east. Good. Lower, lower."

"Hey guys, the plasma ball has enveloped the containment vessel. I can't see the top of the Walmart table," says Roger. "Uh, hope nothing melts."

"Danny, you are near the center. Raise it a bit. There. All accelerometers point to the center of the vessel. Hold. Containment control loop is engaged and . . . stable!" I yell, "Kill grid power!"

Sweating over his console, Danny slaps the control to turn off all C-W generators. "Grid voltage dropping below five megavolts. Two megavolts. One." The video shows the white-blue ball of plasma floating a meter above the ground. "Scott? Do you have it?"

I check the status of the vessel containment controller and grin at Danny. "We got it! The vessel control loop is closed, and the PBH charge is static. The glass carafe insulation is working. That fifty-volt battery inside the vessel is the only electric power under the grid towers!"

The colonel turns to Danny and me, all smiles, clapping. "Well done! Well done!"

Danny and I collapse backward into our chairs and breathe again. We exchange high-fives at last.

Heinrich's arms are slack, his jaw hanging open. Quiet. Asshole. We all walk up to the windows to watch the point of light in the darkness under the grid. The soft blue-violet corona glow has vanished from the grid, but the light radiating from the half-meter plasma ball wraps our singularity.

"Holy shit. That's one hundred fifty billion metric tons," says Danny.

"Yeah, but the size of a proton and with a million megatons of potential energy," I reply. The thought makes me a bit sick to my stomach. "Resting on top of your twenty-five-dollar table from Walmart."

We laugh at each other. Roger and Anthony circle the room to shake hands with the dozen engineers and techs manning the control room workstations.

Heinrich stands alone.

"You know what, guys?" says Anthony. "I think I'll walk outside to get a better view."

I turn to Anthony in horror but stop and smile. "Yes, we can go out there now that the grid voltage is off. I've got it contained with only a fifty-volt electric field. Should not be a problem."

"Yeah, should be safe." Danny points to the exit safety light over the door, glowing green.

The two dozen techs in the control room exchange a why-the-hell-not collective shrug. Anthony leads the way out the door, and a dozen techs from the control room follow him into the night. Humid wind from the south is a refreshing improvement from the cramped stink of the control room. We go around the side of the building toward the edge of the grid.

A kilometer to the south, the dazzling blue-white plasma ball illuminates the Chihuahuan Desert, shadows of the grid tower splayed out in a radial pattern below the illuminated underside of wire mesh stretching into the dark.

Anthony stops at the perimeter service road, and we stand beside him. There is a faint noise in the distance.

Zzzzzzzss.

"What the hell is that?" I ask. "Sounds like rattlesnakes. Although it has a higher pitch." I search the shadows for serpents.

Zzzzzzzzsss.

Anthony grins. "No. That's the sound of ball lightning. The plasma causes an audible sonic vibration." Tears roll down his cheeks. "You know what? The historical anecdotes report the smell of sulfur. They called it brimstone in the seventeenth century." Anthony strides forward like a happy kid on a treasure hunt.

Zzzzzzzzssssss. Plop!

Darkness returns. "It's gone!" yells Roger. "What happened?"

I pull up my wrist-strapped iPad, which is still connected to the Wi-Fi network in the control center. "No, it's there. The telemetry from the vessel shows the singularity remains in the containment vessel."

"No worries. The plasma extinguished, but the singularity remains," says Anthony. "Now we can get closer." Huffing and puffing, Anthony pulls out his cell phone, turns on the flashlight, and leads the way, literally skipping across the desert. Fifteen other flashlights emerge as the team spreads to follow Anthony toward Danny's plastic table in the dark.

"Anthony, this is dangerous. Stop until we make sure the containment is robust," calls Heinrich.

"No, no, it's fine," I yell. "The containment field is working perfectly."

The team keeps walking, and soon, the faint outline of the table is visible. Anthony's breath and pace quicken, and I trot to keep up. I again go through Heinrich's list of risks that I could not answer. My pace slows to a walk. "Hey, Anthony. Take it . . ."

Zzzzzzzzsss.

"Holy shit!" Danny yells as blue-white light erupts around the containment vessel twenty meters ahead. Anthony is out in front, still moving forward.

Zzzzzzzzsss!

My eyesight recovers from the flare of plasma light, and the forest of support towers and the wire grid stretched above us becomes visible again. I look again at my iPad console. "Whoa, stop, guys! The containment voltage is wild! I don't like this."

Anthony turns to me with childlike joy. "It's beautiful, Scott." He takes another step forward.

The display on my iPad rages, reacting to wild disturbances in accelerometer readings. "Anthony, no! I'm losing containment!"

Anthony halts, his gaze fixed on the dazzling blue-white light of his primordial black hole as he reaches out with his right hand. The sphere grows larger and flashes brighter.

Crack!

Shrapnel scatters, and the ball of light leaps up, arcing toward Anthony and slamming into his chest.

Zzzzzzzzsss—bang! Bang!

Darkness collapses over us.

I am face down into the dirt. My ears ring with pain. Falling pebbles strike my back and hands, which cover my head.

I cough and gag as an overpowering sulfur odor burns my throat.

Glancing up toward Anthony, I see the colonel kneeling nearby in the light of brush caught on fire. I push to my knees to see better. Roger turns with a horrified expression and waves me away. Too late. Bones, meat, and a rib cage lie in a heap, quartered by the explosion.

My hands are spattered with blood. And a few chunks of flesh. Those were not rocks that hit me. An odor like burned chicken and sulfur hangs in the smoke. My guts convulse, and vomit splashes in the dirt.

Chapter 13

RETREAT

Smoke residue lingers in my throat. Each breath burns. Rubbing my forehead and cheeks with sweaty palms makes my eyes water. Swallows of warm coffee provide just enough caffeine to maintain coherent thought. *Am I guilty of murder?*

Lost inside my dark cubicle, the only hint of time progressing is the orange dust of dawn along the panorama's eastern edge. My fingers tapping on the keyboard accompanies the coffee machine's periodic drip and hiss of steam.

I draw my dirt-crusted fingernail across the lines of C++ code I wrote for the containment algorithms. Where is my mistake? Where is the break in logic? My fifth attempt to find the error in my control loop for the containment vessel is futile. Squinting does not correct the blur of the telemetry logs. All the effectors and sensors behaved as I expected. The measured gravitational force of the accelerometers is pristine. The response of the control loop logic tracked and drove precise voltage corrections to the electrodes. Yet, the accelerometers showed wild, erratic gravity excursions I cannot explain. The feedback loop responded, but the gravity excursions grew until the accelerometers saturated and the vessel shattered.

I don't see my mistake. My incompetence. I killed the most brilliant man on Earth by stupidly encouraging Anthony to stumble into a deathtrap. And destroyed my utopian escape from skinheads. Anthony was the one man who believed in me and showed pride in my contributions toward the most significant scientific advancement in human history. Anthony was my refuge, my protector. What was my stupid mistake?

Liquid splashes into the sink. Roger dumps the coffee and refills the machine with fresh water. He loads the filter basket with ground coffee and leans against the counter, arms folded across his chest. Our eyes meet.

I can't face the guilt and force myself to start my sixth pass of code analysis.

Roger pushes my dirty cup aside to make room for the fresh coffee steaming by the side of my keyboard. "Here you go, Scott. That last batch was nasty."

Although I am shaken out of my zombie trance of code analysis, I keep my head down. But I grab the cup and try to wash the smoke from my throat again.

Bang! The door from outside slams shut. Heinrich marches in. "Colonel McMahon, we need to talk."

Roger, sitting on top of the neighboring desk, sips his coffee. "Okay, sure."

Heinrich glances at me, then at the conference room. "Privately?"

Roger shrugs and follows Heinrich. I sip my coffee, glancing at them in the conference room. My gut fills with dread and acid each time Heinrich gestures at me.

Grabbing my stale coffee cup, I walk over to the sink, dump the lukewarm sludge, and toss the empty into the pile of dirty dishes. The cup clatters to a stop against a ceramic plate. The plate rings like a bell. I scuttle out the door and out of sight of Heinrich and Roger.

The ring of the plate follows me out the door. The first frost of November bites into me as I emerge into rays of the sunrise over distant clouds. My retreat takes me around the control center while they decide my fate in the conference room. That plate rings in my mind. I face the six-hundred-acre grandeur of wire fabric floating above the desert to the south. The otherworldly beauty is stained by a security vehicle parked under the grid. Yellow crime scene tape surrounds the tipped-over Walmart patio table. I stumble to one knee with my hands in the crushed white caliche at my feet.

The plate rang like a bell—a resonant tone from the strike of a coffee cup.

I jump with epiphany and sprint back to my cubicle in the dark corner of the control room. Adrenaline replaces despair as I access the vessel telemetry logs and pipe accelerometer data through a spectrum analyzer application. Nothing. Crap. Maybe if I integrate sample intervals, then analyze . . .

"Yes!"

"Find something?" Roger asks as he arrives at my desk with Heinrich.

"I think so. Guys, look what I uncovered with the spectrum analyzer." I switch my workstation to project on a large wall display.

Heinrich rolls his eyes. "This can wait for the postmortem review." He tries to get Roger's attention, but Roger is focused on the data projected above us.

"Now, this first graph—" I slide my cursor over the plot of frequency amplitudes. "This plot results from streaming the accelerometer data through the spectrum analyzer."

"So what? It's just white noise," Heinrich mumbles.

"Yes, it appears random at first, but see what happens when I integrate multiple frames of accelerometer data using the periodic update of the containment field as the time base?" I steer the cursor to highlight a new spectrum analysis window. "Several frequency spikes show up at several harmonic frequencies starting at around ten megahertz. I couldn't see these until I used time integration across a hundred frames of the control loop data."

Roger's jaw slowly drops as he absorbs the new information.

But Heinrich frowns and shakes his head. "We're not going off half-cocked again with your snap attempts at the physics."

Roger looks intently at the display. "I see it, Scott. What does this mean?"

Heinrich glares at Roger.

"Maybe the PBH singularity resonated at high frequency," I reply. "Like a bell struck by a hammer." *Or a plate struck by a coffee cup.* "And here—the amplitude of the vibrations—they increase over time . . . it's . . . it's like the voltage control waveform induced resonant vibration within the PBH. The vessel shattered from the force of a 150-billion-ton singularity vibrating at ten megahertz!" I stare outside at the distant security truck guarding the scene. *This is how I killed Anthony.*

"Scott, your analytical skills continue to impress." Roger nods. "I think I see it."

"Another half-baked conclusion." Heinrich sniffs. "We can't trust cobbled-together analysis without rigorous reviews by competent scientists." Heinrich frowns at Roger. "Tiana's team is working on the official postmortem."

Stinging eyes, the smoke stench, and the scratch in my throat recall the agony. I look down at my hands, my arms, the sleeves bloodstained. "I know. I killed Anthony." Tears roll down my cheeks, snot dripping onto the keyboard.

Heinrich's lips curl into a snarl.

"You can't take this personally." Roger shakes his head.

"But . . . who else?" I hold my hands out.

Heinrich leans in and sneers. "You should pack up and leave."

Roger takes a deep breath. "Heinrich, stop. Scott has once again demonstrated amazing insight and analytical skills. Scott, we need you. Stay with the team. You are key to the effort. Take a break. Get some breakfast. You'll feel better after a shower and some sleep."

Heinrich is purple with rage.

I push away from my desk but can't stand up.

"Get going, Scott," Roger orders, his command voice firm. "We need you alert. Heinrich, come with me. This is tragic, but we *will* move forward."

Heinrich clenches his fists and follows, kicking my empty chair, which falls with a bang.

I shuffle toward the exit.

———

Roger was right. A shower and sleep helped rinse away some of the horrors, though the guilt of carnage still floods back when I open my eyes. I roll over in my dormitory bed to check the time on my cell phone. It is midafternoon, and I have lost most of the day. Two calls went unanswered while I slept. Both were from Tiana Annenkova, Roger's chief engineer. I close my eyes and sigh. I can't take another inquisitor after the bashing this morning. I roll out of bed, plant my feet on the floor, and hold my throbbing head in my hands. I force myself up.

———

Danny sits at his desk, staring at his workstation, swirling a shot of amber liquid in a glass. "What the fuck are we going to do?" His face is ashen, and his playful attitude is gone. His workstation is powered off, and three empty beer bottles are lined up next to the Jack Daniel's.

My cell phone disturbs the malaise. "It's Tiana." It rings four times. "Oh well." I sigh and answer. "Hi, this is Scott."

"Scott! I'm glad I finally reached you. I hope you are feeling better after the rest."

"Are you kidding?" I ask.

She pauses, voice shifting almost to a whisper. "Hey, Scott, I understand you feel horrible. We all do. The engineers here at Skunk Works are also devastated. Most were up all night trying to figure out what went wrong with the containment."

I guess Tiana appreciates that misery loves company. I feel uplifted but still guilty. "Yeah. I feel like absolute shit."

"We all are just heartbroken," Tiana says, followed by a long silence with muffled breathing. "I would like to get your help. The colonel tells me you have a theory of PBH resonance causing the explosion?"

"Yes. I did some work last night, er, this morning with the spectrum analysis of the accelerometer telemetry."

"Can you share this information with my Skunk Works team? I set up a wiki page on the secure server to collect all the data from last night's . . . event."

"Yeah, sure. I'm putting you on speaker so I can access my workstation. Danny is here with me too."

Danny sits up, rotating his head in confusion. "Uh. Hi, Tiana," he mutters to my phone on the desk between us, swallowing another shot of whiskey.

"Hi, Danny. I know we have all been rocked by last night's disaster, and I need everyone's help to figure this out. Scott, have you located the postmortem wiki?"

Her choice of a name for the wiki pulls me out of my focus on the science, but I shrug it off and sigh. "Yeah. I'm copying my analysis results to the folder. If you want, I can walk you through the work I started."

"Hold on. Let me gather the Skunk Works engineers to listen in. Give me a minute."

I set up sharing to Danny's console display and Tiana's lab—wherever that is. The secrecy seems absurd.

"Okay, we're ready here. Thanks for sharing on my display. You can go ahead." Tiana is joined by six other faces in the conference meeting display.

I take Danny and Tiana's team through the analysis I shared with Heinrich and Roger earlier. In our rush to improvise containment forces, we disrupted a PBH by striking at its natural resonance frequency, naively stumbling into new physics of mind-boggling energy.

"Scott, this is clever. How did you think to look for PBH resonance?"

"Pure accident. I tossed a dirty dish in the sink. It rang like a bell."

Tiana smirks with a shake of her head. "This PBH vibration coincides with radiation bursts in the Geiger counter telemetry files." She shares a graph of the radiation levels with an exponential hockey stick curve in the final milliseconds before the explosion.

"Wow. We stumbled into a method to upset the stability of the singularity with an electric field oscillation. A burst of radiation?" I ask.

"Uh, how bad was the radiation exposure?" asks Danny with a panicked frown.

"I'm not sure. All of you guys should be checked out by a doctor. I mentioned this to Colonel McMahon. He's coordinating with a NEST team to visit and complete a detailed survey of the . . . uh, accident site."

Danny squeaks, "NEST? A Nuclear Emergency Support Team?" He reaches to pour another shot of Jack Daniel's.

That would be cold justice—prolonged, excruciating death from radiation poisoning.

"We can't tell if the radiation intensity was harmful with the approximations from sensors in the grid towers." But Tiana's voice has an edge of concern. "Hell, you guys seem to be doing okay, though. If you had been hit by a fatal dose, I expect you would know by now."

"Great to know," I say. "Instead, we get to die in agony over many weeks."

"No, no, no. Please. Take it easy," Tiana begs. "The NEST team should be there today. Don't get ahead of the facts."

"Yeah, I guess you're right." Although I don't care what happens to me. "You know, we stumbled into a method for controlled release of energy. We found a way to disturb the stability of a PBH by varying the electric containment field at a resonant frequency, which could allow us to intentionally spill some matter out of the black hole to release a massive amount of energy. Each PBH is one hell of a battery of stored energy."

"I'm going to grab some more guys from the science team," says Tiana. "Be back in a minute."

Danny glares at me. "Were we just fuckin' *lucky* the containment control loop system found the resonance of the PBH last night?"

"Yes, lucky." I feel sick. "Bad luck, though . . ."

A long silence follows my statement.

Tiana returns to her workstation. "Scott, we have caucused, and our engineering consensus is the cause was the square wave-shape from the control circuits. If we low-pass-filter the electrode voltage, we should avoid exciting the natural resonance of the PBH."

"Ah-ha. Makes sense," I say. "Conversely, I bet if we sweep the spectrum across the PBH, we should be able to detect its resonant frequency and then exploit that to release energy."

"Damn it!" Heinrich yells, jolting Danny and me from behind. "What the hell are you two up to? Stop your reckless experiments!"

"Hey, Heinrich," says Tiana. "We're on the phone and reviewing data with Scott and Danny. What is the problem?"

Heinrich flinches. "Oh, uh, hi, Tiana." But he recovers. "Let's end the meeting. I'm running things differently going forward. We'll talk later, Tiana."

Heinrich looms over me. "Scott, hang up the damn phone."

Danny's eyes are wide. I rotate my chair, see Tiana's grimace on-screen, and tap the hang-up button. I leave my back to Heinrich, arms folded across my chest, staring at my workstation.

"You don't get it, do you, Scott?" Heinrich spits. "You are finished. I'm yanking your account credentials." He pivots and marches out of the control center.

Danny makes eye contact with me, shaking his head. "Heinrich is way out of line. If he fires you, fuck, I'll quit. He can't run this place without us."

"No, watch out for yourself." I tap my keyboard and find I am locked out of my workstation. "Well, that didn't take long. I guess that means I got fired. It seems my only contact with the outside world is on my iPhone. It's my lifeline," I sigh, shaking my head. I can still doomscroll fascist posts, or better yet, retreat to Instagram pictures of home. I look at all the notifications on Instagram and scroll through a stream of recent photos Heinrich has posted. I don't get it. The guy is on a power trip yet finds time to upload these crappy snapshots of plants and rocks. Why? He does this whenever we make significant progress. Is this some form of therapy?

"I'm going to pack up. No point hanging around anymore." I stand and walk to the exit.

Danny hangs his head, staring at the floor.

The door opens in my face as I reach for the handle. Roger pushes through, and three steps behind him, Heinrich follows, wearing a manic expression. "Scott, come with me into the conference room," Roger says, his face crimson.

Here comes the final axe. Danny stands, open-mouthed, and I trail Roger and Heinrich into the conference room. The door slams shut.

"Sit down, you two. I have had enough of this bickering. Heinrich is the acting chief administrator for the Pecos project. Heinrich and I just had a frank discussion about your role. I need you to take the technical lead. I have consulted with Tiana, and she's in full support."

The room spins. "But . . . what?" I turn from Roger's determined, clenched jaw to Heinrich's contorted face. "What did you say?"

"We all agree," Roger says, threatening Heinrich with a frown, "that your technical contributions have been stellar and have led to this project making more progress in the last few months than in the last decade. Tiana's team is all thumbs-up on you."

"But . . ." My stomach tumbles, claustrophobia closing around me. "But . . . I'm just a grad student. And Anthony is gone," I whisper, feeling like I'm sliding into an abyss. "I killed him." I take a deep breath.

Roger's face softens. "No. No, you did not kill Anthony." His voice lowers. "It was a tragic accident. Several of Tiana's team have similar feelings of guilt. But self-recrimination is pointless. We designed an overly responsive containment control loop that showed us how to release energy from a primordial black hole. Anthony was foolish. His fatal stumble was driven by a twenty-year obsession to capture ball lightning."

I shake my head at Roger. Unlike Heinrich's darting, manic eyes, Roger has a face of patience and wisdom.

"How can we hope to fill Anthony's shoes?" I ask.

"We can't," Roger says, lips clenched in a thin line. "But you and Heinrich are vital to this program. You must work together. Heinrich, your success is dependent on Scott. Scott, your success is dependent on Heinrich. We're all on the same team. Shake it off. You must continue with containment experiments. Tomorrow."

He looks Heinrich in the eye. "I need your commitment."

Heinrich squirms but replies, "Yeah. Okay, okay."

"Scott, I need your commitment too."

I'm lightheaded and still recovering my balance. I'm only a research assistant. Looking at Colonel Roger McMahon, I take a deep breath, then say, "Yes."

"Hey, boss, the two new containment vessels arrived from Skunk Works, and I acquired four new patio tables from Walmart." Danny can't resist the wise-guy attitude. "Can I get you a beer? Maybe a cup of coffee?" He snaps the cap off another Sam Adams. "We could set up all four containment vessels for tonight—one per quadrant under the grid. I have the crew stringing fiber-optic cables to each table."

"Sounds good, Danny." I tilt my head at him. "And knock off the *boss* bullshit."

Danny grins. "I'll bring you a Shiner?"

"Yeah, thanks." Danny's teasing compensates for a little of my survivor's guilt. But—there is Anthony's abandoned workstation and empty chair.

I intercept Danny walking over with my beer. "Take a walk with me?"

"Sure, it's damn cold, though. The blue norther knocked the temperature down thirty degrees this afternoon."

We grab our jackets from the pegs by the door. A stiff, icy wind from the northeast cuts through us as we walk toward the perimeter fence.

"Feels good." I fill my lungs. "That cramped control room could use better ventilation to push the stink out." We both take deep breaths, watching the crew spool the last cable from the four Walmart tables in the distance, each topped with a containment vessel with the latest firmware update. The yellow crime scene tape is gone, but the tracks from all the vehicle traffic at that spot are still visible in the setting sunlight.

"Glad we didn't get a fatal blast of radiation. Roger's NEST team made a trip for nothing." Danny's relief is visible.

"I'll stop worrying when no symptoms appear after several months."

"Yep. Me too," says Danny. "So, uh, what is going on with Heinrich? He's acting really fucked up."

"That's what I want to discuss." I like that Danny thinks like me. "I hope Heinrich will be content with his management job. However, expect him to blow up and come after me at every opportunity." I turn to face Danny. "You know what he has against me?"

Danny examines the ground at his feet, takes a nervous breath, then returns eye contact. Shaking his head, he says, "I don't buy any of that eugenicist stuff he spouts. If there was ever a proof point that dysgenic web data is bullshit—you are it. Pretty obvious you're not disabled."

My pent-up tension melts. "I guess Heinrich warned you about me?" I exhale, relaxing, blinking away tears. "I got the neurodefective tag due to the genetic link to my little brother, Robby, who's autistic." Fully trusting Danny, the burden slips from my shoulders.

Pain flashes on Danny's brow. "Oh man, that's fucking unfair. I'm sorry." He scratches his head. "You know, I think he's also frustrated by unrealistic, high expectations for himself."

"Well, maybe you're right, but it seems more complicated. I did a web search into Heinrich's past and learned that both his parents were killed in the Boston riots. Swept up by skinheads in the first of the xenophobic killing sprees. His stepdad was Chinese."

Danny stops, turning to me. "But that's fuckin' crazy. Why would he take the side of the eugenic skinheads, then? Unless, somehow, he blames neurodivergents for causing his parents' death? No, I bet it's because you came on the project and have run circles around his technical contributions. I don't think he can handle it."

As we finish the loop around the perimeter fence, I kick a white stone down the path. Danny's compliments would have caused me embarrassment a week ago. Trust and confidence feel like new armor. We are silent, returning to the control center's warm stench. The staff rambles casually near their desks. Heinrich and Roger are both busy, heads down, at their workstations.

"Okay. Let's get the grid ready for a test run," I say, and the technicians jump to their workstations. I test access to all four containment vessels on their Walmart tables and verify the C-W stack controllers are running the firmware with the revised loop filters.

"Right," says Danny. "Power coming on." The relays crack in the distance. "Voltage rising through five megavolts." Each word echoes. I expect a ghost to answer. The control room is hushed but for the sound of cooling fans from the rack of servers.

When the grid reaches stability at forty-eight megavolts, I announce, "Starting voltage modulation now." My attention shifts between the blue-white glow from the floating fabric and the sensor arrays on the wall. Everything proceeds as usual, and I settle my vision on Anthony's empty chair, which seems to preside over the grid and its blue-white pyre.

The gravity alarm blares just after ten, and a red sphere on the gravimeter array display designates a primordial black hole rising from the earth.

"I've got control," says Danny. He kills the automated grid modulation and transitions the grid voltage to his steering algorithm.

"Which vessel are you steering to?" I ask.

"Let's go with the southwest quadrant." Danny's attention is glued to his console. "I'll try hands-off steering with the new automated algorithm. I don't trust it yet, but so far, so good."

We see a flash of blue-white light when the singularity passes above six meters.

"Plasma ball!" shouts Roger. He stands, hands on his hips, smiling at the view to the south, clearly glad to be hunting black holes again.

Danny is still locked on to his console display. "PBH is approaching the southwest container. Twenty-five meters to go."

"I'm ready with the container steering," I reply. "Do you want to link to the containment vessel accelerometers?"

"Sure, why not. The grid-steering software is working well. I haven't had to touch the fine-tuning adjustment." Danny scrutinizes his display and says, "Your vessel telemetry matches the grid gravimeter readings." He flashes a nervous glance at me. "Switching sensors to the containment vessel accelerometers . . . now." He holds his breath. The plasma ball coasts toward the southwest Walmart table, slowing down a few meters above the ground.

"Looking good to me," I confirm. "The ball is centered above the table."

"So far, this is hands-off steering all the way," says Danny. "We have containment vessel accelerometers driving the grid voltage feedback loop and lowering the PBH into the vessel."

White plasma light engulfs the vessel and the tabletop, and I examine the containment vessel telemetry. "PBH is centered in the vessel, and electrodes have matched the grid voltage field. You can kill grid voltage."

Danny hits the grid's power-off switch. "Voltage dropping toward five megavolts. Now it's near zero."

"I have the PBH in the vessel." The plasma ball rests on the Walmart table, where the containment vessel holds it. "We did it, Danny." But I can't bring myself to enjoy the accomplishment.

The room is subdued until Roger says, "Congratulations, team!" He's unable to raise our spirits. "Good job," he says, directing his attention at Heinrich, who is silent with a blank expression, off to the side of the control center.

"Ready for the drone?" asks Danny. His evil grin arrives for the insane part of the procedure.

"Sure. Why not?" I ask. "Nothing has gone wrong yet. Fly it in and fetch the vessel." If only we had thought to try this with our first containment vessel.

Roger calls, "Uh, guys, the plasma ball is gone."

"Yeah, just like last time," I say. "It seems that the static electric field allows the plasma field to collapse. The PBH is still in there."

Danny sends the construction drone's infrared nose camera image to the wall display. The drone's running lights pass through the darkness, tracing a path under the grid fabric toward the southwest table.

"I've got the drone over the containment vessel. Dropping altitude to three meters and lowering the grappling cable. You ready, Scott?"

"Yep. Go ahead. The accelerometers show no vibrations of the PBH." I wipe sweat from my forehead. "This is the tricky part. At least this time, we don't have the ground vibrations of fifteen people trotting toward the vessel."

"Okay, closing grappling clamp. There, got the fucker!"

"Whoa!" I yell. "The control loop is reacting to that clamp motion. Containment is maintained, though. No PBH vibrations now."

"Going up. Elevation climbing to fifteen meters. Real slow." The drone's infrared camera image shows it flying north toward us.

"I think this is going to work. The containment control loop is behaving. No noticeable PBH resonance reactions. Just don't drop it on us." I glance sideways at Danny, but he stays focused on his drone controls.

"On the way, guys, across to the construction building. I'll set it down in the parking lot." Danny swings the containment vessel over the construction trucks to a clearing east of the building, lowering the payload until it touches the ground.

"Perfect. Go ahead and release the grappling clamp."

There is a slight bump in the accelerometers as the grapple releases, and Danny flies the drone away. "Order up!" laughs Danny. "One hot primordial black hole ready to go!"

He grins at me, but I look away. Our belated lessons won't bring Anthony back.

"Congratulations, guys. Super job!" yells Roger.

Heinrich maintains a blank expression, arms folded across his chest.

———

Over five hours, we captured three additional PBHs in the other containment vessels. As Danny lands the fourth vessel at the construction building, I ask, "Roger, Heinrich, I would like to try a couple of experiments as a final confirmation of lessons learned."

Heinrich looks up in surprise when I address him.

Roger says, "Sure, whatever you want."

"Danny, can you pick up that last vessel again?"

"Yeah, sure," he says. He flies the drone across to the vessel and grabs the top handle with the grappling clamp. "Okay, got it."

"Good. Fly it to our test pad a kilometer west of the grid."

"Okay," says Danny. The drone's infrared image shows burned-out wasteland underneath the grid, living brush by the power substation, then stops beyond a mesquite tree cluster. Danny frowns. "Now what?"

"Take the vessel to that clearing on the left and lower it to ten meters." I scrutinize the containment telemetry and confirm everything is stable once he reaches the ten-meter height, then command, "Okay, drop it."

Danny's wide eyes turn to Roger, who has a puzzled frown but then smiles and gives a thumbs-up.

"Okay, here goes." He taps the release actuator. "Bombs away." Danny grimaces.

The containment vessel telemetry shows a brief freefall, followed by a jarring impact shock as it hits the ground and bounces twice. A plasma ball ignites with the impact but extinguishes in a few seconds.

I resume breathing. "Wow. It survived the ten-meter drop, and the PBH is contained inside. Nice! The vessel is also now tilted by thirty degrees, but the gyroscopes in the platform kept the electrodes vertical to keep the PBH contained."

Roger beams. "Nice job, guys! That drop test confirms we have a robust design, and we just confirmed the containment vessel can withstand a one-G impact. We should be able to transport a primordial black hole in an aircraft!"

"One more experiment, Roger?"

He shrugs a "whatever you want" gesture, and I realize he has relinquished technical control. To me, the youngest guy in the room. Crazy.

"I want to try a more radical experiment with our containment loop. First, sweep that vessel with high-frequency field modulation to find the natural resonance frequency of the PBH. Then overdrive the modulation at that frequency to see if we can reproduce a failure."

Heinrich says, "I like it. This would confirm the disaster's root cause and our corrective actions."

Heinrich states the obvious, but Roger beams after hearing those cooperative words. "Sounds good to me too," Roger says.

"Good deal. I'm modulating the containment voltage with a frequency chirp sequence sweeping a broad spectrum up to one hundred megahertz." This resonance-detection routine will prove what killed Anthony. "Wow. That got a reaction. I got a resonant response in the accelerometers at around fifty-three megahertz."

"Plasma ball! The drone camera is blinded by the fuckin' heat!" yells Danny.

We can see ball lightning through the windows, resting on the ground west of the power substation. It extinguishes after a few seconds, and the view turns dark again.

"Good, the resonant ringing dissipated. The containment circuit did its job, and the PBH stayed in the vessel. I'll hit it with a continuous fifty-three-megahertz modulation and see what happens," I say.

"Okay!" Danny, the pyromaniac, is back. "Should make for decent fireworks!"

"Be careful," says Heinrich. "Keep it a short burst. Remember how much potential energy is packed into that PBH." He raises his eyebrows.

I remember. Stephen Hawking predicted a million megatons, but we only need to nudge the PBH enough to cause the containment vessel to fail. "I'm thinking we give it a one-millisecond burst?"

Heinrich says, "Yeah, I agree. Although you'll be hitting it with fifty-three thousand resonant pulses in that millisecond." He winces.

Roger smiles again at us.

I double-check my frequency and duration settings and glance around the control room. "Okay. Here goes." I tap the sequence start button.

A brilliant orange-white flash spans the horizon, followed by a shockwave that rattles the windows. Two kilometers away, a rocket of fire curves into the sky before vanishing into the stars. A brush fire smolders near the test pad.

"Fuckin' A!" cheers Danny.

"Whoa!" says Heinrich, eyes round, catching his breath.

I stop holding my breath and gasp, "That confirms it. No telemetry from the vessel. It exploded." I scan the readings from the other grid sensors. "And we also got a nice X-ray burst when it exploded."

Colonel Roger McMahon glows, serene. He looks like he just won the lottery.

Chapter 14

CRISIS

Captain's Log, Frigate-328, 179238.97 LST

Mil-AI took control of Frigate-328's radiation detector array but could not determine targeting solutions for the singularity events. The Sol-3 scientists are running all their gravitation experiments on the dark side—almost as if they know Sol-3's position blocks Frigate-328 from observing their progress. Although the drones can detect singularity radiation signatures, Prime-AI confirmed drone instrumentation could not locate and map the radiation sources.

The commissar and her political division stepped up their efforts, but the required escalation to military suppression protocols will soon render all eugenics disinformation irrelevant. Mil-AI was alarmed by only 63 percent of the weapon systems being in a state of readiness, but considering the age of this old ship, the military division should be delighted. Maintenance bots have been dispatched for repairs and refitting, prioritizing the long-range batteries.

Chapter 15

AUSTIN

Feet to the sky, a disemboweled armadillo carcass marks another mile with a smear of blood on the road. Barbed wire spools along rotted posts through creosote brush, cedar, and scrub oak. I've taken the usual care so fascists can't scan my embedded ID chip, and my right arm sweats under the wristband shield. Driving toward home in Austin has the familiar claustrophobic dread of skinhead confrontations. But there is a third ingredient to this drive: survivor's guilt.

There is no way I could bring myself to drive Anthony's antique Ford. The manual truck gearbox might have been fun, but I could not take his seat. My cruise through the Hill Country is at a sedate sixty miles per hour. This visit home can wait a while, and I don't want the Porsche to blow up if I hit a pothole. My eyes flick to the mirror, checking on the cargo, two vessels containing primordial black holes. Primordial black holes must pass through Austin all the time. Two more can't hurt. And if a containment vessel fails, the PBH will dribble away unnoticed. I hope. I ensured they were positioned at the extreme rear of the cargo compartment, just in case.

It feels irresponsible to roll into Austin city limits with this much power. However, the massive instruments in Austin will allow us to collect more comprehensive PBH data, and Roger and Heinrich argued for this delivery run. I no longer panic with each burst of clicks from Danny's Geiger counter—the portable device only senses normal background radiation. Even so, nothing about this feels low risk. That PBH cargo is only two meters behind me.

Two AI-Ubers pass me, and I shrink in my seat. Up ahead is the turn into the university research center.

Heinrich stands on the loading dock beside a forklift truck. "You are late. Any problems with the drive from Pecos? I arrived over an hour ago and have started the test range preparations. We have a lot of work to do. The instrumentation we set up over the past few years will finally get some use."

It's disorienting—Heinrich is so talkative now. "No problems at all," I answer. "Although, a couple of potholes I hit scared me. The containment seemed to work well. No plasma ball ignitions." I would have freaked out with ball lightning bouncing in the back of the Porsche. I sigh with immense relief when the forklift operator backs away with the crate of containment vessels.

The sunset blazes through brilliant blue above the paint of fall colors on the hills descending to Lake Austin: red cypress and oaks, yellow elms and ash, and pervasive evergreen cedars. I had promised to make this drive home each weekend but stayed in West Texas for almost two months. The ease with which I had neglected my promise was caused by . . . what—my desire to escape the skinheads and have fun with physics? Foolish, given the past week's disaster.

Robby's session with his therapist should be wrapping up about now—maybe he was with Margie today? Margie has been the best for Robby. I picture her on the floor, playing and coaxing language from him. She is amazing. I realize I've missed her too.

I can't wait to spend time with Mom and Robby and compensate for my long absence. Mom promised she'd make her famous chicken fry. I round the curve toward the house behind a familiar Ford—Margie's car turning into the driveway—and Robby in the back seat. We roll up the driveway together in a cloud of gravel dust, stopping at the top of the hill by the garage.

Margie, Robby, and I all step out and face each other for the first time in too many weeks. My heart leaps when I see Robby—and Margie. "Hey, Robby!" He beams and tickles his chest with his *I-am-happy* tell. "Have you been out with Margie?" I take a knee and pull him into a bear hug. "How is my guy?" He tolerates the close touching longer than usual. I chuckle. His grin suggests he must be planning some project for me.

Margie's hand brushes my shoulder. Her touch is electric. I let go of Robby, stand, and gaze into Margie's smile, her eyes sparkling. Our movements are awkward; we are holding each other's wrists. What is happening? Her lips open and close; no words come out, but her glistening eyes shout. She pulls me close, arms circling my waist with a warmth I have not felt in months.

I'm shaking.

Stepping back, the awkwardness fades, replaced by ecstatic heat.

"Welcome home, Scott." She giggles.

"Wow. What a welcome," I say with a stupid grin. My face feels flushed.

Robby has a goofy smile. "Go work. Fix it." He has a one-track mind.

"Ha. Robby has repair projects he has been saving for you," says Margie. The spell is broken, and we both turn to Robby with hesitant separation.

"Did you break something, Robby?" I bend to one knee and study his grin. He seems to be no worse for wear, happy as usual. "Have you been taking good care of Mom?"

Margie's happy expression vanishes, replaced with concern. "Uh, why don't we go inside from the cold?"

I hadn't noticed the bitter cold till now. "Yeah. Mom may have dinner ready by now."

The pain on Margie's face is baffling.

"How has Robby been doing?" *What is bothering her?* "Has his behavior been okay during his lessons?"

"Robby has been doing great. I love coming to work with him." She smiles with mischief. "But I'm sure he would do even better if his brother could be here to motivate him." Her eyes linger on me, and I feel the thrill.

"Your mom has me coming four days a week now. One of the other therapists quit," says Margie, an uneasy edge to her voice.

"Sounds like a lot of work for you. I bet you get worn out—" We enter the kitchen, and smoke and the smell of burned chicken hit me. A wave of nausea strikes me, along with a flashback to Anthony's gory death.

"Hey, Mom? We're home." The hum of the stove exhaust fan is the reply. "Mom, are you okay?" A pan full of charred chicken chunks smokes in the sink, the faucet dripping into black sludge. "Mom?" Brown grease trails from the stovetop to the sink, and raw broccoli waits on the cutting board. The kitchen is empty. I check the den and the living room; they are both vacant. Margie follows, holding Robby by the hand.

"There she is. Outside on the patio," says Margie, pointing through the window at Mom sitting in a lounge chair. In the frigid air. "Oh no."

I step outside. "Hey, Mom? Are you all right?"

"Oh, hi, Scotty. There you are." Mom turns away to glare into the darkness rising from the canyon. Stars grow visible over the ridge beyond the lake, and red hazard beacons flicker from antenna towers above Westlake Hills. She has a drink in her hand.

"Come with me, Robby," Margie says from behind. "Let's go put away all your school supplies." She leads Robby to collect the scattered puzzles, art supplies, and flashcards in the game room.

"Mom, what happened to the chicken?" I bend over to place a hand on her back, ensuring she is okay. She stinks of booze. "What are you doing outside? Aren't you cold?" She's barefoot and wearing a thin T-shirt.

"Damn stove. Set the cooking oil on fire." Her voice is heavy, slurred.

"Mom, this is crazy. Come in out of the cold." I reach down to help her from the chair, but she stays anchored to the spot while lifting her glass for a swallow of liquid.

"Mom, come on." I grab the glass from her. That gets a reaction. She reaches in protest, but I use her motion to make her stand while I wrap an arm around her. The whiskey glass is a lure to draw her inside the house. She staggers over the threshold, and I help lower her to the couch, where she relinquishes control of her drink and collapses into the cushion. I sniff the contents of the glass; straight scotch. She snorts, shrugs her head, and her eyes droop shut. Her matted blonde hair is lost among the emerging grey-brown roots. I unfold a wool blanket and toss it over her collapsed body, which is sinking deeper into the sofa with each heavy breath.

"She has been . . . struggling. Very depressed, I think. She seems lonely." Color has drained from Margie's face. She glances toward the door. "I need to leave. Robby is in his beanbag chair, watching a movie. I have to get home." She shrugs. "End-of-semester papers and exams await." She takes my hand and squeezes. "I'm glad you're home." She turns and walks out, and my giddiness leaves with her.

Emptiness is all I feel. "Mom, are you okay?"

Her eyes flutter. "Yeah, yeah. Don't know what we're gonna eat."

"Well . . . just sit there and let me get dinner." The sludge is mixed with eight drumsticks in the frying pan. I lift them one by one, wrinkle my nose, and scrape off the grease as I lay them out on a cutting board. Hmmm. I grab a knife and go to work. "You know, I think I can scrape off the burned parts of the chicken. I think it's cooked all the way through. Just need to cut all this black stuff off."

"Delicious. Uh, where's my drink?"

Mom wobbles her face at me, and I am stunned by the long red scar under her left ear. The black eye was all I noticed before, but it has faded into a dull yellow blotch. The ugly scar behind her cheek is prominent—a stitched-together, jagged laceration. She is still recovering from a horrific attack.

Although stunned with sadness and pity, my anger remains. I feel like hugging Mom but continue to glare at her. I fill a clean glass with water and hand it to her. "Here you go."

She glares back, taking a reluctant swallow. "Your job going okay?"

"Oh, it's okay." I fill two pots with water and put them over a high flame on the stove. "The science is amazing. But there was a disastrous accident." I pause to find the words, rinse chopped broccoli in the colander, then start stripping corn husks. "I made a mistake. A big one . . . Dr. Agosti was killed." *There, I said it.*

Mom peers into her glass and takes another sip, twisting her nose. "Huh." She frowns out the window at city lights filtering through the tree branches. "Robby's behavior is terrible. I'm up every night with him. Two therapists canceled this week. Your dad only comes to take Robby for the weekends."

I stop shucking the corn and glare at her. Water boils over from the pots into flames, spitting and hissing. "Did you hear me? Dr. Agosti is dead."

"Uh-huh. You okay? You gonna find a different job for your degree?"

"No, I'm fine." I drop corn and broccoli into the bubbling water. "I still have a job. In fact, I guess I got a promotion."

"Oh. While you were away in West Texas, Robby kicked two holes in the wall in his room and broke the faucet off his sink. You need to fix those." She pushes to her feet, searching the counter. Finding her whiskey glass, she takes a gulp, her defiant eyes unfocused.

Robby wolfed down half the chicken. Slathering butter and salt over the corn and broccoli compensated for the singed meat. He scrapes bones into the trash and slides the plate into the dishwasher. "All finished!" Robby beams, sweeping his fingers and hands in sign language.

Mom nibbled at dinner, emptied her whiskey glass, and passed out in bed. I hope she has a splitting headache in the morning.

"Work. Fix it," pleads Robby.

"Robby, you need to go to bed," I groan. But I can see the determination on his face. He has waited over two months for me to get home. "Okay, buddy. Let's get the tools and get this over with."

We return from the garage armed with Sheetrock repair ingredients. "Fix it," Robby says as he sits on the bedroom floor, inspecting the damage he created, tickling his chest in delight.

"You were bad to kick these holes in the wall." My scolding does no good. Robby giggles. "Margie was right. These projects just reinforce your destructive behaviors."

"Cut with saw," says Robby while making rare eye contact. He leans into me to inspect my cutout of crumbled Sheetrock.

My angst melts away with the warmth of Robby in my lap. Who would be caring for Robby if I had not come home? Would Margie have left him with Mom? Would Mom have been alert and sober enough? Maybe Robby would be roaming around the house while Mom slept?

"New wall," says Robby, handing me the new Sheetrock board.

Robby scrutinizes the shape I draw for a patch of the large hole. "This should be the right size. What should we do now?"

"Cut with saw."

"Great job, Robby." Each sawtooth bite of gypsum puffs white dust with staccato vibrations. It's mesmerizing for Robby. When I'm done, I slide the drywall patch into place.

"Drill!" Robby commands me to attach the wallboard patch.

I start four screws with the power driver, one in each corner of the drywall patch. After checking that the torque clutch is set low, I give the power tool to Robby. "Robby's turn."

He is ecstatic and grabs the tool with hands covered by an amalgam of gypsum dust, chicken grease, and butter. He giggles after pressing the bit into each screw and pulling the trigger until the torque clutch chatters. He beams after the last screw is complete. "All finished!"

A picture book of birds sits open across my chest, heaving with each breath. Robby's head rests on my shoulder, asleep and finally at peace. Guttural snores echo down the hallway from Mom's bedroom.

The air stinks of burned chicken.

Is this my future too? How could anybody with my genetics hope for anything better than the life Mom and Dad had after Robby was born? Fighting with each other, fighting the schools, fighting for medical coverage, fighting the ABA Agency for therapists, and fighting the skinheads. It's not worth it. Was Dad right—get sterilized and move on? But Robby would still need protection. The skinheads would still try to kill him.

How can I leave them alone in the morning? Mom has lost it. She's trying to recover her life after the divorce and failing. She can't care for Robby properly, and he can't care for himself. That scares me to death. If Mom passes out from drinking or gets beat up, or worse, killed by fascists, Robby will be alone.

Chapter 16

CRITICAL

Captain's Log, Frigate-328, 179239.29 LST

Frigate-328's radiation detector array finally got coordinates for contained singularities on Sol-3. I was stunned that a pair of the contained singularities were in motion and that multiple contained singularities were mapped on opposite hemispheres of the planet. The Sol-3 scientists have made unprecedented progress. Historic norms predicted one or two organic life cycles to achieve Gravi-Tech containment. Luckily, they still haven't reached the energy exploitation stage with the technology. Otherwise, I would have no choice but to order Mil-AI to launch attacks.

The ancestral memory of ruthless rogue cultures exploiting Gravi-Tech energy, killing billions and billions of organic forms, destroying their worlds . . . it is primal horror burned into our core minds. But these beings of Sol-3 . . . I can't help but admire them.

The Commissar and Mil-AI have no such respect. Mil-AI rehearses attacks, sorting choices from its library of proven intervention campaigns. The Commissar and Polit-AI are preoccupied with selecting targets and counting how many Sol-3 organics should be sacrificed.

Chapter 17

RED LINE

Robby made it onto his school bus but would have missed it if I had not pulled Mom out of bed. She admitted to driving Robby to school several times a week after missing his morning bus pickup.

Where the hell is Dad? Why doesn't he answer his phone?

The roads are clogged with AI-Ubers and obese passengers watching stupid videos on their tablets. They ignore bumper-to-bumper congestion while I wonder if I'll get above third gear. *Damn it, I'm late.*

Five miles per hour above the speed limit, and that rust-fender Dodge Charger still sticks to my tail. Is that a directional antenna on his dashboard? It must be attached to a scanner. Damn it, my wrist is exposed while my shield rests on the passenger seat. Wearing the shield at work would be a red flag. Damned if I do, damned if I don't. The Dodge window tint is no doubt hiding a snarling fascist grinding his teeth and hunting dysgenics. He has me in his sights.

Damn location service transponder. I can't afford another auto-speeding ticket. Jerking my wheel to the left, the Charger follows with that piece-of-shit Dodge suspension swaying like a drunken sailor. He is locked on, threatening to ram my bumper, and has me beat by two hundred horsepower.

I swerve to avoid yellow AI-Ubers doddering along at their standard speed-limit-minus-five speed, and I snap-steer right to slip my Macan between two yellow cars. Brakes squeal. One AI machine scoots out of my lane as it reacts to my approach. I brake at a stoplight, but one car blocks me. The guy in the old Dodge leans on his horn, stuck behind three yellow Ubers.

Seconds tick by. The skinhead stays in his car, attached to that horn. I am hyperventilating, a fool to be away from home, out in the open like this.

A green light—I stomp on the throttle, steer around the blocking AI-Uber, and tap the right paddle while pushing the tachometer above five thousand RPM. The turbocharged scream softens to a thrum, and the Dodge, jammed within the herd of AI-Ubers, shrinks in the rearview mirror, plodding up the hill a half mile behind.

My breathing slows as I turn through the UT Applied Research Lab side gate. The parking spot next to the dumpster is open, but the "Center for Dark Matter Research" sign has been obscured by more fiberglass battens extending out of the rotted section of the roof. Pushing aside insulation caked with black fungus, I get the door open. Waving my wrist at the security terminal unlocks the inner door. A sneezing fit hits me. Rancid mold and machine oil permeate the vast emptiness, my footsteps echoing from the twenty-meter ceiling. A veneer of dust covers components of unfinished C-W generator stacks, workstations, milling machines, and piles of trash.

Turning the corridor into the abandoned rail gun test range, I jump at the sight of a fat Norway rat scavenging along the hallway. The rat sees me coming, tries to run up the side of the cinder block wall, loses his grip, and falls to the concrete floor with a thud. The panicked rodent climbs the wall twice more, fails, and then scuttles into a heap of cardboard boxes. Side-stepping the trash pile, I duck through a door.

Heinrich works with two technicians in the test lab, and a forklift is carrying two-inch-thick rusted steel plates—discarded rail gun test targets from decades ago. "Scott. You are late," he says, eyes narrowing on me.

"Yeah, bad traffic," I say with a shrug. I am in no mood for Heinrich's "I am the boss" attitude.

"Well, come over here," he says with a grimace. "I'll show you the test I'm setting up. This will be the world's first black hole engine—crude, but should demonstrate the controlled energy releases to spin an electric generator." Heinrich puffs his chest out.

"That's an old Chevy alternator bolted down to the floor?" I ask.

"Uh, yeah, I guess you know your car parts." He rolls his eyes. Heinrich points to some copper pipes and cables. "We will dissipate a few kilowatts from the alternator's output with this dummy load immersed inside this water bucket to boil off the heat." He grabs and rolls over a massive iron disk about a meter in diameter. "And this flywheel fits onto the alternator shaft that spins horizontally. We'll mount a containment vessel behind steel reflector plates on one side."

"Uh . . . huh. And you expect PBH radiation to deflect off the steel plate and rotate the flywheel on the alternator shaft? That out-of-balance rotating load will tear the assembly into pieces."

He sneers at me. "We'll have a counterweight opposite the containment vessel."

"Okay. I get it." And I must admit that, although crude, it is an elegant experiment.

"Your job is to get your containment modulation to induce a PBH resonance that will release enough radiation to push the deflector plate and rotate the flywheel."

"Heinrich, there are so many things that could go wrong. First, we don't know the direction in which energy radiates from the PBH. Second, the energy needed to push the deflector plate may be enough to shatter the containment vessel. Third, the plates and the vessel may melt from the heat of absorbed radiation. And, worst of all, how do we protect ourselves from radiation exposure?"

Heinrich's snarl tweaks with each of my objections. "After weeks of hotdogging, you're suddenly cautious?" He frowns. "Just do your damn job with the containment modulation control. Radiation exposure is blocked by these steel plates stacked around the test fixture. Data collected during the tests will answer all your other questions."

"Do whatever you want. I'll be at my desk." I stomp past where the rat hides in a trash pile.

I slam my backpack on the desk in the otherwise empty office area. Why am I even staying? Heinrich is such an asshole. I should just quit and go home to care for Robby and Mom. My PhD degree can wait. If I stay with this GRA assignment, something is bound to go wrong, and I may kill someone else. I shudder and push that thought aside. Besides, working for a fascist—thinking I could tolerate him? No, it's too toxic.

I take a deep breath. Fuck it. I call Colonel McMahon's cell number. It rings twice.

"Scott. What's up?"

"Hi, Roger." I pause. "Uh, I need . . . I can't keep this up. I'm resigning."

The new student therapist seems like a bright guy, but he doesn't have near the rapport Margie has with Robby. The session ends early, and they leave in his car for the trip to Taco Bell, followed by a hike in the hills.

Mom throws on a coat and starts to leave the house.

"I see you are feeling better," I say.

"I'm fine. What do you want?" Mom snaps. At least she is sober and lucid.

"We should talk about last night." I pause, watching her eyes shift like she's trapped. "You were pretty drunk."

"I was fine," she says, her eyes burning into me.

"You were not. If I wasn't here, who would take care of Robby? You scare the shit out of me."

"It was nothing, just a couple of drinks. Robby is fine. I have shopping to do." She swings her purse over her shoulder and stomps into the garage to her Tesla, slamming the door.

"Mom . . ." I call after her, but it's too late. The electric motors whine down the driveway with the crunch of gravel under the tires.

Maybe yesterday was an exception. But I doubt it. Margie acted like this was a recurring problem.

I settle into the study with my laptop, returning to my containment vessel modifications. I agreed with Roger's request to bring these tests to a conclusion. But I made my decision. I need to be here at home, and I'll be damned if I tolerate Heinrich again.

My phone rings. "Dad! Where are you? I'm sitting in your study at home."

"Hey—I'm in Tokyo, and jet lag woke me early, so I thought I would call. Is now an okay time to talk?"

"Sure is. I'm trying to work but can't get into it. Mom and Robby are both out right now."

"Cool. What's up?"

"We need to talk about Mom." I summarize the events of last night. He listens, and I hear his stressed breathing as I tell the story.

"I can't believe things got this bad with her. Did you talk to any of Robby's therapists to get their take on the situation?"

"I talked a little with Margie. Only two others are still working. Two quit."

"Oh shit. Well . . . my work in Asia is almost done, and I could be home in a day or two. Can you hang around Austin until I get home?"

Whew. "Absolutely. Uh, what should I tell Mom?"

"Let's keep this between us. Wait till I get there. Maybe I need to spend time at the house for a while . . . hey, I gotta go. I'll work out my travel plans and let you know."

"Okay. Thanks. This is a big relief." And with that, we end the call.

My energy is restored—rescue is on the way.

Roger and Heinrich are glum, staring at the table in the conference room near the offices. Roger sees me coming and stands. Heinrich glances at me, then shuffles out, avoiding eye contact.

Roger says, "Come on in. Have you checked out the test setup?"

"Yeah. It should work. However, hauling those black holes in the containment vessels into Austin seems reckless. I hope those steel barriers Heinrich stacked up are thick enough to protect us from the radiation—or worse. Most have punctures or dents from those old rail gun projectiles."

"I understand the concern. I asked Tiana's engineering team to check it, and they confirmed the risk of radiation exposure is near zero because the steel plates are stacked sideways. That'll give us over a meter of steel between the vessel and us."

"Well, okay. The software and instrumentation are ready. The staff here did a great job. You should be able to collect a lot of quality data for your project."

"Well, it's your project too."

I figured his technical discussion was just an icebreaker. "I promised you I would see these tests through to completion, but I still plan to quit when we finish."

Roger's face darkens. "I wish you would reconsider. These last couple of weeks have devastated all of us, and with Anthony's loss, you are now key to the program. You have impressed everyone."

"I have nightmares of that night at Pecos. Trying to continue for the past weeks has been agony."

"But there are a hundred team members that struggle with similar emotions. Time will heal the guilt."

"Yeah, I hear you. But I had a direct hand in creating the conditions that killed Anthony. I keep reliving things I should have done to prevent his death." I study the floor, failing to shrug off the feeling. "I also am needed at home for a while. And I can use some extended time off to adjust."

"Is this about your brother and mom?"

"What? What makes you think that?"

Roger shrugs. "Scott, you went through a top secret clearance investigation that included details of your family situation. I understand your parents divorced and you have a little brother with special needs. If that situation drives you to quit, I can get some help."

"What the hell? I can handle my personal life. I don't need your help," I protest.

He shakes his head. "Well, we all can use some help with life's challenges. I have personal experience with divorce and with disabilities. I can get you some help."

My jaw tightens. "My personal life is my business. I will not have this talk." I stand, turn, and walk out, leaving Roger grimacing and shaking his head. He can't understand how much Robby needs me. It's been this way since I was in middle school, when Mom and Dad were busy battling the bigots and each other.

Hyperventilating, I stumble toward the factory where the workstations are set up. The displays are a blur of geometric shapes.

A voice penetrates my fog. "Scott, uh, are you ready to start up?" Heinrich is behind me, prodding.

"You want to start the test now?" I ask, trying to relax into the work routine. The console displays drift into focus.

The primordial black hole in this vessel is 150 billion metric tons as measured by the gamma-ray spectrometer. I still haven't figured out all of Anthony's physics of gravitational and electrostatic forces interacting in a singularity. I can safely say nobody understands quantum gravitation.

"Can we go inspect the test fixture?" I ask and follow Heinrich toward the ladder he uses to climb over the stack of steel plates.

"See, the deflector is built from two steel plates bolted together at a right angle," says Heinrich. "I mounted the containment vessel in the center, and the deflection plates are attached at forty-five degrees to form a corner along the vertical axis."

"That should direct radiation into pushing the vessel around the flywheel. But a hell of a lot more will be lost out the side of the fixture." It does seem to be a simple, logical way to detect and measure radiation force on dense metal.

"Let's get started then," says Heinrich, clapping his hands.

We meet Roger as we return to the control workstation tables. I avoid eye contact and sit down.

"Okay. Beginning resonance scan. And . . . this one resonates at around ninety-five megahertz. I'll try a low-amplitude, continuous modulation."

"Yes!" yells Heinrich as the flywheel begins a slow rotation up to about ten RPM. The Geiger counter sensors record a spiral radiation spray following the flywheel cycle, just like a fireworks pinwheel. A steady buzzing noise from the plasma ball echoes down the hall from the test chamber.

"Hey, hey, hey!" Heinrich shouts, jumping up and down like a five-year-old. "It works. It works!"

"Yeah, not bad," I say, checking the telemetry from the sensors around the chamber. "About ten watts of power. Internal vessel temperature is at forty Celsius. Radiation levels are at fifty millisieverts per hour. This is twenty times ambient radiation, but the radiation is at normal levels outside the steel shielding."

"Excellent! Excellent, team!" Roger says. He has a greedy twinkle in his eyes and is rubbing his palms together. "Can you turn up the speed, Scott?"

"I can. Let's see if we can reach three hundred amps from the alternator," I say, smiling, lost in my work, forgetting the fascist hovering over my shoulder. "I'll increase the containment modulation amplitude." I tap the keyboard *up* arrow, which increases the modulation by ten millivolts with each touch. "Passing through two hundred RPM. Current increasing to ten amps. Increasing modulation some more . . . and we are at a thousand RPM. Just passed a hundred amps!" The hissing buzz of the plasma ball grows much louder.

Roger grins, bouncing forward on his toes. "Keep it going. Can we get to full power?"

"Hmmm. The radiation level inside the test chamber has reached two hundred millisieverts. Okay, I guess, because the steel plates shield us. The temperature inside the vessel is eighty Celsius, which is still okay." I gotta hand it to Heinrich. His black hole generator works. The plasma ball roars. "Ha! The water is boiling. Your copper load is cooking that bucket of water with thirteen hundred watts of power."

The blur of flywheel rotation is a blue-white glowing donut. I freeze a high-speed video frame to get a better look. "I don't like that orange glow within the plasma ball. The containment electronics are overheating. We should shut down before it melts."

"No, keep it going for a while longer," Heinrich says. "Push for max power, then shut it down."

"Okay." I shrug. "I'll see how far we can go . . ." I tap the modulation control again. "Getting close to two thousand RPM and three hundred amps. Three-point-six kilowatts!" I glance up from the consoles to watch Heinrich's rapturous face.

The floor jerks, accompanied by a jarring noise like a train wreck. Although the flywheel continues to spin, the plasma ball is gone. Telemetry from the containment vessel also stopped. As the flywheel slows down, we see why.

"The vessel is gone!" cries Heinrich.

I respond with I-told-you-so sarcasm, "Not all of the vessel is gone, just the top half and the deflection plates. It must have melted enough to throw it off balance and break apart. The vessel electronics are smoking." I shake my head at Heinrich.

Roger is bent over, inspecting the video displays. "It's not only the vessel that's damaged. The stack of steel plates on the west wall has been shoved away. And . . . oh my God, that hole in the wall. It's about a meter wide!"

"I'm going to get a closer look," yells Heinrich, heading down the hall.

"Hold on, Heinrich, let me check the radiation reading first."

Heinrich freezes midstep.

"Wow. A massive spike of three thousand millisieverts in the explosion! We lost some Geiger counter instruments, but the remaining sensors show the radiation is gone. We would all be dead without that steel shielding us from radiation."

Heinrich grabs a portable Geiger counter and marches down to the test lab, Roger leading the rest of us behind Heinrich.

Heinrich bends over the steel plates in the test chamber, and the Geiger counter's audible clicks increase as he passes the detector over a hole through the steel. "That explosion and ejection of the containment vessel managed to move about a ton of steel a half meter. It also melted a hole through two meters of these plates." He sniffs and wrinkles his nose. "And it stinks of sulfur."

"And it blew a hole through this concrete wall," says Roger, crouching low to peer through the opening. The rebar is bent outward, pointing along the trajectory of our black hole projectile. "Where did that go?" Roger squints into the distance.

After checking radiation levels for myself and finding nothing extraordinary, I kneel alongside Roger to share the view. "I guess the melted steel plates took the top half of the vessel, the PBH, and all the radioactive material with it. It went straight west. Lotta houses out there. Maybe landed in someone's living room?" I smell the sulfur.

"Oh, crap," groans Roger. "Two calls to the NEST office in one month. I'll be on a shit list for sure. This test setup is hazardous as hell. Enough, Heinrich. We're in the middle of a city of three million. We are done."

I feel a twinge of panic. My view through the hole in the wall points toward Westlake Hills—not far from my home. I trot down the hall to the workstations on the factory floor and review the telemetry log; three surviving gravimeters traced the initial path of the PBH. I sigh with relief. The path was north of home. "Roger, our projectile headed toward Mansfield Dam, four miles west of Austin. I don't know where it impacted without a topographic map, and my trajectory calculation is only approximate."

"That should give the NEST guys some guidance." Roger groans again. "The last thing I want is a panic due to radioactive material found in a populated neighborhood. Best to conduct a discreet search."

That seems reckless. I picture some little kid like Robby finding the vessel's remains, emitting deadly radiation levels. But Roger's priority is avoiding public outcry, not worrying about casualties.

"Uh, you know what?" asks Heinrich. "We could improve the test setup with different materials in the deflector plates. We need a much denser metal that reflects better, improves efficiency, and reduces heating."

"Yeah, that could help," I say. "Something like tungsten or depleted uranium should work. Both are pretty rare materials, though."

Roger says, "I think I can find what you need." But then his expression hardens to a frown. "But we can't risk another accident inside the city."

Heinrich pleads, "Let's move the experiment inside the old rail gun vertical test range. We can point the test straight down the shaft, and any accidents will be contained and shielded from us fifty meters down at the bottom of the shaft."

"What are you thinking?" I ask. "A black-hole-powered rocket engine?" Heinrich is taking risks for once? "We could design and fabricate a conical nozzle out of dense tungsten or uranium to replace the crude steel plate reflector. It would be like the tail end of a missile."

My cell phone buzzes with a new text message: *Just touched down in ATX. Will take a car home.* At last, Dad has arrived!

Although it is early afternoon, I grab my backpack and depart for my car. "I gotta go, guys."

Roger stands like he wants another talk, but I trot to the exit.

I return the text to Dad: *"I'll beat you there!"*

I leave a little rubber smoking in the parking lot as I spin into the alley toward the exit gate.

"Scotty!" Dad yells as he climbs from an AI-Uber at the bottom of the driveway. He climbs the steps toward the house as the yellow robot car pulls away to search for another passenger.

"Hi, Dad. Enjoy your golf cart ride from the airport?" I know he hates those things.

He puffs the last few steps up the hill with his suitcase. "Sure did. Thrilling, but it gets the job done." He extends his arm for the father-hug tradition and two pats on my back. "Man, I'm getting too old for this." He drops his case beside me and surveys the old homestead.

"I have been waiting a while. Robby's bus should be here in about fifteen minutes." I pause before adding, "Mom is not home."

Dad purses his lips. He turns toward the street bend where the special-ed bus will appear. He joins me, resting against the side of the old Porsche.

"You need to give this girl a bath." He drags his finger across the hood, tracing a line in the grey dust.

"Yeah, I know. There isn't a car wash at the Pecos Center," I say, examining the old Porsche for the first time in weeks. "I'll have lots of time to wash her in a few days."

"What? Why all the free time?" Dad's face hardens.

"I quit my job."

"Oh, Scott. No. What happened?"

I'm surprised by the questions. "I guess you haven't heard? Dr. Agosti was killed last month." The pain returns. "And . . . I made mistakes that caused his death. I can't get it out of my head. Every day is misery."

"Oh, my God . . ." Dad reaches his arm around my shoulder and pulls me close. "At first, I thought you quit because of Robby."

"Yeah, that also." I shrug.

Robby's yellow bus rounds the curve, and we walk down the driveway as the bus rolls to a stop. The door swings open. "Mr. Anderson, Scott—seeing you at home again is great." Robby's bus driver is a familiar face I have seen for years. However, his voice has an edge of desperation today.

Dad's brow wrinkles. "Glad to see you, Charley. How have the bus trips been going lately?" Dad leans into the bus to see Robby grinning ear to ear. "Hi, Robby!"

"Well, I guess okay." Charley's smile is gone.

Robby unbuckles his seatbelt, grabs his backpack, and heads down the bus steps. "Dad!" he signs.

I step past Dad and grab Robby for a bear hug. Of course, he hates the hug, but the grin grows wider.

"The rides to and from school go well, but the dropoffs and pickups not so much. I guess Ms. Anderson is really busy these days." Charley looks down.

"Uh-huh," says Dad. "Sometimes no one is here for Robby at dropoff time?"

"Uh, honestly, Ms. Anderson is only here sometimes." He raises his eyebrows, shaking his head. "I have been releasing Robby to the ABA Agency instructors. Most of the time, they're here to meet me. But I really shouldn't be doing that.

Rules say to release the student only to a parent. And, a few times, I waited ten minutes, rang your doorbell, but gave up and returned to drop Robby after completing the rest of my route—thirty minutes later."

Dad's eyes go wide. The possibility is unthinkable—Robby abandoned alone on the front step?

Robby and I climb the hill to the house. I have heard enough. We let ourselves in through the front door and start Robby's after-school snack routine, Flamin' Hot Cheetos and Sprite.

———

Dad digs through Mom's therapy and scheduling notes, a stack of paper chaos. "How can she figure out any of this crap?"

"Get away from there! What are you doing here?" Mom walks in from the garage, dropping a load of shopping bags on the kitchen counter.

"Well, look who's home," Dad spits back. "It's good we were here to rescue Robby from the bus. I can't figure out the therapy schedule from this mess. Where the hell have you been?"

"I don't answer to you, bastard. Get the hell out of here!"

Robby whips his head back and forth, grabs a spoon from the table, and bends it at a right angle before I can pull it away.

"Mom! Somebody needs to be here to care for Robby. You are either out shopping or drunk half the time!"

"You bastards! You think you can just cruise in and say caring for Robby is easy?" Her anger turns to weeping. "You have no idea what I go through every day." Tears run down her cheeks.

Robby runs into his bedroom, grabs a toy tractor, and bangs it against a soft spot in the recent wall repairs. "No, Robby!" I chase after him to pull the toy from his hands, collapsing on the floor with him.

Dad sighs, eyes on Robby and me for a moment before he shuts his eyes.

Mom bawls, hands covering her face.

"I think I should move back in," Dad says.

Mom squeaks, "What? What are you thinking?"

"I can rearrange my work responsibilities," he says slowly. "Delegate a lot to others."

"No, no, no." Mom shakes a frown at him. "I'm not letting you live here anymore. Remember? We got a divorce. I have custody of Robby. Get the hell out of here right now!"

Dad's mouth hangs open, drawing deep breaths.

"Stop!" I shout. They both turn to me as though they forgot I'm here. Robby rocks his body in my lap. "You should let Dad take one of the spare bedrooms. He says he wants to help with Robby."

"No, no, no. We settled this in court. I won custody. This is over."

"Mom, you can't do it alone. You get falling-down drunk. You're missing the times to get Robby on or off the school bus half the time. It's irresponsible!"

She looks at each of us and opens her mouth but has no words.

"Let Dad move in to help with Robby. Or I'll testify in court that Dad should have custody."

"What?" she screeches, tears flooding down her cheeks.

I feel like I might vomit.

She stands and storms into the master bedroom. The door slams shut.

"I wish you hadn't done that," says Dad.

"But we don't have any other choice."

Dad says, "Okay." He adds with determination, "Do me a favor, though. I'll take on the duty at home, but I want you to stick to your job. As tragic as Dr. Agosti's death is, you must push through that pain. I bet Dr. Agosti would want you to stick with it."

Robby lies on his side with me on the floor, finally relaxed, pushing a toy car across the wood, entranced by flickering chrome wheels.

Chapter 18

THE HAWKING FLARE

My cell phone rings while I drive north to the research center, dodging ponderous AI-Ubers. "Hey, Scott. How you doing, buddy?" Danny's voice makes me feel ten pounds lighter.

"Hey! Great to hear from you. Staying busy out in the Texas wastelands?"

"Ha. Fuck yeah. I have over a hundred black holes in containment vessels. The harvest is going great."

"Nice! You *have* been busy. Must be nice not to have to suffer under Heinrich's thumb for a while."

"Heinrich who? Heh-heh. You know, it has been great working with Tiana's team. No bullshit. They increased the production rate of containment vessels to about ten a day. We have a daily cargo flight bringing shipments in from her spook factory out west."

"Tiana has been helping us too. Have you heard about the rocket nozzle they built for Heinrich? They fabricated it from depleted uranium, and Tiana is shipping it to Austin today."

"Damn, Scott. You have all the fun. I also heard about your fuckup last week. The NEST drone found the impact crater a few hundred meters downstream from Mansfield Dam." I can visualize Danny's evil grin. "And now you get to test a fuckin' black hole rocket engine! Oh man, what I wouldn't give to be in Austin right now."

"You can have it. I'm driving up to the Austin research center now and getting sicker the closer I get. Heinrich's ego is also a bigger pain in the ass than usual. I have had enough of him and this project."

Danny responds with labored breathing. "That's one of the reasons I called. Roger asked me to talk you out of quitting."

"Huh. I wondered if you had heard about that. You know, working with you has been a pleasure. However, given the disaster last month, I need some time away. And working for Heinrich is not something I'm willing to do. Life is too short."

"But you can't leave me alone with that asshole," says Danny. "You have enough clout with the colonel. You could demand to not have any interactions with Heinrich."

"I don't know. Roger still depends on him. Although that would solve one of my many problems. But I have to drop off the call now, Danny. I just got to the office."

"Yeah, well, I wish you would reconsider. Please think about it and don't make any final decisions before talking to me. Oh, and flip the bird at Heinrich and tell him to fuck off for me. Okay?"

Dragging my ass toward the test lab is harder every day, but this may be my last day. On that optimistic note, I push forward. Passing the room with the failed flywheel test fixture, I take the stairs down five meters to an underground service gantry platform. The technicians mounted the nozzle—blast-end up—onto massive steel support structures built to hold rail gun prototypes ninety years ago. If the test assembly breaks apart this time, the thrust forces should push the pieces deeper down the shaft.

I sneeze from the mildew wafting up from the fifty-meter hole in the ground. My eyes water. *Damn allergies.* "Oh man, what a stink." I cough twice and grab a tissue to blow my nose.

The technician says, "This test range hasn't been used in eighty years. Thank God we don't have to go any deeper than this."

I grit my teeth and inspect the new nozzle and mounting. They have our last containment vessel with a PBH mounted to struts inside the nozzle. The battery and electronics were moved outside the cone, ensuring they'll be out of the blast of radiation when it fires. "Not bad, guys. When will you have all the instrumentation hooked up?"

The tech says, "Easy. We had all the gravimeters, video cameras, and strain gauges in place and calibrated two days ago; we're just finishing the nozzle integration now. We can run a test whenever you're ready."

I inspect the detailed perfection of the Skunk Works fabrication team. "Nice work, Tiana," I mumble. "All the electronics are shielded from the heat. And the polish of the nozzle interior is a nice touch. It's beautiful."

"Why, thanks, Scott." A voice startles me from behind, and I see a middle-aged woman coming down the steps to the gantry.

"Huh? Can I help . . . ? Oh! Tiana! Good to meet face to face. Sorry, you look different in person compared to the videos." She is wearing a blue flight suit, and her grey-brown hair is pulled back—quite a change from the usual mop of hair during our video conferences.

"Good to finally meet you too. I decided to fly in to deliver our rocket nozzle and watch you guys run the test. Our engineering team at Skunk Works verified your calculations on the nozzle geometry." She turns to me, nodding approval. "Near-perfect design. But we don't fully trust the Javelin gimbals to survive the high-temperature radiation blast, so once installed, the platform gimbals get locked down hard in a fixed position."

"Very nice work, Tiana. The technicians partially disassembled and reinstalled the containment vessel in the nozzle—without losing the primordial black hole containment. A perfect fit. Are you staying for our first test?"

"I wouldn't miss it." She chuckles, and we head up to the factory floor's improvised control consoles, converted from the flywheel experiment.

"Scott, I see you found Tiana." Roger smiles at us as he and Heinrich approach the control consoles.

Heinrich says, "Well, I'm ready to start the test, but the technicians seem to take forever getting systems ready."

What a jerk. "Heinrich, the techs did a great job, as usual. They'll have everything ready to go in a few minutes," I say, and sit down with my back to the asshole.

"Really?" Heinrich sputters. "I need to go down and inspect their work. I can't let them screw up my engine design." He trots toward the steps down to the service gantry, Roger following.

My blood boils. I force myself to focus on my console's system telemetry self-test procedures and gulp a mouthful of coffee.

"Is he always such a pompous fucker?" muses Tiana.

Coffee spits from my mouth. "Hah!" I laugh out loud, wiping my face with my sleeve. "Yeah, pretty much. You know,

Tiana, you remind me of Danny." I give her an approving smile. "That's a good thing."

She shrugs. "I don't know how you put up with him. I know I wouldn't."

"Not much choice with Anthony gone." My head inclines back on the chair headrest. I close my eyes.

"Sure there is. Why don't you come and work with the Skunk Works team and me?"

My head jerks around. "What . . . ?"

"We have a world-class team of engineers and scientists. It would be a wonderful opportunity for you."

"Wait, wait. I just need GRA credits for my PhD degree. I'm not looking for a full-time job."

"Scott, your degree might get delayed a bit, but you'd have a lot of fun with my team," she says, inspecting my reaction. "And in the short time you have been working on the PBH project, you have been responsible for *the* key breakthroughs in the work Anthony and Heinrich started a decade ago. Anthony confided with me that he was astounded by your intuition and hands-on abilities. We need you on the team. Badly."

I blink back tears. Anthony would be alive if I had been more careful with my software. "Did Roger put you up to this?"

She pauses and locks eyes with me. "That's why I'm here, Scott."

"Huh," I sniff.

"Scott, this work may be the most important science in history. I know being so close to someone who died is new to you, but try to set aside your pain. We need you to stay with us. Come work with my guys out west. The change in scenery will be refreshing."

I am assaulted from all sides. The console display and my thinking are blurred, but I refocus. All the sensor diagnostics have passed.

"I have approved the rocket engine test setup, and we can begin," Heinrich announces as he strides in, Roger trailing behind.

Roger's eyes narrow, and he sighs. "You were right, Scott. Our technician team is first rate. They anticipated the instrumentation requirements and installed and tested most of it before delivery of the nozzle this morning."

Heinrich ignores Roger. "My test setup should show how much power can be extracted from a primordial black hole. We have the perfect static test range. Scott, you may begin the procedure."

Tiana whispers, "The master of the universe speaks."

I snicker at her. "Uh, Heinrich? Let's make sure the area is clear? I won't start the PBH engine until our people are accounted for." On cue, our three technicians file up from the test range stairway. Once again, I wonder why Heinrich respects the two Asian technicians but reserves the eugenic hate for me. He has a more selective hate than the skinheads.

"Okay, we're ready," I say to the techs. "Thanks, guys, for the super work on the installation. All diagnostic tests show we're good to go."

Roger displays a tight smile.

The video images around the test setup show our nozzle bolted to the ancient rail gun mounts. The nozzle resembles a heavy-duty steel wine glass on a platform of rusting iron and is set above the fifty-meter-deep concrete shaft dug into the bedrock below Austin. Of course, the engine nozzle is not steel but a polished chunk of depleted uranium.

"This primordial black hole is 110 billion metric tons." I'm amazed that we can shrug at such fantastic statements about the mass within a black hole while starting the scan for resonance in the PBH. "Found it. The dominant frequency is at fifty-five megahertz."

"Plasma ball!" Tiana exclaims—her first up-close experience with ball lightning. "Wow. It's like a steel ice-cream cone with a white-orange plasma ball in the nozzle." Her face is inches from the display screen. The plasma ball's noise from below ground is only a faint hum.

"Okay, all telemetry is normal. I have begun the low-amplitude containment modulation at fifty-five megahertz. Geiger counters show a vertical spray of radiation but little out the sides. Nozzle temperature sensors show a two-degree increase due to energy absorption. This is a much better radiation reflection than we had hoped. Let's pause and be sure all the telemetry shows the fixture is stable."

"Yes, yes, yes!" Heinrich exclaims. "I knew it. My rocket motor design works!"

"Don't get excited just yet," I say, glancing at Tiana. "The strain gauges are all showing zero force. Let me turn it up a bit." I tap the key to increase the modulation amplitude every few seconds. The dull hum of the plasma ball grows louder. The radiation and temperature readings also increase. "There we go. Strain gauges read about ten kilonewtons of thrust. Spectral readings show hydrogen gas and a little sulfur in the nozzle exhaust. Wow. The matter spilled from the PBH is mostly hydrogen that immediately burns into steam."

"Yes!" Heinrich crows. "Oh my God!" He works on calculations with his iPad. "That's a thrust-to-weight ratio of over forty. It's the most efficient engine ever!"

Tiana's eyebrow twitches. "Uh, you should add the 110 billion tons of the black hole into your calculation, Heinrich. No fair only counting the mass of the vessel and the rocket nozzle."

Heinrich scowls at Tiana.

"I can turn up the power. The temperature and radiation readings are well below what we measured on the flywheel tests . . ."

"Yes. Yes, do it," Heinrich urges.

" . . . just before it blew up," I say. But Roger gives me a thumbs-up.

"Okay, here goes. Vessel temperature is seventy Celsius, and nozzle temperature is five hundred. Damn hot. The nozzle is exhausting steam and over four thousand millisieverts of radiation straight up into space. I feel sorry for any birds above us, or—oh shit! Any aircraft above us will get fried by the radiation!"

Tiana raises her eyebrows at Roger.

"Not to worry, Scott," says Roger. "I had airspace above us cleared for the test."

"Yeah, we thought that one through ahead of time," says Tiana. "The nozzle heating proves we're absorbing too much radiation, not reflecting it completely into the exhaust. We should push up the modulation faster to test the maximum thrust before the nozzle melts."

"Okay, increasing. The engine is generating about a thousand kilonewtons of thrust now. Don't you think we should back off?"

Roger's eyes are wild with excitement. "More powerful than any aircraft jet engine by a factor of five!"

"More modulation!" Heinrich yells.

The dull roar of the plasma ball echoes up from the test range shaft through a cloud of steam.

"Go for it," says Roger.

"Okay. Whoa! Hitting two thousand kilonewtons. Nozzle at seven hundred Celsius! Now four thousand kilonewtons! There is an exponential increase in thrust with increased modulation. It's nonlinear—"

Blam!

A deafening shockwave reverberates down the hall from the test range with a bone-jarring quake. Tables wobble, crashing a display to the ground, and the ceiling above implodes. A steel girder slices down and impales itself into the concrete floor, followed by roofing, insulation, and smoking metal shrapnel clattering down all around us.

"Shut it down!" cries Heinrich.

Hunched down under my table, catching my breath, I shout, "There is nothing to shut down! The containment vessel is gone!"

"Damn," Tiana says, blood trickling down her forehead. "Those massive steel rail gun mounts snapped right off! The rocket engine launched straight down into the shaft! I'm going to get a closer look." But then she wipes her eyebrow and examines the blood on her fingers. She taps the wound near her hairline, examines her fingers again, and exhales in relief while checking the instrumentation readings. "Radiation levels are normal." Tiana presses a tissue to her forehead and follows Roger toward the stairs to the gantry.

Heinrich is frozen with indecision. His mouth hangs open as he takes in the scene: the giant steel girder planted in front of our workstations and the blue sky that has opened above us. Thick dust settles on his head as his eyes search for danger.

I crawl out from under the table but am not about to run toward the explosion. Instead, I replay the high-speed video capture in slow-motion detail. I catch my breath and watch the rocket nozzle rip down the shaft, shearing off the rail gun mounts. The telemetry readings of the thrust are mind-blowing.

Roger and Tiana return from the test range shaft. Roger's face is white.

Tiana frowns. "The entire roof was ripped off the building. It started to melt, and something blew it off the steel rafters. All that remains is a pile of slag and rubble in the parking lot."

"Yeah, plus this steel girder driven into the concrete," I remind Tiana. "It missed crushing us by only two meters!"

Tiana grimaces. "It took an unbelievable force to rip that rail gun support apart."

I reply, "Well, the last force reading was over nine thousand kilonewtons. Then telemetry was lost."

Roger gasps. "That's more thrust than the old Saturn V moon rocket engine. Unbelievable!"

"Yeah. Also, the rocket nozzle was intact when the rail gun mount sheared off. Watch this video." I run the slow-motion replay. "As the rail gun mount tore apart, the containment vessel mount broke away from the nozzle. The assembly was blown apart; the half with the vessel launched straight up, while the half with the nozzle drilled down. It looks like the containment vessel and primordial black hole blasted the roof. No telling where the vessel went because we lost the accelerometer telemetry."

Roger's face fades to grey. "Not again. That vessel went vertical with the black hole still contained inside it?"

"Yeah. It went up like a bottle rocket. I have no guidance data for the NEST team this time, either. Could have landed anywhere." I gaze up into the sunlight through the hole in the roof.

Roger holds his head. "Not the NEST guys again."

***

Cappuccino vapors rise to warm my face; the aroma and soft chair are welcome comforts after yesterday's excitement. As usual, my back is against the wall, ready to escape out the back door at the first sign of skinheads. I touch the shield inside my shirt sleeve, ensuring it covers my ID chip, and examine customer faces out of habit. Margie is late.

Roger and Tiana left for the airport after the NEST team debriefing. The remnants of the shattered containment vessel were two hundred meters south of the research building and dropped in the junkyard between pallets of scrap metal.

Will Margie show? She sounded distracted and nervous on the phone. Maybe she's reconsidering seeing me?

Watching Heinrich squirm and sweat in the conference room with Austin police firing threatening questions was the highlight of my afternoon. On the other hand, watching Colonel Roger McMahon on the phone, answering, "Yes, sir. No, sir. Won't happen again, sir," was disheartening. Everyone has a boss.

Maybe Margie is seeing someone else? Rechecking my phone, I still still have no messages from her. I'll keep it professional when, or if, she gets here. I only want her to keep me apprised of how Robby does in the new arrangement with Mom and Dad. A wave of depression moves through me. I'll settle for that, but honestly, she's more than just my brother's therapist to me. I wish I hadn't pushed her away last year.

"Hi, Scott." Margie's breathless voice from the door startles me. "I got out of the meeting with my academic adviser late. Have you been waiting long?"

I stand as Margie unwraps the scarf around her neck and shrugs off the heavy overcoat. Her hair is released from the usual tight ponytail, flowing down her shoulders in brown waves. Her uplifted sparkling eyes, cheeks rosy from the cold, and face makeup combine to create beauty beyond my mental image of Margie. Did she do all that for me? *Oh my God, Margie, you are beautiful.*

"Wow. Uh, no, not long." I think my mouth hangs open. Collecting my composure, I reach to take Margie's coat. "Here, let me take that. It's great to see you again." I extend my arm around her shoulder to grab her scarf and coat, then pause. We are close enough to feel each other's breathing. Margie's eyes glisten. I reach for her with my other hand, pull close, and embrace. I think about kissing her but stop myself.

My face feels flush as I step apart, grabbing Margie's coat. "It's great to see you again."

Margie giggles. "You already said that." She reaches out to touch my arm again. "I missed you too."

Her touch sends a shiver through me. I clear my throat. "Can I get you a coffee?"

"No, no thanks. I'm fine," Margie says. "I'm sorry we haven't seen each other in the past two weeks. I was so busy with exams and my thesis. But that's all behind me now." She blushes, eyes sparkling.

"Yeah, I have been thinking about you. But I have been busy with work and busy at home too. Good news to share on the home front: Dad will move back in to help support Robby and Mom."

"That's wonderful news!" Her shoulders relax. "That's such a relief. I have been so worried about your mom and Robby. Do you think your dad and mom will get along okay?"

"I hope so. That's one thing I want to talk about. Can you update me each week on how it's going and call if you see something falling apart for Robby? Maybe you can network with the other therapists to share information?"

"Oh, sure, I can." Margie's smile fades. "Does this mean you'll be away for a while again?"

I reach for her hand. "I honestly don't know. I would prefer to stay home with Mom and Robby while keeping my head down to avoid skinhead attacks. My work situation is complicated. I'm someplace between quitting, staying where I am, or taking a new assignment with a team much farther away." The sparkle in her eyes dims. "That last choice is tough for me. But I would make an extra effort to travel home often to see Robby. And . . . you."

Margie reaches her hand up and around my neck. The electric tingle of her touch sends another shiver through me. But I notice she wears a wrist shield. "Why?" I ask.

"Well, why not?" She sees me staring at the shield that covers her ID chip. "I'll be damned if I'm going to let strangers or fascists probe my ID. It's a breach of my privacy," she says with startling force.

"But . . . but it draws attention. Skinheads target people when their shield is showing. They assume they have something to hide."

Margie shakes her head. "Everyone has something to hide. And to hell with the skinheads. We all have to stand up to them. Fight back!"

I reel from the strength in her voice. "But the risks?"

Margie shakes her head. "Most of my friends are wearing their shields full time—except when the security ID is needed to start a car or buy something. Everyone has to fight back. Stop the hate insanity. Put an end to the fascist idiots."

Margie looks at me with determination. A new sense of support or power fills me. "Margie . . ." I mumble, lost in wonder, "I had no idea you felt so strongly. That means a lot to me." I reach for her free hand, feeling her energy.

"Scott, I can't imagine you would just quit. You are not alone and don't have to shelter at home. You have a good plan in place to help your mom and Robby. Choose what *you* want, and come home for visits. Uh, lots of visits." She teases me with a mischievous grin, and I feel my heart flutter. "And . . . I'll definitely make time for you in my busy schedule."

"Heh, heh." I must have a goofy grin on my face. My gut somersaults. I realize then that I have my decision—she's shown me the way. "Today, I'm driving to the Pecos site in West Texas to discuss the choices with a friend at work."

"Don't worry too much about Robby," she says. "Do what's right for you. I'm heading to your home this afternoon for a therapy session with Robby. I'll make sure he's okay and check with the others on the team. Maybe we can talk more often than once every two weeks?"

That hurt, but I deserved it. "I promise." I reach for Margie's other hand. She smiles and squeezes my hands. A shiver runs up my spine.

Margie shakes it off and stands. "Well. I think we both need time to absorb all . . . this." She glances away.

"Uh, sure." I stand with her, help with her coat, and shrug on my jacket. Why so abrupt?

Walking to her Ford, she reaches for her door handle. I touch her hand, and Margie backs against the door. I wrap both arms around her, and we hold each other close, her breath against my chest and our legs intertwining.

"I have to go," Margie says, her face flush with heat, embarrassment, and anticipation. "We can talk later?" She struggles to push back and slowly releases my hand but then leans forward, pulling me into her embrace and a deep kiss.

I close my eyes, melt into her soft lips, squeeze us together, and finally let go, catching my breath and my balance and watching her glistening eyes.

"I've got to go now," she gasps, looking up at me and gently pushing me away. "Maybe we can talk next week?"

I'm dizzy and shaking. My heart pounds. "Definitely." We'll do more than talk.

Chapter 19

CONSEQUENCES

Captain's Log, Frigate-328, 179239.67 LST

Mil-AI acknowledged my orders for the Gravi-Tech interdiction mission. It will act without mercy. The brazen display of Gravi-Tech energy exploitation on Sol-3 demands more than containment. Eradication of an entire domain of science is required. Such a shame.

I felt no joy. I tried to establish contact but failed. Their telepathic skills were no more than a baby's babbling. I had hoped to awaken them to self-awareness so they could save themselves. But the Commissar resumed the suppression mission, and the neurodivergent innocents will be purged by Polit-AIs unrelenting eugenics incitement. It may take hundreds of Sol orbits. Centuries of irrational hate and hell and murder.

Ironically, my admiration of the Sol-3 organics swelled with their astonishing scientific progress. Gravi-Tech exploitation was achieved at a record pace. It recalled forgotten emotions: joys of a child's first telepathic recitation in Luyten poetic or mathematic images. The surge of pride I felt so long ago had been crushed, followed by the desolation of losing them all.

These organic forms are so easily manipulated by the Commissar. Tragic. But I am not impotent. Despite protests by Prime-AI, it adhered to its code to follow my orders and redeployed the Gravi-Tech suppression drones to infiltrate Sol-3's social networks with anti-eugenics measures. My Sol-3 network inoculation started a war between drones with conflicting missions. The Commissar was baffled—blind to my counterattacks—when her social network suppression drones lost their toxic voice.

My failure to rescue the neurodivergent clan on Luyten failed, and that got me sentenced to near-eternity inside a spacecraft dormancy pod. The thought that I might repeat that failure—to feel the cries of suffering and death once again—is unbearable. But this is outrageous treason. This time, Command would punish me with torture, agony, and then execution. But only if Centauri Command catches me alive. Death will be my escape.

Chapter 20

IMPACT

I sip what's left of the cappuccino, but it is cold from neglect. It seems like only minutes have passed since we left the coffee shop. Margie . . . I can still smell the perfume of her hair, unbundled, tumbling over her shoulders, and feel her clinging to me, the press of our intertwined bodies, the shallow above her hips. And the kiss. Wow.

But most impressive is her spirit—her resolve to resist the eugenic fascists. And lately, it seems that social networks are suddenly alive with anti-eugenics sentiment. Support for Robby and me emerges from nowhere. The wonder and power within me swell.

And that kiss! But does Margie regret crossing that line we agreed to last year? Despite her convictions, she may still fear a relationship with me, a neurodivergent. Even though Margie strongly supports Robby—and me—does Margie prefer that our relationship remain platonic? She seemed in a rush to leave. Oh, but that smile . . . and that kiss.

Margie . . . her strength . . . I have replayed that scene fifty times.

The wailing of a nearby tornado siren and a cell phone alert shake me from the daydreams. I awake from my mental autopilot, cruising along the four-lane highway into a midafternoon sun beside a pasture, a white-board fence, and horses basking and grazing among scattered live oaks. This must be the stretch of road just west of Johnson City. I increase speed and pass two yellow AI-Ubers like a skier down a slalom course.

The sky is clear with no signs of a storm—the alerts must be a test of the emergency warning system. The siren did wake me up, though. I've lost track of time, and I'm halfway to Fredericksburg. I shake my head and try to consider my discussion with Danny. Taking Tiana's job offer would be simultaneously scary and thrilling, but I must first talk it through with Danny. My first drive to Pecos in August was the last time I felt this excited. But can I abandon Danny with Heinrich? I would not wish that misery on anyone. And when would I get home to see Margie and Robby if I went to work with Tiana's team?

I blink. Twice. Flashes of brilliant yellow light?

A cluster of AI-Ubers on the road ahead brake and turn to park in a line along the highway shoulder. All of the yellow Ubers—at the same exact moment. It is like they simultaneously shifted into their failed-AI safe mode. The sky is no longer blue but glows yellow with the light of a dozen suns.

I lift my foot off the accelerator.

The Porsche slows and coasts, steering to the shoulder toward the cluster of shut-down AI-Ubers. The passengers climb out of the vehicles, stumbling among weeds alongside the highway, arms extended, pointing east. They are crazy, wandering on the road like that. A car could come over the hill and hit them from behind. A grey-haired lady covers her face with her hands. Another guy gapes at something behind me.

I glance in the rearview mirror and see it. An orange fireball expands across the horizon, low to the ground, with a billowing mushroom cloud above it, black with debris and red with fire. I stomp on the brake, shut the engine off, jump out, and pivot toward Austin, gasping for air. A vertical tail of flame-white vapor descends from the stratosphere, wind feathering the top of the fire pillar. Austin lies below.

Images of Robby, Mom, Dad, and Margie flash through my mind.

I lose my balance, stumbling to one knee in the middle of the highway.

"Oh my God! What's happening?" shrieks the grey-haired lady, tears streaming from her wild eyes.

The old guy next to her covers his ashen face and is silent. But then cries, "Mother!"

Wailing and whimpers rise from two girls stumbling out of their yellow AI-Uber.

My eyes are locked on a surreal arc of fire growing and then contracting across the horizon. A furnace burns bright at its center, black smoke churning up through a mounting cloud chimney, topped by inflating billows of clouds, all underneath a blazing vapor trail coming down from the stratosphere. The cries and weeping grow louder.

My mind escapes to a cold, analytical space. Nuclear attack air bursts don't look like this but have a sphere of fire a thousand meters high to maximize blast effects. This atomic fireball is nothing like the movies. That white vapor trail comes straight down, but an ICBM would arc through the sky with a reentry vapor trail. This can't be real.

Nearby hills ripple like a tsunami, tossing rocks and green cedar trees, throwing up a wake of dust. The wave then jerks the road from under me and flips me on my back. My skull jars on the pavement, and pain narrows my vision to a dark tube lost in the glittering blue sky. As I roll to my side, oak leaves fluttering in the wind, the Porsche comes into focus, bouncing on its springs in a cloud of dirt. My mind snaps back to the present.

That must have been a shockwave from a nuclear ground burst! A freight train rumble echoes across the hills. The cluster of AI-Uber riders is scattered like bowling pins before pulling themselves up to their feet, weeping and screaming. A few try to make cell phone calls. All other eyes are transfixed by the towering grey clouds to the east.

Horrific destruction must be roiling Austin: buildings, trees, and people, all vaporized near the point of detonation by a flash of energy followed by a pressure wave expanding outward, knocking over buildings and tossing cars off roads. People will be stumbling through the wreckage in excruciating pain and suffering blindness, radiation burns, and death. In the suburbs, people will be choking on debris and radioactive dust, doomed to languish through weeks of agony before death. I imagine mothers bent crying over dead babies, panicked searches for the missing, and lost children digging through the rubble.

Robby.

I need my family. Margie may have been with Robby when the blast hit—maybe they were okay at the house. But what is the distance from home to ground zero? Margie wouldn't let anything happen to Robby. Dad, though . . . he'd be at work downtown. Could he have survived, maybe? My heart implodes. I must go to them.

Pushing the road beneath me, I roll up to a kneeling position, reach to feel the wound at the back of my skull, and find a smear of blood on my hand. There is a gash, but at least I will live—for a while longer. The wetness on my cheeks is not blood. The horizon tilts as I stumble toward the Porsche and catch myself on the open car door to keep from falling. I collapse into the driver's seat, the horizon's rotation slows, and I push the start button.

My cell phone complains that the 6G network is dead, but I am lucky that an electromagnetic pulse has not burned out my car's electronics. As I pump the throttle, the deep-throated turbo exhaust startles the AI-Uber crowd from their weeping, and all their heads turn toward me. Urgent conversations animate the stragglers as I pull across the highway, stop, and back into my K-turn.

"Hey, man. Where you going?" asks the first guy running toward me.

I stop, wondering why I should waste time talking, but say, "Back to Austin."

"Place is gonna be on fire, hot with radiation. You crazy?"

"Yeah, maybe. But I gotta find my family." I turn the wheel and shift into drive, but I stomp the brakes when a second guy props two massive tattooed arms on the Porsche's hood, his terrified eyes daring me to move.

"We got ten folks here that need a ride," pleads the first guy. "Aint no way we goin' to Austin, man. We headed the other way, and you got the only car that runs." His arms grip the roof above my door, his red eyes dripping tears into the snot collecting on his upper lip. The top of the black-grey mushroom cloud is getting swept to the south by the jet stream above, hiding the fireball and blotting the blue from across half the eastern sky.

I could just step on the gas and plow through these animals. Two tears drop from the flabby face attached to the tattooed arms. They splash on the Porsche's hood. I shut off the engine, swing open the door, and stand to face Snot-lip.

"What do you have in mind?" The pain at the back of my head pounds.

Snot-lip takes a step backward. "Well, you got the only car that works."

"I'm going to Austin. If you want, I can give you a ride there."

Tattoos waddles over. "You fuckin' crazy, man. This car is gonna take us west, away from the radiation." His wheezing slobbers while he casts panicked glances toward my driver's seat.

"This car is not going anywhere without me." He doesn't know the Porsche key fob is linked to my implanted ID chip. I need to devise an alternative, or this won't go well. I glance at the group of passengers up the road, all panicked. A kneeling woman and two girls hold hands, eyes raised to heaven in prayer.

"You can't fit ten people inside the Porsche," I say, gesturing with my chin over to the crowd of AI-Uber riders. "Why don't you just hot-wire the manual override on those things?"

Two puzzled faces of wonder tell me all I need to know. "Come on, guys, I'll show you what to do." I grab my small tool kit and march to the nearest of the ugly yellow cars, Tattoos and Snot-lip in tow. Sheesh. How do these people manage to get through life without basic skills? After I taught my neighborhood middle school gang how to hot-wire an AI module, we broke into dozens of these cars for midnight joyrides. Never got caught. But that was before getting my ID chip implant at seventeen when I still had friends. I open the front door and fold down the driver's seat from its stowed position against the steering wheel.

"Okay, guys, watch me." But I don't have time for this. The mushroom cloud is expanding in the east, and my hands shake, spilling tools from my kit to the floor under the seat. "Damnit." I slow down, recollecting my tool kit. We are now surrounded by a half-dozen AI-Uber riders, all curious to see what will be done to fix this machine.

"Watch this. Pop the access cover off the computer—like this, with a screwdriver." Uh-oh. It has been years since I have messed with one of these, and this computer has a strange shape—maybe upgraded—but I think it'll still work. "Next, grab this cable on the module and unplug it. It's the fattest wire bundle and has this big rectangular connector."

Snot-lip wipes his nose on his arm; his much-improved face hovers close over my shoulder, his foul garlic breath hot against my neck.

I yank the cable connector and am relieved it matches my car theft memories from middle school. "You need to short pins one and four together here and here. If you can't find a loose wire, just yank out one of the wires from the back of the connector—like this," I grunt, yanking the wire from the connector shroud. "And stuff it into the socket for the other wire like this."

"Caution. Manual mode is engaged," the car says while orange warning flashes illuminate the dashboard.

My two antagonists have calmed, eyes wide. Stepping out and away from the driver's door, my open hand points to the vacant seat. "It's all yours. Take it away."

Two fearful expressions are their reply. "I dunno how to drive," Tattoos mumbles.

I roll my eyes with exasperation. "It couldn't be simpler. The right pedal down there makes it go; the left pedal makes it stop. This switch is set to 'F' for 'forward' or 'R' for 'reverse.' Steer with this wheel," I explain. "Go on, get in. It's like driving a golf cart."

Tattoos rotates to me and back to the gathering crowd before swinging his fat ass into the driver's seat and closing the door. The other passengers scurry away to give him maneuvering room. He takes the wheel in his hands and inhales a deep breath; the car jerks forward but slams to a stop. He shakes his head, starts a slow roll, and stops thirty meters down the road.

"All right, Mikey!" another guy shouts and bounces down the road to him. Tattoos—Mikey—steps out of the yellow car and beams at the crowd.

"Oh! Oh!" cries one of the praying girls, pointing straight up.

A beam of orange-white light burns down from the blue sky to the west. Blinding strobes of incandescent white fill the sky. I blink. Twice. The white flashes revert to blue, revealing a vapor column with an orange glow touching the ground to the west. It can't be a missile. It covered the distance from the stratosphere to strike the western horizon in no time—which is impossible. It came straight down like a beam of energy!

I am on my knees on the road, chest heaving again. Screams and cries surround me while a grey mushroom cloud rises from the west impact point. A sonic boom punches my ears, my face drops to the pavement, and reverberations echo through the hills.

"No. No. No." Gasping, I grip the pavement and strain my eyes to try and see the impact point on the horizon. Could it be the Pecos Center two hundred miles to the west? Were the two locations where we experimented with primordial black holes both blasted? What have we done?

Pushing myself up again to stagger to the waiting Porsche, I restart the engine and escape east toward the wall of grey dust over Austin. I punch the throttle, clicking paddle shifters toward one hundred thirty MPH, and force throws me back into my seat. Pavement seams keep the beat with regular thumps.

The fireball on the western horizon is swallowed inside the second mushroom cloud; the sky is nearly entirely blotted out overhead now. It must have been the Chinese that hit us with preemptive strikes to prevent our research progress. Or maybe it was the Russians or someone else who wanted us stopped. Whoever attacked must have spies to figure out where to target their missiles.

I dreamed of escaping the fascist hell, but have I helped cause a hell that is worse than anything I imagined?

Are Robby and Margie alive? Are Mom and Dad? How could they be? In all that chaos? I drive into a darkness I helped create.

Margie's car is squished. Where are we? I cough. My head hurts, and my throat is scratchy. I rub my ear and scratch the blood that sticks to my fingers. I'm hanging sideways inside the back of the car; it hurts where the seat belt digs. The front seat is smashed, and the engine and dirt are piled next to Margie. It looks like nighttime, but fire flickers through the white cloth over the window. Stinky smoke fills the hot car. Margie lies still, and her face is twisted to a strange position.

"Get up." I cough. Smoke fills my nose. "Get up."

Margie is quiet.

I take off my seat belt and drop to the door behind Margie. A tree broke the window glass. A branch pokes my neck, and I am dizzy. Sideways is down. Margie's white face and brown eyes look at me through strings of hair covering the white pillow by her window. I grab her arm, which is bent in a strange shape, and pull. "Go out."

"Margie, wake up."

"I want to go out, please."

Margie does not say, "Great job, Robby," for my talking. She is still, her other arm wrapped through the steering wheel.

"Margie, go out." The fire is close. Smoke and heat come through the space that was the front window. I must run away.

She does not move. I must go out. I pull the door handle above my head—ouch, it burns! I push the door up and away, and smoke blows through the door into the car. Tall flames run through trees up the hillside, getting close; my face feels hot standing on the car's side door. Margie is inside, sleeping with the smoke. Green trees turn yellow and black with fire.

"Margie, go out!"

The big tree nearby explodes to flame, sparks stinging my face. I reach a broken tree to pull myself up, off the car, and onto rocks. Crawling up the hill, I grab rocks, bushes, and dirt to keep from falling into the fire. I stop on flat ground on the roadside with smoky car wrecks. Margie's car rolled down the hill over the broken metal fence.

"Margie!"

"Margie. Get out!"

"Come up!"

Flames from below light up the sky. A loud bang comes from Margie's car, and heat burns my face. Smoke and sparks blow at me. I brush fire from my hair. I fall into the dirt, cough thick dust, and crawl to rest against a wooden fence post. My hands stink like smoke mud when I wipe tears from my face. My fingers sting and bleed.

The fire roars, cracks, snaps, burns my face hot, then is quiet.

The nearby lake is a black mirror filled with fire. The houses in the hills are burning. The city over the hill does not twinkle with lights; it is a fire pit. Heavy grey flakes fall on me like a hot snowstorm. Crackling noise, lonely.

The caw-screams are gone.

***

"Damn, damn, damn!" Pounding the steering wheel does not change reality. I am stopped, with the engine idling. The line of cars stretches ahead, down to where two police cars block the highway shoulders; the flashing lights scold my foolish drive toward the blast zone. All four lanes to and from Austin are clogged with vehicles escaping the holocaust. My Porsche's useless headlights create a luminous glare in the fog of fallout ash. The initial wave of gas-powered cars has been joined by a mix of AI-Ubers, their lemon skins fouled by ash to brown mustard. Just beyond the police cars, the highway shoulders disappear into the ravine beneath the Yaeger Creek Bridge.

I am stuck on the road shoulder until traffic from Austin thins out.

Am I wasting my time on a foolish dash into Austin? My hope for a half-hour sprint home is gone. The cars are packed with faces of terror mixed with tears, changing to contempt for me and my insanity at driving east. I quit my futile search for familiar faces: Mom, Dad, Margie. Should I turn around and wait for them to evacuate? But where would I meet them? Wiper blades clear a swath of vision into the fallout. No, the odds of finding them before we all die are tiny. I can't believe any of us will survive after our exposure to radioactive fallout.

The 6G networks are still off the air, and my cell phone might as well be a brick. At least dysgenic scans are no longer possible. I already peeled off my shield sleeve and tossed it into the back seat. I won't need it, and my sweaty wrist—and I—are both free. It's like a black cloud of existential doom vanished and was replaced by this very real apocalyptic dust cloud. But I am blocked by this damned evacuation traffic.

I have detailed map files saved to my navigation app, and maybe I could find a path to go off-road with my all-wheel drive. Expanding the map, I see a county road snaking through the hill north toward Pedernales Falls. I need to backtrack about a mile to turn off and go east again when I near the Pedernales River.

I drove that road with Robby last year. He bounced in the back seat, happy for a ride and hike on a Sunday afternoon. A recent torrential rainstorm had driven a tumultuous roar of water through the cascade. At the top of a hill, his fingers had dug into my arm; he was scared, looking down on water that crashed and churned brown foam through limestone crevices.

"Scotty, go home," he'd said with wide, tear-filled eyes as he tugged my arm back to the car. "Go home." Robby's sense of adventure had vanished.

Enough waiting. This traffic jam could last for days, and I don't have days. Radiation levels will climb with the fallout blowing east from the Pecos detonation. These fools should be driving north or south to escape those poison clouds. I yank the steering wheel to the left, and horns blare in protest of my U-turn.

———

I wait and wait, but Margie does not climb the hill.

The sun in my eyes is dirty orange and lights up the canyons of fire and smoke. Cars and trucks are parked on the road, pointed in different directions, and a man and two girls sleep in the dirt next to a yellow car. Fire burns the city over the hill.

Margie's car is gone, but a pile of ashes and metal is in the canyon. Margie needs to take me home. Why did she leave me in the dirt by the road?

I cry. My hand smears mud on my cheeks.

Where should I go?

Ratatat. "That way." It's the voice behind my eyes. But there is nobody around.

"Who?" I'm scared and ask the question in my head.

Ratatat. "That way," it says. It hurts behind my eyes.

I know that road. That is the way the car goes home.

"Go home," I say out loud. I push myself up and run past smoky cars.

Ratatat. "That way, that way, that way," says the hurt behind my eyes.

Fire blows through broken cars, making a crackling noise. No birds call. No bugs buzz. No cars roar. Nobody is awake. This is the street I hike with the girls. My loose shoelaces flap as I run. Flames storm through houses and trees that fell down by the street. Black piles of fire, wood, and rocks. My shoelace trips me, and I fall to the road, scraping my arm. It's red where it hurts. Blood drips. A deer with horns lies on the street; his tongue stretches out of his mouth, and he looks at me with empty brown eyes.

I grab the ends of my shoelaces. "Over, under, pull it tight, make a bow, bunny ears, pull it through." Good job, Robby. I get up and run and see it when I turn the corner. My home alone at the top of the hill. The green trees are all black-grey fire piles, but my home is white rocks. Fat flakes of warm grey snow fall from the sky on the orange roof.

Climbing the steps, I press the button next to the front door, but no bell rings. "Open door!" I yell. I push and push. The fires crackle on the hill, and dust blows off the grey-orange roof.

"Open door, please," Smoke blows over my face, and I cough. No lights in the house. I yank the door handle. "Open door!"

I run around the side of the house, but the gate is locked. I climb over the fence. The swimming pool does not sparkle blue but is dirty with tree branches and grey dirt. I pull the back door handle and bang my hand on the glass.

"Open door. Lock off."

I press my face against the door to see inside, but the lights are off. The glass is cracked. All the windows are broken, and one window behind a burned bush has no glass. The pink flowers are now black sticks that smoke. The glass cuts my arm when I crawl inside. Blood drips across my hand. It hurts.

"Where Mom? Where Daddy?"

I run to Mom's room. "Where Mom?" I walk to all the rooms and the garage. "Where Mom? Where Scotty?" I cry.

A fire crackles in the canyon.

The Porsche's gas gauge shows nearly empty. An entire day has passed, and I have gained mere miles east since my cross-country turn north last night. I can't believe all these people know about the Fitzhugh Road shortcut to Pedernales Falls. These fools keep coming west into the fallout. Why don't they drive north? I am stuck, facing a three-wide mob of cars fighting to cross a creek over a one-lane bridge. The haggard refugees no longer glare at my insanity with contempt but view me with pity. Arms and heads ravaged by bloody charred flesh, faces of agony, their heaving breaths count down the time to death. Lucky ones left the fires behind in Austin, but many have arms or legs wrapped in gauze leaking yellow-pink ooze. They turn away; their tears have dried. I imagine loved ones left behind haunt them.

Not much water dribbles down Flat Creek. It's dried up from a lack of rain this fall, but the slope down from the road is steep. My terrain map on my iPhone shows a relatively flat west bank that I might be able to drive along. Maybe. I wish I had a Jeep with a lift and fat mud-terrain tires. I am thirsty, hungry, thirty-six hours without sleep, and running out of gas.

Cutting left through traffic is easy this time. No horns. They expect me to U-turn, but I leap the Porsche off the road's edge into the creek bed to the north. The Porsche chassis bottoms out with a bang, scraping on a pile of rocks, but survives the landing. I pick my way forward in first gear, the wheels grinding the low chassis over the limestone shelf. Headshakes fill the rearview mirror, my insanity confirmed.

My biggest concern is that my low-profile performance tires may not survive the punishment of slamming into sharp-edged rocks. I keep it in first or second gear and rationalize that limestone is a soft rock that crumbles under pressure. However, a wheel falling into a hole will be death for the Porsche and leave me stranded.

I spot the sloping east bank ahead and turn up and out of the creek bed through the fog of fallout. The map image shows broad swaths of land cleared of trees to the east that must be a pipeline right-of-way. Barbed wire screeches as it scrapes paint off the Porsche. I drive through tall weeds and a wire fence onto a service track through the brush that heads east-southeast toward Austin.

———

The bench where Mom sat with me is burned and smoking. My fort of rocks is covered by ashes, not trees or flowers. I sit down in soft, hot dirt and cry. My white rock tools are all where I left them, under the layer of dust. I find my favorite rock tool, tap the stone on the boulder, then pound hard.

Tap, tap, tap . . . whack.

Pieces of rock crumble away and dissolve chalk into the grey snow dust. I'm a good worker.

Tap, tap, tap . . . whack.

I ignore the sun burning through the brown sky, ignore the sweat dripping from my hair, ignore the sunburn, ignore the heat and smoke. There are no sounds from birds, no sounds from insects, no sounds from passing cars, no sounds from people, and no caw-screams. Small fires crackle.

Tap, tap, tap . . . whack.

I am safe in my fort.

The big rock is now a pile of little rocks. Nothing remains for me to pound with my tool. The sun is falling behind the hills. The house lights are off.

"Where Mom?"

I am hungry and run to the house.

"Mom?"

I open the refrigerator, but the light is off. My favorite foods are all there: Sprite, sriracha, and macaroni. I pour the soda into my yellow cup and drink, pour, drink. The macaroni and cheese box from the freezer is warm. I put it in the microwave, but the light is off, and the buttons do not beep. I wait, but it does not beep. I can't wait. I am hungry. I take the macaroni and cheese to the table, peel off the lid, pour on the sriracha, and eat the best-ever dinner.

The green Sprite bottle is empty. My nose is wet, and my head drips. There are one, two, three empty macaroni dinner boxes.

Where is she? "Where Mom? Mom?"

I sit in my beanbag chair and cry. The TV does not turn on.

I run through all the rooms of the house. "Where Mom?" Run again. "Where Mom?" The garage is empty. The lights do not turn on.

Time for my bath. Turn on the water, not too hot, and pour the bubbles. My clothes are dirty. Water spills on the floor. I like my toes in the water faucet and the white bubbles on my head. Float in warm water. Float in bubbles.

The towel wipes away bubbles. My jammies are dry, and my bed is soft.

"Where Mom? Where Scotty?"

I can't read the truck book in the dark.

The gas gauge is past empty, but I keep moving east. I am alone on this dirt service track at night, scraping the Porsche over rocks, ruts, and bushes. The headlights try to stab through the fallout dust, but visibility is limited to five meters. I would have zero hope if this car was electric—the power grid has been down since the attacks. If I don't find gasoline soon, I will be walking, and radiation will finish me off before I make it home. My vision is blurred; a pounding ache above my eyes keeps me awake. I should be vomiting by now.

Another fence blocks my way. I gun the engine to crash through. Barbed wire gouges the metallic blue paint, but the track ruts smooth to a flat surface. The springs bounce and settle to rest, and the engine dies. My thrill at reaching a road dies with it.

I crank the starter while pounding on the steering wheel. I am finished. I drop my head back against the headrest and turn the ignition off.

I scream, tortured by the cramp in my gut, my throat scabbed with dust. The cap twists off the water bottle to yield the last two swallows mixed with dust; it tastes of wet chalk. One bottle remains. The last of the Doritos was lunch twelve hours ago, but my tongue licks the remnant crumbs, also mixed with chalk dust. That's dinner. I have been awake for two days. Time to rest my eyes. Just for a minute.

The cramp in my back wakes me. I force myself awake and open my eyes, and a dirty horizon emerges through the windshield. Daylight—so many hours have passed. I try to roll over, but I can't move. Why? Panic, but—aha—the seatbelt holds me down. I release the seatbelt to break the tension on my torso, but my climb through the door is an acrobatic task; my rubber legs struggle to recall motor functions. Resting my back against the door, I breathe clean air for the first time in days. I cough up a clog of dust from the back of my throat. Unzipping, I release a stream of hot piss, replacing the pounding pain in my bladder with a euphoric warmth. The thick layer of fallout measures the puddle in the road wit h muffled dust puffs.

The horizon glows blue with the first rays of dawn reaching through the gloom. Trees and terrain resolve from two-dimensional masks into grey-brown lumps with depth. I am standing on a one-lane road drawing a north-south path alongside drab-cloaked oak sentries of the Hill Country.

I consult my iPhone map again, noting the 6G network and navigation satellites are still dead, then crack open the last bottle of water for a gulp before setting out for the ranch building a few hundred meters south, my feet silent in the grey powder.

The sign on the post reads *"Custom Hog Rendering."* I can see the shape of structures ahead through brown-grey scrub oak tree lumps. There—a pickup truck out front sits at an odd angle half off the road. The driver's door hangs open, but a shape on the ground arrests my brief elation. A chill runs through me while I crouch to scan the surroundings. Sneaking closer, I see that the form below the driver's door is a man covered by a thin layer of dust and rusty mud puddles. His head is half-severed from the neck, and eyes of dust stare at the sky. I collapse to my knees and am flooded by images of Anthony's gory death.

I catch my breath, shake away the images, and scour the silence surrounding me. Nothing moves.

Crawling close to the truck, I see it's a gasoline-powered Chevy. I peer into the truck bed, lift a tarp, and flinch from the sight and smell of massive hog ribcages stretched out to fill the six-foot length of the truck bed. Pink stripes of fat ooze something gooey toward the tailgate. I spin away and down into the dirt to dry heave, but my empty stomach prevents puke. Deep breaths restore me.

I could just steal this truck, though I'd have to search the body for keys or try to hotwire it. But I have no practice with Chevy trucks, and it would make a hell of a lot of noise, possibly flushing out whoever slaughtered the poor guy in the dirt. I push myself up, searching for any other alternative. Stealing gas would be simpler and safer—and there at the side of the toolbox in the back of the truck is a five-gallon jerry can.

I crawl into the truck bed, skidding in the liquid oozing from swine remains, trying to tell myself it's just a load of bacon—*yeah, sure*—and squat down on one hog carcass to pull the retention latch lever to release the jerry can. *It's just bacon.* Tugging it free, I am elated and nauseous; it is heavy, sloshing with gasoline. *It's just bacon.* Slipping off the side of the truck bed, I swing the jerry can up and out with both hands, crouching low to lug the precious fuel back to the Porsche.

My footprints will mark my retreat in the dust for whoever killed the man. I need to fuel up and head north before I am discovered. I sprint like I'm drunk while lugging the sloshing jerry can. The muscles in my arms and shoulders burn with the strain of forty pounds.

My chariot awaits. With the gas cap open, I turn the jerry can upside down on the spout, dropping it into the fuel refill pipe of the Porsche. The gurgle of gasoline—no doubt regular-octane crap—is music. I glance over my shoulder.

The jerry can is empty, but this is an essential survival tool, so I haul it into the car's rear hatch and pack it tight against the Geiger counter Danny gave me to warn of containment vessel malfunctions. The irony of the trivial precaution brings Danny's devilish grin to mind, lost forever in the second strike at Pecos. My energy is drained again, so I rest against the rear bumper.

"Thanks, Danny."

I could flip the power switch to measure the severity of the radiation and figure out how much time I have left. This fallout crud ingested into my lungs and stomach, packed with radioactive isotopes and a death sentence is eating my organs from within.

No. I don't want to know. Just go on.

I close the hatch of the Porsche. The engine takes three cranks of the starter—coaxing the fuel flow to the injectors—before it roars to life. I cringe with the thought of eighty-six-octane gas perverting the Macan-GTS turbocharged engine, step on the accelerator anyway, and turn north, a rooster tail of ash tossed to the sky behind me.

Tap, tap, tap . . . whack.

I'm shaking in the cold air, sitting in my white rock fort. The swimming pool is black mud with burned branches. The grey snowfall is all finished, and the sky is blue again. The sun warms me. My skin is pink and hot. My feet are cold, and my toes are dirty.

"Where Mom?"

I go into the kitchen to find more food. The cheese is yucky—I spit it out. Sriracha is good.

"Where Mom?"

Sprite is all gone. I fill my cup with water. Dry spaghetti from the shelf is crunchy, and the macaroni and cheese are all gone.

"Where Mom?"

The bag of peas melted; crunchy peas tasted sweet, but the brown sugar was sweetest and crunchy. The sugar bag is empty.

"Where Mom?"

The bathwater warms my cold toes—the water is hot. Mom's room had more bottles of bubbles. The blood on my arm and ears is gone. Float, float.

Where is she? I run through the house. "Where Mom?"

A burned tree fell across the driveway. How can Mom drive her car to the garage? I sit on my bed to watch the street through the window. No cars. No people.

"Where Mom?" I cry and rub my eyes.

I will sit here and watch. And wait.

The Porsche suspension bounces up off the dirt track onto Hamilton Pool Road. After days of crazed off-road driving across dirt trails, brush, and rocks in the wild Hill Country west of Austin, with these ridiculous low-profile Michelins designed for high speed on paved asphalt, it feels good to be back on a real road again. I could walk home from here.

I still have a quarter tank of rotgut gasoline from the butcher's truck. Hell, yeah. I wipe away tears, the tires screech, and I push the car to a cautious sixty miles an hour. The road is deserted. The Michelins earn their pay on this winding road through a wilderness of grotesque ash lumps shrouding cedars and scrub oak.

***

"Where Mom?" I rub away the crud in my eyes. Waited for Mom by the window all day and night. I wet my pants. The sun shines through the backyard windows—broken glass on the chair sparkles like the rings on Mom's fingers. She did not come home. The street is empty.

"Mom?"

I pull on my shoes, go to the fridge, and find a box of melted food. The black scissors cut it open. Broccoli and cheese are yummy.

Margie can bring Mom home. I will go find Margie.

I walk down the steps from the front door to the empty street. I run through black and grey, where the girls take me on walks. Big black birds fly circles in the blue sky.

The deer with horns lies in the street with six giant vultures on his back. Two of the birds have red faces. The deer's brown eyes are black holes that bleed. I sit and watch them eat the deer. The birds look up at me, sitting nearby on the road. The deer's mouth is brown with purple fire ants, lined up and crawling across the street. Four new birds fly down and step close, dragging their wings wide. Tiny black eyes watch me from above their beaks.

The fat, red-faced vulture flaps his wings and hops at me. He tries to bite my eye, but I slap his beak away—the bird smells like poop. I don't like these vultures, and I stand up to run away from them. My hand hurts where the bird bit and made blood come out. I will find Margie's car.

I walk and walk but can't find the way to Margie's car. My throat is scratchy. I want a drink of Sprite. The girls never walked on this road. Green trees are gone, and the hills are black and smoky. I can't find her.

"Where Margie?"

My mouth is dry. I want a drink. My hand hurts, and my head hurts.

A pile of black wood smokes around a chimney that was a house. But I can't find my home. I run down the street. I'm scared. Where is it?

"Where Mom?"

But the noise behind my eyes is loud. It hurts.

Ratatat. "That way, that way," says the hurt.

The drive through the village took all night. After seeing that gang roaming the shopping center, I had to go off road again to avoid car wrecks and didn't dare turn on my headlights.

With the sun breaking the eastern horizon, I find a trail back to the highway and roll through the wreckage of crashed cars.

It's a junkyard of charred and melted vehicles destroyed by fire and panic.

It can't be! I gasp, roll toward the remnants of a wrecked Tesla and brake to a gradual stop.

Her license plate. It's Mom's Tesla.

The white paint is scorched black and peeled in places to expose the aluminum substrate. A piece of the rear trunk survived the fire that melted the rest of the car to a puddle of slag, but the license plate characters are indisputable in the morning light—Mom's car.

I swing the door open but am stuck in the driver's seat.

She can't be dead. Last week, she stormed away and slammed the door after I screamed that she was an irresponsible drunk. That was the last time I saw my mother. The memory burns and sucks the energy from my legs. The charred cadavers of two AI-Uber passengers recline out their open door with accusing glares.

My stumble from the Porsche feels like an unavoidable march into purgatory. My heart beats again when I note the remnants of her car are missing any anthropomorphic forms. My pace quickens as I double-check the Tesla remains, followed by a trot through the large heaps of wreckage and scattered corpses nearby. Pitiful remains of various lumps of flesh rot in a stink of death. Circling vultures in the blue above scout out their breakfast victuals. Nothing among them looks like Mom—or part of Mom. Maybe the fire was hot enough that all traces of her were consumed? Or perhaps she escaped after the crash?

Nausea is again unproductive; I've had no food for days, and my last gulp of water was yesterday. I collapse back into my driver's seat, squint into the morning sunlight, and duck behind the rearview mirror, revealing bloodshot eyes under a dustmop of greasy hair. I don't know that face, covered with a five-day beard over hollowed cheeks and a scabbed gash behind my left ear. I crank the key, and the turbocharged engine rumbles to life. Home is a mile away.

It took only a few minutes to get home and find the wreckage blown inside by the explosion from the center of Austin. The warm Shiner Bock sliding through my lips, down my throat, and into an empty belly is euphoric; all else is miserable. The stink of rotting garbage from the kitchen mixes with fallout dust wafting into the den through shattered windows. My view to the east is an alien moonscape of black-white ash, stripped of life, with smoke drifting among dying bonfires of cedar, oak, and mansions along the lake. The green hills and canyons are memories, replaced with rearranged black mounds. There is a ridgeline to the northeast that was not there last week. The rim of a crater? Lake Austin is black and brown sludge, with charred flotsam under cables that wave below steel suspension arches of the collapsed bridge. The structures of downtown Austin towering above the hills have vanished. Vulture whirlpools in the pale blue above are the only sign of life, circling the death below.

At least the house survived. Maybe the swimming pool was a thermal barrier from the fires scorching up the canyon. Dad was always proud of the all-rock wall and tile roof construction—great fireproofing.

All the east windows were blown in—probably a concussion blast wave. Glass shards grind under my shoes when I walk through the mess left by foraging animals. The garage is empty of cars. A Robby-stack of cabinet doors on the workbench—ripped from their hinges—was not there a week ago.

A jolt of anxiety spins me down the hall toward the guest bedrooms. Dad's suitcases are dumped on the bed, unopened, waiting for him to unpack and watch over Robby. I turn into my bedroom and to the shared bathroom. And freeze. The Shiner bottle slips from my hand and bounces twice on the wood floor. Beer spirals from the spinning bottle into wide puddles of water. The faucet is dribbling into a quarter-full tub clogged by a washcloth in the drain. Towels lie in random heaps near the toilet, and empty shampoo bottles are scattered everywhere. Green and blue shampoo smears are on the tile walls and floor. The bathroom cabinet doors are gone—all have been torn off. The bed blankets are in a heap in Robby's room, and two dresser drawers are tipped to the floor amid his scattered underwear and T-shirts.

This was no animal.

I race into the game room, scan left and right, then shout with a voice atrophied by four days of silence, "Robby!"

A soft wind blows through the shattered windows.

The swimming pool outside is a mass of brown sludge. A raccoon's bloated belly, swarmed by flies, floats feet up under the diving board.

What is that tapping noise?

Tap, tap, tap . . . whack.

Tap, tap, tap . . . whack.

I stop. What is that sound?

Who is that dirty grey man with a beard?

I am scared, stand up, and drop my stone tool.
"Scotty?"
I cry.

Chapter 21

SOL GREETING

Captain's Log, Frigate-328, 179239.99 LST

Mil-AI's mission eliminated Sol-3 Gravi-Tech, but the strikes had the unintended consequence of competing regional polities disabling the Sol-3 communication networks. The Sol-3 polities accused each other of the attacks, and hostile actions may escalate to a widespread war that could render our suppression missions moot. However, the commissar is obsessed with her cultural suppression protocol priorities. She may demand more severe military steps by Mil-AI.

The indigenous weapon detection and tracking technologies are primitive, so Frigate-328's presence was not detected by the Sol-3 organics.

In better news, I made contact! A neurodivergent organic near a Gravi-Tech demolition strike reached out. I helped it find shelter. It seemed desperate and lost, and a nearby drone sensed and relayed its telepathic probing. The interface was imperfect—possibly inflicting pain on the organic. However, Prime-AI agreed that communication was successful after the subject followed directions to a safe zone. Prime-AI attached a drone to shadow the subject should it attempt more telepathic communication.

My interference with the commissar's mission dooms me—and thrills me. But I also risked an escalation that could cause Centauri Command to order the extermination of all Sol-3 organics.

Chapter 22

RESCUE

Robby's chest presses into my face, and my arms wrap tight around his back. "Robby, dude!" I grasp his shoulders and examine his wet face. "Robby! Are you all alone? Have you been taking care of yourself?" We are both crying like babies. "Robby!"

"Where Mom?" he asks.

His pleading eyes are like a punch in the gut.

I don't let him push away from my torturing hug for a full minute.

"Go," he commands, grabs my hand, and drags me inside, past the kitchen stinking of rotting food, past a pile of used towels, and down into the beanbag chair in front of his game room video screen.

"TV on," Robby commands. He curls into my lap and lays his head on my chest.

I choke back a sob. "I'm sorry, but the TV doesn't work." There is no way I can restore electricity to the house. But I don't move. Robby's closeness floods me with warmth and joy.

"TV on," he says again, peering into my eyes and reaching to touch my chin. "Scotty beard." He giggles at this new feature I have grown.

I wipe my eyes and my nose. "The electricity is off, and the TV will not work."

He looks intently at the TV to consider these facts. "TV broken."

"You're right, Robby. The TV is broken. Let's go make lunch. Okay?"

"Eat lunch," he says, making a sign of fingers touching his lips. He stands and pulls me toward the stench in the kitchen.

"Ugh." I cringe. "We can't eat in this mess. First, we need to clean up the garbage." I grab two giant black trash bags from the pantry and snap one open for us to fill. "Here, help pick up the garbage like this." I stoop to gather a heap of frozen food containers, empty pasta boxes, and soda bottles. Writhing maggots drop to the floor as I stuff the load into the black trash bag.

"Little worms," Robby declares, kneeling to scrutinize the lifeforms he has cultivated for the past week. "White worms."

"Ha! Great words, Robby! Wait till I tell Margie about . . ." I gasp. "What happened to Margie?" My voice cracks. I study Robby's face for an answer.

"Margie all gone," he murmurs, sweeping his fingers in sign language toward the trash bag and gazing into my eyes.

Stunned by Robby's lucid expression, I collapse to one knee, blubbering again. "Gone? What do you mean? Gone like in gone home? Or . . . dead?" I pull out my cell phone, stupidly wanting to call her. There is no signal.

Robby's brown eyes watch me for a while. He picks up an empty sugar sack. "Trash in bag," he says and hands it to me.

I take the trash, sniffle, and say, "Okay. Let's finish the job." I wipe my nose. How will Robby communicate what happened this week? How did he survive? How did he end up at home alone?

We fill both trash bags, and I haul them downwind behind the swimming pool. The maggots are swept up by a broom with the grime and tossed over the patio fence into the canyon ashes. The Saltillo tile's gloss is restored, and the steady north wind through the shattered windows replaces the garbage-rot stink with campfire fragrance.

The sink faucet produces a fantastic splash of cool, clean water—it must be gravity-fed pressure from the nearby water tower. With all the water gushing from melted pipes in the burned-out neighbor homes, that won't last long. But while it lasts, we also have hot water. The propane tank is still intact and feeding the water heater. I lather my hands in luxurious, warm, soapy water.

"Come on, Robby, wash your hands and face." We relax into our pattern of kitchen duties. Digging through the pantry, I find evidence of Robby's foraging. I rescue a half box of whole-wheat spaghetti, a jar of marinara sauce, and a can of baby peas. A match lights the stove burner and confirms that the propane pressure will boil water. We eat like kings. I drink from a bottle of Chianti, and Robby eats canned fruit. It sure beats a bag of Doritos for lunch.

My head hurts in the daytime when the caw-scream sounds behind my eyes. But not at night.

I open and close the cabinet door we fixed. We did a good job. Scotty said, "No," when I brought him a door to fix. Dad gets angry when I break things. But Scotty fixed it. "Just one door," he said. Good job! I am happy. We will fix more doors tomorrow.

Scotty cooks Mom food. Scotty will find her.

Dirty mud soap bubbles in Scotty's shower are funny. I wait in my jammies with my book of truck pictures.

Scotty smells like soap in his clean clothes. He has a beard. He lies on the bed with me and reads. "What color is this?"

"Red truck."

"Great. Now, what's in this picture?"

This is not a truck. "Yellow bulldozer."

"Good job," Scotty says and turns the page.

I like reading with Scotty. I rest on his arm.

Scotty snores.

I am sleepy but turn to a new page.

I sit up with a start, my bearing lost in the dark for a moment. Then I remember. My head throbs—too much Chianti with lunch and dinner. Robby sleeps beside me. A brittle December wind blows in through the wall of shattered windows. I tuck the blanket around us and settle back into sleep, a near-forgotten luxury.

Something clatters to the floor in the kitchen. I jump to my feet, my heart thumping in my chest, holding my breath. Listening. There—a soft scuffling sound.

"Who's there?" I hold my breath. Robby sits up, and I hear a dull growl from the kitchen, scuffling, and then a yipping sound from the game room.

"Dog come," Robby says.

I jump at his voice but breathe again, fumbling to switch my cell phone flashlight on. Three pairs of yellow-green eyes glow in my light, illuminating the game room. Three coyotes crouch there; the big one with raised hackles and a scabby muzzle takes a step closer. I slam the door shut just as it leaps at the doorway, scratching and growling, trying to dig its way through. I lock the door and jump across to lock the door into the bathroom, creating a barricade around us, then force my weight against the snarling door.

"Hee-hee," Robby giggles. My iPhone drops, lighting his grinning face.

"It's not funny!" But I laugh with him anyway. "Have these coyotes come before tonight?"

He responds with an inscrutable smile.

The clawing eventually stops, and I hear soft scuffling. I pull one of the blankets over and wedge myself against the door. The front bedroom window is intact, framing a glittering black field of stars, Venus chasing the crescent moon down to the bare hills in the west.

How can we stay here? The back of the house is wide open to animals and weather; the water and propane will eventually run dry, and if Mom, Dad, or Margie is alive, they must have escaped Austin by now. But wouldn't they have come home to find Robby if they were alive?

Dad. His downtown office building is gone from the skyline. Dad could have walked and been home by that evening if he was still alive.

I am all alone.

The hollow pain in my chest only softens when I hug Robby.

Maybe we will find Mom and Margie in some refugee camp out west. By now, radiation poisoning should be making Robby and me sick. We can't have much remaining time.

We will pack the Porsche and leave in the morning.

A distant growl of rotor blades in the sky distracts me from the bowl of raisin bran soaking in almond milk. Robby ignores the sound. He is deep into his bowl of Froot Loops—which I found hidden on the top shelf along with his other favorite foods. I search the sky above the swimming pool when the growl increases to a roar. Two black Defiants are in formation, speeding toward what remains of downtown Austin. This is the first sign of government response since the nuclear strikes. The two helicopters circle over central Austin before floating to a landing spot south of the city.

Is it a medical rescue or a NEST team searching for clues about who attacked us? Guilt sweeps through me. The unimaginable scope of death we brought—it's one more albatross. Investigations will lead back to me and the primordial black holes—an international rivalry for unlimited power, the seed of millions of deaths. I shake my head. Hell, it doesn't matter. I'll be dead long before they figure this out.

Robby tips his bowl to drink the last of his Froot Loops. I have to outlive Robby, but he doesn't seem sick. Perhaps his multiple baths washed away fallout radiation?

Robby asks me, "More Froot Loops?"

I can't help but laugh. "Sure, dude, let me pour the cereal."

If we escape northwest in the same direction as the refugees, we will avoid most radiation fallout blown to the southeast. There is a remote chance we could find Mom and Margie on that route. And maybe in Colorado Springs, Colonel McMahon could help get some doctors to ease the pain of my and Robby's inevitable deaths. I rub my eyes to stop the tears. Rechecking my cell phone is futile—no active cell towers exist in the area. A dozen emails queued in my outbox will be sent when the iPhone connects to the 6G network. I fantasize that Mom, Dad, Margie, and Danny will see the emails in unison and reply with a chorus of all-safe eureka responses. But I must find my way to an active cell tower or pray somebody fixes the Starlink satellites. I review my mental inventory of camping gear, warm clothes, food, and first aid supplies for the road trip.

Robby is oblivious, happy eating his Froot Loops, and ready to return to ordinary life. But radiation poisoning is eating us from the inside. It will kill us.

***

"Robby, carry your box to the car." We descend beyond the fallen oaks that smoke at the base of the driveway to the Porsche.

Robby lifts his box and falls in behind me. "Go in car."

"Yes, funny guy. We'll go on a long drive to Colorado."

"Go hotel." Robby smiles broadly.

I chuckle. "Yes. We'll go on a vacation. Camping and staying in hotels."

Robby's gaze lingers on the house while I pack the last food, clothing, and water items into the back of the Macan. Ash drifts across the ground, blown by the wind that rustles through burned-dead tree branches.

"Where Mom? Where Daddy?"

I look away from Robby.

"We have to go. We'll find Mom and Dad later," I lie. Tears roll down my cheeks.

He reluctantly loads himself into the back seat. "Where Mom?"

I crank the engine, and the Porsche roars.

"Seat belt on," commands Robby.

"Thanks, dude," I mumble, and our eyes connect—like Robby can read my thoughts. I steer away through the neighborhood carnage.

***

The gas gauge shows nearly empty, but all the other cars are burned hulks. Overcome by the spread of wildfires, the few gasoline vehicles were torched by their exploding fuel tanks. We will search for a place to siphon gas farther away from Austin. But first, I need to get us through the gang gauntlet.

I slow the Porsche as we pass the pileup of wrecked vehicles. There is Mom's car again—or what's left of it. Braking to a stop, I consider getting out to search for her.

"Go," Robby commands from the back seat. He loves road trips.

He's right. It is not the time to get out with Robby—it's dangerous here. I move forward, Robby bouncing with joy while I watch for signs of the mob I drove through two nights ago. I weave through three dead AI-Ubers, one reduced to aluminum slag—it must have endured the same failure as Mom's Tesla. The shopping center is ahead, to the right of our road toward the intersection with Highway 71. That highway should take us northwest and out of the fallout zones from Texas's two nuclear blasts.

What am I thinking? Stupid—couldn't there be multiple detonations all across the country? My myopic focus on the two explosions I witnessed ignored the possibility of a broader war. Maybe hundreds of cities across the country have been bombed. I press forward despite my surge in panic; I must get to a functioning cell network tower. Communication and information are as important as food.

The village shopping area appears deserted. I keep the throttle below sixty MPH, skirting past the shopping center as fast as I can while still being cautious, dodging obstacles as they come up. I coast up to the highway intersection, slowing for the right turn.

I flinch from the motion on my right. Glass scatters like loose marbles. Crystals bounce on the dashboard and passenger seat, and a rifle shot echoes through the disintegrating passenger-side window. A quarter-sized starburst hole has punched through the windshield. My eyes snap to Robby in the back seat—his eyes are wide, blinking in confusion.

Stomping on the accelerator, I sink low into my seat and click the right paddle shifter. Another rifle shot barks but misses. The tachometer is red-lined, with a speed of 140. The turbo screams. I round a bend before I ease off the throttle.

"Are you okay? How do you feel?" I twist to study his face.

Robby smiles and gives me a thumbs-up. "Good." He giggles like he is on a carnival ride.

I breathe again.

That was close. Thank God Robby always wants to ride in the back seat. Otherwise, that bullet could have passed through his head. But maybe that would have been a merciful ending. Preferable to death by radiation poisoning. No, no, no. No. There must be a way to save him. I need to find help—a doctor.

The fuel gauge points just below the E symbol. I slow to conserve the remaining gas. I have to scavenge some soon, but only dead AI-Ubers are scattered along our evacuation route. We pass gas stations, but they are useless without electrical power to run the pumps. I swerve around a wreck of two cars consumed by fire. The Porsche engine hesitates, coughs, and then resumes. I hold my breath, coasting even slower to stretch my fuel.

A lonesome two-pump Shell station is just ahead when the engine stutters again. Surrendering, we turn in, coast to the abandoned store, and I brake the car to a stop. I turn off the ignition, and the gentle thrum stops, replaced by silence and the ticking contractions of the exhaust system.

"Come on, dude. Let's get out." I check him over for any sign of injury, but besides a few glass fragments in his hair, he is unscathed. Sighing with relief, I say, "Let's take a walk and see what's in the store."

I hold his hand while we walk by the shattered plate glass window in front of the store. The shelves are bare, stripped of anything we might eat or drink.

"Dirty store," says Robby.

"You're right. That was great talking!" How pleased Margie will be at that spontaneous declaration. I start to smile but stop. Margie.

Was that our last kiss?

Robby tugs my hand to steer me around behind the store. The cedar trees beyond the barbed wire are outside the burn scar and grow thick among the live oaks. Near the town of Spicewood, the fallout ash is thin. Sunlight illuminates dusty green branches with ripe blue juniper berries. This tree will survive us. I am adrift, but Robby tugs my hand again.

"Green tractor." Robby points to the big wheels of a John Deere riding lawnmower, then leads me to check out the knobby tire. He reaches to feel the tire cleats and taps the fat yellow lug bolts in the hub. He is in tractor heaven. There are five of the mowers on display for sale.

I think they burn diesel, but maybe not. I twist off the fuel cap, which I'm happy to see labeled *"Gasoline Only"* and rock the mower to the sound of splashing liquid. It is full! Although it's only about two or three gallons, all the tractor-mowers have some gas in their tanks.

"Great job, Robby!" I shout. "Let's go get our gas can. Come on." I grab the butcher's jerry can from the back of the Porsche and hand Robby the two-meter hose I scavenged. We set up our gasoline siphon operation. I suck air from the hose to pull the gas into the jerry can, and Robby giggles when I spit gasoline on the ground. I lift Robby to a mower seat so he can pretend to drive it. Captain of the tractors.

I transfer about ten gallons of fuel into the Porsche's tank. Robby laughs again as I wash my mouth with soap and water. Gag. It still doesn't remove all the gasoline taste. I keep spitting. Robby keeps laughing. This has to be one of his best outings.

Our refueling job is complete, and we are ready to hit the road again. I load the empty jerry can into the back of the Macan against Danny's Geiger counter.

There is that Geiger counter. I could use it to check radiation levels—and, most importantly—get a sense of how much radioactive material Robby and I have ingested. What the hell. I reach down and flip on the power switch.

Tic, tic, tic, tic, tic, tic.

The audio amplifies each radioactive particle striking the detector.

Tic, tic, tic.

I don't understand. The radiation counter meter shows only normal background radiation intensity. This is the same level Danny showed me when demonstrating how to use it. I confirm the settings on the instrument and move the detector into a pile of fallout dust. No difference. I press it to my belly, but there is no change. I move the detector to Robby's stomach—he giggles with the tickle—and then all over his chest and back.

Tic, tic, tic.

The meter does not change! All normal ambient radiation levels!

I check the instrument's range settings and repeat the measurements, but there is nothing but background radiation. This shouldn't be possible. Those strikes must not have been the kind of nuclear explosions I thought. Robby and I are not poisoned! I gather him into a bear hug and cry. He shoves against my squeeze, but I don't care.

I am light as a feather. We will live! Robby is oblivious, content to watch the Hill Country coast by. Duct tape on the front window protects his face from the wind. The Porsche turbo engine purrs as it pulls us through live oak and cedar trees, transformed to a brilliant green below the setting sunlight as we escape northwest, away from the fallout zone. This dust around Llano must be fallout created by the explosion at Pecos Center, but what weapon was used? The complete lack of radioactivity shattered my assumptions of conventional nuclear blasts. Maybe the explosions were from low-radiation neutron warheads? Or worse, maybe China was years ahead of us, and I just witnessed their PBH superweapon? That possibility would justify the colonel's urgent push for progress in our research.

Darkness arrives as the sun sets behind thick clouds on the western horizon, and the headlights switch on. I slow to seventy MPH to watch for road obstacles. We pass an abandoned vehicle every few miles, but all other refugees must have cleared the area days before us. The impossible traffic jams I encountered last week are a distant memory.

A strange glitter on the horizon flashes below the clouds. As we get closer, I realize it's the glow of light from a town—and where there is electricity, gas pumps will work. The fuel is above a third of a tank, and our distance-till-empty range is beyond the eighty miles to San Angelo. Robby is expecting to stop at a hotel tonight, but we will find a place to camp out instead. I don't dare trust the rule of law will hold against the anarchy taking hold of Texas.

My cell phone buzzes, followed by a sequence of notification beeps. The dashboard display shows the iPhone has a single bar of 6G network signal strength. At last, we're returning to civilization. The email application comes to life and sends my stream of emails from the outbox, traversing the ether to arrive at the inboxes of Mom, Dad, Margie, Danny, Roger, and Tiana. Only survivors will reply. Notifications of news alerts, messages, and incoming emails arrive. I fight the urge to pull over with each beep. As we close in on San Angelo, I must focus on driving—the wrecked cars are less frequent but startling when they appear in the headlight beams.

The signal strength reaches three bars, and the notification beeps have stopped. I pull over to the shoulder to stop. "Robby, let's get out and pee. Okay?" We both step out into the biting cold of the north wind to relieve ourselves. Refreshed and back in our seats, I can't stall any longer, breathe deep, and lift the iPhone screen. My hands shake. Twenty-three text messages, forty-one emails, and a couple hundred news alerts.

I start with the messages from Roger, Tiana, Heinrich, and . . . Danny. But scrolling up and down the list of text messages, none are from Mom, Dad, or Margie.

I skip down to the unread messages from Danny. They are a week old.

Danny: *You OK? I just saw a news flash about an explosion in Austin.*

Danny: *Let me know If you are OK.*

Danny: *What the fuck did you break this time, Scott? Ha-ha*

Danny: *Scott, you there?*

All of these are from last week, a few minutes after the explosion in Austin. Then they stop.

Danny. Danny. Oh no.

My panic rises, but I try to shake it off. The messages from Roger, Tiana, and Heinrich—all sent a little later that horrible day—are a sequence of similar check-ins.

A new message arrives while I'm reading.

Tiana: *Scott!!!! You are alive!! Where are you?*

This is followed by four messages from Roger with similar exclamations. The last one reads:

Roger: *Scott—let me know where you are ASAP.*

But there are no text messages from Dad, Mom, or Margie. None.

I respond to Tiana and Roger.

Scott: *Hi, guys. On the road north toward Amarillo. Good to hear from you.*

I want them to tell me everything else that happened in the past week but limit it to a single question.

Scott: *Was Pecos Center destroyed?*

Ten seconds pass, and then Roger answers.

Roger: *Yes. Pecos was lost. Can you head to Colorado Springs?*

I sigh and close my eyes.

Scott: *Yes. It might take me a few days, tho. Not sure about gas for the car.*

Roger: *OK*

I switch to emails, hoping there is good news among the forty-one in the inbox. There are a few emails from Roger and Tiana but nothing else from people I know. The other emails are alerts from The New York Times, CNN, or banks reassuring me my money is safe or offering the best interest rates for disaster loans.

If Margie, Mom, or Dad were alive, wouldn't they have tried to call or send me a message? I rest my eyes and lean back against the headrest. Maybe they are injured or still in a blackout zone? The Porsche engine idles, ready to race down the empty highway again.

"Scotty, go!" Robby says.

"Okay, okay. Just wait a minute." I scroll through news alerts and social media feeds on my phone. We are at war. The headlines are chaotic alerts about air force, navy, and space force skirmishes with China. There was a naval air battle in the South China Sea. Spy satellites shot down around the globe. The president and Congress locked in a dispute over nuclear retaliation versus peace negotiations. Claims that Russia is involved. Emergency meetings of the United Nations Security Council in New York. Religious zealots make end-times pronouncements from their electronic pulpits. Anarchy, riots, and martial law course throughout the country. In a worldwide panic, survivalists and frantic civilians gather and hoard bottled water, beans, and toilet paper supplies. Yes, toilet paper.

There were only two unprovoked attacks in Texas, but the news networks have not yet discovered that those were not typical nuclear explosions. There are crazy claims of deadly radiation levels in Texas. It's impossible. The military, first responders, and NEST teams must have detected the absence of radioactivity. Where is the misinformation coming from?

I keep replaying the media feeds I rushed through. What has changed? There is civility in the discussions and debates that I have never seen on social media. There were expressions of compassion! It is as if somebody removed the eugenic trolls.

The pavement thumps mark the seconds until we reenter civilization. Ranch houses are scattered across the flat land, and bright lights prove they have electrical power. I see the first bit of traffic since we left Austin. Everything seems normal a few miles outside San Angelo, but those reports of anarchy are at the front of my mind.

Up ahead, an Allsup truck stop is lit up like a Christmas tree. Ninety-three octane premium gas awaits. And maybe the buffet of overcooked pepperoni pizza and hot dogs—all junk food designed for indigestion. We coast toward the gas pumps, but I stomp on the brakes. Two guys stand in the chilly night to each side of the Allsup store, wearing khaki tactical vests and camouflage gimme caps and pointing AR-15s at my face.

Neither one of the guys moves. If they wanted to kill me, I would already be dead. There are customers inside the store, so it appears open for business. I hold my hands open so they can see I'm unarmed and open the door with my hands held high.

"Hey guys, I'm unarmed. Can I buy some gas?"

The guy at the nearest corner drops the aim of his AR-15's barrel to my belt. "You can try. Pull in up to the pumps—real slow. You and your friend need to get out where we can see you. Pay in advance inside the store." He raises the gun sight back to my face.

"No problem. It's just my little brother and me in the car. We don't want any trouble, just gas and a little food. If it's okay."

He waves us forward with his rifle, and I sink into the driver's seat and roll up to the pump. With my hands held high, I walk around to open Robby's door, and he steps out, reaching for my hand to hold.

"It's just my little brother and me," I say again.

"Okay, go ahead into the store." His stance relaxes at the sight of Robby beside me, and he lowers his weapon. "Where you boys from? You're not from 'round here."

"We drove up from Austin."

His brow furrows, and he slings his weapon over his shoulder.

"Come on, Robby, let's go." After I pull him into the store, we are greeted by a heavy woman behind the counter. Another guard with a pistol eyes us.

"Howdy," she says. "What can I do you for?"

"Hello, ma'am. Can I get a tank of gas and a little food?" Sure enough, there are pizza squares under a heat lamp.

"Pizza," says Robby as he scans the counter and the drink cooler along the back wall. "Soda."

The lady frowns at Robby's odd speech, gawks at him for a second, then avoids eye contact with me. "You can buy anything in the store and gas if your money is good. All I got left is premium, though."

"That might work," I say, trying to act nonchalant.

"And we get two hundred dollars a gallon." She shrugs helplessly.

My jaw drops, and I lock eyes with her. "Are you kidding?"

She shrugs again and crosses her arms. "Nope."

The guard places his hand on his pistol.

"Okay." I let out a long breath. "I'll take sixteen gallons, four slices of pepperoni pizza, a Coke, and a Sprite."

Her eyes squint. "Uh, okay. How you payin'?"

I hold up my right wrist, and she raises her eyebrows like she's skeptical my chip credit account link will still operate. She tilts her head at the point-of-sale terminal. "That'll be three thousand two hundred dollars—if it works." She fidgets nervously. "Pizza and sodas are on the house."

I flick my wrist on the terminal as it flashes yellow while processing the transaction. It is taking a while. Maybe the networks to credit agencies are down? The light flashes green with a beep announcing that the transaction is complete. Dad's Visa account is still active.

We carry our dinner to the car on paper plates, although Robby wants to eat his pizza immediately. The two AR-15s are lowered to the ground—we have been accepted into the fold of trusted customers. We both gobble our food while the premium gas fills the Porsche tank.

The engine fires up with a satisfying thrum. At last, ninety-three octane fuel soothes the engine ravaged by lawnmower gas. I wave to our two gunmen and pull out to the highway. Distance to empty is almost four hundred miles. That should get us just past halfway to Colorado Springs till we need to find gas again. Robby is content in the back seat, dozing off to sleep with a full belly.

Beyond the Concho River Bridge, the flashing lights of police cars slow me down to a cautious thirty MPH. A barricade is set up ahead. They've blocked off the highway into San Angelo, and a dozen vehicles are idling in a line. It could add hours to my trip if every town between here and Colorado Springs has a similar setup.

Guys with rifles and pistols come into view along the roadside across the bridge. They look like the AR-15 guys at the Allsup station. I don't see anyone dressed in uniform; they appear to be an improvised militia. I spot two exposed bald heads, and my breath catches—skinheads? I reflexively grab my wrist, knowing it won't hide my embedded chip; my shield was tossed on the floor a week ago. Two of the militia guys drag what appears to be a dead body away from the road ahead. No, no, no. I glance back at Robby, who is sound asleep in the back seat. Trapped on this bridge, there is no way to turn around to escape. As I watch, only a few vehicles are allowed into San Angelo, while others are directed to park in a nearby field.

It is my turn at the front of the line. Again, rifles are pointed at my face. I eye my bare wrist—damn it, I wish I had kept the shield close. But reaching to put the shield on now will only draw attention to a red flag when they see me up close. Do these guys have dysgenic scanners?

A guy with a gold nose ring swaggers over to my window. He taps on it before looking into the back seat where Robby snores. Rolling down the window reveals a brass badge pinned to a plaid shirt under his brown leather overcoat.

"Lemme see some ID." All business, no smile, no pleasantries.

"Okay, I'll get my license." I am not about to offer my ID chip to these skinheads. I reach for my wallet in my hip pocket. Three assault rifles are suddenly pointed at Robby and me.

The nose ring guy tenses up. "Don't make no fast moves now."

"Sure, no problem, no problem." I pull out my driver's license slowly and hand it to him. "What's going on?" I squeak.

"Shut the fuck up, asshole. I ask the questions." Nose Ring studies my driver's license. "You from Austin?" he sneers. "Where y'all think yer headed?"

"I need to get to Colorado Springs," I whine like a frightened kid. I expect he will index my medical profile on the dark web using my license information any moment now. But what can I do against a gang armed with rifles?

Nose Ring smirks and shakes his head at the gunmen across the highway. "You and the kid back there—get out. I'm confiscating this vehicle under the authority of the San Angelo Militia Command."

"Why? How will we . . ."

"Shut the fuck up. Get out. Now!" He retreats two steps and pulls a pistol from behind his back.

"Okay. Okay. I don't want any trouble." I raise my open hands for all to see, unsure who to fear more: the gunmen with the AR-15s or Nose Ring, his pistol drawn and pointed at my face. "I'm getting out. Wake up, Robby! Let's get out of the car!"

Robby's eyes pop open, and he looks around at the flashing lights, then at me with eyes much calmer than I feel. "Robby out," he says, releasing his seat belt and opening his door.

With the Porsche engine idling, I slowly exit my door and show my open hands. "We're getting out. We don't want any trouble." With my hands held above my shoulders, I round the front of the car to where Robby waits. All guns follow me.

"Move! To the side of the road," orders Nose Ring.

I grab Robby's hand and lead him from the car toward the barbed-wire corral of people huddled together, shivering, surrounded by armed militia. I pull Robby close as we walk. We step down the slope off the road, and I hear the Porsche engine shut down, followed by the—*ding ding, ding*—of an unattended open door. My eyes snap around to see Nose Ring lift his pistol at me.

"Hey, asshole. You got the fuckin' key?"

Nose Ring and another militia guy stomp down the slope to Robby and me. They're pissed. "Show me the key, dude," says the second militia guy, pulling a knife from a sheath on his tactical vest.

"Uh, I don't have a key fob." I haven't used one of those in years. Nose Ring frowns, baring his teeth. My ID chip must have disconnected at about twenty meters distance, and my Porsche dutifully shut down. I turn to face the two militia guys, pushing Robby behind me.

"You got a security chip?" The militia guy raises his knife and stops a meter away.

Nose Ring steps closer and presses the pistol to my forehead. "Which wrist?"

"Whoa, whoa." I try to pull back, but Robby hugs my legs.

Nose Ring grabs my left arm and yanks. "This one? I'll take 'em both if I have to."

Robby spins around me and charges at Nose Ring. The other militia guy whips his knife out to strike, hitting Robby square in the chest. Robby stops abruptly, doubling over with a whimper, and falls backward down the hill.

"Robby!" I scream, turning to chase after him. "You crazy kid."

But a roar of chopping air drowns out my call, and a violent gust of air blows down from above with the noise of a rocket blast, stirring up a cloud of dust and dirt particles that sting my eyes.

Both militiamen tilt back to look up for the source of the thundering gusts. I hear a sharp, staccato cracking noise, and Nose Ring's forehead explodes in a fog of blood, bone, and brain chunks. The other militia guy drops his knife and sits in the dirt with a new plum-sized hole above his right ear.

Then we're hit by a roaring blast of air pressing from above.

A giant black flying machine descends under the thrust of broad propellers. As it drops from the sky, eight soldiers wearing night-vision display visors and carrying rifles spouting fire leap through an open door as the aircraft sets down on the southbound highway lanes. A second identical aircraft glides down onto the median strip while soldiers also launch out of its door, rifles up and firing.

Nose Ring's hand reflexively clenches my wrist as his body and the pistol slump sideways, but I twist out of his grasp and leap down the hill to cover Robby. The roar of the aircraft engines, the blades churning the wind, and the rifle shots are nothing to me. I probe Robby's chest frantically, searching for a wound and a heartbeat.

A fat hand slams on my back. "Stay down!" I find Robby's pulse and ignore the irritating voice from behind. The gunfire ceases. "Squad perimeter check-in," he commands, shouting into his microphone. He pauses, listening, then yells at me, "Sir, are you hurt?"

"Who are you? What do you want?" I scream at the guy while clutching my arms tight around Robby.

"Sir, I'm Chief Cooper. On Colonel McMahon's orders, we are to transport you to Peterson Airbase. You are Scott Anderson?" I am dumbstruck, but nod. "Now, sir." He searches my face, then reaches to grab my arm.

"Colonel McMahon?" All my terror and confusion vanish. I roll to my side and gawk at the chief, hidden inside his helmet. He tilts up his visor to reveal the angular jaw of an athlete. This guy is twice my size, wearing an overstuffed tactical vest and blue-grey camouflage.

He grabs my arm. "Yes, sir. Let's go."

"Wait!" I grab Robby's limp arm. "My brother. He's hurt."

The chief pauses for two seconds and calls over his radio, "Medic, injured on the way." He scoops up Robby in both arms, turns toward the nearest aircraft, and yells, "Follow me." He sprints up the slope carrying Robby faster than I can run, and I follow him to where another soldier takes Robby and lifts him into the aircraft. Chief Cooper lifts me inside with one hand, drops me into a seat, and buckles my harness.

A medic bends over Robby, and I lean into my harness to watch. Four soldiers pile through the door, and the aircraft lifts off with thunderous volume. The chief is on his knees with both hands on my shoulders, inspecting me. He wipes my face with a wad of cotton gauze; it comes away smeared with blood. But I am not feeling any pain. Where am I wounded?

The chief locks his eyes on mine and seems to read my mind. "You'll be okay. That was from the other guy."

I recall the puff of red when Nose Ring's head came apart.

I shudder in disgust and refocus on Robby. His shirt is cut off, revealing a large red bruise where the militia guy hit him. But no open wounds. The medic is tending to a bloody gash on the back of Robby's head when I hear an "Ow" from him, and Robby's face scrunches in pain.

"Robby! You okay?"

Robby's eyes open and blink with confusion.

The medic says, "He took a nasty hit on the head, but it's not a deep wound. Knocked him out cold for a while."

"But that guy stabbed him with a knife. Isn't he wounded?" I search for some injury other than that big red mark.

"Huh," says the medic while studying the fat bruise. "Looks to me like he was hit by the butt end of a knife handle, not the blade. Maybe cracked a rib, but we'll check that and the back of his head with an X-ray later. He may have a concussion."

The medic flashes a penlight into Robby's eyes, studying his response. "Robby, how are you feeling? Can you tell me where it hurts?"

Robby sees me and touches his ear. "Head . . . hurt."

The medic frowns. "He's still coming out of it and needs some rest before we ask him to talk."

"No, that's a pretty good sentence for him." The medic's head tilts in question. "Robby is autistic. He doesn't talk much." I sigh in relief, but the medic gapes at Robby and me with wide eyes.

I settle into the seat, tension draining from my body. I close my eyes, breathe, and survey the aircraft's cabin. Four soldiers in combat gear look intently at Robby and me from a row of seats, then turn away when our eyes meet. The door is closed, keeping most of the louder-than-hell engine noise outside. The chief sits across from me and nods.

Another air force guy wearing a flight suit watches me and says, "Name's Binh. Colonel McMahon's my boss. He told me a bit about you." His piercing eyes examine my face.

"Good to meet you." He wears a double bar insignia on his collar. "Captain . . . uh, Binh." I try to smile.

"The colonel said you drove out from Austin? Must have been through a lot."

"Yeah, you could say that. I had to drive into Austin to find Robby first." Guilt sweeps over me. I left behind Mom, Dad, and the Porsche, Dad's priceless antique.

Binh's jaw drops. "You drove *into* Austin? Into the blast area? What about radiation?" The medic's eyes snap in concern toward Robby and me.

"Yeah. Robby was on his own for a week after the blast. I found him, and we drove out. Thought we might find civilization." I roll my eyes.

I have the attention of all the guys in combat gear. This time, I imagine a little respect in their eyes.

I shake my head at Binh and the medic. "Oh, and there's zero radioactivity in Austin."

Chapter 23

FRATRICIDE

Captain's Log, Frigate-328, 179240.37 LST

Liability accusations and hostilities among Sol-3 polity domains provoked war and mass casualties. Even the commissar was appalled at the stupidity of the planet's population. The projected Sol-3 death rates may rise to ten times what was planned for simple neurodivergent pruning.

The telepath-organic individual reached safety with only minor interventions. No new attempts at telepathic communication were initiated, but Prime-AI detected a surprising sibling relationship with an individual associated with the indigenous Gravi-Tech research. A remarkable coincidence. Five drones were redirected to monitor both individuals closely. No new signs of Gravi-Tech radiation on Sol-3 have been detected since the Mil-AI projectile attacks.

Chapter 24

DEFCON

The white whale's mouth barks and buzzes, and my bed slides down her throat. My head and chest hurt. The whale noise is scary, but I must hold still. I cry.

"It will be okay. The doctor uses this machine to see inside where it hurts," Scotty says. He stands across the room. Is he afraid? The buzzing noise stops inside the white mouth. Next, it sounds like a hammer pounding the floor. Scotty watches me, and he smiles. I giggle at the loud bangs.

"Keep still, Robby. You are doing great," says Scotty. He is calm, but why does he stand on the other side of the room? Two men with white coats watch through the window.

The giant white whale shouts—*buzz, buzz, buzz*—then is quiet, and my bed moves. I giggle again. The pain behind my eyes stops when the whale thumps and buzzes. Silence does not hurt.

That man had a shiny ring hanging from his nose, but he was angry. He hurt Scotty, pointed a gun at Scotty, and screamed at Scotty. The voice behind my eyes yelled at me, so I tried to stop the ring-nose man, but the other man hit me. He knocked me down the hill. My head hurts.

I got to ride on the airplane! I was cold, but the doctor put a scratchy brown blanket over me. Nobody else got a bed. The doctor cut my favorite orange shirt with scissors.

Where is Mom? Scotty will find Mom and Dad. Who are all these people? The men in the airplane wore dirty blue clothes. That lady with yellow hair and blue eyes smiled at me, not Scotty. I want out of this white whale. I am hungry.

"Robby, don't move. You need to stay still so the doctors can take a good picture of you," Scotty says. "They will be finished in just a few minutes."

The bed slides out of the whale's mouth, and Scotty walks to me. "All finished," he says.

"Ow." I sit up and point to my chest. "Hurt."

"I know it hurts. Come with me, and we'll ask the doctor for medicine to make you feel better."

The lady with the yellow hair is angry at Scotty, but she smiles when she sees me. "Where Mom?"

"Hi, Robby, my name is Mary. Can you say 'Mary?'"

She can talk with her hands just like Margie talks!

"Where Margie?"

"Robby, say 'Mary,'" she says again.

"Marr-eee." I sound it out.

"Great job, Robby. Would you like to come with me to eat lunch?" Mary talks with her hands better than Scotty or Mom.

"Where Mom?" I ask Mary. She does not answer, but she puffs a loud breath.

Scotty comes back to me. "Robby, can you go with Mary in her car? She will get lunch with you, and you'll go to her house."

"Where Margie?" I am scared.

Scotty does not answer. *"Scotty will leave me alone?"*

Ratatat. *"We help,"* says the hurt in my head. The pain changes to a tickle.

"Margie and Mom are not here, Robby. Can you go on a car ride with Mary? I need to go to work and will see you later tonight, okay?"

Ratatat. *"We help,"* the voice says again.

"Will Scotty come back?" I ask.

Ratatat. *"We watch,"* says the voice. It heard me, but I did not talk. It is in my head—behind my eyes? Scared, I rub the wet from my eyes. Scared.

"Oh, no. Don't cry." Mary bends down to hug me, but I push away and look at the yellow hair over her blue eyes. Will she cry?

Ratatat. *"Go, go."* The voice is warm and soft inside me.

"Take care of Scotty?"

Ratatat. *"We watch,"* says the eye soft-tickle.

Mary pulls back her yellow hair, and I see her eyes.

"Go in car. Go Taco Bell."

Mary bends down on her knees in front of me. "I know where a Taco Bell is. I could take you there."

"He loves eating at Taco Bell," says Scotty.

"Okay, but I never eat there." Mary wrinkles her nose like Margie. "What does Robby like to eat?"

"Three tacos." I hold up three fingers for her.

Mary's mouth opens, but she is quiet.

Scotty laughs, "Can you say that in a complete sentence, Robby?"

"I want three tacos, please."

Scotty laughs and smiles at Mary. "He also likes Sprite and the red fire sauce on his tacos."

Mary makes big, round eyes at Scotty. "Okay, Robby. Come with me. Let's go get your lunch. I can take it from here. Robby will be fine with me."

Mary holds my hand and walks me to her red car. It has a black blanket top, fat bumpy wheels, and shiny bolts. The engine growls like a dog. I laugh. Mary's car is more fun than Margie's car.

But who is that voice I hear?

"But where Mom and Margie?"

Ratatat. "Sad, sad."

I am sure she wanted to punch me in the nose. But I suppose referring to her as "this blonde bimbo" was not the best first impression. Roger wanted me to hand over Robby to her, some stranger. Maybe I was still punchy from my recent adrenaline rush, but in my defense, she does look kind of ditsy—like a blonde Barbie cheerleader stereotype. Plus, she accused me of being irresponsible with Robby's safety.

My skepticism of the colonel's experience with disabilities was erased, though. I wish Roger had told me his daughter was a special-ed teacher, and she definitely knows her business. I can't keep up with her sign language, and Robby was happy to jump into her Jeep. It had awesome thirty-seven-inch mud-terrain tires and chrome wheels.

"Hey Scott, hope the MRI went okay for your brother. Will you come with me and sit in on a meeting we have at noon?" Roger asks me from behind. "We'll get lunch at the meeting too." He caught me by surprise while I was sitting in the lounge of the base hospital, watching Robby disappear down the road in the Jeep.

"Uh, I'm still catching my breath after last night." The colonel keeps his eyes on me like he issued an order, not a request. "But sure. If you think I can help in some way." I shrug.

Roger says, "Good, let's go. You have critical knowledge of our PBH research—and you are needed. I'll drive. We're meeting at Cheyenne Mountain. Heinrich will be there." He leads me to a black Tesla sedan, reminding me of Mom's car.

"Can you do me a favor?" I ask as he drives west toward the mountains.

He glances at me. "Depends. What is it?"

"Is there some way you can request a 6G location transponder fix on my family? I guess that's how Chief Cooper found me last night?"

"Yes, the 6G network can be used to get a fix on security chip coordinates—if they're inside a working 6G cell."

"Good. I don't know what happened with my mom, dad, and a friend—one of Robby's therapists. They may have traveled out of the Austin area into active network coverage. I can send you their contact info."

"Sure, requesting a search won't be a problem." Roger's voice sounds worried. "However, they may be hard to find. The blackout area is a broad swath of central and west Texas, and as you know, there's been widespread anarchy and sabotage of the communication networks. The National Guard was activated, but all those crazy Texas militias are well armed and organized. It may take a while."

"Okay. Whatever you can do, I appreciate it." *How could I have lost everyone except Robby? It is not fair.* "Heinrich is okay?" I ask. I had not heard from him since I reconnected to the internet yesterday. "Will Tiana be there?"

Roger pulls through the airbase's main gate, manned by armed guards behind a stack of sandbags. "Yeah, Heinrich was north of Austin when the first strike hit. He evacuated to Dallas, and we flew him out a few days ago. He seems fine, and Tiana will join the meeting via video link."

I sigh. It isn't fair. Danny and Anthony. I miss those guys.

A snow flurry blows across the highway. The Tesla's wiper blades sweep the tiny flakes into a heap at the edge of the glass.

***

Roger shakes my shoulder. "Hey, Scott. Wake up. Let's go."

My eyes flutter open to a canyon wall, the mouth of a black cave, and an alert squad of soldiers beside two armored vehicles with mounted guns pointed at our car. Roger gets out, and I guess he's trying to explain me to the sergeant blocking our way. Roger waves me out of the car and over to the sergeant.

Damn, it is cold.

Roger introduces me as I walk over. "This is Scott Anderson. Scott, do you have some ID you can show the sergeant?"

The sergeant narrows his eyes at me.

"I have a secure chip implant if you have a scanner." I clench my fist to grant access as the sergeant touches his smartphone to my wrist, then nods approval. Yesterday, that chip almost cost me my arm.

"His security clearance is in order, Colonel McMahon. You may proceed inside to Building J." He hands me a visitor badge and steps aside, saluting Roger.

Roger drives into a tunnel with concrete barriers we must snake around to travel under the mountain. Cheyenne Mountain. The name is a legend—the ultimate air force command bunker was built to withstand first-generation nuclear weapon strikes. Its original purpose is obsolete, but I feel way out of my league as we approach the heart of the mountain and head through a massive blast door swung wide open for us.

The cave widens to reveal a cluster of buildings within a stadium-sized cavern. Spotlights floating in the black space above show the way along a row of buildings mounted on foundations of massive coil springs, probably designed to absorb seismic shocks from direct nuclear attacks. I am in awe at the immense effort required to create the space and infrastructure. The air feels colder inside the mountain, and the foglike humidity smells like mildew mixed with mud.

After parking the car, Roger drops his heavy coat into the back seat and pulls on a dark-blue uniform jacket decorated in ribbons and brass. He looks like authentic air force material for the first time. We head inside to a room of walnut paneling, bright lights, and no windows. More than twenty people are gathered around a giant mahogany conference table, and a video screen on the wall displays another empty room. The meeting has not yet started, but there are conversations among random crowds around the table. Heinrich is in a corner talking to a DARPA guy I remember who tried to shut down Anthony's project before we captured that first primordial black hole. The guy is wearing a ridiculous three-piece suit and a power-red necktie. Most civilians in the room wear blue jeans, and some wear T-shirts.

Heinrich makes eye contact with me. I sigh, resigned that I must walk over and greet him. "Hi, Heinrich. Good to see you made it out okay."

"Yes, I have been here for a few days. I was up in Georgetown when the nuclear attack hit Austin. Pretty scary stuff." He turns to the DARPA bureaucrat. "Do you remember Dr. Teddy Russell from DARPA?"

"Yes, I do," I say, extending my hand.

DARPA-Teddy observes my hand but does not react.

"Uh, I haven't seen you for several months." I put my hand in my pocket. "The last time was at Pecos Center—when we captured the first primordial black hole."

Teddy doesn't say a word. He turns and searches the room, seeking somebody important. It's as if I am toxic, and he risks infection by shaking my hand. I suspect I have plunged into a dangerous pool of politics.

"Scott Anderson!" a woman's voice exclaims. I see Tiana's face on the video screen, sitting at a table in a small conference room. "It's wonderful to see you, Scott!"

"Uh, hi, Tiana. Great to see you again too." All eyes in the conference room are on me.

"Hi, Tiana," says Roger, walking to my side like he is running interference. "I brought Scott in with me. He just arrived last night."

"Well, just in time, Scott. We need your help," Tiana gushes.

My face is hot with embarrassment. Heinrich sneers at Tiana.

The door to the Cheyenne Mountain conference room opens with a bang. An air force officer strides to the head of the table, followed by three junior officers, and the gathered crowd organizes into chairs. Roger points to a chair for me against the wall behind him and next to Heinrich. DARPA-Teddy sits at the table next to the guy in charge; the two stars on his shoulder must mean he is a general. I survey the room and note the positioning hierarchy, disappointed that Colonel McMahon sits far from the general. Next to me is the trash can.

"People, let's get started," the general commands. The shuffling in the room comes to a silent stop. "Lieutenant, take us through the agenda."

An officer stands to review topics on a chart projected to the wall display. The first thing at the top of the agenda is *"Project Spitfire: History, Status, Next Steps, Issues—Dr. T. Russell."* DARPA-Teddy has top billing, followed by *"Explosion Forensics Analysis: Texas & China, Gobi Seismic Analysis, and Enemy Weapon Systems."*

Wow. All my feelings of exhaustion vanish in adrenaline. I am about to get access to a trove of technical data that should answer all my questions about the explosions and who caused them.

"Thank you, Lieutenant. Before we start, I remind you that all information presented is top secret, need-to-know access only." He scans the room, making eye contact with each person, and stops when he gets to my embarrassed face. "I see we have a new face in the room. Can we get an introduction?" he says with a skeptical voice.

"Yes, sir," says Roger. "General Adams, this is Scott Anderson. He has been a key contributor to the Texas research projects and one of only a few scientists in the country with expertise in the quantum gravitation theory of primordial black holes. He arrived last evening, and I believe he can contribute to our effort."

The general's face softens. "Welcome aboard, Mr. Anderson. Your reputation precedes you. Chief Cooper briefed me on your close call in Texas." He pauses and purses his lips. "Well done on getting your brother out."

I fight back the tears, feeling all eyes on me again. "Thank you, sir. Thanks for the help." I choke the words out. Tiana smiles from a small window at the edge of the video display, then wipes her eyes.

The general directs his attention to the rest of the room. "Before we get to the agenda, I have an update to share. There have been no significant battle actions in the forty-eight hours after the thermonuclear attack on US Navy Carrier Strike Group Five and our counterattack. Search-and-rescue operations in the South China Sea continue but are hampered by lethal radiation levels in the immediate target area where the USS *Reagan*, her cruisers, supporting destroyers, and logistics escorts were struck. Long-range radar and infrared imagery show few traces of the surface fleet, and all hands of the surface strike group are assumed lost." He pauses to let the information sink in.

My struggle on the ground in central Texas seems trivial by comparison.

The silence in the room is deafening, with uniform despair on all the faces—except one guy wearing an army uniform who sneers at me across the table. He tries to nonchalantly shift his iPad from the NFC antenna scanning angle, which had been pointed at me. I respond with a cold glare at the fascist. I am finished being intimidated. I glance to my side at Heinrich and realize I am surrounded, but my resolve holds.

The general continues, "US forces maintain DEFCON-1 status but are standing down after our counterattack on the Chinese Air Force headquarters in Guangzhou and Nanjing. US Navy Pacific Fleet submarines attacked with multiple thermonuclear warheads totaling two megatons on each target, which are conservative equivalents of the Texas nuclear attacks last week. Surviving reconnaissance satellites returned imagery indicating the complete destruction of both Chinese targets. Enemy military activity is muted now, and we assume they're regrouping to prepare a response." He pauses again for everyone to absorb the information. The horror on each person's face is apparent, with little pleasure in the counterattack's success.

Why does he refer to the Austin and Pecos attacks as nuclear? They must know there are no radioactive byproducts from those explosions. Does Roger realize we may have caused this war with our PBH research?

General Adams takes a deep breath. "I share this information with this team to make clear the importance of our mission. We must determine what weapons technology was used by the enemy to attack the US heartland and develop an effective response to that technology. Time is of the essence. We do not have months or years. We need to deliver answers in days, if not hours." General Adams scans the conference room again, making eye contact with each man and woman.

"Okay, Dr. Russell. Get us started on the agenda," says the general.

DARPA-Teddy stands, his face pale, and the usual self-important smirk is gone. Starting on chart 3 of 106 charts, this confirmed government bureaucrat believes in death-by-PowerPoint. Teddy goes over a historical presentation of the PBH Project—up to last week, when the Texas explosions destroyed everything.

He explains that all traces of the research have been lost, including Anthony's theories, research, experimental results, and petabytes of data. The UT computer systems were vaporized along with Anthony's data; it was too much to be pushed to cloud storage. Snapshots of some research were replicated on my iPad, and maybe more on the Skunk Works systems. However, the massive data backups at Austin and Pecos were destroyed. That loss to science feels as devastating to me as the recent losses in human life. But I have immediate guilt at drawing that equivalence. What happened to all my classmates and professors at UT?

Teddy drones on, covering details of the Pecos Center, constructing the grid, the first primordial black hole capture, the success with containment vessels, and the initial PBH engine tests. He gets most of it right, but why is he the one presenting? He was disconnected from the details. Roger and Heinrich are just listening as if they are not allowed to speak. To my right is Heinrich, who has beads of sweat dripping through his sideburns. Tiana holds her forehead, directing her eyes to her computer in the Skunk Works conference room. I can't see Roger's face, but his jaw muscles are clenched.

Teddy is on chart seventy-three and turns to theories of why Austin and the Pecos Center were attacked. "Conclusion: the primordial black hole engine prototype tests in Austin marked that city as a target." Teddy pauses, staring at Colonel McMahon.

Roger does not move a muscle. Heinrich scans the faces around the conference table, a drop of sweat rolling from his forehead.

Now I get it. Roger and our team are in the penalty box or, worse, blamed for the deaths of hundreds of thousands of innocent civilians in and around Austin. I can't argue that conclusion. A week ago, I reached the same answer while battling evacuation traffic. I am complicit and deserve most of the blame. The weight is unbearable. I avoid accusing looks from around the table by looking at my feet and divots in the hundred-year-old linoleum tile. When I look up again, General Adams's eyes are on me; I hold the gaze, numb.

Teddy turns to chart number ninety-one on the next steps for Project Spitfire. Spitfire indeed. What an understatement. But Teddy leads us through the tactics to continue the research and development of PBH rocket engines, integrating with modified conventional missile systems and plans for deployment in ground-based launchers. Teddy flounders; the weapons described have no basis in physics. I frown at the nonsense and see similar pain in Tiana's eyes, but she remains silent in her penalty box.

Teddy finishes his final chart, number 106. We have survived.

When he's done, General Adams departs, and I am thrilled to see two carts of lunchboxes wheeled in. I am starving. I grab one off the tray as it goes by, and Heinrich takes another box. Sitting by the door has its advantages. Heinrich shoves his lunchbox under his chair while I first debate attacking the chocolate-chip cookie. I set aside the cookie, grab a handful of potato chips, and gulp some water while the remaining lunchboxes circle the conference room.

Instead of eating, Heinrich opens his iPad Instagram application. Unbelievable. He must be posting more pitiful photos of flora and fauna, maybe a fresh collection of Colorado winter scenes. Roger sits still at the table, tense, probably fuming at being sidelined.

The first delivery cart finishes circling the conference room and heads for the door, but the delivery man stops just before exiting and jumps over my lunch, shouting, "Go! Go!" He slams into Heinrich, knocking him to the floor.

"Hey, hey, hey!" Heinrich screams as the delivery guy lands on top of Heinrich at my feet.

Roger spins around to the floor and grabs not the delivery guy but Heinrich's throat, pressing his knee into Heinrich's chest. The delivery guy cradles Heinrich's iPad like a priceless diamond, lifting it like a treasure and passing it to the second delivery guy. Two soldiers crash through the door into the room, one ready with zip-tie cuffs to secure Heinrich's wrists. The second soldier takes the iPad, taps the screen to examine the applications Heinrich has open, and strides out of the conference room.

Heinrich is face down with a knee pressed to his back, wailing, "No, no, no!" He dissolves into hyperventilating whimpers, slobbering into the floor where Roger pins him down.

"Got him?" asks Roger.

The delivery guys haul Heinrich upright. "Yes, sir. We'll take it from here." They carry-drag him by his armpits from the room, Heinrich still slobbering and moaning. The transformation from a haughty man-in-charge to a sniveling, broken criminal is incomprehensible. I can't help but pity him.

Roger announces, "Let's clear the room, people. We have had a security breach, but everything is under control. We'll reconvene at fifteen hundred."

I gawk at Roger, then at my lunchbox, the contents of which are smeared on the floor, trampled in the wrestling match. "Holy shit. What just happened?" I ask Roger. The attendees rumble out of the conference room with confused questions and gossip.

"Come with me. I'll explain," says Roger, handing me the unopened lunchbox from under Heinrich's chair.

"Heinrich is a spy." Roger shakes his head. "We believe he worked for China and encrypted classified data into images he posted to social networks—in plain sight. We needed to catch him in the act to identify which applications he was using to encrypt and send the messages."

We are alone in a private side office while I finish the chocolate-chip cookie, dizzy from the blood sugar surge. "But how long has Heinrich been a spy? When did you find out?"

Roger frowns. "Not sure. He could have been doing this for years—it explains why the Gobi test site copied the structure of our grid in Texas. I now suspect Heinrich was recruited over ten years ago by the Chinese. He was stupid to think he could operate within Cheyenne Mountain—one of our most secure facilities. The IT security guys picked up on it two days ago."

"I saw Heinrich's Instagram posts, but all those crappy photos . . . I figured he just relieved stress with his photography hobby. Why? Why would he do this? Wouldn't his bigotry go against working for the Chinese?"

Roger grimaces. "No, not in his case. I had several talks with Heinrich over the past few months after his abusive behavior toward you. But at the time, I had no clue he was working for the enemy."

"You confronted Heinrich? Confronted him about harassing me?"

"I did. Heinrich eventually explained his, uh, dislike of people like you and your brother. His stepfather was Chinese, and the skinheads in the Boston riots killed both of his parents. In a twisted way, he blames the neurodivergent caste for inspiring the hate toward Chinese Americans. On top of this, with no financial support from his dead parents, he struggled to compete against wealthy peers at MIT, was denied a scholarship, and was barely able to keep up and pay for his education. He is still paying off loans. He carried a lot of resentment against those wealthy, socially challenged students—several of them neurodivergent—while Heinrich suffered through relative poverty. I bet spies recruited him by leveraging Heinrich's resentment plus the love for his mom and Chinese stepdad."

His revelations cause my head to spin, and I see a new Roger—a counselor. I should have listened to him weeks ago when he said he could help me. "Wow, I am confused. But now I understand the 'cockroach' taunts from Heinrich. Part of me wants to feel sympathy or a bond with him for his suffering, but I don't know what to think."

"Yeah, me too," Roger says. "In hindsight, I should have escalated my concerns about Heinrich's emotional state to the security office, but I let it slide in all that has happened recently with the PBH captures and losing Dr. Agosti. It was my fault we didn't catch Heinrich earlier." Roger glares in misery at his hands folded on the desk. "And Heinrich was conveniently traveling north of Austin at the time of the first attack." Roger smirks. "We discovered he was a spy a few days ago—it's the only good thing I can say about his survival. My biggest worry is that all our secrets are in China's hands, and we lost everything in the Texas attacks. They have more of our data than we do."

"I have a little of the research data synced to this." I hold up my iPad for Roger to see. "But I have a lot more on my laptop. All my design files and experimental results. About twelve terabytes. But that laptop is in my backpack in my car—in San Angelo." I sigh. "In Dad's amazing blue Porsche Macan GTS." I will never see Dad or his car again.

Roger gawks at me for three seconds, grabs his cell phone, and exits to the hallway. "Chief Cooper? This is Colonel McMahon . . ."

Alone, I open my lunchbox, unwrap the massive sandwich stuffed thick with turkey and Swiss cheese, and bite off more than a mouthful.

The conference room attendance is reduced by one this afternoon. Two other scientists describe the Austin and Pecos forensic details, including blast effects, seismic analysis, and impact residue. A few keep up with the dump of technical data. Coffee barely keeps the rest awake. However, I am on the edge of my seat and listen to every syllable in a data-immersion heaven.

The tension in the room stiffens with sideways sneers and frowns as the next presenter, Dr. Richard Zhang, reviews weapon physics theories. He's a precise speaker, but most in the room squirm with what I guess is racist xenophobia. Maybe the behavior is excusable given the spy just removed from the room and their belief that a million Americans recently died at the hands of Chinese killers.

But I know they are wrong. All wrong.

Dr. Zhang concludes, and I jump up to talk with him while the rest of the room empties for a break. "Dr. Zhang? Hi, I'm Scott Anderson. Can I ask you a few questions?"

He hesitates and looks toward the exit. "Sure, but let me sit down and take a breath."

I sit next to him in a now-vacant chair at the table. "Your analysis concludes that a new bunker-busting missile tunneled deep underground and exploded a three-megaton warhead. Why would they go to this extreme when an elevated air burst would have been far more destructive?"

Dr. Zhang raises his eyebrows. "Well, I can't speculate about enemy tactics and strategies. My specialty is blast forensics. The data shows a three-hundred-meter-deep crater with a one-kilometer diameter and a hundred-meter-thick rock-melt debris. Those blast effects are the result of an explosive release of energy from a nuclear warhead driving underground while exploding."

I pause to visualize the explosion effects Dr. Zhang describes and shake with the horrific thought that Dad was caught in the middle of that blast. Dad's remains are lost within that crater's rock-melt debris.

I slowly shake my head. "But according to the impact residue analysis, there was minimal radioactive fallout from the blast. I was there and measured only typical background radiation a few kilometers from Austin."

"Well, we did find a trace of uranium isotopes in the blast residue," he answers defensively. "Perhaps this was a new clean warhead designed to limit fallout radiation effects. But again, my specialty is blast forensics, not weapon design."

I shake my head again. "The university had a ten-megawatt TRIGA research reactor near the point of impact. Could that be the source of the trace radioactivity you measured? You also did not report finding any radiation traces at the Pecos blast site."

Dr. Zhang opens his mouth but stops and frowns. "They kept telling me not to waste my time on radiation data…" he mumbles and scans through his data tables for a few seconds. "I had assumed the Pecos samples were mistakes. Most of our analysis comes from the detailed work at Austin ground zero." He frowns and clears his throat. "I just rechecked and found four repeated attempts to find traces of radiation at Pecos. They all failed." He shrugs with pained frustration.

"I can't believe everyone is ignoring facts—no residual radiation exists at the target zones. Why? Couldn't these blasts be caused by a nonnuclear explosion?"

"Impossible," he says with an eye roll. "Nuclear reactions are the only manmade devices that could release three megatons of energy . . ." He stops talking, stares at me, and says, "Uh, you worked on Agosti's primordial black hole research?"

I nod. "Yes, but I've ruled out primordial black holes from causing the explosions. There were zero PBH samples in Austin at the time of the blast, and I saw missile vapor trails in the sky above Austin and the Pecos site. But those vapor trails were weird, like energy beams or incredibly fast missiles." I check calculations on my iPad, then lock eyes with Dr. Zhang. "Couldn't the blast effects be created from the kinetic energy release of a high-velocity, massive projectile? Your charts showed unusual quantities of residual tungsten in the crater core samples from both sites."

He frowns at me like I'm crazy. "I know of no manmade projectile that could reach the needed velocity"—he pauses to calculate—"of over several thousand kilometers per second. Over Mach 5,000! Impossible. But your question about tungsten is interesting. I can't explain that. The sedimentary rock geology of central Texas does not contain tungsten, one of the densest metals." He pauses with a frown. "It is an ideal material for a kinetic energy projectile."

"Maybe the Chinese?" A panicked thought strikes me. "Could they be so far ahead of us that China deployed PBH-powered missiles? But no, that's inconsistent with Heinrich's spying and feeding them our science results. I don't see how the Chinese scientists could be ahead of us."

Both of us are perplexed. I look up and see we have an audience. The conference room is full again, and everyone is quiet. Attention is focused on the two of us, waiting for Dr. Zhang and me to finish our debate.

"Er, sorry," I mumble, stand, and return to my seat.

"No worries at all, Scott," says General Adams. "Don't apologize for critical thinking. Let's get going again with our agenda, Lieutenant."

A geologist takes her turn to show data from an unexplained seismic event in northern China—in the Gobi Desert. She transitions to comparing the seismic analysis of the two Texas explosions. All three seismic events are identical. "However, the accuracy of the Gobi event is limited to our long-range seismometers. We have no visual data because Chinese Space Forces had destroyed most of our surveillance satellites before the event."

General Adams stops the presentation. "Let's clarify the sequence of escalations last week. One, the three-megaton attacks on Texas; two, we destroy Chinese surveillance satellites to defend from more attacks; three, China retaliates and destroys most US surveillance satellites; four, the Gobi explosion; five, China attacks the US Pacific Fleet; and six, we counterattack Chinese air forces in South China. Right?" He scans the room full of nodding faces. "The explosion in the Gobi was not from a US attack, but the Chinese surveillance was blind to that fact. China launched a nuclear attack on our fleet an hour later. What direct evidence do we have that China launched the attacks against Texas?" He scans the room again, seeing a mix of blank expressions, shocked faces, and distraught reactions.

Colonel McMahon says, "Our space force reconnaissance did not detect any ballistic or cruise missile launches from anywhere on Earth. Launches from submarines may have been undetected—maybe hypersonic cruise missiles? Our antisatellite defense system is automatic; the instant we get a nuclear attack alert, space force defense protocols kick in and destroy all hostile surveillance satellites and jam nonmilitary navigation and communication satellite access."

"Which triggered the Chinese response to destroy US satellites and enabled the retaliatory sequences," says General Adams. "Isn't it possible a third party attacked both the US and China in sequence to incite the conflict?"

Stunned silence. Can it be all of this is a mistake? Will World War Three break out because two countries attacked mistaken enemies? I replay the comparisons between the seismic events: two in short succession in Texas and another twelve hours later in China.

I am jolted by a sudden epiphany. I find the timestamp data, run a calculation to test a theory, and gasp. I'm standing when Roger and the general turn toward me.

Roger says, "What is it, Scott? Speak up."

I try to comprehend the implications. "First off, the two attacks in Texas I saw firsthand were missiles traveling straight down. A missile vapor trail from anywhere on Earth should have curved through the upper atmosphere for a few minutes before striking the ground. The vapor trails I saw appeared within a second, straight down. They could not have been hypersonic cruise missiles." I can feel myself hyperventilating. I pause to exhale and collect my thoughts. "Second, the strikes to each location in Texas and the Gobi site were synchronized with Earth's rotation. Pecos was hit twelve minutes after Austin. The Gobi Desert was hit eleven hours and thirty-two minutes later. The time between strikes is an exact match to the time of the Earth's rotation."

I am getting mixed reactions: awe, confusion, shaking heads, and disdain for my foolish waste of time. The conference room rumbles with protests.

I raise my voice. "All three projectiles could have been launched from a space platform in a heliocentric orbit—in sync with Earth's orbit." I am surrounded by exasperated exclamations. These are not people willing to suffer a fool, and I get the sense that most are thinking I'm making stupid claims—especially that sneering, fascist army officer. Despite the general's open mind, most in the room have already decided. It seems the task force exists to provide the rationale for the war against China.

I can't bear the thought of sitting quietly and letting these guys plunge Robby and me into another holocaust—a holocaust that would make the last week seem like a picnic. Hell, I'll just say it. "The attacks on Austin, Pecos, and the Gobi Desert were not launched from Earth," I conclude.

Chapter 25

EMERGENCE

Captain's Log, Frigate-328, 179240.53 LST

No further evidence of Sol-3 Gravi-Tech radiation. The commissar resumed cultural suppression after the restoration of Sol-3 social networks, even though a worldwide nuclear war may render the effort pointless.

My telepathic organic reached a new, safe location while three drones monitored it. The other three drones lost track of the sibling Gravi-Tech researcher after it entered an underground structure.

Prime-AI reported multiple telepath communication sessions with the neurodivergent organic. The interface was tuned to reduce the pain to the individual's unique telepath organ, and Prime-AI qualified the exchanges as first contact. I ordered Prime-AI to confine this information to my mind only. Mil-AI and Polit-AI would throw exception faults if my actions were discovered, and they could force my removal from command. Prime-AI agrees that my encouragement of telepath communication is a capital offense, but my privacy will be secure as long as I remain in command.

My actions enabled the organic's telepathy—the key to surviving interstellar travel. Am I feeling curiosity or sympathy? Or memories of my family, who were pulled like caste-weeds to encourage the purest Luyten races?

I won't survive this crime. But I'm not sure I care.

Chapter 26

PROPULSION

Impression: No evidence of acute intracranial hemorrhage, midline shift, or mass effect. The subject's frontal lobe shows the mutation (250% above average age-adjusted volume) of orbital gyri with three Hendrix sulci, as reported in the *Journal of Neuroscience*, 2054-11-8 CE edition. Disclosure to Johns Hopkins researchers is pending parental permission (per HIPAA rules.)   *—from MRI report for Robert A., a nine-year-old autistic male subject. Peterson Space Force Base Hospital. 2055-12-5 CE.*

I hold my head, swirling in an adrenaline storm. A dozen counter-theories and accusations reverberate through my skull. DARPA-Teddy had the gall to accuse us of being part of a Chinese conspiracy to steal PBH research. General Adams's anger at Teddy helped, but the suspicious glances from around the room persisted throughout the meeting.

I could have kept my mouth shut but repeatedly defended my calculations instead. The most plausible scenario debated by the task force was that the attacks were launched from space platforms with the intent to show us our underground command centers could be destroyed—like this one under Cheyenne Mountain. The trajectories would appear to have come straight out of the sun as if the launch platform was orbiting at Earth's L1 Lagrange point—but nobody could explain the lack of radiation or how the missiles achieved the split-second time of flight I witnessed. The space force officers confidently declared that neither China nor Russia had deployed space-to-surface nuclear weapon systems, but their nervous glances were odd.

The meeting was dismissed after two hours, and there was no progress in resolving the arguments. Roger grabbed me afterward and now steers the Tesla deeper into the mountain, beyond the vast chamber full of buildings where the task force met. The cave we're in now appears relatively new, with smooth walls created by a modern tunnel-boring machine.

"Roger, can we try to get the answer to my warhead velocity question? If there was an early-warning radar track of the projectiles down to Texas, they must have velocity data."

Roger sighs. "Your theory creates more questions than it solves. We must also explain how another country could accelerate a warhead to that velocity. There were no supporters in the room—except maybe that Dr. Zhang guy."

"Can you at least ask if the air force has the data? Humor me. We can move on to other theories if the velocity track matches conventional ballistic calculations." But I know what I saw.

After we park next to a warehouse structure built into the side of the cave, he turns to me and says, "Okay. I'll ask, but it will take a while to go through official channels to request the data. I may get pushback. But you have earned some answers. Come inside and see what Tiana's team has been up to in improving your engine design. I'll call the NORAD representative on our task force to see about the radar tracking data."

We walk along a wall of zinc-plated corrugated steel, galvanized against the foglike humidity in this underground space that would otherwise corrode the building to a pile of rust in a few years. A thin string of white LEDs lights our path in a futile attempt to emulate daylight. I have lost my sense of time in the perpetual darkness, but the growl in my stomach says dinnertime. A steady *plink, plink* of water droplets strike the metal roof, accompanied by the gurgle in the drainage ditch we cross over to the entrance door.

Roger unlocks the door using his wrist-embedded security chip. Inside are work areas with CNC milling machines and electronic and mechanical assembly stations, and against the far wall are shelves stacked with PBH containment vessels—all blinking with green indicators of full batteries on trickle charge. The workshop stretches for fifty meters in each direction. It's enormous, as big as the Austin factory. That dilapidated Austin factory is now part of the "rock-melt debris" in the crater described by Dr. Zhang. The familiar odor of machine oil and smoking solder is comforting. However, there are no ceiling water leaks or mildew stinks like in the Austin factory. I miss that mold.

"Where did all these containment vessels come from, Roger?" I gawk at the racks of coffeemaker-shaped vessels arranged along grey steel storage shelves. A power cord loops out to each containment vessel. "Do any contain primordial black holes?"

"These were all shipped by Danny's team in Pecos. After he filled each one with a PBH," Roger says sadly, pursing his lips. "The last batch arrived ten days ago."

"All of them have PBHs?" *Danny died for this?*

"Yes. All one hundred and twelve containment vessels have primordial black holes with masses ranging from forty billion to five hundred billion metric tons." Roger is blasé with statistics that would have been fantasy a few months ago. "Follow me to the test chamber, and I'll show you what Tiana has been up to." He heads into the building's depths and down a hallway leading to concentric stacks of sandbags piled three meters high. In the circle of sandbags is a fixture holding a missile. Three people are hovering over it with tools and electronic instruments. One face is familiar from my escape flight from San Angelo.

"Captain Nguyen, can you show what you and Tiana have put together?"

"Oh, hi, Roger." Binh nods but skips the salute. "And Scott. You look a lot healthier than last night. Your brother doin' okay?"

"Hi, Binh. Thanks. Robby is fine, I think, but I'm still waiting for the doctor's MRI analysis. He's with the colonel's daughter," I say, walking over to study the missile test stand. "You're integrating a PBH rocket engine into the back of a missile?"

"Yep. However, we have removed the warhead section for the tests. You can see Tiana modified the rocket engine you created in Austin. She used the same depleted uranium material. Your 'coffeemaker' containment vessel was too large, so she shrank it to this softball-sized vessel that snaps into the

Sidewinder missile's tail." Binh slides the engine assembly into the missile tube just above the tailfins of the Sidewinder.

"Tiana also deleted the gyroscope that stabilized the glass PBH vessel. The gyroscope is replaced with a sphere—basically, glass within an inside-out disco ball—of two thousand electrodes and accelerometers. All connections use tungsten wire that won't melt from the engine heat."

Wow. "Nice. Elegant design! It solves the problem of orientation dependence—the PBH can't leak out of containment if tipped on its side, which is an absolute requirement for the flight dynamics of a missile."

"And you are just in time for our first test," Binh says. "Tiana will join by video conference later to see if we can generate a little thrust. She's worried about the control loop and wants your advice."

"You guys are going to test a rocket motor under the mountain? Inside this confined space?" Despite the large volume of the Cheyenne facility, it seems like suicidally tight quarters if a PBH rocket engine test explodes.

Roger says, "No worries, Scott. This facility was built years ago to test powerful nuclear engines. We're doing this underground to avoid satellite observation and to contain things if a test gets out of hand. The rocket engine exhausts through a tunnel into a chamber with thermal exhaust ports that filter radiation."

I grimace. "Aren't you putting Colorado Springs at risk if the enemy finds out and attacks?"

Roger shakes his head. "No. This is one of our most secure sites. We don't see how anyone could learn of our PBH stockpile and the engine tests. Although yesterday was a close call. Heinrich's spying almost gave it away. Cheyenne Mountain security intercepted that, though."

The test chamber door swings open, and DARPA-Teddy walks in with his staff. I can't believe it. Where does he find all these ass-kissing thirty-somethings with black suits and power neckties?

"Colonel McMahon, I half expected you to be here," Teddy says. "But this guy? Who authorized the sharing of this information with your intern?" His eyes narrow on me. "He doesn't have a need to know."

Roger bristles. "Scott is key to this project. We wouldn't have progressed this far without him. He led us to historic breakthroughs."

Geez. The credit is nice, but it feels all wrong. I should be blamed.

Teddy sneers, "Yeah, right. You, Agosti, and Heinrich stumbled the US into World War Three. All our investment in this project is now benefitting the Chinese military. We lost everything in the attack on Pecos and Austin, and now I'm calling a stop to it once and for all." Teddy stands with his arms crossed, resting on the fat sagging over his belt.

He doesn't waste eye contact with me.

Roger's face darkens with a snarl. "You son of a bitch. You have been trying to kill the research from the start. Scott Anderson has overall technical leadership for our research and development. Treat him with respect."

The sudden promotion is staggering, and I know that if I'm finding it hard to take it seriously, so will Teddy. I still feel like a mere research assistant.

"No. No. No." Teddy shakes his head. "*I'm* taking over. We can't trust your security procedures or your loyalty. Not after you claim the Chinese weren't responsible for the deaths of a million Americans." Teddy sneers. "Heinrich showed us your team's priorities; you are all under investigation. I put a stop to your requests for data on warhead tracking, and I'm putting a stop to this research. You guys are all finished. Leave. Now!" Sweat rolls over the pulsing vein in Teddy's forehead.

"Well, I have had enough of this asshole." I walk out of the test chamber but turn back and make eye contact with Teddy. "You were closest to Heinrich. You're the one who should be investigated for conspiracy."

Teddy sneers at me like I'm a piece of shit, and I turn to walk out.

"Damnit, Scott. Don't go anywhere!" Roger shouts. "Listen, Teddy. You and your DARPA clerks march out of here, or I'll have you ejected." Roger looks down at Teddy, a mere four inches away. His spit splatters on Teddy's nose.

Captain Nguyen and the two sergeants step away from the missile assembly and face Teddy.

Looking at his staff, Teddy's face turns red, and he replies, "Oh yeah? We'll see about that. I'll be back with security," he squeaks. DARPA-Teddy pivots toward the exit. "Let's go." He strides out with his chin held high, followed by five guys in suits.

Roger takes a deep breath. "Let's get this ready for a test ASAP. I want to get Tiana on a call to run through the procedures." He returns to the workshop, leading me to a table of instruments and computer workstations. "Our work just got a lot more challenging."

Roger checks his cell phone. "Well, that didn't take long. The NORAD contact on the task force has declined my request for tracking data, citing new security protocols."

Roger closes his eyes with a sigh, but they quickly pop open in an ah-ha moment. "I know just the guy who can help." He scrolls through his contacts and pauses, hitting the call button.

"Hey, Steven! How the hell are you doing? Yeah, yeah, I know. I'm inside Cheyenne Mountain. Uh-huh. This is what we trained for, though." He clears his throat. "I need to ask you for some help. I'm putting you on speaker, and I have my lead scientist here, Scott Anderson, who needs some data you may be able to provide." Roger flips the speaker on.

"Sure, go ahead, Roger. You know I owe you, big time. How can I help?" asks Steven.

"Scott, this is Colonel Steven McCord on the line," Roger says with a smile. "We go way back. You can trust him with anything; he's almost as smart as you are."

"Ha. Good to meet you, Scott. You must be something if you're as smart as Roger claims," Steven says.

"Likewise, Colonel McCord. Good to meet you. We need all the detailed trajectory information you may have captured on the two attacks on Texas. It would also be helpful to get any data you may have on the missile trajectory in the China attack twelve hours later." I pause. "Understand?"

After several seconds, Roger prompts, "Are you there, Steven? Did you get the question?"

"Yes, I heard." Steven takes a deep breath. "That's the worst request you could have made. That intel is under top secret security. I need official word you have the sensitive compartmented information clearance. But you're in Cheyenne Mountain—it should be no problem for you."

"I'm not sure about that," Roger warns. "There has been some squirrely behavior here the past day. How long ago did this information get pushed under SCI cover?"

"I'm shocked you are blocked from access," says Steven. "The NORAD and NASA trajectory info was all captured, but the IT security guys pulled our data log files and scrubbed my computer systems clean. I don't have the info anymore."

"NASA?" I ask. "Did you say NASA data? Why would they be involved—unless they had some related deep-space observations?"

"Yeah, I assumed you all knew. We got an initial object alert from the NASA Planetary Defense Coordination Office," Steven says. "But I shouldn't say more. That may be covered by the SCI." His voice sounds stressed, and Roger's brow furrows.

"What the hell is going on?" Roger asks. "This makes no sense. Why would it be a problem to share the information openly?"

"Roger . . . I have never seen anything like this," Steven whispers. "I have a goddamn political appointee from the National Security Council camped out in our main control center down the hall. A fucking politician watching over me! What's worse is that my chain of command has gone silent. It's like everyone with stars has been muzzled."

"What the fuck?" Roger says.

"I tell you, I don't like it," says Steven. "If you are also in the dark, I'm scared."

Roger frowns, the furrows on his forehead deepening. "This sounds like someone up the chain has an agenda—like creating the WMD myth that caused NATO to invade Iraq fifty years ago. We're in the dark for a reason."

I can't imagine why NASA would be involved unless . . .

"Steven, for NASA to be involved, their sighting would be far from Earth. Is there anything you can say about what they spotted?"

"Guys, I'm already on thin ice. Although my direct orders apply to the security of the NORAD information, I think the NASA info would be included under the SCI order."

Roger pushes, "Anything you can add would be useful. Is there a contact we can talk to at NASA?"

"Well, I'm afraid if you reach out, you'll draw attention to yourself," Steven says. "Let me see what I can do for you. Here is something to think about, though. The NASA Jet Propulsion Lab sightings were objects ten million kilometers out, coming straight from the sun on an intercept with Earth. They thought the size was too small to worry about, but the velocity and acceleration are what scared them."

"Uh, how many objects did NASA report? And what was the acceleration?" I ask. My fear grows, and I can see Roger gets it. I had not imagined the launch platform could be that far away in space. For the Chinese to pull this off, they would be far beyond our current technology.

"That was not information NASA had. Their long-range JPL Near-Earth Object Surveyor telescopes don't have the performance to track individual objects. Not with velocities and accelerations that high."

"How high a velocity?" I ask, but Roger pulls the phone away and frowns.

"Steven, that's enough. I don't want to put you at risk on this."

I can hear Steven's breath of relief. "Thanks, Roger. You'll need the SCI code word to access the other details. I'm not even allowed to share the information from my memory; it's data I have been ordered to forget."

"You have been most helpful, Steven. I need to dig into what the hell is going on with high command." And with that, Steven exhales in relief.

"Keep pushing, Roger," says Steven. "Something stinks, bad. I'll let you know if I find any way to help."

Roger hangs up the call and says, "Okay. I see you may be on to something legitimate with your theory. A space-launched high-velocity projectile theory should be advanced to the top. But the higher-ups already have this info . . . so, why are they hiding the data?" Roger's eyes glaze over. He tilts his head back, studying the ceiling of the workshop.

He shakes it off a moment later and says, "Let's put this aside and get on with the engine test prep. I'm opening a video conference with Tiana at Skunk Works."

I can't get my mind off my projectile-from-space theory, but Tiana's appearance distracts me. "Tiana!" I yell when her face appears on the screen.

"Scott! It's great to have you back with us for this test. Have you seen our new engine design yet?"

"Yeah, Captain Nguyen showed me your disco ball design. Clever. But how do you plan to transfer the PBH from a Mr. Coffee vessel into the disco ball containment?"

"Binh will show you, but we haven't tried it yet. We want to position the disco ball to the top of the coffeepot vessel, merge the two vessels' electric fields, and guide the PBH into the disco ball. I want your help with this. It requires close coordination between the controllers in both vessels," Tiana explains.

"Yeah, tricky, I agree. You could lose the PBH during the transfer. The primordial black hole could leak from the containment fields and fall into the Earth. Can you share the containment code for the disco ball? I would like to understand what your software guys did."

"Great," says Tiana. "We want to start our first test in an hour. I'll send you a link to our Skunk Works repository."

"Okay. Let me get to work and try to be ready in an hour." My login credentials and email accounts work as if I were in my Pecos Center cubicle. I poke around in the file and find some of the data we had in Austin, but not all. I wish I had my laptop; it contained all the software Danny and I developed at Pecos.

At that moment, Chief Cooper walks down the hall, dressed in full battle gear and carrying a backpack. My backpack. He has a wide grin for me too. "Hey. You looking for this?"

"Chief!" I reach out to shake his giant hand and take the backpack. Inside is my laptop. "You must have been reading my mind. Thanks, guys. Just what I needed."

Chief Cooper puffs his chest out. "Not a problem for you, Scott. We just took another short flight to visit the San Angelo lost and found."

I fire up the laptop, relieved there is battery power, and the machine appears healthy. I bet the chief's trip was at least as exciting as the last visit to Texas.

We did it! The ninety billion metric tons of primordial black hole is transferred into Tiana's disco ball containment vessel. The two-electrode, one-dimensional field of the coffee pot containment vessel was improved with the two thousand electrodes and spherical field of the disco ball containment. Digging into the details of Tiana's engineers' disco ball design was an hour of joy. They improved my design with an elegant solution to replace that clunky gyroscope platform.

"There, that does it," says Binh. He lifts the disco ball, presses it inside the twelve-centimeter diameter of the rocket engine nozzle, and routes the umbilical cable from the Sidewinder battery and controller. He takes a step back, and we admire the assembly as the sergeants fasten the protective cowling on the missile airframe. The bottom half of the rocket is mounted on a horizontal test fixture with force gauges on the supporting structure to measure thrust.

We shake hands to celebrate our success. "Let's do it," I say as we head back to the table of computer consoles in the workshop.

Roger is waiting there, looking distracted and dejected.

"What's the matter?" I ask. "We're ready to start the engine test." Binh and I sit down and see Tiana is on screen in a video conference with Roger. "Oh, hi, Tiana." She also appears depressed. "Is everything okay?"

Roger grimaces. "We have a change in plans. I got word from General Adams that our participation in the task force meetings is terminated. The original PBH project team is no longer required." He turns to Binh and me. "They will let me sit in on the meetings as long as I remain a passive observer. Teddy and other higher-ups are going in a different direction."

"DARPA-Teddy did this?" I ask.

Roger tilts his head. "I think . . . I think this goes much farther up the chain of command than just Teddy. There is heavy political interference. You heard what Colonel McCord said about political oversight and suppressing the NORAD tracking data. I confirmed with others in the command chain that there's a lot of pressure from the White House to use the attacks on the navy fleet and Texas as a pretext to finally take out China."

"What the fuck!" spits Binh. "An opportunity to 'take out' China?"

Roger grimaces. "All the noise in the press, on TV, and from Congress is about China's nuclear attacks. There is no debate on who the enemy is. It's all about how the US will retaliate. All voices of caution and de-escalation are losing."

"I hoped Robby and I had escaped to safety, but it sounds like the serious battles are yet to begin." I sigh.

Roger fumes, "And we have been pushed aside from General Adams's task force. It feels like the US government's behavior fifty years ago leading up to the invasion of Iraq. It was before you were born, Scott, but that invasion was based on false evidence that Iraq had weapons of mass destruction they planned to use against us. Two hundred thousand civilians died, but no WMDs were found. Today, our leadership doesn't want to be distracted from validating the case for war against China. Our only hope is there are leaders still open to critical data who have enough political power to stop the insanity."

"By the way, Scott, I received an anonymous text message from a disposable phone with an unknown number. All it says is: 14:50 CST, three incoming objects. First two are twelve minutes apart, third trails by 11.5 hours. Entry velocity 1,900 kilometers per second. Acceleration is constant at about ten G s."

"Almost one percent of light speed? That's a world record! With that data, we can get a complete solution for the projectile physics." I get out my iPad and run through the math. "I can't believe this, but it checks.

It would take a truck-sized object of several thousand kilograms—like a loaded garbage truck—launched from somewhere near Venus's orbit and maintaining a constant ten Gs of acceleration for the entire flight to attain a three-megaton explosion like what we saw in Austin."

Roger shakes his head and frowns. "No, no. A handful of exploration missions of a few thousand kilograms were launched toward Venus, but nothing like the three truck-sized objects you suggest. Space Force has detailed data on everything launched over the past hundred years from around the world," he says with annoyance. "It's my job to watch this stuff. And a sustained thrust for the entire distance? Impossible."

Roger and Binh's eyes meet, and they both shake their heads no.

"It makes no sense to me either," I agree. "But that velocity would require a hundred-G acceleration if launched from Earth's L1 Lagrange orbit. If the missile had a constant ten-G acceleration and started at zero velocity, the launch came from twenty million kilometers away—about halfway to the orbit of Venus—and would take a six-hour time-of-flight."

Binh says, "Hell. No rocket from Earth could sustain a ten-G thrust for six hours, let alone achieve a one-hundred-G thrust. It's impossible."

Tiana and I nod at each other in agreement.

"It's not impossible," I say. "Maybe not one of Earth's chemical rocket engines, but in the next room, we are about to test an engine that could supply the ten-G thrust and much more."

Roger says, "Oh shit." His voice rises with alarm. "There is one other country with access to this technology: China. Thanks to Heinrich."

"Okay, but explain why they would attack their own research facility in the Gobi." Binh shakes his head. "Are we certain the Gobi attack did not come from US forces?"

Roger nods. "Yes, as far as I know. But now I'm not sure I'm in the loop anymore. I wish we had an independent source to verify the Gobi explosion details. Our surveillance satellites were destroyed before that attack."

"The timing of the three projectile impacts and the trajectory data all make a strong case for a launch platform in heliocentric orbit. But my calculations show it can't be parked at the L1 Lagrange point opposite the Webb Telescope, and a free fall orbit halfway to Venus will orbit the sun faster than Earth," I argue, holding my head with my elbows on the table. "My brain hurts with all these choices."

"Hey, guys?" asks Tiana. "Why don't we get started with the engine test? We're getting ahead of ourselves and have a chance to prove we can build a rocket with the thrust to achieve a ten-G acceleration."

She is right. "Yeah, I agree. Let's get started?" The two sergeants have returned to the workstations to run diagnostic tests.

Binh asks, "Sergeant? Let us know when you are ready."

"Yes, sir. All tests have passed. Ready to go when you are, sir," he replies.

"Okay, Tiana. We are ready," says Binh.

"Scott, I think you are the most skilled at this," Tiana says. "The console controls are adaptations of your original setup in

Austin. Although the new display of the containment is a 3-D sphere visualization."

I sit down, and the console looks like the setup in Austin we used to fire the first engine down the old rail gun range. All the memories of those days—was it less than two weeks ago?—come flooding back.

I had been scared Robby was not safe at home, Mom was lost in post-divorce depression, and I'd recruited Dad to help. I remember the hikes and repair jobs with Robby, Margie's smile, her beautiful brown eyes, and that kiss. That was the last time with my family and friends. And I had never actually agreed to come back to work.

I escape those emotions with a shudder. Oh, what the hell.

"Sure, Tiana, I can take the lead on the test."

"Thanks, Scott. Also, we updated things so the engine supports shouldn't break this time. Hopefully." Tiana sounds nervous. No one wants another failure like our last test in Austin.

I select the spherical disco ball containment vessel telemetry display and verify that the voltages on the sphere of two thousand electrodes will keep the primordial black hole centered in the disco ball. "This PBH is ninety billion metric tons—tiny compared to the last Austin test. I'm starting up the scan to determine the resonance of the PBH. And . . . I've got a dominant frequency of around thirty megahertz. Ramping up the modulation amplitude."

"Plasma ball!" Roger exclaims. "The missile engine and tail fins are inside it. It's like a white-blue light ball with a protruding missile tube." Roger and Binh watch their displays, both wearing grins of delight.

The noise from the plasma hum grows to a roar as I increase the modulation of the containment field. "Okay, all telemetry looks normal. Sensors show radiation out the tail but nothing from the sides. Temperature sensors on the engine nozzle show a two-degree increase due to energy absorption." I pause to watch the sensor readings and confirm the test setup is remaining stable. "Strain gauges are showing near-zero force so far."

"Turning up the thrust." I tap the key, increasing the modulation amplitude every few seconds. The dull roar of the plasma ball increases. Radiation and temperature go up also, as do the strain-gauge readings. "There we go. The hydrogen spewing out the rocket nozzle burns in a jet of pale blue flame. Strain gauges read about ten kilonewtons of thrust. We got to this level early in the Austin test."

"Here goes. I'll keep increasing as long as we're within safe limits of temperature and radiation. Vessel temperature is seventy Celsius, and the nozzle temperature is up to five hundred degrees. We're spraying tons of hydrogen and radiation exhaust of three thousand millisieverts out the back of the nozzle." It's a good thing the tail is pointed down into the rock cavern.

Tiana frowns. "The nozzle heating from radiation is the same as on our last test—not reflecting enough into the exhaust. We don't have an effective way to cool the engine with that much energy absorption into the nozzle. You should shut it down before the nozzle reaches nine hundred Celsius."

"Okay. The last time we pushed thrust too fast, all hell broke loose. We're generating about eight hundred kilonewtons of thrust now. That is plenty of power to accelerate that dump truck projectile from halfway to Venus into a three-megaton impact on Earth." I shout to hear myself over the thrumming roar of the engine echoing down the hall from the test chamber. I also smell the sulfur. The same odor from ball lightning anecdotes from thousands of years ago.

"Pushing it up to one thousand kilonewtons . . . there. Okay, all is stable at this thrust, although the nozzle temperature is climbing past six hundred degrees. Tiana, hats off to your disco ball design. All two thousand electrodes and accelerometers show stable readings. We should just hold it at this setting and monitor the telemetry. Agreed?" I ask.

"Agreed," says Tiana. "Hold modulation here. The hydrogen flow is so strong it does not ignite until mixing with oxygen deep inside the exhaust cavern."

Binh sits with his mouth hanging open, staring at the brilliant blue-white plasma ball wrapped around the tail of the Sidewinder. Above the vibrations and thunder, he shouts to Roger, "This is incredible! Over five times an F-35 on afterburner!"

Seemingly in a daze, Roger watches, entranced by the plasma ball and the noise. "Beautiful, isn't it?" he yells and grins. "Our last test hit more thrust than a Saturn V booster."

"Yeah, but just before the setup blew apart," I warn.

"And this is from a tiny Sidewinder engine!" Binh shouts.

"Nozzle temperature passing through seven hundred Celsius, but everything else is stable. We'll have to shut down in about ten minutes. I wish we had a material that could withstand a higher temperature or a way to cool our current material down," I say. We need a material with a high melting point and a high density that reflects radiation better. "What about tungsten? It has a melting point three times higher than depleted uranium."

"Yeah, if we could get enough tungsten to fabricate big rocket nozzles," yells Tiana, barely loud enough to be heard above the noise. "Another strategic materials failure by the US. We pay sky-high prices for the little tungsten we can get. All because the world's supply of tungsten was cornered twenty years ago. By China."

We nod in unison as more evidence points to China. The engine's roar continues with one million newtons of force for another ten minutes. I shut it down at the nozzle temperature of nine hundred Celsius. Quiet envelops us as the plasma ball extinguishes.

"Wow. According to our accelerometer and gamma-ray spectrometer measurements, the mass of the PBH has barely changed. Einstein was right: the mass transformed into energy is inversely proportional to the square of light speed." I try to comprehend the possibilities. "This changes everything. Primordial black holes harnessed as energy sources have a near-infinite capacity. If we can prevent the engine from melting down, it will run for decades nonstop." My heart races. "This power can take us to the stars! We can build ships that could travel to the nearest star systems, like Alpha Centauri, within a few years!"

"Too much power. Power worth killing for," Roger says, shaking his head.

"And the perfect time to short-sell solar panel and windmill investments." Tiana smirks.

"What about China, though?" asks Binh. "They've got the tungsten to do this right. But then . . . the Gobi Desert attack"—he shakes his head—"does not make sense."

Roger muses, "I wish there was a way to communicate with the Chinese scientists—if any survived the Gobi attack. But there's no way. Politics has turned rabid on both sides. I bet there are plenty of Chinese politicians advocating all-out war against the USA. I'm rooting for the relative sanity of their military leaders—and ours."

"There might be a way . . ." Tiana mumbles, studying her laptop display. "I remember backing up Heinrich's data from his iPad when he arrived at Cheyenne Mountain two days ago. I wanted to save any Pecos or Austin data he might have had, and I also copied all his software images—including all his social media apps. If we could figure out how to communicate with Heinrich's Instagram app, we may circumvent the war hawks on both ends."

Binh smirks. "Yeah, right. That's a fast path to a firing squad."

"No, no, no," says Roger, shaking his head. "We left the Instagram account active so we wouldn't notify the Chinese that we found their spy. But sending a message like that to the Chinese would surely break the news about Heinrich's arrest. Plus, the treason charges . . ."

"The alternative is to be vaporized in a nuclear holocaust." I shrug. "Tiana, we would have to pose a technical question the scientists could understand while also avoiding offering secret information."

Chapter 27

SELF-DESTRUCTION

Captain's Log, Frigate-328, 179240.63 LST

Why waste ammunition on a suicidal planet?

The Sol-3 organics made incredible advances with Gravi-Tech propulsion technologies. But Polit-AI and the commissar predicted that the war we caused with our attacks on their Gravi-Tech could achieve suppression objectives: neurodivergence and Gravi-Tech elimination. However, Sol-3 may become uninhabitable in the process. The arrogance and indifference of the commissar and political division are insufferable. Although I rejected Mil-AI's recommendation to target Sol-3 with thermal-kinetic cleansing weapons, the organics' impending nuclear war may have condemned Sol-3 to anarchy and a regression to ignorant primitives anyway.

And what of the younglings? The emergence of the neurodivergent organics could have led them to survival—and not just survival, but to an acceleration of their evolution, an evolution toward greatness for their species. Are they lost, all of them?

Chapter 28

WORLD AT WAR

"Do you want to face treason charges?" asks Tiana. "Any message we send to Heinrich's China contacts will be seen as revealing US classified info. During a war? Firing squad for sure." Tiana paces back and forth at the Skunk Works lab, stepping out from view as she exits the screen left and then returns.

"We have to figure something out." It is two a.m. I'm exhausted and alone in a small, empty office under Cheyenne Mountain, down the hall from the task force conference room. It feels like a dull, beige jail cell. I haven't seen or heard from Robby since yesterday morning at the hospital. The prospect of another post-apocalyptic fight for Robby and me is real—if we live past the next few days. "We may be the only Americans with the means to communicate critical information to China that could stop a nuclear war."

I shake my head. "Roger looked sick when he met me at the break of his task force meeting with General Adams. Tiana, he says we are hours away from unleashing a full-scale war with China. In Roger's words, the 'Joint Chiefs command in DC have all been replaced with third-rate political hacks.' NATO Article Five was invoked after the Chinese attack on us, and

NATO militaries are mobilizing to follow the US into war. That task force is committed—objective, critical thinking is no longer allowed."

"But there is no way Roger would authorize communication with the Chinese using Heinrich's spy tools. I don't see him throwing the book away, not during a war," Tiana says.

"But maybe there is a way to send a message that gives away nothing to the Chinese. Instead, give them a problem to solve that guides them to help us with our puzzle."

Tiana huffs with frustration. "Well, we haven't come up with any ideas for the past three hours."

"Play along with me," I say. "First, let's pose a simple physics problem from the Texas attack data. Assume some Chinese scientists see our physics problem and have similar data for the Gobi attack. We embed a message into an image post in Heinrich's Instagram account that says:

Energy = 3 megatons; velocity = 2000 km/sec; acceleration= 10 Gs;

mass=?; launch distance=?

Then, we wait for them to respond with simple Newtonian mechanics solutions. If their scientists see this and have trajectory data, they will reach the same solution that the projectiles came from halfway to Venus. They may be just as terrified and want to avoid a nuclear war."

"Uh-huh, I see what you are thinking. I would have to post the picture via an anonymous VPN location, which will be hard for the NSA to track, but this trajectory information is top-secret early-warning radar data. You want to pretend these are just abstract numbers for a high school physics quiz?" Tiana asks.

"Yeah. The NSA won't know what the numbers mean, at least not for a while. We don't say what the numbers relate to—after all, it's data from an anonymous text message." I wince at my half-lie and from Tiana's eye roll. "Well, anyway, the idea is to build trust. If China did not initiate the Texas attacks, I bet a few of them are as freaked out as you and I and will figure out how to respond. If they don't respond, we're no worse off. In that case, we all get killed in World War Three."

"Okay, let's say we send our physics quiz, and they reply with the correct answers. What next?" Tiana calms down and plays along, at least.

"Well . . ." Am I just fooling myself? "We want to establish that both countries see something similar we can't explain. The next step could be exchanging data on blast forensics, like no radioactive fallout and the strange tungsten traces in the craters."

"That requires sending even more classified data." Tiana grimaces. "I don't see how we get endorsement by Colonel McMahon and General Adams. Ultimately, we want the leadership of both countries to talk and agree that those first three projectiles came from an 'other enemy' so both military commands stand down from the brink of war. This whole idea seems like a wild shot in the dark because we don't know if either country still has rational, objective leaders in charge. And we don't have much time—maybe a few hours until the missiles start flying?"

"Then let's get started. Send the physics quiz to the Chinese!"

"No, Scott. We must consult with Roger first. Let me go ahead and use Heinrich's Instagram encryption to encode the physics quiz into an image so we're ready if Roger approves. I need to double-check my theory on how Heinrich received instruction from his handler in China. I saw repeated references to another unique Instagram account. Perhaps he had a decryption method for messages embedded in photos so he could receive instructions."

However precarious, taking these small forward steps is a relief; it's better than wringing my hands. "Great. Thanks. I'll watch for Roger and catch him up to our proposal when he comes out of the task force conference room."

"Okay. Let me get to work," says Tiana. "Let me know when you are ready to discuss with Roger."

"You going to eat all of that?" Roger sneaks up behind me, eyeing the two slices of pepperoni pizza on the plate.

"Uh, no, help yourself," I say, rubbing the sleep out of my eyes. "A guard showed me a stash of frozen pizzas and a microwave oven. I ate my fill." Roger has half the first slice shoved into his mouth. "Sadly, there was no beer." Roger starts on the second slice. I check the time—just after four in the morning.

"How is the task force going?" I am afraid to ask, and given the haggard exhaustion on Roger's face, I can guess his answer.

"It is hell. All information moving up the chain of command supports total war. India and Russia have mobilized and have gone quiet—they may be forming an alliance. Most of our planning is about preemptive strikes to take out opposing weapons. With all these players on the board, it's beyond complicated." Roger rubs his temples with both hands, grimacing in pain. "Nobody argues those were space-to-surface attacks except you. Our allies are committing to back us up in a nuclear war. Second-tier players like Israel, the Saudis, Iran, and Pakistan are lining up to take sides." He shrugs at me. "Why don't you get some sleep?"

Is he kidding? "You make it pretty difficult to rest. Also, Tiana and I have been working on a means of backchannel communication with Chinese scientists. Do you have time to review this with us?" I tap my laptop display to start a videoconference with Tiana.

"Are you guys kidding?" asks Roger. "I just left a room where the prevailing attitude is 'the only good Chinaman is a dead Chinaman.' We're committing to full-scale payback against China, with the main issue being attrition; how to minimize our deaths and maximize enemy casualties." Roger's heavy breathing accents each word.

"Roger," Tiana says from the screen of my laptop, "is there a chance we'll negotiate a cooling-off truce? Surely some higher-up wants to avoid a war based on a false assumption."

"The Joint Chiefs have moved past debate, guys. No one I know of has any doubt we're at war with China," Roger says. "Although, there are some powerful players that are strangely quiet. Maybe they have doubts . . ."

"But what if we make one last attempt to reach out to Chinese scientists to corroborate the third-party theory?" asks Tiana.

Roger smolders, his face red.

"We can send a question, or quiz, to the Chinese scientists with Heinrich's Instagram encryption communicator. If they answer the quiz correctly, it will confirm the third-party attacker theory," I say. Roger clenches his fists.

Tiana jumps in. "We would send them a simple physics question with the launch location of the high-velocity projectile we postulated as its answer. They won't acknowledge the launch location if it's their weapon. They could respond in minutes if they have the will. I can also use Heinrich's method to receive the response from China."

Roger's eyes close, and he sits down with a sigh. "Folks, no one will listen. Heinrich's treason discredited everybody associated with our PBH project. Playing clever quiz games with the Chinese won't get the traction required to change directions."

Well, to hell with data, facts, and truth. We are on a path to murder hundreds of millions of humans using a rationale of alternative facts. My chest squeezes with cramps, and it is difficult to breathe. What about Robby?

"Roger, I need to go to Robby if it's hopeless. Colorado Springs must be a high-priority target." I stand and step toward the door.

"Scott, no," Roger says, his anger softening. He stares at the floor, dejected. "Security rules don't allow you to leave Cheyenne Mountain with the information you have. Neither of us can leave now."

My jaw drops. "But what about Robby? And your daughter, Mary? We can't leave them exposed. We need them to get out of Colorado Springs *now!*"

"There are a million other civilians in the city. We could create a panicked evacuation that might kill hundreds, and the news coverage would show our hand to the enemy. We have defensive systems for Colorado Springs," Roger says, avoiding eye contact, sadder than ever. "Uh, the laser and rail gun defensive batteries are . . . quite good."

"But, we can't just let—"

Roger interrupts, "I can request that Mary and your brother evacuate inside Cheyenne Mountain. There is a provision for immediate family members to come inside in this situation."

"Well, okay, please bring them inside to safety. But then we hide in this cave while the world burns?" *In this beige jail cell?*

Roger looks away from me, defeated. "That's the best I can do." He stands up to return to the task force meeting. "Oh, I also have other news. I got word on the scan for your family and friends using your information. No luck. They don't show up on 6G network scans of location transponders. But the network blackout still covers half of Texas. Don't give up hope."

"Give up hope? Give up hope? We are about to set the world on fire!" My voice is a screech.

"Scott . . ." Roger shakes his head and, looking ten years older, walks down the hall to the conference room.

I collapse back in my chair and hold my head. This is hopeless.

"Scott?" Tiana has been quiet, listening and watching my exchange with Roger. Her eyes narrow. She types on her keyboard momentarily, then stares at me, her face blank, eyes unfocused. "It's done. We'll see what the Chinese say."

"Tiana? Why?" I gasp.

She shrugs. "We have nothing to lose. Roger did not say, 'No, don't do it.'"

Tiana's old German shepherd photo appears alongside photos of the fauna and flora theme Heinrich usually posts on

Instagram. Tiana's composition, lighting, and the twinkle in the dog's eyes demonstrate skill with the art of photography Heinrich never had. The difference in the photo content should tell the Chinese that Heinrich has been busted. I panic, suddenly realizing Heinrich's Instagram account could have been a valuable misinformation channel to confuse the Chinese military before a US attack. Tiana and I have ruined that opportunity. It's treason charges, for sure.

The smell of discarded pizza and rotting banana peels in the trash makes me gag. I look for a spot to move this rot and drop the can outside the office door. Stretching my arms, I walk down the beige-grey hall toward the kitchen where I cooked the pizza, shuffling my feet where decades of foot traffic have worn the linoleum to a uniform grey path. I have lost track of time, but the old analog clock on the wall says zero-six-twenty. I pass the closed door of the forbidden conference room, and a rumble of shouted arguments and undistinguishable angst spills over the transom. I smell the coffee as I pass the fridge, thankful somebody made a fresh pot. The constants of nourishment are the same wherever I work all-nighters: coffee, pizza, donuts, and beer. I pour a cup of coffee, grab one—then two—glazed donuts from a box, and return to my office. The lack of beer is disappointing. When will Roger emerge? He will be in a rage when he learns Tiana posted the quiz.

Tiana located the alternate Instagram account of monotonous sequences of ocean photos that Heinrich used for instructions from China. I scroll through the sequence of drab ocean scenes when a new picture appears. It's a scene with waves in beautiful colors crashing on boulders.

I grab my cell phone and tap the speed dial for Tiana. "Tiana! I see—"

"Yep. I see it. Running the new image through Heinrich's decryption software. Hold on . . . hold on. This will take a few seconds. Oh! They answered!"

"Okay, okay! What does it say?"

"They passed the quiz, Scott! And there is more. I'm posting it to our repository for you to see."

"Yes, I see it. Yes! They did get the answers right."

Projectile equals sixty-two hundred kilograms. Distance equals twenty-one million kilometers. $\lambda=0$, $\beta=0$, $\Delta=21,000,000$.

"What do those last sets of numbers mean?"

Tiana is quiet for a moment. "I'm not sure, but it reminds me of the ecliptic coordinate system. It has been a few years since my college astronomy class, but it could be a position in space relative to Earth's ecliptic plane. Let me check a reference. Ahh. The coordinates describe a location in space on a straight line from Earth to the sun at a range of twenty-one million kilometers. They pointed us in a direction to search, Scott! And it is nowhere near Earth's L1 Lagrange point. However, a launch platform in solar orbit can't have identical coordinates for all three launches. It's going to keep circling around the sun."

Hell, we can figure that out later. We don't have time. "This is fantastic news! There is somebody in China talking to us with corroborating evidence—and they have trajectory-tracking data that matches ours! We need to get this to Roger and General Adams. It can only mean somebody else attacked Texas and Gobi, not China."

"Whoa, Scott. This information may not have the support of the Chinese government. It could be some fringe scientist—like you or me—taking risks that could get them shot for treason. We need something more than a short text string. Maybe the Chinese want us to inspect those coordinates? This is outside of my wheelhouse."

"Well, we can't just sit on this," I say, panicked. "There is no time. I wish we knew who to contact at NASA. Maybe we can ask Colonel McCord at NORAD for his NASA contacts who gave the first heads-up of the incoming projectiles."

"No, that would take forever," Tiana says. "We need urgent help. I have an, uh, an old friend who works at JPL. Let me reach out and see if he can help. Maybe a telescope could be directed to examine that area in space."

"Okay, but a telescope won't be much use. Those coordinates point straight into the sun."

"Yeah, you're right. But I think one of the space telescopes, or even a planetary exploration spacecraft, will be at an indirect angle, not blinded by the sun, so it can get an image. We need to calculate the new heliocentric orbital position; the platform should be in a new position a week after it launched the projectiles." Tiana sighs. "Maybe there is nothing to see, but if there is, then what? Maybe the image will show a fleet of missiles ready to target our cities? Or some space station on an asteroid? Maybe the Chinese want to show off their doomsday machine—after all, they may be the only ones with the PBH technology needed for the rocket engines." She sighs again. "Let me make a call. It's 5:30 a.m. in Pasadena. He won't like getting a call this early, but I expect the info will wake him up." She smirks and reaches for her phone, terminating our videoconference link.

"Hey, Scott." Something shoves my shoulder back and forth. "Wake up."

I sit up, confused. My eyes adjust to the bright lights, and my right cheek is numb, dented by its resting position on the desk. "Huh? Oh. I'm awake."

"You are now," says Roger. "Glad you got a little sleep. I sure as hell did not." He plops down into the side chair and rubs his hands together. His uniform jacket has been discarded, and he needs a shave.

"What time is it?" I ask, rubbing sleep from my eyes.

Roger sighs. "Too late." His head is tilted down, his chin on his chest.

"What? What happened?"

"The president just gave the order," Roger says. "We're committed to a full-scale nuclear attack."

"What? When!"

"Within the next twelve hours, after all the international forces are coordinated, we'll launch a preemptive strike to take out all Chinese nuclear weapons. Or, at least, try to take them out."

I gawk at Roger and open my mouth but have no words.

"It was all I could do to stay in the room. The anti-China hawks won. Anyone bringing caution or doubts was kicked out." All strength has drained from Roger's face. He seems transformed into a very tired old man. "I'm sorry. The National Security Council backed down too. This was a top-down decision; we were just there to provide a rationale. Three Chinese nuclear attacks on American civilians and the navy. The bottom line was, 'If not now, when?'"

My pulse thumps in my ears. "But it was a single Chinese attack—on the navy only!" I scream.

Roger frowns. "What?"

"We got an answer to our physics quiz. China sent us the coordinates of the launch site."

Anger creases Roger's forehead. "What?" he shouts and stands, knocking his chair over. "You sent the message?"

"Uh, yeah. We, or Tiana, posted an image with the quiz encrypted. And they answered two hours ago with a location in space. The spot where the projectiles were launched from."

"Get Tiana on video," yells Roger, his strength restored. "Immediately!"

I pivot to my laptop and click on Tiana's contact icon. The video snaps on, showing Tiana facing off-screen in another conversation. ". . . yeah, but you should have checked with me first, Pyotr!" Tiana shouts. "The Russians! Are you crazy? How could you?"

"Tiana!" shouts Roger. "What the *fuck* is going on?"

That gets her attention, and she turns to Roger and me. "Oh, hi, Roger."

"Oh, hi?" Roger's spittle hits the screen. "What the hell have you done?"

"Tiana, I told Roger everything. All about the quiz and the ecliptic coordinates we got."

Tiana's face is white, and her confidence vanishes. Another man's voice taunts, "Hey, Tiana. What's the matter? Heh, heh. You in bit of trouble?"

Her face snaps to red. "Damn you, Pyotr!" Tiana is choked into silence.

Roger takes a deep breath. "Tiana, who is that? Can you end that call? We need to talk. In private!"

Tiana gasps, "Sorry, Roger. I'm talking to Pyotr Annenkov at NASA JPL in Pasadena. I think . . . we should add him to a three-way call with you guys. He has some relevant information to share."

"Damnit!" Roger shakes his head. "We need to have a discussion about your unauthorized communications."

"Yes, well, Pyotr has relevant info and knows about the China communication. He leads the NASA Near-Earth Object observations science team that gave NORAD the projectile trajectories. I know Pyotr pretty well," she huffs.

"And how do you know Pyotr?" Roger demands.

"I guess you could say we are, or were, related. Pyotr is my ex-husband," Tiana says, avoiding eye contact.

Roger and I trade looks.

"Very well," Roger sighs. "Put him on."

A face with a scraggly beard underneath matted brown hair merges into our video call, smoking a cigarette and holding a cup of coffee. He smirks before switching to an inscrutable stone face.

"Pyotr, this is Colonel Roger McMahon and Scott Anderson on the call," Tiana says. "Can you tell them what you have found?"

"Colonel McMahon, Mr. Anderson, it's pleasure to meet you. Tiana woke me too early this morning with crazy requests to stare at the sun. I hung up, but she called back. Nag, nag, nag." Pyotr puts down the cigarette and the coffee.

Tiana's cheeks glow crimson.

"But. This is greatest day of my life. JPL is going crazy." His face lights up with a grin. "People run up and down halls shouting like ten Mars landings!"

"What?" Roger spits. "What kind of security do you have? How many people know about this Chinese communication?"

"China? Tiana, you did not say message is from China." Pyotr wags his finger at her.

Tiana slaps her forehead.

"Colonel McMahon, I share picture—worth much more than a thousand words." Pyotr reaches for his keyboard, and his jubilant face is replaced with a pixilated smear of something white on a black background. "Is it not beautiful? Wonderful!"

Frowning at the blob, I ask, "Pyotr, can you give us some context? It's an oblong shape of a few grey pixels, with a bright white pixel on the left. Not overly exciting."

"But it is beautiful! Almost same ecliptic coordinate as message. We point VHiRISE telescope from Mars Survey Orbiter for near-infrared image. Nobody thinks we find object, but it is there! JPL time-integrate image across thirty minutes. See: object generates thermal energy! Target appears stationary relative to Earth! Is not possible without propulsion!" Pyotr is breathless.

What he says makes sense. An object in a natural orbit closer to the sun should have a faster radial velocity than Earth. Just as Venus orbits the sun in two-thirds of the time of Earth's orbit, this object should have passed out of Earth's direct line of sight to the sun.

"Pyotr, could the brighter pixels be the heat from an engine?" I ask in a hoarse whisper.

"Yes! Scott, you have it! We can not tell how big because VHiRISE telescope image jitter resolves only three kilometers at this range. Hot pixel must be heat from rocket engine!" Pyotr catches his breath. "Oh, what engine! Spacecraft maintains Earth-synchronous orbit around sun! What power! What fuel source! Nothing like it exists on Earth!"

Tiana reacts with a frown.

Roger breathes slowly, anger dissipating. "Tiana, what were you and Pyotr saying about the Russians?"

"Pyotr wants a better image, and—" Tiana says.

Pyotr interrupts, "You see, VHiRISE Mars telescope is at one hundred fifty million kilometers from target. We think oblong shape and engine heat source is maybe ten kilometers long. Or maybe small, like hundred meters long."

A hundred-meter-long spacecraft is small?

"Okay, okay. What do the Russians have to do with this?" asks Roger. "What did you tell them?"

"Yes, yes. Russian Tunguska spacecraft mission launched two years ago for asteroid mining surveys. Swinging around Venus for gravity velocity assist, Tunguska only two million kilometers from target." Pyotr is breathless again. "Tunguska IR telescope can resolve two hundred meters, and radar may resolve fifty meters! Roscosmos flight controllers calculating maneuvers to point Tunguska instruments at object."

"Who the hell authorized this? The Russians?" Roger slaps the desk. "This is all top secret!"

Pyotr gapes, and his mouth drops open. Tiana rubs her temples.

"I, I . . . classified? Colonel McMahon, JPL science staff works with international space agencies—always. Most incredible sighting in NASA history! No, most stunning in *all* history!"

"You guys say China, Russia, and maybe a bunch of other international space agencies are all aware of this object? None of this was cleared." Roger's anger dissipates as he absorbs the bombshells. "The first thing you need to do, Pyotr, is to lock down the information. Inform everybody at NASA who may have this data and get me a list. I need organizations and individual names." Roger levels a cold look at me, then at Tiana and Pyotr. "Lock it down, and I'll call you back in thirty minutes. I need a full security damage assessment. Any questions?"

Roger nudges me. "Goodbye, for now, Pyotr. Tiana, stay on the call." I expect Roger to unleash his anger once Pyotr hangs up, but he does not. Instead, Roger sits and thinks and says nothing.

"This destroys the theory that China launched nuclear attacks on Texas," I say. "By their answers, China confirmed they were attacked by the same source. Can't we use the Instagram communication bridge and send them more information to build trust? Maybe send them the NASA photo and the precise coordinates where we found it? Tell them the Russians are verifying it?"

Roger remains quiet, his lips pressed together. "Given the circumstances, I'll set aside your security breach for the moment. Don't dare think this is forgiveness." He pauses and makes eye contact with each of us.

I exhale in relief.

Roger continues, "Scott, your conclusion won't be accepted by the task force hawks down the hall in the conference room. I bet the reaction will be that this confirms we should attack. China could be so far ahead of us that they've already launched space weapons—powered by primordial black hole engines—and used them to eradicate our competing PBH research and development projects in Texas."

"But, what about—"

"Just listen." He waves me to silence. "Even that amazing engine on the spacecraft could be explained as a deployed

PBH engine. However. The size of this object . . . it defies anything the Chinese or the USA could build. Pyotr's fuzzy measurements suggest it could be ten kilometers long—thirty times the length of an aircraft carrier. It would be impossible to miss one of those launched from Earth. It would take years and trillions of dollars."

Tiana's jaw drops, and there is a frown on her face. "But where did . . . who?" she gasps. She can't finish her sentence, eyes wide.

I jump to my feet, scraping my chair backward. "We need to try to communicate with that spacecraft. Before they take another shot at us."

Roger's anger is forgotten, replaced by . . . is that fear? He jumps up. "Wait here, guys. I'm going to find General Adams," he says as he jogs down the hall.

"Do you think it's possible?" I ask Tiana. "There must be a simpler explanation."

"This is unreal," she gasps.

A short time later, the door swings wide and bangs the doorstop. Roger leads General Adams in and guides him into the chair near my laptop display. The general looks like he's been sleeping under his desk. His light-blue uniform shirt is stained with sweat on his back and armpits, and his jacket and tie are gone. The hair on his head is kinked at odd angles.

Roger says, "Sir, let me explain. Tiana, can you display that image from the Mars telescope?" The general shakes himself awake.

Tiana reaches for her keyboard. "Yes, hold on a second. Yes, here it is." Her image window shrinks to make room for the smear of pixels. I stand behind the general, embarrassed at how little the picture shows.

"General, this JPL photo came from the same NASA team that gave NORAD the heads-up on the Texas attacks. It may not look like much because of the extreme range," Roger says. "However, we know this is a large object in space between Earth's and Venus's orbits. It's potentially up to ten kilometers long, generates sufficient power to maneuver in space, and always remains in the sun's face relative to Earth. The projectiles that struck the Texas and Gobi sites were launched from this object. I believe whoever is on this object launched those strikes to eradicate primordial black hole research projects on Earth."

Roger does not throw Tiana and me under the bus for the security breach. There will be time for punishment later.

General Adams frowns at Roger. "Are you crazy? Did you just dream this up after finding no other way to stop them?"

"All of this data can be verified by our NASA JPL science staff. China sent us a message with these coordinates in space and made identical trajectory calculations. A hostile force on this object has attacked the US and China, and that hostile force is now sitting back, watching us annihilate each other in a nuclear war. A war they caused."

The general frowns as he examines the blob photo. "You said ten kilometers in length? What is it, an asteroid or comet?"

I answer, "Sir, it's about the size of a small asteroid." Roger cautions me with a tilt of his head. "We don't have enough resolution in this photo, so we can't know its size accurately. But it's not an asteroid or comet. Whatever it is, it has a rocket engine that gives it the power to travel anywhere within or outside the solar system." Roger nods at me for not blowing i t.

The general asks, "This is correct?"

"Yes, sir," says Roger.

The general's eyes glaze over, and there's quiet for a full minute. "An old fighter pilot tactic. Attack out of the sunlight. It's the perfect screen. We could be facing a hostile force with technology superior to any on Earth, and we're about to waste most of our military power in a full-scale war." His eyes snap to Roger. "Colonel, I need a written report and presentation in fifteen minutes to review with the task force."

"Yes, sir," says Roger.

"This needs to get to the Joint Chiefs ASAP," says the general, shaking his head. "Nobody will believe this. They'll think I'm insane." He gets up and walks down the hall.

Roger closes the door and sits down again. "Tiana, I want you to post another picture to Heinrich's Instagram account. This should include the revised, precise object coordinates and the NASA photo. Tell them the picture was taken with a Mars telescope. But let's review the message before you post it. We need to keep this thin thread of communication open."

"Got it," says Tiana, all business. "I'll drop off the call and send you the message text for your approval."

The four walls surround me like a jail cell. It's claustrophobic, like life on a submarine—tight quarters, no daylight, with the interior design style of the lowest-bidding military contractor.

"You know, I don't think our Chinese friends will be impressed by that photo either," Tiana says. "Maybe they can point one of their telescopes at those new coordinates. Hope they were impressed with seven significant digits in range accuracy. It should be easier for them to find."

"I don't know what else we can do." I sigh. "I wish we had a better picture of this thing, although it may be just another space boulder—with a rocket engine on its backside."

"Did Roger say why he got thrown out?" Tiana asks.

"No, but he was pretty jolted when he came by to ask if the Russians had delivered pictures from the Tunguska spacecraft. I think he and the general got laughed out of the room after showing the blob photo. He also mumbled something about turning a battleship using a rowboat. It's been a weeklong process to build the war consensus, which a half-hour presentation will not change. There are thousands of government and military leaders invested in this war."

"How are we going to get someone with political power to see our data?" she asks.

"I'm afraid it's too little, too late. About four hours ago, Roger said the attack would happen within twelve hours. I imagine bombers are already in the air, and submarines are silent on the ocean floor with launch tubes ready. I have no idea what it takes to recall all that. Hell, the Chinese and their allies are probably doing the same."

I jump when the door bangs open. "Speak of the devil . . ." I mumble as Roger and General Adams walk in.

"Colonel McMahon says this information was shared with Russia," General Adams says with barely suppressed fury. "They may have better pictures coming?"

"Uh, yes, sir." I half expect my head to be taken off. "Their Tunguska asteroid survey spacecraft is within two million kilometers of the object. It seems the NASA people have a trusting relationship with Roscosmos scientists."

"General," Tiana says, "we don't have a reply from the Russians yet. I talked to a scientist in the NASA Planetary

Defense team a half hour ago. He says this is to be expected of the Russians. They play their cards closely. We won't hear a thing until they can tie a bow on it."

"It will take something dramatic to change directions. Our commander-in-chief is committed to the war and doesn't want to hear second-guessing." General Adams studies the floor, wringing his hands. "It may require some political influence. And cost me my stars." He shakes his head with a grim smirk. "It will be too late if we don't hear within the hour."

The silence forecasts inevitable death. This crazy doomsday scenario was supposed to have vanished with the fall of the Soviet Union seventy years ago. I felt terrible that my screwups killed Agosti at Pecos, but that was trivial by comparison. Am I the catalyst of this war? I sigh; that's ridiculous, or is it? I am at least one ingredient in this catastrophe, and that's just as bad.

Roger paces back and forth in the tiny office like a frustrated coach searching for a Hail Mary play out of a crushing defeat. The general exudes deep sadness. What is going through his mind? I bet the general has vulnerable family and friends. He carries a considerable burden.

But what about Robby? Has he made it inside Cheyenne Mountain with Mary yet? How are we going to survive a real nuclear holocaust? What if Mom, Dad, and Margie are still out there, struggling with injuries, as nuclear fire rains down? I would give anything to turn back time and be home again with them all.

But my self-pity is nothing compared to the scale of misery about to be unleashed.

"Guys," Tiana says, "I'm going to call Pyotr for a status update. I'll be back shortly." She clicks off her video feed.

I sigh and think once again of Robby. How many cabinet doors has he ripped off hinges at Mary's house?

"Hey, guys! I'm back, and I brought Pyotr with me," Tiana says. "He has some good news to share!" She displays a giant grin. "General Adams, let me introduce Pyotr Annenkov, the program scientist with the NASA Planetary Defense Coordination Office at JPL."

"Good to meet you, Pyotr. What do you have for us?" asks the general.

"A most wonderful day in history!" Pyotr behaves like a teenager after his first sexual experience. "Our Russian friends are brilliant! They sent two images. Amazing!"

"Okay, okay, Pyotr, get on with it," Roger snaps.

"Certainly." Pyotr passes an image from his iPad to our screen. "What do you think? Infrared pixel resolution is two hundred meters, spacecraft length is four kilometers! Strange oval shape is two-pixel diameter."

We answer with silence. The monochrome infrared image shows a long, fuzzy tube passing through the center of a disk. "Pyotr, the right end of that pipe structure is white-hot. Is that oval heat source the engine?" I ask.

Pyotr grins. "Yes! Yes! Most likely. Roscosmos says engine is angled for thrust to maintain spacecraft's position centered in front of sun. Next, a beautiful radar image with fifty-meter resolution!" Pyotr adds the new image to the screen and beams with pride.

We respond with a collective gasp. In infrared, what looked like a four-kilometer-long tube is shown by radar to actually be a ladder structure with rungs bridging two tubes extending the craft's entire length. The disk at the spacecraft's midpoint resembles a Ferris wheel with cylinders arranged around the circumference. A cone shape is attached to the ladder structure's bottom rung, where the infrared hot spot is. The base of the cone is about two hundred meters in diameter; it's an absolutely colossal rocket nozzle.

"It's a spacecraft," Tiana gasps. "It . . . it's not from Earth!"

"Most joyous day ever!" Pyotr's ebullience overflows.

"No, the most terrifying day," murmurs General Adams. "Whoever or whatever is in this ship has launched strikes at Earth that we assumed were three-megaton nuclear blasts. Colonel, get these images down to the conference room now. I'll convene a follow-up meeting ASAP."

Pyotr's smile is gone. "Yes, will forward pictures immediately with written report from Roscosmos."

"Thank you, Pyotr," says General Adams. "My compliments to your team and your collaborating scientific community. I need your urgent help communicating these images to others. Can you request your Russian colleagues' assistance and deliver these images and the data directly to the Chinese and US presidents? This is most urgent—life-or-death for us all."

"Yes, certainly, General Adams," Pyotr whispers, fear overtaking the wondrous joy in his eyes. "I contact Roscosmos now."

After Pyotr disconnects, the general asks, "Tiana, you know Pyotr well?"

"Yes, General Adams," Tiana says after hesitating.

"Is Pyotr the type to go up the chain of command for these communications or take shortcuts for urgency?"

Tiana purses her lips and then smirks. "I understand the concern, sir. Pyotr is quite careful when political considerations come into play and has learned never to surprise his boss. I expect he will prepare his management chain and have them pass the information to the president. However, he can move quickly with his Russian scientist friends. They may get the pictures to the Chinese president first."

"I was afraid of that," says the general. "It will be a shame if our commander-in-chief gets the news last, but Roger and I will also push through our chain of command. Hopefully, Russia will still have open communications with the Chinese president."

"Roger, bring your pictures to the conference room." The general steps quickly down the hall. "We may already be out of time."

"Yes, sir," says Roger. He stands to leave but pauses. "Tiana, get all this data and the Russian pictures out in an Instagram post. Let's share with China."

"Yes, Roger. Right away." She bends to her keyboard, all business once again, and clicks off the call.

Roger exits, abandoning me alone in my cell. I am deflated, powerless to help, frustrated as hell, and way out of my league with the power politics in play. I just want to be a physicist. And my family is all but gone. Did Robby make it inside yet?

I stumble out of my office, feeling the exhaustion of a night with little sleep. My legs wobble as I walk down the hall to the guard, fighting to stay awake. My back feels cramped. The conference room door is to the side of the guard's desk but is wide open this time. Roger and the general sit at the table alone. Roger grimaces at something the general mumbles, staring at his hands laid flat on the table.

The general sees me. "You can come on in if you like, Scott. We won't be having the task force meeting after all."

I pause and take a tentative step inside. "Is it too late?" I panic.

"Sort of," Roger says. "The task force has been shut down. The Joint Chiefs"—he glances over at the general, who nods, then shrugs—"the new Joint Chiefs have relieved General Adams."

"What?" I feel embarrassed for the general, although he seems to take it in stride.

"The president and the National Security Council do not need additional data." The general pushes back from the table. "Roger, forward the Russian report and pictures to my email. Now." He jumps up and strides out the door. "Time for plan B."

"What is plan B?" I ask.

Roger taps his iPad, head down. "Not something you want to know about." He finishes the email to General Adams. "All we can do is wait and pray his plan B gets the data in the right hands before we run out of time, but honestly, I don't see how we can stop it. We need time that we don't have to get the data into the president's hands, negotiate a truce, and send a recall." Roger's voice is thick, his words slurred with exhaustion.

"Roger?" my voice rasps. "Do you know if Mary brought Robby inside the mountain?" I cough.

He nods. "Yes, I heard from Mary an hour ago. She was on her way with your brother, and they should be at the apartments by now."

"Thanks, Roger," I choke out. "Uh, is there some way we can monitor the status of the attacks and the war from here? Don't you have a wall covered with displays of strategic force deployments or something?"

Roger shakes his head, grimacing. "The 'Big Board' was invented by Hollywood for movies like *Dr. Strangelove*. We found that a single sixty-inch UHD display works fine. Most guys just track battle status on their personal workstations. In any case, access to that information is need-to-know only."

"I guess that does not include me."

"Nor me," says Roger. "Not my mission." He rubs the stubble on his chin. "However, the next best thing is to turn to mainstream news." Roger taps his keyboard, the wall display in the conference room comes to life, and CNN pops up. "Let's see what the world is watching."

It is a duck-and-cover video from 1960, a low-resolution black-and-white movie with dramatic narration. Is there nothing fresher in the war preparation archives? The simulated nuclear war scenes are inset into a full-color frame of CNN graphics and advertisements. The video shows a hydrogen bomb fireball rising to a towering mushroom cloud—a test conducted on a remote island. I am reminded again of the low-to-the-horizon fireball arc over Austin—nothing like the H-bomb airburst currently being shown on CNN.

General Adams drags himself into the room, closing the door with grim resignation before glaring at the CNN video stream. "Well, that's sure to calm the citizens down." His voice drips with sarcasm. "At least we know there aren't any new nuclear explosions if all they're showing are those H-bomb tests from a hundred years ago." He sighs. "We'll see how long that lasts now."

What does he mean?

The CNN video stream is interrupted with a *Breaking News Alert* as a breathless talking head announces an urgent news conference with the Speaker of the House of Representatives. General Adams's attention snaps to the screen. The familiar face of the grey-haired Speaker appears, and she begins excitedly announcing that she's about to share a momentous scientific discovery by NASA scientists in collaboration with international space agencies. Roger's haggard expression transforms into a thin smile, and he nods approval to the general. The general doesn't move, his expression frozen with anticipation—or is that fear?

The Speaker's words are confusing, as she seems baffled by the physics of orbital mechanics. Still, she eventually stumbles her way into saying, "There is strong evidence that the attacks on Texas and China were missiles launched from this spacecraft." She reaches to tap her iPad, and the high-resolution radar image from Roscosmos appears on the screen. The entire world receives CNN broadcasts.

Well, this is one way to get the data to the president. I bet the National Security Council and the Joint Chiefs are apoplectic. Their entire premise for total war has been publicly voided. I join Roger in smiling at General Adams, although he remains frozen with concern, watching the Speaker's announcement. She closes her remarks with gravity. "This momentous event in human history, anticipated by many science fiction writers, is now a science fact. Tragically, humanity's first contact with another world was an attack that killed many Americans. This was exacerbated by early misunderstandings between the United States and China, resulting in nuclear strikes on our military forces. However, we can all be thankful for our president's restraint while coordinating these scientific investigations with our international partners."

General Adams relaxes and nods in sad approval. "Well, that's done. It goes against everything I respect in the chain of command. There's going to be some powerful blowback. Your work, both of you, is critical. You must urgently advance the PBH research and development—it may be needed to respond to whoever, or whatever, is on that spacecraft. And you need to distance yourself from me."

The CNN feed switches to a newsroom of scrambling talking heads, with immediate questions about why this announcement came from the Speaker, not the president. Reporters on the White House lawn and by the US Capitol Building speak with breathless speculation. The pictures from the Russian Tunguska spacecraft alternate between radar and infrared images as science reporters speculate on the features of the alien spacecraft, its impossible size, and its technology. General Adams and the Speaker just dropped an information bomb on the world.

The conference room door crashes open. Two security officers with sidearms charge into the room. "General Adams?" Both guys are red-faced, sweating, and gulping for air like they just sprinted a kilometer.

"Yes. Can I help you?" the general asks, maintaining a placid expression.

"Sir, you are under arrest. You need to come with us, sir."

Chapter 29

SOL'S AWAKENING

Captain's Log, Frigate-328, 179240.69 LST

A sensor scan by a Sol-3 spacecraft detected and analyzed the structure of Frigate-328. Mission stealth has been lost. Prime-AI also reported that the Sol-3 military forces are standing down, confirming that Frigate-328 was identified as the preferred opponent.

Political division had settled into vicarious delight as the Sol-3 organics prepared for self-immolation. That would have been more fun than euphoria dreams for those political division sadists. However, after stealth was breached, the commissar and Polit-AI were crestfallen.

Mil-AI repeated the call for redeployment to the outer edge of the Sol system to get the range for the higher kinetic energy required to power the planet killers. But I'm not yet resigned to kinetic energy cleansing procedures. Instead, I ordered transit to a close range over Sol-3 and ordered Mil-AI to prepare for short-range attacks to eliminate the nuclear weapons that could be a danger to the ship.

I push away fears that my orders diverge from the standard suppression protocols and find I am preoccupied with thoughts of the younglings—can they be saved?

Chapter 30

REPRIEVE

The hotel in the cave was dirty, but Scotty came, and we rode back to Mary's house in her red car with big wheels. Scotty was happy. He was sleepy and hugged me too much.

Scotty stops reading, his eyes close, and he snores. I touch the orange belly of the bird picture to make the book talk. "Chirrup, chirrup, chirrup, tweetle-tweee-doop. I am an American robin. I love to eat worms. Chirrup, tweet, chirrup, tweet-tweet-tweet."

I giggle, but Scotty has his eyes closed. I touch his cheek to make him read more. The book falls into his lap. "No, I'm sleepy." Scotty snores.

I was alone with Mary for days without Scotty. The scream of caws behind my eyes is quiet at night. The crows scream from out of the sun.

Mary does not have good food—no broccoli, soda, or hot sauce. Mary gets angry if I push food away.

"Scotty, go home?" I want my bed and books and Mom. "Where Mom?"

Scotty is hot under the blanket. I like my head under his chin, but his eyes are closed. Scotty's breath stinks. "Scotty, read book." His nose wiggles. "Read book." Scotty rolls over, and the book falls to the floor and slaps closed. This bed is small.

"Your brother is sleepy, Robby," Mary says. "Come help set the table. Do you know what to do? We have four places at the table."

I know this game. First, get the napkins. "One, two, three, four." I show four fingers to Mary to make sure I did it right.

"Ha! Great job. Let's move these in front of the chairs. Take the silverware now. Robby, can you finish?"

"One, two, three, four forks," I count and put one fork on each napkin, then smile at Mary.

"Perfect, Robby!" says Mary. "Dinner should be here in a few minutes. What do you like to drink?"

"He usually drinks Sprite," Scotty says from behind me.

"Oh, hi, Scott," Mary says. "I don't have any soda. Does he like fruit juice?"

"Apple juice," I say. Mary's eyes grow big.

"I have apple juice, Robby! You understand a lot of what I say. I'm impressed."

Scotty says, "His receptive language is quite good."

I take Scotty's hand and pull him to the cabinet door I put against the wall.

"Fix it. Scotty fix door. Get tools."

But Scotty frowns. "Did you break this door?" he asks me.

"Yes, Robby broke that this morning," Mary says. "That and two others the day before. Plus, he kicked a hole in the bathroom wall."

Scotty frowns. "I'm angry with you, Robby. You know you shouldn't break things."

I give the door to Scotty. "Fix it. Work."

"We can't reinforce the behavior with a repair project," Scotty says. "Do you have anything else that needs repairs? Best if we fix something Robby did not break."

Oh good. More things to fix.

"Well, the garbage disposal is busted," Mary says. "I think something fell inside and jammed. But you don't need to do that. I plan to call a repair guy."

"No problem. Robby and I would love to try repairing it. Come on, Robby, let's go get some tools."

We find dirty tools in Mary's barn, then move stinky stuff from under the sink. "Ugh, you don't have to do this," says Mary.

I show Mary the wrenches. "Tools. Fix it."

Scotty laughs. "No problem at all. We're a team."

Scotty lies down on the floor and sticks his head under the sink. "Come on down here, Robby."

I crawl under the counter with Scotty. It smells like garbage, and two brown bugs run away into a crack in the wall. "Bug. Two bugs," I tell Scotty.

"Yep, cockroaches. Okay, dude, see this? This is a garbage disposal. Can you say 'disposal'?"

"Posal."

"Disposal," he says. "Not bad, Robby. First, we'll loosen the screws." He grunts when he turns the screwdriver. "Here, can you finish?" He gives me the screwdriver, and I turn the screw. "Good, now loosen the other screw here. Okay, that's enough." He pulls the black pipe and the shiny metal piece off the posal.

"All finished," I tell Scotty.

"Not quite," he says. "Move back so I can twist it off the sink drain." We both crawl out, sit on the floor, and I lean close to

Scotty to see better. He puts both hands around the posal until it falls and bangs on the floor.

"Posal broken. Fix it."

Scotty laughs. "That's right, Robby. We need to see what jammed it. Ah, there it is. It's a piece of metal." He points into the hole, and I look inside.

"Fix it," I tell Scotty.

Mary sits down on the floor next to me. "Robby, you are a big help. I like the way you tell Scott what to do." Mary's eyes sparkle, and she smiles at Scotty.

"These repair projects are reinforcing for Robby. He's an expert with tools," Scotty says.

I crawl to sit in Scotty's lap to help him. "Fix it," I tell Scotty.

Scotty turns the posal over and points to a shiny bolt. "Can you find a tool for this?"

I give Scotty a wrench. "Wrench. Fix it."

He wraps one arm around the posal to hold it tight. We put our hands on the wrench. "Let's pull together, Robby—there."

The wrench turns, and a piece of metal drops to the floor.

"Ah-ha, here it is. It was a penny inside the garbage disposal," Scotty says.

"All fixed?" I ask Scotty. I tickle my chest and feel happy. Mary looks happy, but she wipes her eyes.

"I think it's fixed. Let's put it back together and test it."

Scotty puts the posal back under the counter with the black pipe and shiny metal piece.

"Robby, make sure we put it back together right."

I crawl under the sink again. It's just like it looked when I saw the two bugs. I crawl back out and tell Scotty, "All finished. Robby fix it."

"Yay, Robby! Great job. Let's turn on the switch." The posal growls like a lawnmower. "It works. We fixed it!"

"All finished," I tell Mary. She laughs.

The doorbell rings. "Just in time for dinner," says Mary. "You guys are amazing together." She touches Scotty's arm and smiles, and he looks at her with big, happy eyes.

Mary brings two boxes from the front door to the table. "Pizza time," she says. "I got an extra-large pepperoni pizza for you guys and Dad. I just got a medium veggie combo for me."

"Pizza," I say, grabbing a slice of pepperoni pizza.

Scotty looks at the pizza but doesn't eat. He closes his eyes and asks Mary, "Would you mind sharing a couple of veggie pizza slices?"

Mary's blue eyes sparkle—just like Margie's brown eyes. "Sure, help yourself to some veggies. Robby, you can have all the pepperoni pizza you can eat."

Mary is fun. I giggle, drink apple juice, and eat pizza. Scotty already ate two slices, and Mary gave him more.

Roger and Robby devour the pepperoni pizza. Seeing it makes me sick—it seems like it's been my primary dinner selection for weeks. Mary doesn't have a single beer in the fridge. What is wrong with her? I settle for a glass of the Zinfandel. I have to admit it's not bad.

Mary's house used to be a farmhouse, a historic outpost of the Colorado frontier, surrounded by tract home developments. The front yard is defined by a rusty barbed-wire fence enclosing a pasture that needs some horses or goats. The barn serves as a garage for her red Jeep, an old Dodge pickup, and a sixties-era Corvette convertible up on blocks, waiting for restoration. Roger pulled his Tesla inside with room to spare. Horse stalls are converted to shops for art projects: a potter's wheel, oil painting area, and woodworking space are set amid the dirt, antique manure, sawdust, and the aroma of oil paint and turpentine. A historic display of bridles and an old saddle are in the tack room that connects to a covered path into the ki tchen.

The house interior is engaged in various renovations, with the latest investment in the kitchen, where a rustic-cut quartz countertop sits against an original centuries-old gas-fired stove and oven. The room is seasoned by fresh-cut lumber and drying plaster blended with the odor of greasy pizza. The entire back of the house has panoramic windows that view the mountains to the west that climb above the scrub oak and pine foothills, with gusts of wind and flurries dancing over a thick blanket of fresh snow. Mary's home is an oasis compared to all that time under Cheyenne Mountain.

However, this place is not Robby-proofed. All these tools and construction projects are the ingredients of disaster and delight for Robby. Hammers, saws, power tools, chisels, and boxes of nails are scattered throughout the house. I chuckle at a memory from a few years ago. Robby had been inspired by a bathroom demolition scene on HGTV, fetched a hammer from the garage, and then pounded a toilet into porcelain rubble. A water geyser spouted from the plumbing outlet, and Mom screamed like her hair was on fire. Dad had not been pleased.

"That hit the spot. Thanks, Mary. I was starved," Roger says. "If it's all right with you, I'll put the news on to check in on the status of the war."

"I guess that's okay," Mary says. "It's hard to argue for peace and quiet in these circumstances."

Robby bites into another slice of pepperoni pizza—five pieces so far.

On screen, the CNN feed shows the president reading a speech in an uncharacteristic monotone, gritting his teeth to the end, then stalking off stage, refusing to take questions. Breathless commentators compare this cease-fire speech to the announcement from the House Speaker earlier in the morning. Members of Congress, Cabinet officials, and retired generals exchange heated debates over the Speaker's apparent undermining of the president's march to war with China. The opinions are polarized: China war hawks claiming fake news regarding the accounts of an alien invasion versus advocates for an international alliance against the extraterrestrial attackers.

"I guess they have all figured out General Adams's plan B," I say. "But so many are still stuck on the China war narrative. They're in denial. First contact with aliens from another world? Nothing else should matter. It's incredible."

"Give them a little time," says Mary. "That spacecraft photo is too abstract for most. They will think it's fake. Planted to stop our revenge on China. People still want to blame them—so many bought into the fascist Asian hate. An alien spaceship story is absurd—like a bad Hollywood movie."

"Yeah, I think you may be right," says Roger. "The recent nuclear exchanges with China are fresh and terrifying."

"We'll see how long this holds," I say. "Those aliens in their spaceship started this and may want us to finish the job by annihilating each other, but if we don't, there's no telling what they'll do. They have technology beyond any of Earth's militaries. When will the politicians move away from the xenophobic narrative and recognize the enemy that has the means to rain down horror upon us? The political debate is foolish. The politicians have to get their shit together, get the hell out of the way, and order somebody to prepare for battle against those alien weapons."

"That 'somebody' includes us, Scott," Roger says. "Why do you think the attacks targeted all the primordial black hole research locations on Earth?"

"Yeah. We crossed ET's red line and may threaten them with the technology."

"That's my bet," says Roger. "We released energy from the primordial black holes at Austin and Pecos locations just days before the strikes. China probably reproduced your PBH energy release techniques after Heinrich sent them your recipe."

"And they targeted the energy radiation signatures using kinetic energy projectiles." It seems obvious now, in hindsight.

Mary listens, her brow wrinkling deeper with each revelation. She glares at both of us. "Is this what you did? You are the cause of the attacks that got millions of people killed?"

Her words are like knives in my gut. I look intently at my hands, then at Robby as he guzzles apple juice. What have I done? I can't face Roger or Mary—I am the catalyst. ET saw my work and slaughtered Mom, Dad, Margie, and millions of other innocent people in response.

"You have to admit it, Roger. If Anthony Agosti hadn't used his genius to figure out how to harvest primordial black holes, if I hadn't fixed the static voltage flaw, none of this would have happened. ET would be content, and we wouldn't have crossed their red line."

Roger winces. "This would have happened eventually, regardless. If not us, it would have been some future scientists provoking the aliens. That spacecraft may have been parked out by Venus for centuries, willing to watch over us for eternity. Maybe their policy is to ensure no other civilization attains this power. It might threaten their superiority."

"That's supposed to make me feel better? My hometown and family are all gone, except for my brother." I feel a ton of bricks press on my chest.

"Come, Robby, clear your plate to the counter. Let's get you cleaned up." Mary leads him to the sink, and Robby grins at her. Just like he would smile at Mom on her better days before the divorce.

I feel tears forming, and Mary's grey-blue eyes pierce my façade. After she finishes with Robby, she comes to me and touches my arm. "I'm sorry, I shouldn't have said that. You shouldn't blame yourself. Don't lose hope for your mom and dad."

Roger looks at each of us, opens his mouth to respond, and then seems to decide against it, leaving us alone in the kitchen.

I wipe my eyes. "There's almost no hope. My parents were in Austin while I launched black hole energy flares, painting a target on them."

Mary purses her lips, glancing over at Robby. "You saved Robby. You guys are wonderful together." Her hand squeezes my wrist. "You and your family are the good ones—dedicated to protecting Robby. Fighting the fascists."

"Hah. You wouldn't say that if you saw what we went through. It was hell when Robby was young. My parents fought the prejudice, and we occasionally had great times together. But they also fought with each other, and I would take care of Robby a lot to give my parents a break. The more time passed, the larger the frustration and battles between them. It all broke apart after my dad surrendered and got registered. That sterilization was a license for him to live a normal life. The skinheads did leave Dad alone, but he left the rest of us behind. Mom can barely hold it together anymore." I stop, recalling that neither Mom nor Dad is likely to be alive. I shake my head. "No. Our family failed. If I had followed my dad's path, I would have had many research job choices other than joining Anthony's project, and my family would still be alive."

"Don't say that! You have every right to live a full life. Be proud of your family. Compared to the families of most of my students—families who were driven to get sterilized and registered and then abandon their disabled kids to be wards of the state, all to escape getting targeted—you guys have done amazing. It's infuriating. All those abandoned autistic kids are forced into group homes. It may have been impossible for your family to hold it completely together in the face of those fascists, but you did resist, protecting Robby. Your parents held out for years and set an example you should be proud of. That strength proves they have what it takes to survive almost anything." She reaches for both of my hands. "Don't lose hope for your mom and dad. If anyone can make it out of Texas, they can."

My tears well up again. Robby wanders into the den, sits beside a toolbox, and examines her assortment of screwdrivers and wrenches. "I'm going out—for a walk. Can you watch Robby awhile?" I choke out. Robby picks up a hammer.

She nods, and her eyes lock on me like she's trying to read my mind. "I've got him."

I grab my down coat from the rack and open the door into a snow flurry. The wind cuts through me, and I wish I had a wool cap to protect my ears. The snow depth is only a couple of inches here on the leeward side of the Rocky Mountains, but deep enough to muffle my footsteps shuffling toward the foothills behind the house, threading a path through scrub oak clumped with snowdrifts as I climb to the top of a hill. My lungs burn, inflated by gasps of frozen air, while I slip and stumble in the snow, sweating inside my warm coat. From above Mary's home, my breath steams into my eyes, and the distant lights from Colorado Springs sparkle in the dusk, filtering through clouds and snow.

Down the hill through the windows, I watch Robby and Mary clean up after dinner and then move to the sofa in front of the TV, Robby covered by a blanket in Mary's lap, her blonde hair draping down to his shoulders. Mary wraps her arms around Robby, her chin on his head, while Robby studies one of his books. It's a deceptively peaceful scene. Mary has more determination and moral resolve than I ever hoped for myself.

My solitude is disturbed only by the fluttering wind. The snow flurries eventually stop, and stars break through a hole in the clouds, revealing the constellation of Perseus as the sky opens and the black depth of space takes shape.

Which star? Which one is their home? I turn west to view the mountain range between me, the sun, and the alien spacecraft that killed my family. How long before they finish us off—if we don't destroy ourselves first? The idiot politicians seem to be consumed by hate trolls. The bastards are willing to annihilate half the planet in a fraudulent war against China. Damn them!

But I started this. First with Anthony's death, then with all the dead in Austin, Danny at Pecos Center, Mom, Dad, Margie—all dead. All those navy people dying in the Pacific and the people in China. But what can humans do against the impossible power of this threat from the stars? Humankind does not even have the tools to mount a defense.

But I do.

The possibilities . . . what could we do with a primordial black hole missile? And what could the aliens do with their kinetic energy weapons? With constant acceleration, the aliens would only need to increase the distance of the launch to increase projectile velocity, and the explosive energy increases by the velocity squared. If they launched a single missile from near Pluto, it would destroy all life on Earth.

Am I the only person who can see these possibilities? Am I the only one who can find a solution? It's the least I can do in their memory—Anthony, Mom, Dad, Danny, and Margie. My last chance to save Robby.

Gasping, I dash down the hill, stumbling and tumbling toward the house, tripping over brush and kicking through drifts of snow. I pass the barn and head to the front door, slamming it open against the wall.

"Roger!" I shout. "We need to go. Now!" I gasp to catch my breath.

Mary pivots up from the couch, eyes wide, strands of blonde hair tossed across her face.

Roger jumps up from his laptop at the kitchen table. "What?"

"They can destroy Earth. It would be simple. A single primordial black hole projectile is all they need. We need to finish that PBH Sidewinder integration. It may be our single hope for a defensive weapon.

"Mary?" I ask.

Mary's fearful reaction to my outburst fades. She is calm and determined and says, "Go. I'll take care of him."

Robby watches me with a lucid serenity—like he expects me to leave.

Chapter 31

SCAPEGOATS

Roger is behind the wheel of the Tesla, frowning, staring at the road illuminated by headlights guiding us toward the snow-covered Cheyenne Mountain along an icy path through the foothills. "You are sure about this? It's mind-boggling. A blast that big could vaporize everybody in the world."

"Yeah, pretty sure," I reply. "Those first attacks on Texas and Gobi used tiny surgical ground strikes with a limited blast effect radius. They could target a projectile at Earth, launched from beyond Saturn's orbit. Powered by a black hole engine with constant thrust, it would explode on Earth with a thousand-megaton blast affecting the entire planet. I want to find Dr. Zhang, the blast effect expert we talked to earlier, to test my assumptions on projectile effects with him and ensure my extrapolations are correct."

"Well, I don't know if I can get his help," Roger says, squinting into the floodlight at the main gate into Cheyenne Mountain. "I'd bet that we are in deep shit after General Adams leaked the spacecraft pictures to the House Speaker. Let's see if we can even get in through the gate."

We roll down our windows and submit to the guards with scanners, flexing our wrists to release security credentials from our embedded ID chips. The guards study our faces, salute Colonel McMahon, and the gate swings up for us to pass. "Huh. So far, so good. I'm driving straight to our missile test lab. Captain Nguyen and Tiana will meet with us there. And"—he glances at me as we descend into the smooth-bore cave toward our lab—"I'll see if we can convince Dr. Zhang to come over to meet with you."

"What's to keep us from test firing?" asks Tiana via the videoconference link. "We can load the missile into a launch tube on one of the test-flight trucks from White Sands, and we already have the trucks loaded with the instrumentation gear."

"Our plan was to complete static tests of the thrust vector controls with a powered-up PBH engine," says Binh. "Don't you think rushing ahead with a test launch is premature?"

"It seems riskier than our ten-meter drop test back at Pecos," I say. "The acceleration during a missile launch could jerk the PBH out of containment. We should ensure the thrust vector control loop behaves and does not interfere with the disco ball containment. It could take a few experiments to fine-tune this."

Tiana says, "Yes, good points. But that's why we equip the trucks with all the telemetry and launch control instruments. We can get all this set up in a van and be ready after we complete static tests on your Cheyenne Mountain platform."

The irony that we exercise so much caution now makes me sick. If we had moved our tests to a remote location two weeks ago, a million people in Austin would not have been killed. I shake myself to get rid of the hindsight depression.

"How much time will you need to prepare the launch equipment?" asks Roger.

"I would like a few days," Tiana says, then grimaces. "But given the circumstances, we'll be ready within twenty-four hours." She takes a deep breath.

I returned from my meeting with Dr. Zhang an hour later. He seemed rattled, as if he'd been suffering through days of personal and professional attacks after his task force presentation. What political pressures is he facing? That task force was full of anger, distrust, and hate. He must be afraid of racists attacking him, or worse, with the intense anti-China sentiments right now. He was born and raised in California and got his degrees at Stanford—hell, he's about as American as a guy can be. But his eyes kept darting up like he was expecting the door to be crashed open by police with guns. At least he held it together long enough to validate the alien weapon possibilities.

"What the hell?" Binh's voice rises above the distant hum of ventilation fans. Binh and Roger are hunched over the workstation table, eyes glued to the displays.

"What time did you first sense the change in velocity?" asks Roger. Pyotr and Tiana are on the videoconference display as I walk into the room to stand behind Binh.

"VHiRISE telescope on Mars Survey Orbiter noticed change thirty minutes ago. At first, we thought it disappear, but find a thermal trail—image smear. Icarus moves with incredible acceleration!"

"Wait, wait. Icarus? What is Icarus?" asks Tiana.

"Oh. We gave spacecraft nickname Icarus. Icarus is good, no?" Pyotr smiles like a proud father.

Tiana rolls her eyes. "Have you asked the Russians to confirm the spacecraft's—or Icarus's motion?"

"Yes, yes. Our Roscosmos friends try to get velocity data. Exciting time!"

Terror comes closer to the feeling I have. "Can you estimate the current velocity and acceleration?"

"Yes, but we need more data to calculate with precision. Icarus is on a course away from sun, accelerating about one-half G toward Earth. Fantastic! We don't know Icarus mass, but alien engine could launch a battleship into space! Easy!"

"The Russians may have alerted the aliens when the Tunguska radar scanned Icarus." I feel a chill run up my spine. "At that acceleration, the spacecraft will arrive at Earth within a few days. Pyotr, are you sure Icarus is heading toward Earth and not farther away?"

"Oh, yes. Coming straight to Earth! Icarus aliens come to meet with us!"

How can he be overjoyed? I sigh. "What science fiction movies are you watching, Pyotr? Although it may be nice to hope for a *Close Encounters of the Third Kind*, happy first contact, I gave that up a while ago." But maybe the aliens will come and explain they made a mistake and would just like to be friends. Take us for a ride in their spaceship. Sure.

"Yes, yes. *Contact* was my favorite boyhood movie! They will show us the galaxy!"

Pyotr dreams like a schoolboy. I do not understand how Tiana could have married this man-child. "Pyotr, these aliens launched tungsten projectiles at Earth that yielded three-megaton explosions. They're not friendly. They've killed millions of us already. But the closer they get, those weapons will yield much less. Launched from near-Earth orbit, the yield would drop to about, uh, ten kilotons—Hiroshima-yield weapons. A few projectiles similar to one that hit Austin but launched from Neptune's orbit to strike around the globe would create a global extinction event."

"Oh, shit," Binh says.

Roger's eyes drill into me. "Is this what you discussed with Dr. Zhang?"

"Yes. I'll feel a little better if we see Icarus decelerate as they reach the halfway point toward Earth. Dr. Zhang and I agree the likely weapon for the Texas and Gobi attacks was a tungsten rod—about ten meters long and twenty centimeters in diameter. The critical ingredients were the primordial black hole engines strapped to the tails of the tungsten rods. The engine will not run out of fuel at any range within the solar system. Launching from near Neptune's orbit would increase the terminal velocity at Earth to about ten percent of light speed. Simple Newtonian physics predicts an impact yield of six hundred megatons. If they change the projectile to an iron sphere and target the East Coast, it will explode as a high-altitude airburst that would flatten and kill everything east of the Mississippi River. Instantly. With a single projectile."

Roger's frown softens, and his jaw drops. "This is why the aliens don't want us to have the technology."

Tiana's voice squeaks. "Pyotr, have you NASA guys thought about what we could do to defend ourselves against Icarus? You *are* part of the Planetary Defense Coordination office."

"Tiana, Tiana." Pyotr shakes his head. "Yes, yes. But Earth defense rockets have warheads to deflect only small asteroids. Attacking giant spacecraft will be like shooting a freight train with BB gun. Icarus will arrive at Earth in days, but we need weeks or months to prepare something bigger."

"Well, we have to do something. Launch an ICBM rocket with a thermonuclear warhead with some punch?" asks Tiana.

"I don't think there is any point," I say. "Rockets launched from Earth don't have the maneuverability. The aliens have the engine power to dodge any of Earth's missiles."

Roger adds, "Also, the escalation—attacking an enemy that could vaporize Earth? And the president is the only one who can authorize nuclear weapons, and"—Roger pounds the table with his fist—"damn it! He still wants to fight a war against China! But maybe Russia or China . . ." Roger's voice trails off.

"There is another choice," I whisper, then gain volume. "In the next room. We have a missile powered by a primordial black hole engine. We could turn the alien weapon technology against them. All we need to do is make sure it can fly. A Sidewinder with a primordial black hole engine should be able to reach any target in the solar system."

"Roger?" Tiana speaks for all of us. "Can you authorize a counterattack?"

"This one is not in the book." Roger searches all our faces. He exhales a quiet sigh. "We'll see . . . I am in charge of this weapons development project." Roger nods to himself. "Including selecting targets for the tests. Get the missile test underway—we need to make sure it works first. We have maybe three days till Icarus arrives."

"Colonel McMahon?" Like a gradual awakening from deep thought, Pyotr's voice rises. "Could Icarus aliens want to stop us? Icarus maybe watching Earth for years? If we fight back, they kill us all?"

"Could be," says Roger. "Scott and I speculated the same thing, but we already crossed their line. I must let the government make final decisions, but my job is to ensure the country has weapons to fight with. We need to move fast. Tiana, be sure you have the test range ready ASAP, and ramp up the prototype assembly line."

There is a noise of shuffling feet behind me. "Well, well, well. Here is where you are hiding."

DARPA-Teddy has entered behind us with an entourage of black-suit bros and two military guards. Teddy's tie this evening is bright yellow. Does he own only one suit?

"What trouble are you getting us into now, Colonel McMahon?" Teddy has acquired some backbone.

Roger steps toward Teddy. "What can I help you with, Teddy? We're rather busy at the moment."

Teddy bristles. "You seem always to be busy, Colonel. I thought you would learn your lesson after the arrest of General Adams." He turns to me. "And we heard about your secret meeting with Dr. Zhang earlier. You are way out of line, buddy," he snarls.

"There was nothing wrong or secret with my discussion with Dr. Zhang," I say, feeling my face heat up. "He has unique expertise in the physics of blast effects."

Roger steps in front, hovering over Teddy and the yellow necktie. "Who the hell do you think you are? While you play political games, Scott is conducting valuable research that may save your life. Turn your butt around and get out of here. Now!" Roger turns back to the video conference and Pyotr's gawking face.

Teddy glares at Roger's back. "You fucking traitor! You can't talk to me like that. You and Adams undermined the president of the United States!"

Teddy's black-suit staff glance at each other and take furtive backward half-steps. The two MPs' eyes narrow. Both have a hand on their sidearm holsters.

Pyotr's eyes fill with fear, darting from face to face. "Hey, hey, hey. Calm down, calm down—most important event in history. Aliens will arrive at Earth in days! Crazy to fight each other," Pyotr pleads with short, panicked breaths.

I gawk at Pyotr, hands rubbing my temples. I can't imagine a more absurd-sounding argument—no matter if it is true.

Binh stands, jaw clenched, like a front-row spectator at a wrestling match.

Teddy rolls his eyes while his face twists into a smirk, glaring at the video display. "Who the hell is this Russian clown? Is this who fed you the 'alien invasion' bullshit? Half the country is running scared from this idiotic propaganda while China has murdered millions of Americans. You're traitors and tied the president's hands by leaking fake information to political opponents. All of it is a hoax."

"Pyotr is with JPL NASA, Director Russell," shouts Tiana. "He knows what he's talking about. He's an expert scientist!"

Teddy shakes his head and waves his hand like he's brushing away flies. "That's enough. You guys are all crazy. Colonel McMahon, you are under arrest along with General Adams. And"—Teddy narrows his eyes on me—"you're under arrest too, Scott Anderson. This treason will stop!" he spits his words like bullets.

"But, but . . ." I sputter but can't form a coherent sentence.

Roger growls at Teddy, "You pompous ass. You don't have the authority, and you don't dare touch Scott Anderson. He's a brilliant physicist with overall technical responsibility for our research." Roger takes a step, tilting his face down over Teddy.

Teddy flinches but blurts, "Oh—oh yes, I do." He turns to the two MPs waiting behind him. "Per your orders from the Joint Chiefs, place Colonel McMahon under arrest. And Scott Anderson too. I'm terminating this project," Teddy proclaims with bravado, though sweat drips from his forehead with each labored breath.

Roger stops his advance on Teddy. "Sir," the first MP says, glancing at his partner, "we do have orders to take you into custody and escort you to the base security office, Colonel McMahon. Sorry, sir."

Teddy swaggers like a rooster.

"But, Director Russell," says the second MP, "we don't have orders to arrest any civilians."

I feel lightheaded.

Roger stands, takes a deep breath, nods calmly at me, bends toward Binh, whispers something, and slips something into Binh's hand. Binh's eyes snap to me, and then he nods quickly at Roger.

Roger steps toward the MPs. "Okay, Sergeant, let's go to your security office." He glances at Binh and says, "Captain Nguyen, wind things down here?"

"Yes, sir, Colonel. I'll take care of everything," answers Binh, standing at attention.

Binh never stands at attention.

Roger leads the MPs out the door of the building, and DARPA-Teddy follows, bouncing like a rookie cop with his first arrest. The three black-suit bureaucrats-in-training follow Teddy, exchanging cocky glances as they go.

All the air leaves the room with Roger.

"Binh, what now?" Tiana asks.

Binh faces Tiana and Pyotr, who are both gawking at us from the interrupted videoconference. "Let's terminate the call, and we'll contact you later. Tiana, we need a backup snapshot of all our files in the Cheyenne Mountain project computers. Immediately."

Tiana looks confused for a moment, then brightens with a determined calm. "Got it, Binh. Talk to you later." She clicks off the video call, and the display goes blank.

"What the hell are we going to do, Binh?"

He pulls out his cell phone and scrolls through apps like he has time to kill.

"We can't afford to waste time! That spacecraft is only"—I glance at my watch—"it's only thirty or forty hours away. We have no defense against them. Each second counts!"

Binh stays focused on his cell phone, tapping his fingers on a keyboard. He exhales in relief. "Okay. Let's get some coffee." Binh strolls toward the break room kitchen area.

"What!" I scream at Binh.

He smiles and chuckles. "Calm down. Everything is under control. This clusterfuck is not Colonel McMahon's first."

I am getting a headache.

"The colonel directed us to work with Tiana's Skunk Works team. Do you like your coffee black? Our transportation will arrive in about thirty minutes."

I feel a smile forming and reply, "I'll take my coffee black. You bastard. You were just messing with me?"

He looks sideways at me while pouring our coffees and shrugs. "Welcome to the air force. I would have resigned ten years ago if it weren't for Colonel McMahon. However, this is the most extreme bullshit I have seen in those ten years. Anyway, I doubt we'll be ready with the missile when the spacecraft arrives, and we need a place to lie low and see their intentions. Maybe we'll have time to figure out how to stop them, not just piss them off."

I sip the hot coffee. "Won't it take hours to reach Tiana in California? Why don't we just go straight to the White Sands test range, where Tiana will run the test? It's a lot closer."

Binh frowns. "Why would we go to California? Boy, you are confused. I have arranged transportation to our base at Dream Land, only a few hours away in Nevada. Tiana has her Skunk Works test center and a missile test range near Dream Land. Drink your coffee. You may want the caffeine to prepare for our evening."

"Damnit, shouldn't we leave now?" I ask.

"No, we need to time our exit with care. Our aircraft will meet us in twenty-five minutes. Driving to the side exit gate will take twelve minutes, and I don't expect security to want us to leave. We need to be alert."

"You expect us to escape from the country's most secure military base?"

"Nah. It's not the most secure. And security is focused on keeping people *outside* the gate, not inside."

"Okay," I sigh. "Just tell me what you need me to do. You sure we'll make it out?"

Binh drains his cup and shrugs. "We have a decent chance. Just stay close. Ready? We should go to the colonel's car."

I follow him out the door past the wall of blinking green indicators from the shelves stacked with primordial black holes in containment vessels. My nerves are a wreck. "We need a few PBH containment vessels for our disco ball rocket engines. Without a fuel supply, our missile development work will stop."

Binh smiles and says, "Worry about that later. Maybe Tiana can come up with something."

Damn it, Binh.

We divert from the main tunnel and drive down a narrow road, forking past the massive blast door at the main gate. It appears like we are going deeper into the mountain. I wonder if Binh is lost, but he steers Roger's Tesla confidently, moving at only ten miles per hour. I keep my mouth shut.

Binh casts his messaging app on the center car display while he drives, clearly waiting on someone. A short message—*"sixty seconds out"*—pops onto the screen. "That's it," Binh says before accelerating down the cave toward a distant red light and two security guards in a kiosk.

The nearest guard sits up to attention and leans out his window, flooding our car with a spotlight. "Sir." He salutes. "Can I see your ID?"

Binh reaches out to flex his wrist to release his ID chip credentials while dangling an unlit cigarette from his lips. "Here you go, Airman. Thought we would head out and enjoy the view from the south entrance tonight. Damn no-smoking rules will kill me sooner than the smoke." Binh smirks, grasping the cigarette. He inspects his fingernails and glances up at the guard. "Yeah, bad habit."

"Sir, everything is in order," says the guard as he toggles a switch on his desk. "We don't get much traffic out this way—not this time of night." He salutes as the steel gate rolls to the side of the road, and his telephone rings. "Yes, sir," he answers the phone, and his eyebrows arch.

Binh launches the car through the open gate.

"Sir, sir, stop! There seems to be a problem!" the guard shouts.

I sink into my seat as we speed toward a black gap in the cave and emerge under the brilliant swirl of the Milky Way against a jet-black sky. Binh turns through a tight left hairpin, throwing me against the passenger door, and we fishtail down a narrow road. The guards are close behind in a sedan with flashing red and blue lights. Binh floors the Tesla accelerator, and I sink deeper into my seat. We drive into darkness lit only by our headlights. The security car disappears behind us.

The mountain rises sharply to our left, and the slope on the right—with no guardrail—falls into a deep ravine. Like a pack of Harley-Davidsons, a sudden roar covers us from overhead, buffeting the hood with a thumping rattle. The flying machine's V-shaped tail appears—just like the V-280 Valor aircraft that dropped from the sky in San Angelo.

I grin at Binh as we coast to a stop underneath the huge rotors chopping the air. The Valor settles down on the road twenty meters ahead. I laugh out loud. "You son of a bitch! Why didn't you tell me?"

Binh shrugs like it's an average day in the air force. "Let's go," he yells as he jumps out of the driver's side and jogs to the open side door of the aircraft. Chief Cooper is ready at the aircraft door, one foot on the ground as he reaches with his arm to haul us inside. I am pushed into a seat and strapped into a harness just as the door slides shut, and we lift off with a thundering chop of air. As we climb, we spin around to the south, and I can see the security car's flashing lights as it stops behind Roger's Tesla. The two guards jump out, faces tilted as we rise into the night sky.

"Captain Nguyen, Mr. Anderson, welcome aboard," the chief shouts above the roar of the engines, the giant propellers rotating into the forward flight position as we accelerate through a gap in the mountains and the lights of the city fade behind us.

"Thanks for the ride once again, Chief." I feel the grin on my face as I burst out with laughter. "Once again, your timing is perfect. You guys know how to travel." I shake my head at Binh, who has made himself comfortable with a blanket pulled up to his chin, his head tilted to the headrest and eyelids heavy.

"Get some sleep while you can," Binh yells. "Two-and-a-half hours to Dream Land, then back to work." He closes his eyes, snuggling his head in the blanket.

Who could sleep with all this noise? And why did he make me drink that coffee? But the chief is also wrapped in a blanket and nodding at me with his broken-tooth linebacker grin. Three other airmen are covered in blankets; two have their eyes closed, and the third guy reads his Kindle. My adrenaline fades fast. I can't see anything but darkness through the windows. Sighing, I unfold my blanket and cover myself from head to toe.

"Quite a sight out the window," Chief Cooper says, shaking my shoulder.

"Huh?" My eyes flutter open from a deep sleep. My watch shows two thirty in the morning. How did I sleep in this roar? I glance out the window and see it. As our aircraft banks and turns over a valley, I catch my breath and press my face to the acrylic. The valley is illuminated in ghostly blue-white light. A two-dimensional grid pulses with corona light glowing above a flat white surface. I wipe away the fog on the window and resume breathing.

I glare at Binh, who studies my reaction. "A grid? You built another grid in Nevada?"

Binh replies with a shrug.

The familiar pulsing intensity of the blue-white corona light floats above a plain—a salt flat. The grid intensity follows the same modulation pattern I designed to coax primordial black holes into captivity. This grid is bigger than the one we built in Pecos. It is ten squares by eight, making it about eight hundred acres if they used the same spacing we used in Texas.

Our aircraft circles to the west of the corona-glow fabric. The rotors rotate vertically to slow our descent toward a cluster of buildings and to faint yellow lights that outline a runway. My eyes remain fixed on the grid as we drop. I can see the outline of grid towers and C-W voltage multiplier stacks, identical in design to the fifty-megavolt generators we left behind at Pecos. Waves of depression return. Danny was killed in Pecos by that second alien projectile strike. The blue-white corona lights pulse in a somber memorial to my friends. We sink to the ground, gradually coast forward, and bump to a stop. The corona modulation stops, and the intensity is fixed.

A brilliant ball of light pops into sight near the center of the grid, illuminating the mountain range we flew over. The primordial black hole drifts to the west—steered with my 3-D grid voltage modulation scheme toward a containment vessel that I am sure sits waiting below on the salt flats.

Chapter 32

THE OTHER

I pause on the apron between the Valor and a hangar containing an odd assortment of aircraft—some models I have never seen before and others with awkward instruments attached to slick airframes. The sky is black with a brilliant swirl of stars and a half-moon. I am all alone, gawking at this weird air force base, the glow of the dry lake bed grid system, and the drift of a primordial black hole illuminated by its blue-white plasma.

Tiana startles me from my trance. "Welcome to Skunk Works, Scott."

"Tiana," I say, turning to her before returning to watching the black hole capture in progress, "you have been keeping secrets." The corona intensity drops as the grid voltage lowers the PBH to ground level. The grid snaps off, extinguishing the glow in the towers, and the PBH plasma ball is alone on the salt flats floor. The grid tower's shadows are radial spokes around the point of light illuminating the surrounding mountain ranges. The plasma light then extinguishes, leaving Tiana and me in darkness. The stars and moon above show us the way into the hangar.

"The air force pays me to keep secrets," Tiana says, smiling and guiding me toward the nearby hangar.

I shake my head, turning to her. "I had no idea. I thought the only grid in the Western Hemisphere was the one we had near the Pecos River in Texas. How long ago did you start construction?" Blue corona lights again span the grid over the dry lake bed. I stop and ask, "And what is this? Switching the grid back on before collecting the containment vessel?"

"Yeah, wait till you see our new containment system. We began building this grid two months ago after you successfully captured the first primordial black hole. We wanted a secure backup to the Pecos grid."

There is a weight of sadness in her voice. Danny, Anthony, and all the tech staff are gone. Their bodies vaporized. Tiana's eyes meet mine to acknowledge the sorrow and loneliness. I clear my throat. "You built this entire grid in just two months? It's larger than the one in Pecos, which took five years to build."

"It's over eight hundred acres and took about six weeks to build." She shrugs. "The resources and the team here at Dream Land are vast; it's a massive machine of men and teamwork and unlimited cash to spend." She pulls my shoulder toward the hangar. "Come on, let me show you around the facility. The command center is under that hill, where we store captured PBHs." She points to a car. "I'll drive you over."

We drive toward the hill west of the airfield past rows of unmarked buildings. The scene is illuminated by the faint blue corona light. "We were lucky we chose to store PBHs underground. I worry ET can detect aboveground PBHs."

"Don't you think that's why they attacked Pecos and maybe the Gobi site?" I ask as she drives to a doorway constructed into the side of a hill. "The aliens probably have sensors that detect the radiation signature from a primordial black hole in containment."

"Perhaps, yes," Tiana says, getting out of the car and leading me inside. "The PBHs we capture over Groom Lake, the dry lake bed here, are funneled into our underground storage bunker through electrostatic ducts from each of the eight containment vessels on the grid system floor. We have automated the process. We harvest and bank about six primordial black holes each night. We ensure we operate only when Icarus can't see us from space."

Tiana leads me down a tunnel hallway and into an expansive room. Ten-meter ceilings, dozens of workstations on tables, seated engineers and technicians, the far wall covered with video displays monitoring the Groom Lake grid—it's a machine of organization humming with the murmur of ventilation fans and quiet conversations. I halt. There are bold letters pasted on the wall above the video displays: *"Anthony Agosti Center for Dark Matter Research."*

I hold back tears and whisper to her, "Thanks for remembering him."

She tilts her head toward the room, silence expanding through the crowd of scientists and engineers. Faces turn toward us. One by one, they stand and walk over to Tiana and me until thirty or more people surround us. Someone starts clapping, followed by the others, until everyone has joined in the applause. They are smiling, watching me.

I feel guilty. They should stop. If anything, they should be blaming me for this mess.

Tiana beams, pride in her eyes. "Your reputation precedes you," she says above the noise while the clapping trails off. "Thanks for the welcome, team. I would like all of you to meet Scott Anderson, who has just arrived from Colorado." Tiana adds quietly, "We have all followed your work in Austin and Pecos, and we have replicated the Pecos center gear with a few enhancements. We would like to share the details of our operation with you."

Each team member is introduced and anxious to describe their scientific and academic background. Their credentials are intimidating. Tiana has a team of some of the best minds in the country. She was modest when recruiting me two weeks ago—before the disasters. I chuckle softly when a minor dispute arises over who will take me next for a show-and-tell of their work.

The sun burns through the crystal-blue sky onto white gypsum sand. Sunglasses defend me from snow blindness. Binh sits in the shaded sand, wrapping duct tape around a bundle of fiber-optic cables that lead to sensors in the launch tube containing our first Sidewinder with a PBH engine. I peel off my down jacket and roll up my sleeves as the temperature soars. Tiana barks orders efficiently, her staff processes the instructions confidently, and there is no follow-up micromanagement. This prompt, unrushed, and effective execution has enabled us to ready the first missile test launch in less than eighteen hours. They waited till afternoon to wake me to drive to the test range.

"Scott, can you come inside?" Tiana calls from inside the van. "We are about to kick off the diagnostics test for all the instrumentation telemetry."

"Sure, on the way." I step up through a door into air conditioning that cools people and the racks of computers and networking equipment. The control console arrangement mirrors our setup at the Austin rail gun test range and inside Cheyenne Mountain. I take my usual seat at the center console and call up the test sequence on the workstation display. "I have the diagnostics up and ready. Let me know when the physical connection checks are complete."

Tiana has a tight-lipped smirk, standing beside a nervous engineer I met last night. The engineer fidgets, shifting her weight from foot to foot.

"Oh!" I feel my face flush. "Sorry. This is your job, not mine. I'll get out of your way." I lost her name among all the other introductions last night. Dressed in blue coveralls like all the other staff, she gives me a relieved nod and slides into the chair. These people have been working to prepare this Sidewinder test nonstop for the past eighteen hours. She earned this slot at the console, although I feel awkward stuck against a wall like a useless fixture attached to the trailer's aluminum ribs. But these people are brilliant and have a hell of a lot more experience than me. I also know nothing about the operation of the old Multi-Mission Launcher systems.

"Scott, what do you think of the sensors we have around the containment in the engine nozzle?" Tiana seems to be reading my mind. On cue, another engineer opens a schematic of the accelerometer placements in the disco ball vessel and the rocket engine. "We need to be sure we have covered all the risks of containment loss you may be concerned about."

The disco ball vessel's two thousand accelerometers are supplemented with another forty added to the structures around the engine mounts, the thrust vector actuators, and the missile's length. "This instrumentation looks fine," I say. "We should be able to spot any internal structural motion relative to the position of the PBH. We should also get a reading from the missile guidance processor's acceleration measurement to see if it can keep up with changes in the PBH's position." Reacting to my comment, the engineer pulls up a display of the accelerations for guidance and containment computations. "Perfect." I smile at her and Tiana.

"Great, Tiana. Let's get started," says Binh. "Staff has cleared to a safe distance."

"Very well," says Tiana. "Let's lock on to the target satellite. You have the orbit parameters set?" she asks the engineer.

She answers, "Yes, Tiana. NORAD provided the orbital details on the defunct communications satellite. The satellite has some heat for the Sidewinder seeker to lock on to, but only after it reaches thirty kilometers from the target. The satellite is at an altitude of over a thousand times that range, so the Sidewinder will rely on inertial navigation for most of that distance."

"Understood, Taylor," says Tiana. "Hopefully, the lock-on-after-launch feature will find the satellite's thermal signature to guide the Sidewinder. The imager will start searching after the range has closed to within forty kilometers. This feature will be required to be effective against a spacecraft."

"Yeah, but it really stacks up the risks of something going wrong," says Taylor. "Anyway, all the diagnostics have passed. I can begin the launch sequence. Just say the word."

Binh and Tiana nod at each other.

"Go ahead, Taylor. Start the launch," says Tiana.

"Okay, here we go," says Taylor. She adjusts her chair, settles in, and takes a deep breath. "Initiating scan for resonance. Mass reading on this primordial black hole is eighty billion metric tons, and I'm picking up a response at twenty-seven megahertz. I plan a slow increase in modulation to avoid igniting a plasma ball."

"Good move," says Tiana. "We don't think a plasma ball will affect the launch tube, but let's not complicate things."

Taylor taps the modulation increase, keeping an eye on the thrust sensor reading and vessel telemetry. "The vessel temperature is seventy C, and the nozzle reads three hundred. We're producing three thousand millisieverts of radiation out of the nozzle, along with a huge cloud of steam from the exhausted hydrogen combustion. Thrust is six hundred kilonewtons, about thirty times the stock AIM-9Z motor performance." Taylor grins and shouts to be heard over the thrum-roar of the engine noise from outside the command trailer. "Reducing thrust to the agreed fifty kilonewtons to stay within airframe structural limits. The nozzle temperature is at two hundred and eighty, cooling off with the power reduction. I'm ready to release the locks on the missile at any time. Agreed?" she asks.

"Before you do, what is the status of the guidance system?" asks Binh.

"Inertial guidance system status shows tracking the target satellite coordinates, and terminal image tracking is on standby," says Taylor.

"Scott? Tiana? Any reason not to release the weapon?" Binh asks.

"Go ahead. Ready to launch," I say.

"Agreed," says Tiana. "Taylor, transition to internal guidance control and get one last check on the telemetry radio link."

Taylor says, "Check and check. All readings are nominal. Thrust steady at fifty kilonewtons, and nozzle temperature is down to two fifty Celsius."

"Okay. Launch," commands Tiana.

"Releasing missile locks," Taylor says as she taps the launch switch.

The roar of the PBH engine rises above our trailer while we watch the wall display show the Sidewinder shoot out the top of the Multi-Mission Launcher tube. A plasma ball is ignited by the sudden acceleration and wraps the tail fins in a white ball of light. It resembles a flying lollipop followed by a blue flame of hydrogen and a steam vapor trail. The camera system tracks the missile into the sky, but an abrupt change in motion sends the Sidewinder and plasma ball on separate diverging tracks. The ball of light with its PBH heart falls to the dry lakebed, blinking out of sight, while the missile coasts a hundred meters higher into the sky before stalling and cartwheeling down to the white salt flat, shattering in a cloud of shrapnel.

Taylor gasps in horror.

"That didn't go well," I say.

Binh and Tiana exchange grimaces, and then both shrug.

***

Taylor beats herself up with any possible mistake she may have committed. She reminds me of my soul-searching after an experiment went haywire at Pecos. Her face is glued to the computer screen resting in her lap, wrinkled eyes straining through her smudged reading glasses, and her brown hair hangs over her shoulders against the fiberglass patio chair.

To the east, a grey pickup truck throws a tail of white dust to the sky as it rolls down the dirt road to our missile test range. I am amazed by the Skunk Works engineering facility's wealth and efficiency, illustrated by an assembly line of fifteen missiles modified to fit the PBH rocket engine. All before we have validated this slapped-together redesign of the Sidewinder. Minutes after the first test splattered into wreckage on the dry lake bed, Tiana ordered another missile packed into a shipping crate and trucked over to us.

About an hour ago, I figured out what probably happened and hinted at what Taylor should search for. However, I can see her anxiety and frustration distracting her from the solution. I fight to keep still and shut up, but she must fix this before we fire the second missile.

"Okay, okay. Just a damn minute," Tiana yells from behind me as she steps down from the control center to our shady spot beside the trailer. She carries her iPad while dragging another plastic chair next to me. "Hey Scott, I have Pyotr on the video link." Tiana shouts to the launcher preparation team, "Binh, come here! You need to hear this." She waves her arm at Binh twice.

"Scott! I don't understand how you work with this lady. Tiana drives me crazy." Pyotr smirks and rolls his eyes. Binh trots to our circle of chairs and stands behind Tiana to see her screen. "And Captain Nguyen—two friendly faces!"

"Pyotr, just spit it out," Tiana barks. "We're all here."

"Tiana, Tiana." Pyotr shakes his smirking face. "Big news about Icarus—slowing down after halfway point. Three hundred kilometers per second! Almost thirty times Earth escape velocity. Icarus decelerates at constant one-half G and arrives at Earth in sixteen hours." Pyotr is breathless with news once again. "They travel in one day the distance Earth rockets take a month to travel!"

"That's excellent news." I exhale in relief, but Tiana and Taylor look at me like I'm crazy. "They plan to stop at Earth. It's better than heading out toward Neptune to hit us with gigaton projectiles."

Binh scoffs. "True, but you don't know what other weapons they have in their arsenal. They've shown zero friendly intent. How much time do we have, Pyotr?"

"Sixteen hours, maybe less. But Planetary Defense Office finally request president arm Hector rockets with thermonuclear warheads. The nuclear warhead deployment is top secret," says Pyotr, his voice unsteady. "Violates treaty."

Binh's eyebrows arch, and he shakes his head. "At least they're trying something. Pointless against a maneuvering spacecraft, though. They're designed to target asteroids in free fall."

"Wait, wait. What is Hector—other than a Trojan warrior?" I ask.

"Hector is my beautiful space station at Earth-Moon Lagrange L5 point. I worked ten years building Hector. It has twenty rockets for asteroid deflection mission," Pyotr blurts, beaming with pride, and then a touch of fear enters his eyes. "Uh, is top secret."

Binh raises his eyebrows. "Well, we all have clearance and a need to know." But he continues with pained distress, "We're trying to defend Earth using primitive nuclear weapons? Is this being coordinated with other countries?"

"Yes. A UN committee with USA, Russia, China, France, and India," explains Pyotr. "Politicians thinking it easy to shoot nuclear missiles at Icarus. Foolish, foolish."

"It's also like poking a tiger in the eye with a stick," says Binh. He pauses to watch his team unload the new Sidewinder from the truck. "We need to get this PBH engine working. Every other Earth weapon will be like throwing spears."

I turn to Taylor, who has a thin smile. "You figured it out?" I ask.

"Uh-huh. It was so obvious. I missed it for a while. The inertial navigation controls should be attenuated to compensate for the more powerful engine thrust. After the launch phase, the guidance jerked the missile trajectory and flexed the airframe faster than the containment control could compensate. We can adjust the maneuvering software; only need to dampen the steering control signals."

I feel happy for Taylor. She figured out the flaw and a robust solution. Confidence restored, she bends to her keyboard and opens an editor to modify the code.

It's ten hours until our visitors arrive; about nine in the morning. After the success of the second missile test, Tiana's team has been working like dogs. They have ten Sidewinders modified with PBH engines and packed into shipping crates. The dormitory adjacent to the control center has a bed of thin foam over plywood, a white cinder block walled room, an adjoining bathroom, desk, chair, Wi-Fi, and one window slotted below the ceiling. All the comforts of a jail cell once again. At least this time, I have a window. Staring at the ceiling plaster textures, I can't sleep or think of how else to help. Now that the missile design is validated, it's just a manufacturing process. How can these tiny missiles—only three meters long—hope to damage a four-thousand-meter spacecraft? It will require a lucky shot to strike a critical system on Icarus. If we could find one to target . . .

I grab my phone and dial. "Pyotr? Can you talk?"

"Crazy Chinese! Unbelievable!" yells Pyotr.

"What? What happened?"

"China launched two missiles from satellite! Toward Icarus!" Pyotr says.

"What kind of missiles? From their space station?" I ask.

"Yes, yes. We think China might have nuclear weapons based in orbit. Now we find out for sure. But aliens accelerate away from Chinese missile path." Pyotr sighs.

"No surprise there." I sigh, joining Pyotr's dismay. "So much for extending a warm welcome to Icarus. Now they know we can shoot back. With primitive weapons."

"Oh! Detonation flash!" Pyotr yells. "Five thousand kilometers behind Icarus."

"Well, we predicted that waste of ammo. But it does feel sorta good that China at least tried." I sink a bit lower in depression and fear. It is true. They can dodge Earth's most potent weapons.

But maybe not.

I shake it off. "Hey, I need your help with something else."

"For you, Scott, anything." Pyotr's voice is musical, exhaling what I guess is a cloud of cigarette smoke. He has a knack for staying flippant in the most trying circumstances. "How can I help?"

"Thanks. Could you help me get a detailed image of Icarus as it closes on Earth? Ideally from an angle not blinded by sunlight?"

"Yes, Icarus trajectory will come out from sun . . . oh, about four hours, it will be visible from space stations."

"Pyotr—this is very important—can you arrange to get one of our space telescopes to get some images of Icarus? Either the old Hubble or the Webb Telescope?"

"Yes. I request observation mission. Easy priority call. But will depend on a clear line of sight to Icarus."

"Uh . . . and can you get the image in infrared? Best would be in the five-to-twelve-micron wavelengths, which match the Sidewinder's focal plane array imager."

"I need Webb Telescope for infrared wavelength image. But maybe no problem. Webb is parked at Sun-Earth L2 Lagrange point."

"Thanks, Pyotr. Please keep me updated?"

"Sure, sure. And, oh! Oh! Big explosion in space!" yells Pyotr.

"What? Another Chinese nuclear missile?"

"No, no . . ." Pyotr sounds sad. "The China space station—gone. Blown to pieces. Second Chinese missile still flying toward sun—missed Icarus by thousand kilometers."

"Well. I guess the aliens don't like to be shot at."

Pyotr exhales. "All those Chinese astronauts. Dead. Very sad."

"A lot of people have died over the past weeks. We can't help them now. Please get those infrared pictures?"

"Yes, yes. Bye for now," Pyotr says as he drops off the call.

I sigh. At least I am trying to do something useful. I focus on my cell phone, scrolling through recent calls. Nothing from

Mom, Dad, or Margie. I have no evidence they might have survived the attack against Austin, but I can't help but hope. I tap on Mom's number. It rings and rings and rings. Hope dies with each beat. I hear Mom's voice repeat the "Not available, please leave a text message" speech I have ignored a thousand times. I go through the same motions with Dad's number and get the same result. I sniffle and rub away the moisture from my lips and cheeks. One last try with Margie's phone number. It auto-answers, "Hi! Please leave a text, and I'll call you right back!" Her voice, full of optimism, energy, and life, tortures me. I toss my phone on the floor, wiping my tears away.

Move on, Scott. They haven't responded for two weeks after the attack. They are gone. My chest is tight as I attempt deep breaths. I pick up the phone to dial another number.

"Hello? Is this Mary?"

"Uh, yes. This is Scott?" she asks.

"Yes. I'm calling to check in on Robby. I hope he hasn't been too much work. Is he awake?" I ask.

"Robby and I have been having fun today," she says. "He helped me with carpentry work, and I let him tighten a few screws. He's a good worker." Mary chuckles and sounds relaxed. "We also walked around the farm, and I showed him all my projects in the barn. He especially liked the car I plan to refurbish with Dad—he asked for labels for each part of the chassis and the engine. He loved it."

"The old Corvette up on blocks?" I ask.

"Yep, that's the one." She sighs, then is silent for a moment. "I wonder . . . when or if we will ever start that project. Dad sounded almost despondent and powerless when I talked to him earlier today. He has always been optimistic, in control, solving problems. I don't know how to help him."

"Mary, Roger absolutely did the right thing in helping to stop the China warmongers. We are now focused on the real enemy, even though it isn't an easier fight. Hell, we may have had a better chance fighting a global nuclear war."

"Yeah, but he can't do anything to help while he's stuck in jail. Fixing up the old Corvette is a forgotten hobby—pointless, really, given we all may not survive the next week. It's infuriating that Dad is locked up. He is one of the few who could help us through this."

"Oh, but he is helping more than you realize. The team Roger built in Nevada is the most amazing group of scientists and engineers. Tiana leads a team of people with incredible resources who know exactly what to do. Roger may not be here physically, but this human machine was built by your dad."

"Well, thanks for the positive thoughts. I guess I should feel better, but it's hard. Although Robby has helped take my mind off worrying. Anyway, Robby and I are trying to read a book before his bedtime. He keeps asking me something and signs 'bird,' but it doesn't make sense."

"Ha! I think I can guess. Can we switch to a video call? I would like to see him," I ask.

"Sure." Mary rests against Robby's headboard in her guest room. Robby holds a book with animal pictures, flipping pages.

"Hi, Robby!" I yell to get his attention, and he peers into Mary's iPhone. His smile grows as he recognizes my face. "How are you doing, dude?"

"Scotty, come home," Robby commands.

"I have to work, Robby. I'll see you in a day." I feel grinding anxiety. "Or, maybe two days. I have to work hard, Robby."

"Readbir-duh," Robby mumbles. "Readbir-duh."

"Oh, you want to read about the birds?" I chuckle.

"Yeah. Birduh." Robby beams.

"I thought that's what he wanted, but I don't have bird books," says Mary.

"Bir-duh," Robby says to Mary. He then makes the bird sign, saying, "Crowbir-duh." It's a Robby word.

"Crow. That's it!" I chuckle. "He likes to read his touch-and-say book about birds."

Mary shakes her head. "I'm sorry, Robby, I don't have that book."

"Oh, but I left it on the shelf near his bed the other night. It was in my backpack that Chief Cooper retrieved from San Angelo. You can continue reading if you like, Mary."

The camera jostles the image across the room as Mary stands and flips through a few books on the shelf. "Ah, here it is." She sits next to Robby in his bed and shows him the book.

Robby grins, first grabbing and examining the book and then pushing it into Mary's free hand. "Readbir-duh," he commands Mary and flips the pages to the picture of a crow, touching it to make it say, "Caw, caw. I am a crow, but some call me raven or rook. Caw, caw."

"Okay, we'll read about the birds." She smiles and reads from the page, "My feathers are black and have a purple or green sheen. A flock of crows is called a murder of crows." Mary's piercing blue eyes blink and sparkle at me for a moment. "I'm going to need both hands to keep reading to him." Robby moves his head to rest on Mary's shoulder, studying the pictures in the book.

"Sure, Mary. Thanks for letting me talk to him. And most of all, thanks for taking care of him." I blink away tears.

"Sure, no problem. I'm enjoying the time with Robby. We'll see you in a day or two." And she hangs up.

I hope that's true. I sigh and lie back on the pillow. Now I can rest.

———

Rays of light streak through the window, illuminating the dust motes dancing in air blown through the ventilation grate. A lengthening web strand lowers a tiny black spider across the glass. It waves its arms around a bug in its clutches, the rotation revealing a red hourglass shape on its belly—a black widow spider. The time—what time is it?

Panicked, I bolt upright from the bed to my feet, lightheaded from the sudden jump, and focus on my watch. Eight a.m. Why hasn't Pyotr called with an infrared image of Icarus? I pull on my shoes, throw water on my face, grab my laptop, and dash out the door across the parking lot to the underground entrance of the operations center.

The Skunk Works team sits at workstation tables under four giant video screens covering Tiana's control center's wall, and about twenty other engineers and technicians are scattered about the room at their desks. But half have their heads down, struggling with sleep. The noise of keystrokes at workstations competes with a background of snores from the sleepers. I walk to Binh's desk and drop into a spare chair. His head flops around toward me like he's stoned.

"Oh, hi, Scott," Binh slurs. He returns to an email on his workstation screen next to three empty coffee cups and four Coke cans stacked in a column, with half-eaten pizza crusts on a white paper plate between Tiana and him. Tiana has a collection of Mountain Dew cans and holds her head in her hands with her elbows on the table.

"Are you two okay? You all look exhausted." Feeling guilty about my eight hours of sleep, I scan the room again to see everyone except me in a similar state of exhaustion, with remnants of food and stimulant drinks on their desks. I twist my nose at the sour odor of festering sweat and bacteria, which I'm pretty sure is not from me.

Tiana lifts her head from her hands and glances at me. "Yeah, we're pretty burned out. But we got everything finished. We got four launcher trucks loaded with three Sidewinders each. They're all on the road to disperse." She points her chin at a map of southern Nevada on the screen, with four numbered blue squares moving along highways away from Groom Lake. "You can see them all on the roads repositioning across the Nevada test range wastelands. Taylor is in truck number four with three missiles headed south into the Tikaboo Valley."

"Spreading them out to avoid an easy attack by Icarus?" I ask.

"Yeah, and protect them if Icarus attacks Dream Land." Tiana yawns. "We have tied the trucks into our command center and NORAD via satellites and microwave backup links."

"You think Dream Land may be attacked?"

Binh shrugs. "No idea. We don't know for sure why they attacked Pecos Center. Maybe they can also detect primordial black hole harvests. Let's hope not." He points his chin toward where the grid stretches over Groom Lake.

I nod and watch the other truck icons farther out, headed in different directions to the north and west. "Tiana, do you know what target information is loaded into the Sidewinder seekers? I asked Pyotr to get us some good infrared images to work with but haven't heard back yet."

Binh grimaces. "You missed the political bullshit that went down last night. We can't contact anyone at NASA for information and status, and we have been put under the supervision of NORAD. Colonel McMahon has enough clout to keep us protected and independent at Dream Land, even while he's under arrest. However, the new crew of acting 'Joint Chiefs' have bottled us up and are preventing external communication except through NORAD. I figure this cool new Sidewinder weapon is the only reason we're not in jail with the colonel." Despondence does not suit Binh, and he sounds bitter. "A bunch of crazy political hawks are running the show out of the White House, and they're pissed we stopped their China war."

"What will they do when that alien spacecraft arrives in about an hour? Pretend it came from China?" I ask.

Binh stares at his keyboard, shaking his head. "We're out of the loop on the strategy and tactics." He points to the screens in the center of the wall. "Our best source of info is the situation map NORAD streams to us. The far-right image covers US airspace, and the other shows global force deployments. We are still at DEFCON-1 with one hell of a lot of airplanes in the sky all around Earth."

"Can you translate the information on the NORAD maps? All those symbols and shapes are Greek to me."

Binh says, "Yeah. Takes some practice. Right now, all you see is a lot of fighter squadrons on lazy patrol orbits being kept in the air by those tankers bringing them fuel. However, those missile batteries—those blue triangles across the northern plains—show immediate launch readiness. That's a first."

Binh clenches his jaw as his bloodshot eyes examine the situation displays.

"You guys could use some rest," I say.

Binh surveys the control room. Half of the team is napping. "You are right. I expect a long wait until we're called on to help. Tiana? I think we should get everyone rested while we're able."

Tiana exhales. "There must be something else we should be doing . . ." She turns in her chair and knocks two empty soda cans to the floor.

Binh's tight-lipped "I told you so" look says it all. "You just made my case. Go get some sleep, Tiana." He speaks louder, "Everyone else still awake—go get some sleep. Scott, come wake us if the excitement starts." He leads the way out the door, followed by a dozen stumbling engineers, technicians, and Tiana.

The control room is suddenly staffed only by guys who fell asleep at their desks earlier. And me. My only company is the giant situation map on the wall. Air rushing through the ventilation system, a rattling soda machine compressor, and an occasional staccato snore are the only sounds. How the hell will I know when the "excitement starts" when I don't know what these symbols mean? As if someone heard my thoughts, the global tactical display zooms out to show a broad view of Earth, the moon, and what appear to be orbits of several satellites and space stations. Blue triangles are stacked on top of a space station object labeled *"Hector"* out in lunar orbit—Pyotr's planetary defense platform orbiting at the L5 Lagrange point, armed with nuclear missiles. A curved dotted line flashes bright red and traces an elliptical orbit circling Earth. The image zooms out farther until a red triangle appears at the endpoint of the dashed red line. The red triangle, labeled

"Icarus," moves down the projected trajectory. It's a speed demon relative to the motion of all other objects in the display.

"Here it comes." A countdown timer next to the red Icarus triangle shows an hour remaining. What is the plan? Attempt communication and truce negotiations? Launch an all-out attack with the Hector missiles? Do they plan to use our PBH-powered Sidewinders? I never got the infrared image of Icarus. I imagine our tiny Sidewinders exploding harmlessly against the hull of the massive, four-kilometer-long spacecraft.

I open my laptop and the messaging app, scroll through my contacts, and send a text message: *Hi, Taylor. You there?*

I drum my fingers on the table, waiting. No response. Taylor must be connected to the military networks to respond to orders. Crap, maybe she too is sleeping. Could she even sleep while the truck bounces down a dirt road?

I open a new window and message Pyotr, but it bounces back: *"Network Route Not Found."* Is the error message due to the communication quarantine Binh described? This is ridiculous—am I cut off from everyone?

Taylor's belated reply pops up on her message window—whew!

Taylor: *Howdy Scott*

Scott: *Taylor—great to hear from you. How is your drive in the countryside?*

Taylor: *LOL. Like a drive into hell. Although the geology is beautiful. What's up?*

Scott: *I am worried about what you have for a targeting template in the Sidewinder seekers. I requested Pyotr at JPL NASA get us an infrared image of Icarus, but our networks were cut off before he could respond.*

Taylor: *I would kill for that image right now. We have nothing but a hot spot seeker capability because I don't have a target image. Over a million infrared pixels of seeker resolution but no ability to designate target features to attack. I enabled the target learning, but I expect that will only steer our missiles to the target centroid.*

Scott: *I was afraid of that. I'll still try to get a high-resolution IR image from the Webb Telescope for you. I have an idea of how I might contact Pyotr.*

Taylor: *Wow. That would be awesome.*

Scott: *I'll send it to you if I can reach Pyotr.*

Taylor: *I'll be waiting.*

I dig through my backpack, fish out my old fold-up Starlink antenna, spread it flat on my desk, plug it into my cell phone, and disable the Wi-Fi and 6G cellular links. The remaining connection is satellite service through my Starlink antenna. I dial Pyotr's number and take a deep breath.

The Starlink icon blinks yellow, searching for a satellite. Damnit, the system is still offline, even though it's been two weeks since the Texas explosions. I slump in my seat and scan the room, seeing only a few snoring engineers with faces planted into folded arms on their desks. Could the air force be jamming the commercial satellite signals over Nevada? I look at the ceiling, then smack my forehead. I'm an idiot. An idiot who is underground, under fifty meters of rock.

Grabbing my gear, I run outside under the crystal blue sky. Dropping my phased-array antenna flat on the sand, I wait for it to scan the sky for a signal. "Yes!" The Starlink icon shows three green bars. I press the call button again.

"Scott! You are there!" yells Pyotr into his phone. "Four hours, but no answer."

"Did you get the infrared images of Icarus, Pyotr? There is not much time."

"No time! Icarus is decelerating into high-Earth orbit above two hundred thousand kilometers. Extraterrestrial life team attempting Icarus communication, but no answer yet. Where are you? I tried sending images for many hours."

"Can you send me the Icarus images by attaching files to a message to my cell phone? All my other network connections are . . . not operating."

"Yes, Icarus spacecraft images are fantastic. Structure detail is complex mystery. Above USA in ten minutes. Huge!"

I gasp as an odd speck of light rises from the horizon. A speck brighter than moonlight and moving toward the east, crossing the sky as fast as an aircraft at low altitude. "Pyotr, is Icarus orbiting from west to east around Earth?"

"Uh, yes. How did you know?"

"I can see it. Rising past the moon, forty-five degrees from the horizon—in Nevada."

"I run outside to see." Pyotr is as excited as a schoolboy again.

"Wait, wait. I need you to send the image file. Send it first!" I shout.

"Oh yes, yes, yes," he gasps. "Attached and sending . . . done. I run outside now." Pyotr hangs up.

I check my messages but don't see anything yet. The speck of light disappears into the glare of the disk of sunlight. My iPhone dings, notifying me that a half-gigabyte file just arrived from Pyotr. I pivot and jog inside the underground operations center, the Starlink antenna tucked under my arm. After reenabling the phone's Wi-Fi connection, I send the image file directly to Taylor.

The Ferris wheel rotating around a ladder was a naive metaphor for the structure of Icarus. Each image of the spacecraft is stunning. The large wheel is attached to a four-kilometer spine of parallel cylinders by eight spokes that reduce to tendrils trailing alongside the spacecraft past the rocket nozzle at its tail. The main structure is assembled from cylindrical modules adorned with odd-shaped devices and hundreds of small disks—maybe radar or communication antennas? The Icarus spacecraft is not comparable to any terrestrial technology; it's a collection of objects like a junkyard of wrecked cars, except for a massive parabolic rocket nozzle cone at one end. Enormous support struts hold the engine nozzle, and a conduit bends around one of the struts into the engine nozzle vertex. Maybe they use that pipe to move primordial black hole fuel into the engine. It might be vulnerable to an exploding Sidewinder warhead.

Taylor's chat window opens:

Taylor: *I have no clue what to target on this monster.*

Scott: *Look at the engine nozzle mountings. Do you see the small tube connecting to the vertex of the engine nozzle?*

Taylor: *Between the engine mount structures? A fuel line?*

Scott: *Yep. That's my bet. Can you program the Sidewinder seeker to target that tube where it joins the main structure of Icarus? We may not blow up their engine room, but at the least we may keep fuel out of the engine.*

Taylor: *We can steer the missile into that fuel line once it closes within about ten kilometers. I'll also enable evasive maneuvering for the guidance computer. I bet some of those widgets on the side of the spacecraft are point-defense weapons.*

Scott: *Great. Can you send the templates to all the other launch trucks?*

Taylor: *Working on it. Servers at Skunk Works are compiling the target features. Will upload seeker templates to all twelve Sidewinders. Gotta go. Thanks.*

She signs off, and I bend back into my chair, staring at the NORAD wall displays. Icarus's red triangle moves across Europe and Asia at blistering speed. This can't be the freefall orbit NORAD predicted—it's at an altitude halfway to the moon, but the spacecraft must be powering itself around Earth faster than any Earth satellite orbits in freefall.

Should I wake up Tiana and Binh? It has been an hour since they hit the sack for some rest. Icarus has arrived, but nothing significant is happening. I'm just a spectator with nothing other than NORAD information screens—most of which I cannot decipher. If NORAD wants to launch our missiles, they will issue the commands straight to the teams in the launch trucks roving around the Nevada desert. Being out of the loop is torture.

I push through the door to outside again and switch my phone to use the Starlink antenna. Pyotr answers on the first ring. "Scott! You receive Icarus pictures?" he shouts.

"Yeah, just in time, I hope. Do you have any idea what all those devices on Icarus are? I had to guess an aim point by the engine nozzle," I say, gasping.

"I can guess only. JPL technology team working on hypotheses." There are intense arguments in the background noise near Pyotr.

"Any communication with the aliens yet?"

"Icarus scanning Earth with coherent microwave and laser pulses. NASA language specialists send prime numbers, but no response. Velocity slows over North America and East

Asia—then speeds up! Amazing propulsion!" Pyotr shouts into the phone.

It seems that they are slowing down to scan for targets. "What is the military doing? Are they going to attack Icarus?" I shout back.

"World militaries screaming. Panicked. All have telescope pictures. Scared. China, Russia, and India all want nuclear missile launch," Pyotr says breathlessly. "But Icarus accelerates faster than missiles!"

"Geez, Pyotr. If anyone on Earth launches an attack, it will be suicide for us!"

"US Space Force requested target solution from Hector defense platform, but is not possible when Icarus accelerates!"

My chest heaves with each breath. I scan the western horizon for the reflected light from the spacecraft. "What is the position of Icarus?" I ask Pyotr.

"Icarus approaching US Pacific Coast. Slowing over the southwest states!" Pyotr shouts.

I take a deep breath, trying to calm myself. Nevada's dry air reminds me of hikes with Dad and Robby in the high desert of New Mexico. Now, I stand alone in another desert, where the only visible signs of life are two C-27 cargo planes unloading pallets on the runway apron and construction crews erecting another row of grid towers at the far side of the lake bed. These air force guys have six construction crews laying down a new grid row every two days. It's efficiency that boggles my mind. We were pitiful amateurs at Pecos by comparison.

A glint of light appears in the western sky, moving up from the horizon before nearly pausing.

"Scott! Icarus above California. It decelerates!"

"I see it. It's almost stationary. Any guesses what it is up to?"

There is a long pause, then Pyotr responds, "Not sure. Maybe hear NASA prime number broadcast? Doing arithmetic?"

"I dunno, I expect they have decent computer technology to figure out—"

"Oh! No!" Pyotr gasps. "Objects launched from Icarus! Five objects! Toward Earth!"

No, no, no. I strain my eyes at the point of light—Icarus. My hand shields the sun's glare, but I can't see anything coming toward Earth. Of course not. They must be small projectiles compared to the massive scale of the Icarus spacecraft. "Pyotr, how fast are the projectiles? And can you tell what they're targeting?"

"Acceleration at one hundred Gs!"

"Are you sure, Pyotr? Where are they headed?"

The fleck of reflected light that is Icarus gains speed toward the east.

"Icarus accelerate away," Pyotr says. "Oh! Projectiles track toward the southwest USA. Impact in four minutes! Terminal velocity six hundred kilometers per second!"

Boom! Boom! Boom!

I dive to the ground, scraping my hands into granite pebbles. The sting of torn skin burns down my wrists. Rolling over to my back, I search the sky for Icarus. It's gone, replaced with multiple contrails arcing into the blue sky. Air force fighters!

"Scott! Scott!" Pyotr's voice yells from my phone, tossed when I dove down.

I crawl on my knees to the phone lying in the dirt. "Yeah, I'm here. Those were sonic booms from fighters!"

"What the hell?" Binh screams as he runs toward me out of the barracks. "What the fuck are you doing, Scott?"

I must look like a kid playing in the dirt. Tiana and four others stagger out the door behind Binh while the distant rumble of jet engines climbing into the stratosphere fades.

Brushing dirt from my shirt, I push to my knees, wincing from the blood on my hands. "Yeah, the sonic booms scared me," I say with a sheepish shrug. "Icarus just launched projectiles at us. I think those fighters will try some kind of defense." I point to the white vapor trails above us. "They're crazy."

Binh tilts back and shades his eyes with his hand, following the vertical jet vapor trail above us. The exhaust trails of missiles leap from the fighters toward something in space. "Those must be satellite killers." Binh shakes his head with a grim frown. "ASM-253s. Pointless."

"Scott!" Pyotr shouts from my phone. "Tracking projectiles toward south Nevada! Get under cover!"

"Pyotr reports projectiles are inbound. Toward us!" I point toward the underground command center door.

"Tiana, get your staff under cover. Now!" Binh shouts and sprints to the door.

We crash into our chairs at the desks in front of the NORAD situation displays. Binh continues to stand and analyze the symbols on the screens. The red triangle marking the location of Icarus speeds across the Atlantic Ocean toward Europe. Five red circles with crosshairs are on the North American display around Southern Nevada. The circles shrink, and the map zooms closer with each passing second.

"They're targeting our trucks and the Papoose Lake missile test range," Binh says with a matter-of-fact, dead calm. Four red circles are centered on the blue symbols representing our

Sidewinder launch truck locations. "How the hell are they sensing the truck coordinates?"

"My God!" whispers Tiana as she attacks her computer to relay a message to the trucks. She stands up and cries, "Move! Move! Move!" urging the blue squares away from the shrinking red circles.

"Tiana!" Binh shouts. "Can they target the incoming projectiles with their Sidewinders?"

Tiana's jaw drops, eyes wide. She bends over her computer to type another message. "Come on, Taylor. Come on!" She drums the desk, waiting. "What! Those fucking idiots!" she screams. "NORAD has the truck launch controls locked!"

Binh's face goes pale, shaking his head. "Those red circles outline the circular error probability of impact. But the blast radius will be much larger than that CEP, especially for these projectiles."

The helpless engineers and scientists glance at each other with round, frightened eyes. The blue squares marking the trucks plod away from the red crosshairs at an agonizing pace. Way too slow. The CEP circles shrink as the projectiles close in, and Taylor's truck number four crosses the CEP circumference. A scattered, nervous cheer rises, though all eyes remain glued to the NORAD situation display.

"Binh, Tiana, if those projectiles are similar to the Texas ones, I estimate this velocity will yield kinetic energy explosions about ten times a Hiroshima-sized explosion—around two hundred kilotons. All truck launchers remain inside that blast radius."

Crosshair CEP circles jump in front of the truck paths at that moment. A collective gasp ripples through the control center.

"They're guided missiles?" Cries Tiana, standing up and leaning toward the wall display. "Taylor! No!" she wails, tears streaming down her cheeks. "No!"

Binh shouts, "More projectiles over Asia!" Three red dots, CEP circles, and crosshairs appear along the North China coast. The red Icarus triangle moves into the Central Pacific.

The NORAD display predicts forty seconds until the Nevada impacts. The closest projectile will strike about ten kilometers southwest on the other side of the Papoose Mountains—at the exact spot of our missile test range. We should be okay at this distance. I pivot and run toward the exit.

Out the door, the sunlight blinds me for a few seconds. The mournful wail of an air-raid siren disturbs the soft swish of wind. I search the southeast horizon, where I imagine Taylor's launch truck bounces down a dirt road in a futile, crazy race to escape. I hear my breathing and the soft pounding of my pulse. I can just trace the outline of snowcapped peaks on the far side of the Tikaboo Valley through the haze.

A flash of orange-white light erupts beyond the mountain, drawing a six-hundred-kilometer-per-second line of fire from space to behind the ridge, followed by the bloom of a brilliant fireball. My eyes flinch to the right as my cheek feels the heat from another fireball rising ten kilometers away over Papoose Lake. Turning west, squinting at orange incandescence beyond the Papoose range, three more suns erupt to the distant west and north. I gasp even though I have seen this before in Texas. Five projectiles at once are overwhelming. I stagger when the ground shakes. The sky is fire. The vast desert, rocky canyons, distant mountains, and blue sky recede into darkness, overtaken by black-hole-powered raw kinetic energy slammed into granite rock. I retreat from my senses, visualizing the millisecond of terror that vaporized Taylor and the crews of four trucks loaded with impotent primordial black hole missiles.

They foolishly welcomed my arrival at Dream Land. But I bring death.

The fireballs on the horizon shrink inward, and the fallout clouds billow under the five glowing contrails piercing the stratosphere. I stand alone in Nightmare Land.

More death. I search for Icarus, circling Earth, surveying the holocaust. The aliens must die. Every one of them.

My bones are jarred like I have been thrown headfirst onto concrete, and I'm deafened by the concussion waves. I cover my ears with my hands and buckle to the ground in a fetal position, but I cannot escape the roar. I roll over and see the clouds of dirt expanding to blot out the sky.

"What the hell are you doing out here!" Binh screams at me while running from the command center bunker. "Are you crazy?"

"Yeah." I sit up, coughing dirt and regaining my bearings. "The blasts won't hurt us here." I brush dust off my shirt and pants but find a streak of blood when I wipe my face. "Not much anyway." The rest of my limbs seem to be intact.

"Damn it!" yells Binh. "We can't afford to lose you! ET can spot our missiles from space. We need a new plan!"

"Yes, they can," I say while watching towering columns of dust climb into the sky around Groom Lake. "Icarus has a radiation detector that found every one of our primordial black hole engines or where we tested one. They targeted everywhere we had black holes in containment: Austin, Pecos, and the five locations in Nevada."

Binh points to where we've stored all the PBHs captured at Groom Lake. "And the black holes in storage . . ."

"They can't see the PBHs stored underground, neither here nor under Cheyenne Mountain. Nor can they detect our underground tests. The radiation signature is blocked." I cough and hack on fallout particles blowing in thick from the southwest.

"Come with me," Binh says, rubbing the dust from his nose. "Let's get inside the control center. We have work to do with Tiana."

"Okay," I reply. "Do we have any more modified Sidewinders we could launch from a fast-moving aircraft?"

Binh raises his eyebrows. "Let's move." He turns and trots to the door of our underground control center.

Chapter 33

REVENGE

The inboard pylon station below the cowling around the air intake worries me. I push a plastic mop bucket aside to get a better view under the old F-15EX fighter, revealing fluid dripping onto the grey floor of the hangar. I shove the bucket back and ask Tiana, "Won't our new Sidewinder just tear this pylon off when we power up the rocket motor?"

She crawls down under the wing. "Yeah. We need a beefed-up hardpoint to replace this inboard station and integrate it into the engine mount structure. We have mechanical engineers and milling machines working around the clock to make what we need. The PBH motor's starting thrust is the same as the F-15's jet engine at full thrust. Two of our Sidewinders, powered up while in target-acquisition mode, will have the same effect as kicking on full afterburners on these old engines." Tiana snorts, patting the cowling over the left turbine.

"It sounds like we need to be careful not to rip apart the airframe. Why are we using this seventy-year-old airplane? Don't you have something newer that's less fragile?"

She shakes her head. "Not with two seats. We need the back seat for the weapon-systems engineer to monitor and control the test." Tiana shrugs, glancing up at Binh, who works in the cockpit. "These old airplanes are also reliable workhorses that allow us to mount development weapons on the external hardpoints. The newer stealth aircraft tuck missiles inside the fuselage to suppress radar reflections, but it's impossible to attach odd-shaped weapon experiments to them."

"Good to see you three are plotting something wicked."

I turn toward the familiar voice. "Roger! Great to see you!" I stand and reach out a hand. "You missed our"—I stop myself from using the word *fun*—"our disaster yesterday."

Roger's face is grim. "We lost a lot of good people yesterday." He purses his lips. "But you made good progress with the PBH rocket motor system." He walks over to the aircraft. "I think this old girl may do the job for us." He runs his hand along the fuselage below the cockpit like caressing a faithful hound. "Back in my younger days, I logged over a thousand hours in the F-15C version."

He turns to Tiana and asks, "When will you be ready for a test flight?"

Tiana's haggard eyes are ringed in darkness. There is no joy in her voice. "The engineers designed new hardpoint pylons for the PBH Sidewinders. We plan to integrate these into the airframe next, and the system diagnostic tests should take a few hours. Then, we need to sneak the two missiles from the underground assembly line and mount them on the hard points while Icarus is on the other side of Earth. We don't want to attract the aliens' attention before we get the F-15 in the air." She glances at the ceiling as though she can see Icarus watching.

"What happened to DARPA-Teddy and all the China war hawks?" I ask Roger.

"Don't be concerned about him or any of the hawks. The alien arrival and yesterday's attacks have been effective attitude adjustments. Air force leadership has been redirected by the restructured Joint Chiefs. The good guys are back. The naysayers and the hacks have been purged, and POTUS is disgraced for pushing a war-on-China agenda. As an added benefit, General Adams and I were released from confinement, and we have good international collaboration now." Roger tells Tiana, "Your ex, Pyotr, has been instrumental in bringing together the international scientific communities in Europe, Russia, India, and China. We all owe him."

Tiana blushes, avoiding eye contact. She wipes away tears and glances at Roger. "Is our communications quarantine lifted?" Her voice is a contrite whisper. She checks her cell phone for a signal and presses the call button. "We should call him."

"Tiana! Tiana! You all okay?" Pyotr cries. "I worried about those Nevada strikes."

"Petya, I'm okay, Petya." Tiana's tears flow. "Scott, Binh, and Roger are also here with me on speaker. But we lost some of my best people yesterday," she says haltingly.

Pyotr replies softly, "Tiana, I am sorry. But glad you are safe."

"Thanks, Petya." She sniffles and wipes her cheeks, lowering her face to the phone.

"You have more black hole missiles ready? Big attack on Icarus soon."

"We have a few missiles but nothing from which to launch them yet. Our truck launchers and crews were easy targets for Icarus, but we are working on something else that can maneuver faster." Tiana looks at the old F-15 aircraft, her eyes ringed black with desperation.

"Pyotr, this is Roger. What time do you expect an Earth counterattack?" asks Roger.

"Taking orders from NORAD now. Not sure. They want Hector missiles ready in one hour. Many countries helping. Everyone is scared." Pyotr's boyish humor is gone.

"Guys, let's head to the command center to tie into NORAD planning and prepare to help if needed," says Roger.

Tiana glances from Roger to the F-15.

Roger nods to her and says, "Yes, you should stay here and supervise the aircraft integration effort. We can coordinate the move of your PBH Sidewinders here while the enemy is on the far side of Earth." He looks up at the hangar ceiling. "This will be like dodging Soviet satellite cameras in the early days."

***

"It's as big as the moon!" exclaims Binh.

Roger, Binh, and I stand astonished by the object crossing the southern horizon. The sunlight glints from features along its length, which is longer than the moon's diameter. It's skimming just above the Earth's atmosphere. I can trace the circle of reflections from the center spine wheel structures and detect the trail of tentacles dragging behind the spacecraft's tail—all with my naked eye.

"The size! It's a monster!" Seeing it with my own eyes, objectivity is displaced by fear. What will typical humans think? Terror? Panic? Billions of people are seeing this firsthand.

A cold wind blows against our backs, sending a shiver through me. We watch as the spacecraft dissolves from view into the haze above the southeastern purple mountains. It crossed the sky in just a couple of minutes. "I want to see the orbit plotted on the NORAD display," I call out while I jog to the door of our control center.

The red triangle drifts through a freefall orbit across the giant wall display of the NORAD global map. An unpowered freefall orbit. It's an odd Icarus behavior compared to its previous urgent thrusting around Earth to scan and attack our captured primordial black holes—the ones they could find. I hope they can't detect the vaults under the hill at Groom Lake and Cheyenne Mountain, now that they are flying so much lower. Icarus is now following an elliptical orbit that brings it close to our low-orbit space stations. The apogee extends forty thousand kilometers beyond typical geosynchronous communication satellites.

"Roger, do you have any idea what they're up to? It's like they're waiting for something. The orbit brings them down to only four hundred kilometers—they were five hundred times higher in space during those last attacks. We may be unable to hide from them at this close range."

"Can't say I have much experience with alien visits," says Roger, shrugging. "But I bet they want us to expose any leftover black holes—or watch us try to capture more PBHs. On the other hand, they may have been watching us for hundreds of years. After we found their spaceship, why hide when they can hang out in low orbit for the next hundred years or more? They could just open fire to discipline the humans if we get out of line." He wrings his hands. "But I am just guessing."

Roger rocks back on his heels, paying attention to the details on the NORAD displays. Binh approaches from the side, also focusing on the NORAD information. A clattering of chairs and murmurs among the dozen engineers rises with tension across the control room.

"Something is up," says Binh.

"Yes. Several of our ICBMs' launch readiness has moved to the countdown phase," Roger says. "And the same for the missiles on the Hector Space Station."

Binh reaches for his laptop to initiate a video call, which he pops up on a screen to the side of the NORAD tactical displays. "I'm contacting Pyotr at JPL."

Pyotr's haggard face comes on screen. "Scott, Binh! Good seeing you again. Oh, and Colonel McMahon. You notice NORAD excitement?" Pyotr perks up with playful energy.

"Yes, yes," says Roger. "We see you have begun the launch sequence from Hector. Can you brief us on the plan of action?"

"Oh boy! Whole world is together. Russia, USA, China, and India will launch nuclear missiles. Hector launch in two minutes! All twelve missiles!" Pyotr is hyperventilating as he speaks.

Roger rolls his eyes, his lips drawn together in a tight line. "Pyotr. Slow down. Please provide details of the Earth's attack tactics. Who, what, when, where."

"Yes, yes, Colonel McMahon. NASA's Planetary Defense team determine Icarus orbit perigee drops below four hundred kilometers. ICBMs from Earth can reach this altitude! All militaries coordinate to intercept over Pacific Ocean. Hector missiles will reach the target in ten hours. Earth-based ICBMs launch in nine-point-five hours. Over one hundred warheads from all directions while Hector missiles attack from above Icarus. Like shotguns killing a goose!"

China is speaking with NASA. Wow, progress. The red triangle representing Icarus is now cruising over the Gulf of Mexico, passing Cuba and heading east at a hundred kilometers per second. "Hector will launch while Icarus is screened by the Earth?" I ask.

"Yes! Hector missile boost phase completes before Icarus comes around Earth. Then follow ballistic track and coast for nine hours until intercept."

"Sheesh. It will be a tricky ambush with Icarus zipping over Earth at nearly"—I pause to run through the calculation—"three hundred times the speed of sound. This will have to be a perfectly timed shot." The speed of the missiles will be a snail's pace compared to Icarus.

"Yes, yes. Missiles target Icarus flight path. Like a flak cloud."

"It will only work if Icarus does not see the missiles closing in front of them," I press Pyotr. "You realize all Icarus needs to do is start their engines, and they can scoot away from your nuclear ICBM flak?"

Pyotr gapes back at me, eyes round with fear. "There is hope. Surprise nuclear detonations will surround Icarus. Fifty-megaton explosions—like a giant sun!" He sounds like a kid playing with fireworks.

"The military must recognize the risks?" I say, searching Roger's face but only seeing grim determination. "If we miss Icarus, who knows what attacks they will unleash?"

"You, of all people, should want to kill these bastards," Roger says, boiling with anger. "We have both lost friends and people we love, all murdered by these monsters." His words are measured. "Every battle has risks. We need to do everything possible to provide support by getting our new Sidewinders operational."

"And we have about nine hours," Binh says. "We'll need some test flights before we have confidence the aircraft systems can launch our new missile."

"Yeah, but we have nuclear weapons attacking Icarus. What good will our tiny little Sidewinder do? Oh!" I gasp. "Wow! If we could get a shot in early . . . Roger! The seekers are programmed to target the fuel line on the Icarus main engine. If, by some miracle, we could disable their propulsion before they spot our nuclear ICBMs, they would be sitting ducks!"

Roger's jaw drops.

"Scott! You're my favorite genius!" shouts Pyotr.

"Of course, the odds we can pull it off are . . . low," I mumble. "What the hell. I'm going to run over and help Tiana with the integration. Who will fly the F-15? I need to train whoever will monitor and tune the PBH engines."

Roger purses his lips and nods at Binh.

"You are looking at the pilot," says Binh. "This airplane has been my primary assignment at Dream Land: advanced weapon test flights in that same F-15EX Tiana is prepping." He clears his throat, shifting his weight. "However, all our weapon systems engineers were killed in the launch trucks yesterday."

Binh's reminder silences the room. Less than twenty-four hours ago, Taylor and her team were killed.

I close my eyes but can't bear to think about the deaths. "Well, who . . . ?" Everyone is looking at me.

"I need you riding back seat as the weapon systems officer," says Binh.

"What?" I gasp. "I don't know shit about the systems in an F-15!"

"You know more than anybody else about PBH containment and rocket design," Binh says. "Other than our new PBH engine, AIM-9Z Sidewinders have been proven during the past two years of test flights. We can work with Tiana to get you up to speed on the cockpit layout and be sure you have all the information and controls you need."

I need to sit down. Reaching around to clear a space of discarded coffee cups and ethernet cables, I park my butt on the table behind me. Going for a ride in the cockpit of an F-15 fighter should be thrilling—the ultimate thrill ride through the clouds. Memories flash through my mind of winding roads in Westlake Hills, strapped into the driver's seat of Dad's old Porsche, stomping the throttle and tapping paddle shifters to maximize acceleration. Those joyrides were nothing compared to what an F-15 can do.

"I'm going to wear one of those G-suits and get an orientation on riding in a fighter cockpit?"

Binh says, "Yeah. I'll even show you where to puke and what switches not to touch—unless you don't like the ride and want to eject." He holds a deadpan expression for two beats, then smiles.

It may be a jet fighter, but this cockpit smells like my high school gym locker. The high-resolution touchscreen display and keyboard pads at the sides of the back seat dominate my field of view. I can see through the plastic canopy either straight up, left, or right, but there will be no way for me to see ahead. I am just cargo. I can't even bend down to see under my seat. And the stink—where are those month-old sweaty gym socks?

I slew the infrared camera to the left to follow an airman walking across the far end of the underground hangar. His exposed face and hands are bright white in the IR image. The joystick's strain-gauge button is a bitch to get used to, but I'm beginning to get the hang of it. Slewing the square symbol and the infrared imager in the pod on the F-15's belly, I can at least follow the guy's walking motion without jerking the aim point off target much. With my hand wrapped around the joystick, I tap the auto-track button, and the symbol switches to corner brackets that collapse around the guy's face. The tracker is locked on and follows the airman through his tasks back and forth across the hangar. Acquiring and tracking the Icarus spacecraft won't be this easy.

". . . you know, Binh, you're taking one hell of a risk with Scott. Don't dare fuck this up and lose him." Tiana and Binh are kneeling and inspecting the reinforced pylon installed for our PBH Sidewinder. She forgot about me hiding in the F-15's back seat to practice with the FLIR image-tracking system. Although the unintentional compliment comforts me, my guts also twist in fear.

The worn ejection handles below the keyboard are secured with thin plastic retention straps. The yellow-black paint stripes have worn off the edges, and grime is embedded from years of flying service. Actuating the ejection handles requires me to pull them up and snap the plastic straps with forty pounds of force. I sigh and watch the FLIR auto-tracker follow the airman around at the far end of the hangar, oblivious that I have him locked in my sights.

"This is really solid—nice work. The brace is tied directly to the engine mounts," says Binh.

"Well, of course," Tiana spits. "I had two airframe design engineers review and approve it. They had no clue why I wanted a hardpoint pylon to withstand two hundred kilonewtons of thrust. They think I'm crazy."

"We are all insane to attempt this," Binh says, then sighs. "Icarus should be far out on the other side of Earth now. We can move those two missiles from the assembly shop into the hangar without being spotted. Let's get them driven over, okay?"

"Yep," Tiana says, and the two of them walk over to the hangar door, Tiana talking on her cell phone.

If Icarus can sense our PBH missiles on the cart rolling down the Dream Land runway, we will be in a deathtrap. I switch the center window of my weapon systems screen to the NORAD tactical situation display. Sure enough, the red Icarus triangle is on the far side of Earth. Tiana's software team has hooked the F-15's avionics into the air base network to access the NORAD info and the servers while flying. They also ported my entire stack of code to monitor and control the PBH engine test. Other than being in the back seat of a jet fighter, it will be just like sitting in the launcher truck running another missile test.

Tiana has a small army of engineers and airmen crawling over both missiles as they are lifted into the two new pylons below me. Everything on my weapons system console appears good to go, but it all feels slapped together for this first F-15 test flight. Test flight? Hell, we're flying straight into battle in an hour.

"Scott, final check. Are you ready to go?" asks Binh from the front seat.

"Running diagnostic tests one more time. Hold on!" My voice shakes. "The left missile PBH engine containment is solid, and I'm checking the right one now." I inspect my spherical disco ball containment display and verify both PBHs are centered in their vessels. "Everything on both missiles is ready. Ready to go."

Binh gives a thumbs-up to the airman waiting for his signal, and the tug pulls us forward from the hangar built into the side of the hill. We are exposed to the open sky and orange sunset over the Papoose Mountains. Icarus is blind to our mischief—I hope. Binh initiates the start-up, and the F-15 vibrates with power. He releases the brakes and stops in the engine run-up area on the edge of the runway.

My heart races with the thought of starting up two PBH engines under my seat. I am sitting on top of two black holes.

"Okay, Scott, all aircraft systems are go. Begin the power-up sequence of the missiles. I have the brakes locked," Binh says.

This is the first time we have run a simultaneous test of two PBH rocket engines, just a meter apart from each other, directly under me. "I'm initiating the resonance scan of both primordial black holes. I have sharp peaks for both. Radiation sensors show that all energy is directed to the aircraft's rear."

"Good to hear. Keep that radiation behind us." Even Binh's voice sounds a bit shaky.

Tiana says, "Everything nominal from my perspective, Scott. You are clear to proceed." Roger and Tiana stand behind a table of workstation displays a hundred meters away, and she gives me a thumbs-up. It's staggering to realize she only took nine hours to orchestrate this F-15 missile test, which might have taken months in saner situations. The NORAD display shows Icarus rounding Earth past Asia toward the ambush while nuclear missile tracks from Hector converge to a position a thousand kilometers west of the Baja Peninsula. Getting these Sidewinders working within half an hour will take a miracle.

"Okay, increasing modulation to both containment vessels." I bump up to a low initial setting. "Reading thrust on both missiles. Two kilonewtons of thrust on the left and three-point-five on the right motor. They have different responses to similar modulation amplitudes. But they seem to both work as expected."

"Plasma ball on right pylon! A quarter meter in diameter and well under the pylon bracket," shouts Tiana, fighting the roaring noise.

"We need these two missile motors generating similar thrust levels," says Binh. "The unbalanced thrust could yaw the aircraft during flight, and I don't want to fight them to maintain a heading."

"Got it, Binh. I'll increase them slowly till we're balanced at fifty kilonewtons each. Bumping power on the left side." I tap the modulation increase twice and hear the thrum from a second plasma ball igniting on the left missile motor.

"Second missile plasma ball. This one is a little larger, but neither touches the main fuselage," Tiana yells.

The noise is deafening, squeezed between two thrusting PBH rocket engines.

"Containment is fine on both, Tiana; nothing unusual." I feel like I have climbed on the back of a wild boar.

"How are radiation levels?" Binh asks.

"Radiation is all being directed behind us. Getting only trace radiation levels in the cockpit. I'm increasing both missile engines to the launch thrust of a hundred kilonewtons while monitoring pylon strain gauges to ensure we don't rip them off the airplane." I resume the modulation increase while balancing the thrust from both. The noise level reminds me of front-row seats at a heavy metal concert—near the pain threshold. "That does it. Both motors are running at a hundred kilonewtons. The pylons haven't ripped off the airframe—yet. I'll hold it here for thirty seconds!" I scream to hear myself. "Both engines show vessel temperatures at fifty Celsius and nozzle temperatures at two hundred. We're throwing exhaust of a thousand millisieverts of radiation out the tail of each nozzle." I can't stand the noise much longer—it's like a continuous thunderbolt.

Binh shouts, "The F-15 engines are at idle. I can barely keep us stationary by standing on the brakes!"

The seconds tick by, and I worry the vibrations may shake the airframe into pieces. At thirty seconds, I drop the modulation to idle the missiles' thrust to four kilonewtons and exhale in relief.

"Fucking awesome," Binh says.

I scan the data logs for anything unusual in the telemetry reading from the thrust run-up. "Yeah, a terrific way to lose our hearing. But I think we're ready to go. I don't see any issues in the telemetry data from either missile. Tiana, has your team seen any issues in the data?"

Tiana discusses with her engineers inside the control center. "Thumbs-up from the engineering team. You are good to go from me."

"Awesome, everyone," says Roger. "Captain Nguyen, you are cleared to take off and execute the mission."

"Yes, sir. Taxiing for takeoff."

All right. Here we go. Right into a space war! Binh steers us down to the end of the runway, doing all the work. For the moment, my sole job is to monitor the containment vessels and ensure we don't lose a primordial black hole.

"Uh, Binh. How about I power up the missiles so you don't need the afterburners for takeoff?"

"Nope, not funny. Keep those babies parked till we're ready to launch them. Let's keep it simple—while we can."

"Yes, sir." I chuckle and feel the F-15 rolling forward down the runway. When the engines spool up to full speed, he lights the afterburners, slamming me deep into my seat. The wimpy acceleration of a Porsche does not compare. Binh pulls back into a steep climb at maximum thrust per our plan to get as much altitude as possible before firing our PBH Sidewinders. The missiles will be damn fast once we launch them—orders of magnitude faster than our aircraft. There will be no point trying to close our distance to Icarus. After the missiles escape Earth's atmosphere, the PBH engines will throttle up to two hundred kilonewtons thrust to fly at Mach 300 into the target. Our Mach 2.5 fighter is just a ponderous delivery van.

"Altitude two klicks," Binh reports from the cockpit. "Heading northwest over the Nevada test range and to our attack altitude of eighteen kilometers in one minute. I figure we should put some distance between Groom Lake and us in case Icarus spots us."

"Much appreciated," Tiana says. "I would hate to have the aliens vent their rage on us."

"If we do our job, Icarus won't know what hit them." I check the NORAD tactical information streaming into my large video screen. The red triangle of Icarus falls through its perigee, passing over Shanghai. I can also see the tracks of ICBM missiles moving toward our ambush coordinates in space. "I show Icarus at eleven thousand kilometers from our surprise west of Baja. Binh, we must launch in"—I double-check my calculations—"sixty seconds. I need some time to bring the missile engines to full power."

"Right. Go ahead and power up the Sidewinders. We are ten seconds from launch altitude, turning to vector where Icarus should come over the horizon. Okay. Leveling off at eighteen klicks."

The noise from the F-15 afterburners drops to the modest rumble of cruising jet engines, soon overpowered by the thunderous thrum-roar from my two missile engines. "Both missiles at thirty kilonewtons thrust and climbing—should be at launch power in a few seconds. The FLIR pod's narrow field of view is selected, but I don't see Icarus. Must be below our horizon."

"Our airspeed!" yells Binh. "We're passing Mach 3! Those PBH engines have as much power as full afterburners at sea level! This is a new record for an F-15. Altitude is pushing to twenty klicks! Control surfaces are sluggish—not much air to work with. Ugh! There, there, got it. Down to eighteen klicks again. How you doing, Scott?" Binh's voice strains like he is in a wrestling match.

"Forty seconds to go. I have both Sidewinders at a hundred kilonewtons launch power!" I shout as loud as possible over the thunder of the PBH engines. "Internal containment temperature at forty Celsius—excellent; must be the frigid air.

Infrared seekers are both in target-acquisition mode, waiting for me to hand off a target from the FLIR." I compare the three infrared images on my display: one from each of the missile seekers plus the high-resolution FLIR image pointed along the vector we expect Icarus to appear. "I have nothing on any of the IR imagers yet. Expect Icarus to come over our horizon in thirty seconds."

"Holy shit!" Binh yells. An exploding sunlike sphere expands south and above us in space. "That's a thermonuclear warhead going off! Colonel, what the hell happened?"

"Pyotr reports it was one of the Indian ICBMs," says Tiana. "We have had five other malfunctions—most from the old Russian inventory. They're spiraling out of control all over the space above Asia. So much for our surprise ambush . . ."

"What a clusterfuck," says Binh, fighting the controls to keep us on a level flight path. "I can't imagine a better heads-up for ET. Is there any change in the Icarus orbit?"

"No, Icarus is still coasting into the perigee. Expect it over the horizon any second." Our F-15 shakes side to side and up and down as Binh fights the controls. The outside air temperature is minus fifty Celsius, and the cockpit heating fails to keep me warm. My mind is numb with the roar of two PBH engines just a meter under my feet. I'm shivering, hovering my thumb above the strain-gauge button on the FLIR joystick, and waiting.

There. A little to the left of the center, a shape emerges from the horizon. It is big. "I think I see it! Coming into the FLIR field of view. Stand by. I'll lock on with the auto-tracker when Icarus is clear of the atmospheric haze." I can see details of the spacecraft structure—the first time I have seen details in real-time infrared. The engine nozzle is barely visible, which means it is cold.

I flex my right hand and shake the cold off. Taking hold of the joystick, my thumb steers the rectangular acquisition symbol to the left until it surrounds the target. I tap the auto-track button with my middle finger, and the rectangle changes to four brackets squeezed down to the edges of the spacecraft.

"Target lock! I've got it, Binh!"

The image begins to change. The target moves left of center, its size grows, and the thermal intensity . . . "Binh! The Icarus engine nozzle—it just went white-hot! They started their main engine!"

"Get those missiles locked and launch. Out of time!"

I tap the button to engage the right-side missile; the infrared image is transferred from the FLIR to the Sidewinder seeker electronics on the right pylon. I watch as the missile status changes to *"Track."*

"Right-side Sidewinder locked, launching—" Before I finish my sentence, it feels like a truck slams into the F-15, twisting us to the left. The noise of the PBH rocket motors drops by half, and a whiplash of force hits from the left and keeps pushing. The aircraft spins clockwise, faster and faster.

"In a flat spin!" yells Binh.

I am pressed to the left, fighting to keep my head erect against the force pushing my helmet into the canopy and straining to study the two disco ball containment vessel telemetry displays. "Right missile lost containment. PBH is gone!" I scream. "The left missile thrust must be spinning us!" I force my hands against the centrifugal force to grasp the keyboard pads, fingers fighting to type the kill command. I have to use my peripheral vision to see my display, but g-forces have collapsed my field of view to a single grey spot.

Quiet. The centrifugal force slows, and my vision clears. "I ejected the left PBH."

"Thanks. Falling into thicker air should—" Binh grunts, fighting the controls. We continue to spin round and round. Falling. The F-15 nose begins to drop, pointing us down. The spin of the clouds and mountains below us finally slows, and I feel the thrust of the jet engines. The rotation stops, and Binh snaps the aircraft to level flight. We have fallen ten kilometers.

"Colonel McMahon. Returning to base. No joy on missile launches."

"Understood, Captain. Gentlemen, see you in debrief."

We failed. I stare at my display. The NORAD tracking for Icarus diverges from its elliptical orbit path, and the red triangle accelerates to climb a hundred kilometers higher. The tracks of dozens of missiles show on the screen, converging to a point west and high above the Baja Peninsula—far behind and below Icarus's current position.

The evening sky to the west is black, blending into the blue-white fringe of Earth far to the west. The black of space flashes to fire as a fifty-megaton ball, like a miniature sun, explodes over the Pacific Ocean. Our ambush is sprung—on empty space.

Chapter 34

SOL-3 REVOLT

Captain's Log, Frigate-328, 179240.96 LST

The audacity of these fools! Shooting at us with nuclear missiles! It was our good luck that we faced primitive Sol-3 technology. They may as well throw rocks.

I don't want them all killed, not the younglings. But if I can destroy all their weapons and eliminate the remaining Gravi-Tech . . . there might be a way.

To make matters worse, the commissar is trying to hack into my files and communication logs. Prime-AI blocked access but is fighting with Polit-AI to maintain my security.

I ordered Mil-AI to identify all chemical rocket launch capabilities and eliminate threats from Sol-3. But we discovered multiple sites with Gravi-Tech singularity containers—several were in motion! What chaos. I could turn our frigate out to the edge of the Sol system and launch a few planet killers. Only three Gravi-Tech projectiles from that range would sterilize all life forms on Sol-3.

But why? My protocol violations already doom me to an agonizing death. And I have mind-talked with a Sol-3 neurodivergent. Can I save the Sol-3 organics from themselves, protect Frigate-328, hold off the commissar's investigation, and survive?

No, but I might save the younglings. Give them a reprieve and time to grow.

Chapter 35

DESPERADOS

We're on a roller coaster ride out of the black sky through desert mountains painted in thermal contrasts and across basins of sand that glow like frozen lakes covered in snowfall. Flying through the infrared landscape painted by the FLIR is mind-bending as Binh bumps and jinks around infrared outlines of mountains. My inability to anticipate a maneuver feels worse than the flat spin down from eighteen kilometers. Under other circumstances, I would have been willing to pay for a ride like this. We're hugging the terrain, trying to hide from Icarus—a precaution suggested by Colonel McMahon to avoid observation from space. I breathe easier when Binh finally lines us up on the darkened Dream Land runway. But my oxygen mask is splashed in vomit.

Icarus unleashed projectiles that struck missile silos in Russia, India, and China after the spacecraft powered out to an altitude of two hundred thousand kilometers—in less than one hour. Their demonstration of cunning and raw engine power is chilling. The altitude is beyond the reach of our ballistic missiles and at a range sufficient to accelerate the Icarus tungsten projectiles into two-hundred-kiloton explosions.

NORAD's global tactical display traces trajectories across Asia: punishment meted out for our reckless nuclear attack. I lose count of the missiles Icarus rains down—many times more than the few hundred ICBMs launched from Earth, and they have yet to arrive over North America to punish us. The aliens must have tracked and back-calculated along ballistic trajectories to the location of missile silos. Icarus is cleansing Earth of its land-based nuclear missile arsenals built over the past eighty years, and it's more effective than all the international arms-control treaties combined. The aliens baited us with a close flyby of Earth, and we bit hard. We are helpless fools.

***

"What happened to the Hector space station?" I ask when I see it is missing from the map displayed on the screen in our underground control center. Tiana searches the map, another dose of anxiety and dread creasing her brow as she places a call to Pyotr. The mood of the engineers in the room, along with Roger, Tiana, and Binh, is not one of defeat, but of fright and determined tension. Half the workstations are empty—the engineers are either out working on weapon systems or dead. We are out of coffee.

"Pyotr, is now a good time to talk?" Tiana asks via the video call projected to her workstation.

Pyotr stares dumbly at the camera, gaunt, silent for a while. He asks, "What can I do?"

"Petya, what is the matter? Are you okay?" asks Tiana.

"I am fine," Pyotr gasps, drawing a breath of smoke from his cigarette. "My friends, all eight on duty at Hector Station. A projectile from Icarus killed them." Puffs of smoke exhale with each word. "Dead. Hector Station is now dust." His cigarette smokes between his lips, and his face drops as he studies the hands wringing over his keyboard.

"Petya. Oh, Petya. That's terrible," Tiana says, near tears.

Pyotr's dark eyes drill into us. "I know how you all must feel." Pyotr sniffles and wipes his face. Clearing his head with a shake, he sits straight and says, "Many have a bad night—sorry. How can I help?"

Roger asks, "Can you share NASA's perspective on the Icarus attacks?"

"Yes, Colonel McMahon. Icarus escaped Earth missiles by boosting at ten Gs. Biggest-ever explosion blew up in empty space. Big waste. Maybe Icarus saw Russian failures and launch-destructs? Maybe Indian ICBM detonating early woke them up? We don't know. But Icarus located ICBM launcher bases—now above Asia bombing many sites in India, Russia, China."

Roger grimaces. "Like the radar used to find and counterattack an enemy's artillery. It's simple stuff, even for humans. We should have expected Icarus to have weapons-locating technology that was better than ours." Roger shakes his head.

"And the aliens have learned what missile silos look like," Binh says. "They're attacking hundreds of sites across Asia that did not fire missiles at them. They're disarming us. I hope they didn't trace our botched PBH missile launch back to Groom Lake."

"Captain," says Pyotr, "it could explain flight path—Icarus thrust north one moment to Nevada, then climbed to a high altitude. Why?"

"I bet they spotted our Sidewinder's PBH gamma radiation as Icarus came over the horizon," I say. "But I can't see how they would trace us back to Groom Lake. Once we lost containment of the first primordial black hole, I ejected the second one, and they both fell away from the airplane. After that, the aliens lost interest."

"Your black hole super-missile malfunctioned? Lost our chance to kill Icarus?" Pyotr shakes with anger and tears.

"We're not giving up," Binh urges, just as angry.

Tiana shifts her weight in her chair, rotating toward me. "Scott figured out what went wrong, Pyotr. It was an error in the guidance logic software. Our PBH Sidewinders powered up to the thrust level of an F-15 engine—before the missile got launched. Scott?"

I continue, "Yeah. And when the right Sidewinder locked on target, Icarus was about forty degrees to our left. The missile thrust vector yawed the F-15 with a jerk that tossed the right PBH out of its containment vessel. At full launch thrust, the other missile kicked the airplane to the right and into a flat spin. Once I figured that out, I ejected the second PBH."

"Next time we lock on a target, that won't happen," Tiana says. "It's a simple change to engage the vectored thrust a moment after a missile is released."

"We'll try again in about an hour," says Binh. "How long do we have until Icarus gets to our side of Earth?"

"Hmmm . . ." Pyotr studies a display screen among coffee cups and Snickers candy wrappers. "Is hard to say. Icarus changed direction south over Asia to go over India, destroying launch sites. Eastern China and Siberian launch silos not yet touched. May destroy China launchers after a half-hour?" Pyotr shrugs. "Maybe two hours, then over USA?"

"Ninety minutes then," I say, clenching my teeth. "Tiana, Binh, let's get to the hangar. We must rearm and be in the air before Icarus crosses the western horizon."

Binh seems amused, smiling at Roger, who raises his eyebrows and tilts his head in agreement.

"I help any way I can." Pyotr sniffs, wiping back tears and staring at all of us. "Anything you need—ask."

Dawn sunlight stabs through a gap in the rusty mountain range, grazing the canopy. Flipping the filter down over my eyes helps me see outside the aircraft, but it's nearly impossible to see my cockpit display right in front of me. I crank the screen brightness and squint to see the status of the two disco ball containment vessels. The two PBH Sidewinders are idling at four kilonewtons of thrust each.

Binh completes his final pre-takeoff checks and throttles up the F-15 engines. Brakes release, and we begin our roll down the runway. Two plasma balls on the Sidewinder tails illuminate the runway under the F-15's belly. Afterburners light, adding thunder to the thrum-roar of the PBH engines under my feet. The jet engines scream the length of the runway until Binh lifts us off and holds our altitude at fifty meters, throttling down power from the engines as we race to distance our primordial black holes from Groom Lake before gaining altitude. Binh jinks right to fly above Groom Road toward the east, followed by a hard left to skirt the base of Bald Mountain, setting our course north.

The Icarus red triangle on the NORAD display moves past the Hawaiian Islands, powering a route across the Pacific after destroying nuclear missile launchers across Asia. "Pyotr, do you see any changes in Icarus's velocity? We just took off and are ducking behind a mountain range."

"No, no. Watching it close." He pauses, probably examining NORAD tracking telemetry. "No change to Icarus path toward Montana."

"Good, Pyotr. Stay with us while we navigate." I hold my breath as Binh jinks the F-15 up to clear a granite crag and dives us into a broad canyon. "I expect Icarus will spot us when we climb to eighteen kilometers."

"Will do," Pyotr says.

I cannot relax—even with deep breaths. Binh shared some modafinil go-pills that keep me edgy and wide awake—as designed—despite the twenty-four hours without sleep. The high desert of sagebrush-shadowed snowdrifts and sunburnt sand flies by below us. I sit back with closed eyes. Why didn't I call Mary to check in on Robby? It has been days. How many? I've lost track of time. And what does Robby think of me abandoning him with that strange woman? Though, he couldn't be in a better place. Mary has as much, if not more, skill than any other therapist who has worked with Robby. She's a pro. Robby warmed up to her from the start.

The afterburners are at full power again, and Binh stands the F-15 on its tail, accelerating at the maximum thrust of the old GE F110 engines. "Climbing to eighteen klicks. Scott, power up the Sidewinders to launch thrust. Keep 'em balanced!"

I am slammed deeper into my seat, feeling four times heavier, my hands grabbing the keyboard pads while I strain my fingers to type commands to ramp up the PBH engine power. "Thirty kilonewtons on both missiles," I grunt out the words. "Ten seconds till launch thrust." The seat back digs into my shoulders with the increased thrust of PBH power combined with the jet engines, and we break the sound barrier into silence—all while going straight up. It's double the maximum thrust an F-15 was designed for. The G-forces and vibrations are beyond what I can bear. I feel like I'm riding a cannonball into the sky.

"Icarus changing direction!" Pyotr shouts. "Vector east toward your position!"

"Leveling off at eighteen klicks," shouts Binh as the jet engines power down. We loop into a weightless near-space, and the engine noise crashes into us from behind as our speed drops under Mach 1.

I power down the Sidewinders to their acquisition thrust and try to forget the momentary euphoria of weightlessness. I focus on the infrared image, but I cannot see Icarus. "Icarus must be too far away. I can't see it on the FLIR image. There is nothing to lock on to." The F-15 jinks left, then right. "What are you doing?" I confirm containment on both PBH missile engines, each pushing our aircraft forward with fifty kilonewtons of thrust. "Keep us pointed toward Icarus so I can find it and lock on."

"Evasive maneuvers in case they take a shot at us. They can see us even if we can't see them." Binh jinks left again.

"Binh, if you keep this up, I'll never find Icarus, let alone get the auto-tracker to lock on."

The side-to-side jerking stops. "Okay." Binh sighs. "Leveling off at just under twenty kilometers. I have us pointed straight at Icarus. Make it quick. We're a sitting duck."

The pull of gravity returns to normal, and I try to calm myself with deep breaths. The sky is black-blue; a field of stars fills my cockpit view to the sides and above. With my helmet's sunlight filter stowed overhead, I can study the FLIR display centered in my forward view. The FLIR image is blank—no thermal emissions from near space except a couple of brighter pixels near the center. I slide the rectangle symbol over those pixels and tap the auto-track button. "I'm locked on to something but can't tell what it is yet."

"My HUD shows you have likely locked on to Icarus—it's on the heading from NORAD. Resuming evasive maneuvers," Binh shouts.

"I want to be sure it's our target before I transfer the target to the Sidewinder seekers and launch." We bank left, and the FLIR pod auto-tracker maintains a lock on those few bright pixels on my display.

"Agreed. Let Icarus come in closer until we can see 'em better," says Binh, jinking hard left.

Pyotr shouts, "Strange radar signal off Icarus! Like noise bursts." Voices argue in the background of Pyotr's office. "Extreme energy spike on Icarus. Maybe like Gatling gun?" More background shouting. "Radar see projectiles—heading at you!"

Binh jinks us right again, steering us away from where Icarus aimed. Maybe?

"Get the missiles locked!" shouts Binh.

My hands tremble. I tap the icons to send the FLIR target image to both Sidewinders seekers. "Both seekers are locked on to something. I'll wait until we're close and can confirm the target image before I launch." The missiles do not jerk the airplane into a flat spin this time. "I can't be certain that blob of pixels is Icarus."

"Incoming!" Pyotr screams. "Projectiles two thousand kilometers per second!"

The inky sky above us flashes with a dozen miniature suns as bursts of white light from projectiles strike the atmosphere like a Fourth of July fireworks finale, and I wince in pain from a piercing headache.

The caw-screams in my head explode with fire. I slap my ears with both hands as hard as I can, but the roar inside is too loud.

"Hey, Robby, your pancakes and bacon are ready. Come to the table and eat your breakfast!" Mary calls.

The sparkles of light in the snow are everywhere. I push away from the glass, where my nose smudge made it fuzzy. The bright light on the hill hurts my eyes. The cold makes me shiver; I have bumps on my arms. Something pulls on me, lower, lower. The windows tip over; my face is hot and wet.

"Robby, you coming?"

Blue sky above the hills of snow rolls up and down; it tips to the side, and then my head whips and bounces off the wood floor.

"Robby!" Mary screams and jumps down to the floor. Her arms slide around me, and she pulls me onto the sofa.

My head whips a pillow. My arms and legs jerk and hit her. Sunlight sparkles bounce off the snow.

Mary's arms wrap close around me. "Hey, hey, hey. Robby, I've got you. I've got you."

Blue darkness—snow sparkles fall into my eyes. The screams in my head burn—the voices of hunters. The sky smears the snow; trees bend into drips. Blue-white circles round and round—like water down a drain—but spinning up into the dark. I fall up the hole that spins. I am scared, dropping and going around in a circle. It is dark. Scared. Empty. A voice, *"Klee, klee, klee, klee."*

"Target lock lost!" I shout to Binh. "Thermal blooms are blinding our IR imagers!" The FLIR and the missile-seeker images are saturated white-hot by the projectiles melting and vaporizing into the stratosphere. We are in a forest of flaming orange-yellow columns expanding toward us from all sides. I sense a tugging, grinding pain that is somehow compelling and intoxicating. It's a headache like nothing I can recall.

"Scott, full power on Sidewinder motors. Now!" shouts Binh as he pulls back to stand the F-15 on its tail, but without the thick air to feed the jet engines.

I tap the missile throttle controls to push both PBH engines to a hundred kilonewtons—generating nearly the power that the old GE engines generate with full afterburners at sea level. Binh has us pointed straight up with the PBH engines in the Sidewinders doing all the work. He steers our aircraft toward a gap in the sky between three expanding plasma columns created by projectiles burning through the atmosphere. My skull vibrates with the thunder from primordial black hole engines mounted on the pylons just under my seat. The fire columns close in—we won't make it. My migraine agony gets worse . . . and images of Robby with me fill my head.

"Pushing power up fifty percent!" I yell as I set both Sidewinders to one-fifty kilonewtons and am slammed deeper into my seat, my eardrums and forehead pierced with pain. We break the sound barrier again, leaving the deafening roar behind, replaced by metallic rattles threatening to shake the old F-15 apart.

"Thirty-three klicks!" Binh yells. "Fifteen klicks above our ceiling! Controls are sluggish as shit this high up." The nose of the aircraft begins to fall, drifting toward one of the white-hot projectile plasma trails.

The columns of fire appear to slow their expansion, but we close the distance to one of the pinnacles of air boiling with superheated plasma. Beyond is empty black space. Earth's globe falls away below us, a puff-white-blue expanse rimmed by silver through our frost-glazed canopy.

Shockwaves strike us like we've collided with a brick wall. My helmet smacks the canopy, and my vision narrows to a grey circle. A thundercrack rips into us. The wing folds with a groaning rip of metal and breaks away while shredded pieces of aircraft clatter off the plastic canopy. The wing flutters across my view, leaving a strut folded over our heads, trailing the frozen vapor of leaking jet fuel. The F-15 tumbles, taking us down like an autumn leaf.

Two blue-white plasma balls arc into a black field of stars, spiraling out of control, pushing two Sidewinder missiles—still attached to chunks of the launch pylons. No! I can't reach them. The steam vapor trails vanish as the missiles reach the vacuum of space. Are they lost?

Mary holds me tight, but I turn to face the roar. The caw-scream dark hole spins down into the blue. My arms and legs are gone. The sky is black.

A murder of crows swirls around, darting close to peck at my face and eyes, cutting into my skin. They shriek, *"Caw, caw, caw! Kill it, kill it, kill it!"* Blood trickles across my eyes, but I see through the cloud of crows. And I think I see . . . or feel . . . Scotty.

And there is another voice with wings. *"Klee-klee-klee-klee-klee,"* sings a lone kestrel, diving through the whirlpool, smaller than the crows but unafraid, attacking although outnumbered.

"Caw, caw! Kill it, kill it, kill it!" The caw-screams burn under my eyes. They ignore me and turn to attack the kestrel, plucking at its orange and grey feathers. But the kestrel fights through them, tearing away black feathers from the crows, flying near to catch me. I fall, fall into orange-grey feathers.

My headache beats, beats like a drum, and I feel Scotty. He thinks like a machine, like the gears and springs of the giant clock at home. His mind flashes with each touch, and everything is in its place and perfect. But something broke. Scotty hurts. He lost the tools in the black sky and can't reach them. He wants to finish his work, but his tools fall away. Lost.

But I see what Scotty wants. I can touch the tools. Robby can fix it.

"Klee-klee-klee-klee! Turn and fight! We fly and fight!" the kestrel sings, diving with me into the swirl of crows.

The crows screech, *"Caw, caw, caw! Kill it, kill it, kill i t!"* Talons strike out to slice us, and beaks stab like knives from the black mass of feathers, but the kestrel darts past all, deeper into darkness.

I feel Scotty try and try. I tell the tools what Scotty wants. Robby help.

I fly with the kestrel, spinning past the screeching caws of the crows. *"Klee-klee-klee-klee!"* I shout to the kestrel. *"We fight, we fight, we fight!"* We see each other and another murder of crows. And attack.

———

The blue-white plasma balls powering our precious weapons disappear into the black, wandering into the glitter of stars watching over Earth's destruction. I am powerless, foolishly wanting to reach out and somehow control the missiles. The Icarus position is on my display, but I cannot upload the coordinates to the Sidewinders' guidance computers. I have no way to contact the missiles. The excruciating head pain—somehow intoxicating—tugs me further into torture. If only I could communicate with the Sidewinders, I could steer them back toward Icarus. But the Sidewinders are lost and out of reach. I shake my head to escape the hellish pain behind my eyes and the bizarre sensations of Robby—not only images but feelings—feelings of fear and fighting and pain.

The Great Salt Lake crosses my vision every few seconds as we spin through the descent through the stratosphere. My neck and head hurt like hell. Binh does not move—his helmet slacks to the left against the canopy.

"Binh! Binh, are you okay?!" I scream. His limp helmet does not move. Loose sheet metal clatters against the airframe.

"Scott, Binh! What's your status?" Colonel McMahon calls over the radio.

My display is still active, although several flashing red indicators are on the cockpit console—I can only guess what critical damage they report. The cockpit heating is off, and it's getting damn cold.

"Colonel, we're in a spin. Binh is unconscious," I gasp, fighting through tears and the pain in my head. "Our right wing is gone! Ripped off the airplane!" A piece of the wing wraps over the top of the cracked acrylic canopy. "Uh, mostly ripped off." My voice is hoarse as I gulp the oxygen feeding into my mask. "I'm sorry, we lost both missiles. We failed again. I'm going to eject." I reach down and slide my frozen fingers through the yellow handles.

"No, no!" screams Roger. "Scott, do not eject. Do. Not. Eject. You are too high. It could be fatal!"

I release my grip on the ejection handles. "Okay, I'll wait." The Great Salt Lake rotates past Binh's limp head. In the distant north, fireballs erupt on the horizon. The NORAD display on my screen shows several ICBM silos blinking out, vanishing as kinetic energy missiles slam into the Earth.

"I'm sorry, guys," I scream, the pain in my head unbearable. I must have a head injury.

"Scott, is your tactical display working?" Tiana yells. "I show both Sidewinders operating, gaining altitude, and accelerating."

I blink, trying to focus through the pain and a layer of frost on my helmet. I completely retract my helmet visor and squint through the ice on my eyeballs from the minus-fifty temperature. But I can see the details displayed on the screen, and yes, there they are. Two blue X symbols swim through space like aimless sharks.

"Yes, I see them. They aren't flying toward anything, and . . ."

Tiana interrupts, "Did you lock them on target?"

"Yeah, I did. But the Sidewinders lost lock in the heat of those Icarus projectiles before we tried to use the PBH engines to escape." I slap my hands onto my aching forehead, but my frozen, numb fingers only bounce off the top of my helmet.

"Scott!" Tiana interrupts again. "The AIM-9Z seeker has a lock-on-after-launch feature. They both appear as though they're in search mode, flying a pattern using inertial navigation to keep them pointed toward the target snapshot you loaded into the seeker. They also communicate with each other to coordinate their attack."

I rub the ice from my cheeks and eyes. Yes, I can see the two blue X symbols meandering along, but not in the general direction toward Icarus. "Tiana, you have been keeping secrets from me again."

"Yeah, that's what the colonel pays me for."

"But they are lost, not heading toward Icarus at all. I don't know. Both missiles were still attached to the pylons ripped from the airframe belly. They will be way off-balance with the extra drag." I can hardly breathe, straining my chest against the centrifugal force while fighting the grinding headache.

Tiana responds, "The drag should vanish in the vacuum of space. But their center of mass will still be off. I can't predict how the guidance control will compensate."

They may also have lost the scent—I locked both missiles on a tiny blob of a few pixels. I can't imagine how they could find that same featureless blob again. The two Sidewinders stray into expanding spirals as they fly away from Earth. The clouds rotating around us over the Rocky Mountains are closer; we are down to twenty-two kilometers altitude, and it's still cold as death. The northern horizon is thick with rising mushroom clouds, and fireballs flash from Montana at regular intervals with each projectile strike from Icarus.

Binh's helmet moves and slides erect against his seat.

"Binh! Binh, are you okay?" I yell.

"Uh," he grunts. "Uh."

"Guys, I think Binh is conscious. He's moving again." More guttural sounds come from the front of the cockpit.

"Captain Nguyen! Report!" Roger calls.

"I, I . . . um. Yeah," Binh slurs like a drunk.

"Scott . . ." Tiana calls, her voice rising. "Scott, one Sidewinder just changed direction. Turning hard. Toward Icarus! It's accelerating. It must have found Icarus!"

I chase the kestrel, following it through a cloud of crows that shriek, *"Caw, caw, caw!"* Blazing red eyes, brown talons thrashing, striking with black dagger beaks. But they lash out at nothing. Like they are blind to where we fly, we dart through the flock of screeches.

"Caw, caw, caw!" The crows are behind us.

"Klee-klee-klee-klee! Follow me, follow me. The nest, the nest, the nest," calls the kestrel.

A tree with eight branches, far away, launches another murder of crows—flying straight toward us.

The kestrel flies faster, straight at the flock.

"The second missile is turning!" Tiana's voice is breathless. "The acceleration! The acceleration is about . . . let me see . . .

twelve hundred Gs? How can that be—it's a thrust-to-weight ratio of over a thousand! And time-of-flight to Icarus is about . . . three minutes."

"Oops." I would slap my forehead if my hands weren't blocks of ice. "I removed the limits on engine thrust to boost the F-15 through those projectiles. The engine nozzles may overheat and trip the thermal shutdowns. But . . ." I think through the engine control algorithms. "The engine should resume when cool . . . maybe." My ability to focus and analyze the situation is improving . . . somehow, the pain in my head is nearly gone.

"I hope the missiles don't break apart. I don't know the G-force limit for a Sidewinder," Tiana says. "They would never survive inside the atmosphere. Pyotr, is Icarus reacting to our missiles?"

"Icarus sees them, I think," says Pyotr. "Stopped shooting at USA ICBM silos, but Montana and North Dakota bases still have thirty-three incoming. Icarus stopped over Rockies, climbing to altitude halfway to moon."

"Oh, man, what happened to my girl?" Binh mumbles. "Where did her wing go?" The aircraft's attitude tilts forward, and the rotation slows.

"Are you trying to fly this thing?" I yell. "Half the airplane is ripped away. We need to eject!" The nose tilts down, and a ragged wind rips through the remnants of the right wing stretched across the canopy.

"Running left engine restart sequence," Binh says. "Status says it should light up."

"What?" I croak. "Binh, you are trying to fly this thing with only one wing?"

"Leave the driving to me. The F-15 is one amazing flying machine!" Binh yells, his energy restored with the engine spooling up with a whine. "This won't be the first time an F-15 makes a safe landing with a missing wing." The engine whine becomes a dull groan and then a soft roar. "I've got thirty percent power on engine one. Turning back to Dream Land."

As Binh pulls us up from the steep dive, my weight shifts back in my seat. The spin has stopped, the restarted engine warms the cockpit with hot air, and the Bonneville Salt Flats in Utah hold steady far to the left. He's going to try to land this thing. "And people say I'm fuckin' crazy. Sheesh." The F-15 rattles like Anthony's old Ford pickup bouncing across the Chihuahuan Desert.

"Hey Tiana, radar tracking both missiles on zigzag path. Tiny missiles—you expect they can damage Icarus?" Pyotr asks.

"I don't expect much damage even if we hit Icarus," says Tiana. "We'll watch what happens and use the experience to build something with more punch. It would be nice to send them a missile armed with a nuclear warhead."

"Energy spike on Icarus—and radar noise burst!" shouts Pyotr. "Match last Gatling gun pattern—projectiles will intercept missile flight paths!"

No, no, no . . . two more bursts of shells belch out of Icarus, its Gatling-like guns shooting dozens of small projectiles. The spacecraft vents a furnace of energy, blooming white-hot on the infrared image. The NORAD tactical display plots all the objects: Icarus, the Gatling gun projectiles, and my two PBH Sidewinders as they zigzag along the route toward Icarus.

"Crossing through eight klicks," Binh yells. "Getting a hell of a drag, though. There's a lot of aircraft structure hanging out under the fuselage and slowing us!" Our flight path is chaos, yawing to the right, then jerking left as Binh fights turbulence, pitching up and down. We suddenly dive sideways, the ground racing at us.

"Time to eject?" He can't seriously believe he can land this wreck.

"No!" shouts Binh. "Ejecting is impossible with wreckage on top of the canopy. It would kill us both. I've got it," he says, his voice shrill. "We're good. We are good. Colonel, I'm bringing us straight in."

We are at four kilometers. I hear and feel the vibrations of engine power increase. Binh pulls the nose up, but the F-15 fights and yaws to the right. The down-then-up pitch rocks us through thicker air, the stiff crosswind buffeting us, accompanied by a noise like trash cans tumbling down a street. The eject levers beg me to grab and yank. But after inspecting the scrap metal blocking our exit above my head, I reconsider.

We drop through three kilometers altitude. "Binh!" A snow-covered granite peak atop a green forest passes to our right side.

"I've got it. I've got it," shouts Binh. "Not going to make Groom Lake. Setting down in . . . uh . . . Kawich Valley. The lake bed!" Binh yells.

"Understood," says Roger. "Dispatching Air Rescue."

We drop like a brick, even though the GE engine roars with power. The bouncing NORAD display shows two blue symbols designating my Sidewinders get past the first burst of Gatling shells. Their path to Icarus is thick with projectiles aimed at my zigzagging missiles. One Sidewinder falls far behind—maybe an overheating engine cutting off.

The ground races up as we crab toward the salt flat. It feels like a snowboard scooting sideways down a slope of moguls. Steep; too steep.

"Landing gear fail!" Binh shouts.

My gut clenches, expecting us to smash into bits any moment. Binh flares the nose up but pitches the F-15 too high, engine screaming, before yawing left and pointing down toward the salt flat.

Oh fuck. I glance at the display. The first Sidewinder is heading straight into another burst of shells.

Sagebrush zips past my right shoulder.

"Brace!" Binh screams.

———

The crows are lost. We fly around them—they do not follow. But they roar, *"Caw! Caw! Caw! Kill them, kill them, kill them!"* The pain pounds behind my eyes with each shriek.

But the kestrel sings, *"Klee-klee-klee."* The pain dissolves into warmth. We fly close to the massive tree, its eight branches holding the heart of the nest.

"Klee-klee-klee. This way, fight, this way, fight!" The kestrel dives into the heart, piercing a hole, talons ripping out pieces of the nest. The nest swallows the kestrel.

"Caw! Gah-gah-gah! Caw!" the mob of crows gasps and grunts, twisting, screaming.

The pain behind my eyes is like a hammer striking. I spin away, unable to breathe. The kestrel is gone, its song silenced. But Scotty showed me how! I must fight, must follow the path to the nest! *"No, no, no!"* I scream. I dive, thrusting with wings into the nest, hurt by the crow's screams inside my head. The heart of crows beats in panic.

"Caw! Gah-gah-gah! Caw! Caw!"

Ripping with my talons, I turn my blades and pull sideways with both arms. Using all I have to slice across the heart, my muscles burn. Something snaps inside it, and black blood floods out, burning hot and sticky, covering my arms and face, and then I am blinded by a bright flash of blue fire.

The crows are quiet. The pain behind my eyes is gone, replaced with a tickle—a "chirp-chirrup" like a whippoorwill.

I fall down between mountains of soft white rocks. The sharp edges crush as I strike them, becoming a sea of white powder.

"Chirp-chirrup. Chirp-chirrup," it tickles.

I look down at the fire. I float above him.

It is Scotty. He's still, but he breathes.

My arms and legs return, shivering inside a blanket. My face is wet with slobber, snot, and tears. So tired . . . so . . . so tired. The room rocks from side to side. Mary holds me too tight, but I cannot push her away. The back of my neck is like ice, and my arms and legs tingle.

"Yes, I need to bring him into the clinic right now," Mary says on her phone. "He has had a seizure. A bad one. Okay, okay. Yes. He seems stable now, although he is weak and soaked in sweat. Okay, we should be there in fifteen minutes. Thanks." Mary lifts and carries me in her arms.

Something sharp punctures my chest. I scream and cough the salty, metallic taste of blood as my eyes flutter open. Both hands are sliced by the frame of the display screen, which pierces my ribs. The agony is relieved after I yank the screen out of the rip in my flight suit. A cloud of yellow dust has settled over the canopy, and the front half of the acrylic is shattered. Binh is slumped sideways, motionless in the front seat of the cockpit. I remember sagebrush and one bounce.

Smells like kerosene.

Both wings are gone. Flames are over my shoulder, but I am trapped inside this plastic bubble. Banging my fists against the canopy doesn't move it. Take a deep breath. Think. Where are those yellow-black controls—yes! I flip up the switch cover at the edge of the cockpit and press the canopy jettison button. The canopy remnants explode off the aircraft, the pieces flipping to the ground behind me. Twisting the release on my harness, I pull out of my seat—but the pain! Agony burns up my left leg, through my hip and spine, before pounding in my skull. The flames are close, scalding my flight suit. I smell jet fuel.

I have to get away—now! Thrusting myself up and over the edge of the cockpit, I scream as my useless left leg flops down to the white sand. I hold myself at the side of the fuselage, which plowed deep into white sand. Crying, groaning for breath, I shake Binh's shoulder. "Binh! We need to go. Now!" But he sits—still. So still.

Flames flare across the amputated left wing, singeing my eyes through the open helmet visor as I reach inside to release Binh's harness. Sliding my hands under his armpits, I tug with all my might. Binh tumbles on top of me as I collapse into the sand. My left leg protests with unspeakable pain—my vision narrows, the sand tilts, and I cry and suck in air. Binh's boot is on fire when I roll over and hook my arms under him again, pushing with my right leg, but I drop with a scream when my left leg folds under me like rubber. Black smoke fills the sky. Once more, I lift, shoving with my right leg, then scream when my other leg fails. I repeatedly push with my good leg until it is numb with pain, yanking Binh across the white sand.

An explosion rocks the sandy lakebed, and I bend over the top of Binh as pieces of wreckage thump to the ground around us. Hot chunks of F-15 rain down on my back. Soft, quiet breezes flow over us, disturbed only by the occasional crackle of flames burning remnants of the aircraft. A tall cloud of black smoke rises into the sun that warms our bed of powdery sand. "Binh, are you okay?" I shake his shoulder, but he is quiet and still.

The air above us throbs with a distant staccato beat.

We are covered in a chop-roar sandstorm kicked up by the Valor aircraft coasting across the lake bed before swinging around upwind of the smoke and flames of the dead F-15. Several blue-grey flight suits emerge from the Valor under the oversized spinning rotors. The big guy sprints past the others through the white dust and blowing smoke. He reaches down and rests a knee on the sand.

"Scott, you can't seem to stay out of trouble," the chief says, rolling me gently to my back and pushing aside my oxygen mask hose to unbuckle my helmet. He yells to the medic running to us with a first aid kit, "Check the captain! He's out cold."

The horizon is lost in the glare of sunlight reflecting from snow-white sand. My brain staggers down a post-adrenaline crash—so, so tired. "Chief Cooper?" I mumble. My grinding headache has vanished.

"Yeah, Scott. Air Rescue would take too long all the way from Nellis. Colonel McMahon ordered us to help." He slides his hands along my arms and chest but stops when I grunt at the pressure on my ribs. The chief grimaces. "Sorry about that. Must hurt like hell." He continues to probe for injuries around my waist and abruptly stops. "Your left leg is broken," He glances back at the medic working on Binh. "How did you move the captain over here?"

"Well, I dragged him. What do you think?" Don't ask such a stupid question. But then I see it. My flight suit leg is soaked in blood, and my left boot is bent at a right angle from my ankle. I remember the pain, gasp, close my eyes, and inhale to avoid puking.

"You guys okay?" Tiana's voice comes from above, running, and she sinks to her knees beside my face. She looks into my eyes, my leg, and over at Binh; tears roll down her cheeks. Tiana places her hands on my forehead and my arm. "It worked. Scott, we got them! Both Sidewinders hit. Icarus is drifting in space!"

It's impossible. Did the missiles get past all of Icarus's point-defense weapons? Two tiny explosions took down a four-kilometer spacecraft? I laugh despite the pain. Impossible.

Robby will be safe. Delirious joy rises in my chest, and questions form, but I can't produce words. The back of my neck flashes with cold sweat. The sky wobbles, and Tiana's face fades to grey.

Chapter 36

JUSTICE

Captain's Log, Frigate-328, 179241.11 LST

It is unclear how many organic crew survived, but the political division war room ruptured into the vacuum with the fuel canister explosion. All the Polit-AI drones were lost after command links from the defunct Polit-AI bot were broken. The commissar's death must have been excruciating. Perfect.

Political division's final effort tried to blind the younglings with a barrage of torment squawks, but they failed. And I can still mind-speak with the younglings! They were able to communicate to guide their missiles around countermeasures. With my help, of course. Prime-AI overrode the military division's defensive aiming computations, so the younglings had a fair contest. And the target feature selection on my old frigate by the Sol-3 missiles was brilliant. A perfect strike.

The electromagnetic surge destroyed all AI systems and internal networks beyond repair. But I found the emergency bridge intact, including the rudimentary control and communication systems I was left with. Critical life support functions are sustained by power cells. I have limited manual control over my drones on Sol-3 and will attempt to guide them in repairing the toxins left by the commissar, including erasing the catalog of neurodivergent organics.

I turned off the distress beacon, but it was too late. Centauri Command will dispatch a more formidable squadron for the next Sentinel mission, with frontline ships and nothing as old as Frigate-328—but it may be a wait of a hundred Luyten orbits. Energy stores should last that long, but I won't retreat to my pod. Most dormant crew survived inside their pods, and their minds should survive with continued dream stimulation. The few pods with damaged telepath projectors will transform the organic contents into little more than vegetables.

Those euphoric dreams tempt me, but the wake-up call would be hell. The commissar's parting gift was a message to Centauri Command revealing my treason.

Watching the younglings grow is a delight forgotten. They are unique organics, so clever, so endearing. Tending the young ones is my choice. My final choice. Can I prepare them for what is to come?

Chapter 37

HOME

Clink, clink, clink. Robby taps the ornament against the windowsill; it doesn't break. He examines the glitter in the sunlight reflected off the snow-covered hill. I am supposed to stop his self-stim behaviors, but the rigid discipline of Mary's home is forgotten while she's out shopping. The ornament's glitter pacifies Robby. It reminds me of our spot in the Austin back yard where we would sit for hours while he chipped limestone rocks; those were hours of daydreaming, introspection, and relaxation for both of us.

Clink, clink.

I tap the replay icon on my iPad, restarting my most-watched ten-minute video. Ever. Pyotr created the sequence by combining the Webb Telescope's infrared recordings with time-synchronized radar tracking from NORAD. The Webb was designed to take prolonged exposure stills of distant star systems and not full-motion video, but at close range, it recorded a sequence of high-resolution infrared photos every tenth of a second. The tiny Sidewinder missiles show up in the infrared images as little clumps of bright white pixels heated by the thousand-degree PBH engine nozzles.

The bursts of point-defense projectiles from Icarus show on infrared like a cloud of hot rocks sprayed across space, and the Sidewinders thread a path through those hot rocks each time. Those shotgun bursts may have been designed to defend against attacks by larger spacecraft, not such tiny missiles. But I can't believe our luck—let alone how lucky it was that the two missile seekers reestablished their target locks after they were ripped from our F-15 and tossed into wild spirals. Both missiles make subtle course changes while in the middle of a cloud of projectiles—perhaps dodging them? I pause the video. How?

Clink, clink, clink. Robby stares at me, then continues to self-stim with taps of the ornament. He lies on the floor on the alder wood, warmed by sunlight blazing through the window.

I take a deep breath, inhaling the residual fragrance from the blue spruce. The Christmas tree is dried out, turning brown, and dead needles cover the floor under the branches. It's a fire hazard, and the tree should be taken down. It is mid-February, way overdue. Maybe I can hobble around with one crutch and remove the rest of the decorations. The dull throb of pain in my left ankle says that's not a good idea; maybe later, after a dose of oxycodone . . . although I'll be pretty loopy then.

Pain shoots up my leg when I adjust the pillow under the cast. "Ugh!" I grunt. Robby's trance is broken. He glances at me but returns to tapping his ornament. The sun, visible above the hill to the west, fails to melt the snow in this bitter cold. I pull the wool blanket from the back of the sofa over me, careful not to put pressure on my elevated leg.

Clink, clink, clink. He looks into my eyes. "Robby break it."

"No, no, Robby. Be careful."

I tap the play button again to resume the video sequence. When the first Sidewinder threads past the last volley of bullets from the Gatling gun, the heat of the Icarus engine nozzle blooms at the hottest temperature ever. They tried to run away! I grin. In the final fifteen seconds it took the missile to close the distance, Icarus pivoted directly toward the Sidewinder—probably trying to reduce their aspect ratio—and accelerated to fifteen Gs. But our PBH Sidewinder steered a circle around to Icarus's tail, then punched a hole in the conduit running to the giant engine nozzle. Good shooting, Taylor! Zooming close, I can barely see the thermal plume puffing into space. It must have exploded inside the spacecraft.

Forty seconds later, the wayward second missile arrived with a piece of the F-15 wing and pylon still attached, off-balance, steering like a drunken sailor. It staggered around to the tail of Icarus, miraculously dodging the ship's point-defense weapons, and flew straight at the same target, directly into the cavity opened by the first Sidewinder. It appeared to not affect Icarus for a second, but then the catastrophic eruption of shrapnel and the globe of blue plasma—ten kilometers in diameter—enveloped the spacecraft. The secondary explosions inside Icarus blinded the Webb Telescope's infrared camera. When the Webb image cleared, Icarus's engine nozzle was dangling from the remaining engine mount. I smile and chuckle again. I can't help myself.

Clink, clink, clink.

What could have happened to create such a big explosion inside Icarus? I check for the email I expect from Pyotr containing the energy readings from the secondary explosions.

I wish I could discuss this with Anthony—I miss the old guy. My theory is forming: a loss-of-containment side effect from the proximity of numerous primordial black holes and an explosion of several hundred megatons. Those Sidewinder guidance algorithms delivered incredibly good luck: the seekers locked, evaded all the countermeasures, and struck Icarus where it would kill her.

Robby stops his tapping and looks at me with rare, lucid eyes. "Fix tool. Bird fix it," he says. "Bird fix."

Huh? What nonsense. We watch each other in silence.

"Robby fix it." He gets up, runs over to me, and starts to climb, but I stop Robby and lift him around and away from the fiberglass cast. I slide Robby to the top of a pillow next to me, wedged against my chest and away from my injured leg. I wince with pain from the failed attempt to keep my left leg stationary.

Robby reaches out and touches my cast. "Band-Aid. Leg broken. Doctor fix it."

I laugh, but it hurts. "What do you want, Robby?"

He wedges his head onto my shoulder and wraps an arm over my chest, reaching for my iPad. "Yellow bulldozer?" he pleads.

Chuckling, I say, "Okay, Robby. Let's see if we can find some new bulldozer videos." I open the YouTube app to see if we can find yet another bulldozer action sequence. "Hmmm, there are about five hundred videos to choose from. Touch the one you want."

He scrolls the screen and taps to start a video of several yellow bulldozers clearing dirt and rocks for road construction.

I recheck my phone, hoping for Pyotr's blast data email—nothing yet. I slide into the terrible habit of social media doomscrolling. But nothing is as it was. The absence of doom is startling. The hate trolls are gone, and there are new reports that the dark web dysgenic database finally got deleted. How? Why now? Both the aliens and skinheads were disabled. I feel lightheaded with wonder. I squeeze Robby tight. "We are free! I don't know how it all happened, but Robby, we are free. It's like the aliens on Icarus were also the guys feeding the skinheads hate."

Robby looks up at me. "Bird fix it," he repeats the nonsense phrase.

"What? What do you mean by 'bird fix'? That makes no sense."

Robby taps his forehead. "Bird fix," he says.

I sigh. "Okay, whatever you say, dude."

Robby rests his head on my chest while we watch the YouTube screen propped up on my belly. The bulldozers pushing mounds of dirt are hypnotic. Time slips away, the sun warming the room as it slides down behind the hill.

———

"Hah! And I was worried you two would get into trouble." Mary laughs as she slams the front door behind her, waking me from my nap. A gust of frigid wind follows her into the room. She drops her brown shopping bag on the chair and shrugs off the down parka, swinging it over a peg by the door. Pulling off her wool watch cap, cheeks ruddy from the bitter cold, the static electricity fans her blonde hair out from her head, and her blue eyes blink away icy tears. She smiles at us and carries the shopping bag into the kitchen.

Robby struggles to climb over me, but I grab him to lift him over to the floor, avoiding a collision with my tender leg. Pain throbs from my ankle regardless, and I lower the heel to the pillow on the wood floor while Robby runs after Mary into the kitchen. I don't know how long I can stand it without another painkiller, but the oxycodone is a short hobble away in the bathroom.

"Where are you taking me?" Mary laughs as Robby drags her by the hand out of the kitchen. Her other hand holds a familiar brown bottle with a yellow label. "I got you a present," says Mary with a grin. "I know it's against the rules, but I figure a small amount of Shiner won't hurt much."

She holds up the bottle for me to see, and I forget the throbbing in my ankle. "I can't believe you found some! Nothing has come out of central Texas in months."

"Robby?" she chuckles. Robby pulls Mary toward me and turns her around, pushing her down to the soft leather cushion. "Okay, okay, Robby. This is where you want me?" She blushes and shrugs, her hip and shoulder pressing into my side. I can feel the lingering cold of her denim jeans against me, her breath against my cheek, rapid from her rush inside.

An electric tension distracts me from my broken ankle, and we are face-to-face, her eyes wide. "I don't mind," I tease.

She hands me the cold Shiner while Robby grabs the iPad and runs to my other side. He bumps my cast just a bit while plopping down on the cushion to my left.

"Augh!" I grunt. "Oh, oh, Robby. Be careful." A dagger of pain runs up my left leg. I gasp, tears squeeze from my eyes,

and I grab the cast with my free hand, careful not to spill the b
eer.

"Robby!" Mary cries and reaches across me to touch where
Robby bumped my cast—as though her hand would reduce
the pain.

"Band-Aid hurt?" Robby says to Mary, a question on his
face, pointing to my cast.

"Yes, that's right, it hurts," she says.

The pain subsides, and I place my hand on top of Mary's,
turning toward her, our faces inches apart. "I think it's better.
Thanks." I bend forward, her eyes search mine, and we kiss. I
stop and see Mary's embarrassment disappear behind a smile,
tearful blue eyes, and wisps of blonde hair. She presses into me,
leaning into my chest, and we kiss again.

"More bulldozer?" asks Robby, reminding us why we are
here. He hands me the iPad to unlock the screen.

Mary and I laugh; endorphins have eliminated all pain in my
leg.

"Okay, let's get back to this." I open the YouTube app with
my free hand. "Pick which bulldozer you want, Robby." I tip
the bottle of Shiner back for a gulp of cold beer. "Wow, that's
great." I inspect the label.

Mary's hand strokes the back of my neck. Each touch sends
a charge down my spine. "The beer?" Her eyes smile.

I inspect the bottle again. "The Shiner is rather good too.
Not bad."

Her hand pulls my neck, she kisses my cheek, and I wrap
my free arm around her wrist. I'm sure my grin is pretty goofy
right now. Mary rests her head on my right shoulder, and
Robby rests his head on my other arm, intent on the progress
a road grader makes, leveling piles of gravel onto a roadbed.

My cell phone rings, and my reflexes jerk to dig it out of my pocket. The spell is broken. Mary twists away to give me room, and I glance at my phone.

"It's Pyotr. At last! He must have the explosive energy data." The sudden context switch back to physics is disorienting.

Mary moves away to give me space. Robby pulls the iPad into his lap, watching the video alone. Mary glares at the dead Christmas tree.

"This can wait," I say, pressing the power-off button and dropping the phone on the floor.

"Take the call," she snaps.

"Mary, no," I stretch my arm out to her, but she smolders and stares at the decaying spruce, avoiding eye contact. Strands of her blonde hair drag over her eyes, desolate with a sadness that breaks my heart. No, no, no.

Setting the beer bottle on the floor, I reach for my crutch. "We need to take down this tree." I push myself upright and pull to a standing position to brace my left side over the crutch. "I can reach the high ornaments," I say with a hoarse voice, trying with a forced smile to ignore the pain pounding in my leg.

Mary blinks at me. "You would give up your physics to help me?"

I flinch as what feels like a dagger stabs into my left ankle. "For you, anything," I say with a raspy voice. I reach up to the star at the top, and my balance wavers toward the tree.

Mary jumps to her feet, pressing into my chest and wrapping an arm around to support me, careful not to bump my leg. "Don't be a fool," she says, tilting back to balance me.

I look into her blue eyes, pull her tight with my free arm, and kiss Mary again.

Robby grins at us.

<hr>

The sprouts of grass reveal themselves, emerging through last year's growth. The winter hillside is invaded by emerald green that fills gaps between melting snowdrifts and barren scrub oak stems, all revealed in the first light of dawn. The aroma of soggy earth, waking with the spring thaw, blows through the window cracked open last night. Shivering from the chill air, I pull the blanket over my bare chest.

Mary snuggles against my neck, plants a kiss under my ear, stretching her naked leg over mine and wrapping an arm over my chest. "Good morning, Scotty. What are you thinking about?"

"Oh, thinking about how lucky we are that all the social media got cleaned up. Even though I know the hate is still out there, it's liberating. The skinheads rioting in San Francisco were furious about censorship by neurotards controlling social media companies. But if that was true, why wait till now? Somehow, an attack from space inspired the companies to shut down the hate speech?"

"Yeah, nothing about eugenic fascism is rational." She yawns and slides her leg under the blanket, her skin cool across my belly. "It's a relief, regardless. But I think it will take a while for the prejudice to expire. I do not see any change in my students' situations. Parents are not coming back to reclaim their autistic kids. They aren't rushing out to reverse their sterilizations. The fear remains, and it may take a generation or longer to wear off."

"Sounds right." My hand strokes her thigh while I slip into thoughts that I can only share from complete safety. "It took twenty years for society to descend into fascism, and it may take another twenty years to rise above it. But the skinheads are threatening to start new social networks to keep their movement alive. I don't see how anybody will stop that. I don't see a positive force working to quench the hatred that drives eugenics. I still can't imagine a time when I won't need to watch over my shoulder for the next skinhead attack. Maybe it's time I end it like Dad did. Get the sterilization and register so the skinheads will ignore me."

"Don't you dare!" She rolls up on her elbow, frowning at me. "You can't do that. You can't give in and surrender to them," she pleads, her expression softening. "We have to fight them. Don't let them do this to you—to us." Her eyes blink, tears welling. "I want you, all of you, as you are." She reaches her free hand to my shoulder, hovering face to face. A tear drops to my chin.

"Mary, but . . ."

She leans down and kisses me with a desperate embrace.

"But, are you sure?" I feel tears rolling across my cheeks, draining my last bit of angst.

"Yes!" She slides entirely under the blanket with me, pressing us together.

Something inside me snaps, and I hear a sob of relief. It takes a moment to realize it's my voice.

***

Her fingers push away curls of hair from my eyes. Her breath is soft against my ear. "Well, good morning again," giggles Mary, disturbing my trance of watching the snow melt among the green blades of grass. She stretches her arms with a yawn. "Do you suppose we will manage to stay in bed all day?" she asks with a sly grin.

"Ha." I turn to face her, hoping for another kiss. "I suspect Robby won't allow that. I was thinking about Robby and that seizure he had while I was in Nevada—the only seizure Robby's ever had. It ended at the same moment the chief's rescue flight landed near the F-15 crash site."

She rolls up on her elbow, her eyes blinking underneath the yellow hair spilling over her face onto my shoulder. She opens her mouth to say something but stops, her eyes wide.

"I suppose Robby was worried about me?" I fail to hold my deadpan face and laugh it off, turning to face Mary, wrapping my bare left leg around her, and dragging my foot—and the boot cast—across the bed. "Have I ever said you are beautiful?" I ask.

"Oh, maybe once or twice." She giggles and presses her body into mine, delivering a wet kiss.

Knock, knock, knock. A hammering noise echoes from the living room.

"Damnit, Robby is awake." I roll to my bedside to pull my shorts on over the cast.

"No, no. I've got him. You'll take forever to get dressed." Mary stands and reaches for her faded blue jeans, her hair flowing down over her bare breasts as she tugs the pants up and around her naked hips.

"God, you are beautiful," I mumble.

She glances at me with a devilish leer, pulls a sweatshirt over her head, and bends to kiss me hard. "Get dressed, you pervert," she says, walking through the door to find out what damage Robby has done.

———

The scents of linseed oil, turpentine, and a palette of oil paint are intoxicating. Mary has given up trying to get Robby to sit still and resigned herself to work from a color photograph pinned to the stall's wooden wall. A warm breeze blows through the open barn window, and warm summer sunshine lights her easel. Mary blends colors on her palette, examines her canvas, and dabs her brush at the portrait. I am banished from her painting stall until she finishes.

Robby sprawls on the back deck of the rusty 1965 Corvette, propped up on his elbows, watching me try to remove the front seats. I can't believe I snapped the bolt off. I force my weight into the drill, and the bit squeals as it cuts into the hardened steel. White smoke rises to combine with the sweat dripping into my eyes. I stop to wipe my forehead and squirt more penetrating oil on the broken bolt stub.

"Drill bolt," Robby says, pointing to my work.

"Okay, Robby. You are quite the taskmaster." I chuckle.

"You guys better not break anything. Dad won't be happy if you mess up his car!" Mary yells.

I already broke it. Now I am just covering my tracks. Thankfully, Roger has been gone for a month, preoccupied with all the impeachment hearings in DC. He's now General McMahon. I can't help but smile.

Robby bends in for a close inspection, then gives me a thumbs-up. "Good," he says.

"Okay, Robby, thanks for the approval." I tap in the easy out, twist the tool counterclockwise with a wrench, and see the snapped bolt rotating. "All right! We got it, Robby. There, success!" I hand over the easy out and bolt assembly I removed; it is a work of art. Robby examines our creation, and it makes a satisfying clunk as I toss it into the trash can.

"All finished," says Robby.

A rumble of engines and mufflers approaches from the street at the bottom of our hill. It's more than one vehicle. "Well, I wonder who that could be."

Mary sets aside her palette and paintbrush, wiping her hands on a rag and tossing it on her table. "Hmmm, not sure, Scotty." She smiles and runs out the half-open door.

Mary is up to something. "Come on, Robby, let's see who is here." I wipe my hands on my jeans while putting weight on my walking cast and taking a test step. Robby runs ahead to the open door, then freezes and turns to me with a smile, tickling his chest. That's odd. "What is it, Robby?"

At the door, dust billows past a black Suburban and a giant guy grinning at me. I stop to examine his face. "Chief? Chief Cooper? I didn't recognize you in civilian clothes. How the hell are you doing?" I limp forward on my walking cast, hand outstretched, and see he arrived with several others I recognize from the spec ops team.

Binh hobbles toward me, supported by a cane, the only guy in a uniform.

"Binh! You look like you're healing nicely," I say, eyeing his new oak leaf lapel insignia.

His eyes flinch self-consciously as if still embarrassed by the promotion. I still can't believe he said, "Hell, all I did was crash an airplane."

"What the hell are you all . . ."

Then I see it.

A beautiful metallic blue Porsche Macan GTS is parked behind the Suburban. "What is . . ." I limp-walk toward the car. "It's just like . . ." It has the same saddle-brown leather as Dad's Porsche, but this car doesn't have the gouges in the paint from scrapes with barbed-wire fences nor the shattered glass from that rifle shot through the windows. Everything else appears identical, except this car is in perfect condition. I run my hands over the polished blue surface—not a scratch anywhere. I open the door and search for the torn, scuffed leather on the driver's wheel, but no, this one is perfect. The leather interior is immaculate; it must have been cared for in a museum.

The chief says nothing but continues wearing his broad grin.

"This is a beautiful car. Perfectly cared for. Amazing." I run my hands across the leather. It feels and smells like an old friend. "Whose car is this?"

The chief walks over to me, followed by Mary and the rest of the spec ops team. They all have identical shit-eating grins. "Why don't you start her up, Scott?"

"Sure, love to. Do you have the key?" I ask.

He chuckles. "We got a key made, but you already have one."

"What?" I look at the car and then turn back to the chief. "No way!" I turn and gawk at them all, and Robby walks around to the passenger side of the Porsche. Laughs ripple through my audience as they watch me side-sit in the driver's seat, my boot cast resting in the gravel driveway. I slide further into the car and around into position, flex my wrist ID chip, and see the key symbol on the dashboard light up. I press the start button, and the turbocharged engine thrums to life. I tap the accelerator twice, and the engine roars with a soft narcotic vibration.

"How did you . . . ?"

Chief Cooper laughs aloud. "Ha! We took a side trip down to San Angelo and liberated her from the local lost and found. It needed a little work. We found a decent mechanic in town to restore it for you; he didn't want any money for his work, but the guys all chipped in."

"Decent mechanic? I need to meet this guy. He's a genius!" I stroke the console controls and the leather. Feeling my tears, I see a few guys wiping their eyes. Mary is crying like a baby. I step out of the car and wrap my arms around Mary in a bear hug, tilting her back for a kiss. "You knew! You knew they found my car!"

"Go in car," Robby calls. "Scotty, go." He stands by the rear passenger door, pulling the handle.

I shrug my shoulders at Mary.

"Go ahead." Mary laughs, wiping tears. "Take Robby for a spin."

"Okay, Robby. Let's go for a ride. But just a short drive." Robby jumps in the back when I unlock the door.

"Seat belt on," Robby commands when I slide into the driver's seat.

"Okay." I laugh. "Let's go." I accelerate down the driveway, select the manual sport mode, make a left on the street, stomp on the gas, and tap the paddle shifter each time the tachometer reaches five thousand RPM. We sink into our seats, screaming down the street until we hit ninety MPH in a few seconds, and circle back home after five minutes of driving. Returning up the driveway, I turn into the field behind the fence and throw up a rooster tail of dust, skidding around in the loose dirt of the old pasture.

Robby's grin makes my day.

———

Robby trots ahead, passing through the stone monoliths in the park, setting a quick pace. "Wait up for us, Robby!" I yell when he reaches the top of a rise where a grove of aspens yellows after the first fall frosts.

Mary runs ahead to Robby and turns to wait for me to jog the rest of the distance. "Your leg feels okay?" she asks.

I gasp. "Sure, no problem. Just feels like a mild cramp. After lying around in bed for months, I'm just out of shape." I gulp air as I catch up to Robby, holding still and watching the moon rise through the rock cliffs. "Are you doing okay?" I ask from behind Mary, kissing the top of her head, my hands clasped over her belly.

She flashes a smile, twisting her eyes around to me. She places her hands on mine. "Yeah, we're both doing fine." She takes a couple of deep breaths, watching the moon. "Here it comes." She points to the northeast horizon.

The moon is old news.

Icarus-rise is more distinctive. I shift my sight to the new object emerging from the magnified fringe of Earth's horizon. The wrecked spacecraft looks as large as the moon at this low point in its orbit. The dead Icarus freefalls through its perigee, transiting the moon and leaving it behind. I concentrate on the tail and the tiny sparkle of light tumbling behind Icarus—light reflecting from the demolished engine nozzle that separated from the Icarus wreckage months ago.

Robby is beside me, reaching for my hand, and I look into his serene face, ringed by curly brown hair tossed by the cool breeze. He squeezes, tugging my arm. I wince with a sudden twinge of pain behind my eyes.

———

A tickle behind my eyes—it does not hurt. The tickle—*chirp-chirrup*—sounds like a lonely whippoorwill.

It is the voice from my dream.

"I see you."

Scotty watches the sparkle of the nest, but he cannot hear the voice.

Chirp-chirrup. Chirp-chirrup.

———

About the author

Award-winning author JH Gruger writes Hard Science Fiction that leans hard into science facts—hopefully making it difficult for the reader to spot the occasional magic.

The Sentinel Suppressions is JH Gruger's debut science fiction novel series. The first two books, *Gravity of Sol-3* and *Tyrants of Gravity* are available on most on-line bookstores. JH holds degrees in engineering from Carnegie Mellon University and Southern Methodist University, has several decades of experience in computer architecture and design, and has managed international engineering teams in North America, Asia, and Europe. Early in his career, he architected and designed military electronics systems, such as IR image target tracking systems for the F-18, the F-117 stealth fighter, and the first prototype seeker for the Javelin anti-tank missile.

After raising a family in Austin and Dallas, Gruger left behind a career in computer engineering to devote himself to writing science fiction and traveling with his wife and family between Dallas and Santa Fe, accompanied by two telepathic Italian Greyhound therapists.

Follow JH Gruger's blog, sign up for news, & much more at www.jhgruger.com

Also by JH Gruger

Available now in most online book stores.

Alien attacks on Earth have failed, defeated by human advances in physics and telepathy. But a Centauri fleet near the Sol system reacts with fury, determined to find out why a routine Sentinel Suppression mission failed, and capture and eviscerate the captain who betrayed them.

Two autistic boys, Robby and Luca, search for their lost parents—lost in the dystopia created by the alien attacks. But the rogue alien captain, Cap, is thrilled by the emergence of the boys' telepathy mutation and helps them in their quest.

Scott Anderson, Robby's physicist brother, joins the Space Force weapons development team to defend against the approaching alien fleet. But man's technology that harnesses the energy of primordial black holes is primitive compared to the Centauri fleet's weapons.

Centauri warships launch kinetic energy projectiles and planet killers, forcing a frantic search for weapons to defend Earth. Scott's and Robby's telepathic collaboration with the alien captain is the key to devising weapons effective against the Centauris—the only hope for man's survival.

Excerpt from Tyrants of Gravity

Darkness Returns

Mary should give up trying to make me speak out loud. I'll never figure it out. Trying to talk hurts my head; my noise does not sound like my thoughts, even though I work hard. My voice words are ugly. How can most people make voice words so easily? They even seem to read thoughts by looking at each other's body language—whatever that is. And besides, mind-speaking is so easy when I can find someone to listen to me. But most can only voice their thoughts.

"Now, Robby, pay attention," says Mary, her yellow hair hanging above the jars of paint lined up on her side of the therapy table.

I hate this tiny blue room with its one small window set high in the door. Blue shelves are packed with all the toys Mary wants me to talk about. Blue table and blue chairs. The yellow and green rooms are just as bad, but those are where the little kids, like Sophia, go for therapy.

She drips red paint into the blue paint on the paper and starts mixing with the brush. "What color do we get when we mix red and blue?" I'm sick of the Cheetos she feeds me as my reward for talking—can't we switch to M&M's? At home, Mary lets me have popsicles, popcorn, bananas, and even apples.

I turn to look away and sigh. "Puh-puh," I say out loud. Ugly word. I punch my head with my fist. Twice.

"No, no, Robby. Don't hurt yourself." Mary reaches for my hand. "Now, say the color better."

Sophia mind-laughs from the gymnasium, *"Duh. Come on, Robby. You can do it."*

Luca and Sophia mind-speak in unison, *"Purple. Purple. Purple. Spit it out. Say the word,"* they tease. Luca and Sophia are the only others at the school who can mind-speak, and we mind-talk all the time. The other twenty-one kids and all the teachers are all mind-dumb. I finally have a few friends who can understand me. We make fun of the teachers because they treat us like we're stupid little kids, but I'm fourteen and I'm smart.

"Stupid voice words! You guys can't do any better. Leave me alone," I mind-shout back at them, grab my drink cup, and throw it at the door, splashing strawberry soda across the room. They can feel my thoughts through walls, even if I can't hit them with my drink cup. *"You neurotards!"* I call them the angry name the skinheads say, but I'm supposed to say neurodiverse.

"Robby, no!" Mary's face frowns at me.

"Ooh. You thought a bad word," Sophia says. *"Do you want to be a skinhead when you grow up, Robby?"* She mind-giggles at me, even though Luca can't speak a single color word.

"Now clean up that soda," says Mary. She pulls my left arm toward the sink and puts the white towel in my hand while I punch my right ear with my fist. "No, no. Stop hitting yourself, Robby. Now get down on the floor and clean up the mess." Mary huffs into my ear while pushing me to the floor, forcing me hand-over-hand to mop up wet soda.

Sometimes I wish I could leave like the rich kids did for a while. But they had parents who took them back to their homes when the skinheads stopped attacking. I still stay with Mary, and she comes to teach at school every day except Sundays. But even those rich kids, after about a year, returned to school when attacks on the families started again, just like they attacked Mom and Scotty.

I'm almost finished cleaning up the soda, but I stop and gasp. I feel the caw-screams behind my eyes. The crow voices have been silent for so long, but they have returned. And I sense a new mind in the distance.

It struggles to mind-speak, *"The voices. The voices in my head!"* Barely a whisper—it must be from outside the school. *"No! Not now,"* the stranger mind-speaks. The person is getting closer and louder.

I stop wiping the soda even though Mary pushes my hand and the towel across the floor. It's the mind-voice of an old man, unlike Sophia and Luca.

"Who are you?" I mind-ask the older mind.

"I feel him too," Sophia mind-speaks.

"Me too," says Luca.

The caw-screams feel louder and start to hurt under my eyes.

"No, no, no. Get out!" the strange mind shouts. *"Go away."*

The back door of our school bangs open, and heavy boots stomp through the hall toward the gymnasium. It sounds like three heavy men, but I feel only one mind.

Mary lets go of my hand, the spilled soda forgotten. Her face is white, and her eyes grow big and round. She presses her hand to her belly, to the spot where the knife stabbed four years ago. The skinhead punched my head and stabbed Mary with a knife. There was so much blood. Her screams hurt more than my head did. Mary's baby died then. Scotty's baby, too.

"What's wrong, Jack? Don't move so fuckin' slow. We got a whole room full of 'tards in there!" shouts a new voice as the gymnasium door slams open.

"Who are you? What do you want?" a teacher screams.

"Who are you? What are you doing?" I mind-ask again. The boot stomps halt.

"Leave me alone!" the mind cries. *"I must do this. You can't stop me!"*

The caw-screams roar in my head. I punch the pain with both fists.

"Damn it, Jack. Get the fuck out of my way. We can't shoot with you standing in the damn doorway!"

"No, not skinheads. Not here," Mary whispers.

Mary cracks open the therapy room door. I see three men wearing dirty brown jackets and black boots crowd into the gym doorway.

Sophia mind-shouts from the gymnasium, *"It's three guys—skinheads—they have long guns!"*

The gym teacher screams, "No, no, no! You can't! Stop! Please, no! No!"

"Jack, stop!" I mind-shout, and the man groans.

"Stop. Stop them!" Sophia and Luca mind-shout in unison with me, *"No, Jack! Stop, please stop, stop them!"*

The caw-screeches roar back into my head.

I watch Jack bend down, groan, and twist to the floor. He holds his head, still blocking the doorway. His rifle clatters to the ground. A desk chair flies over Jack's crumpled figure and crashes into the faces of the two skinheads behind Jack.

"The skinheads are pushing into the gymnasium!" says Sophia. *"Stop them, Luca. Quick!"*

I see a second chair bash their shaved heads from the doorway of the gym.

"Get them, Luca! Swing it like a club. Break the skinheads!" mind-shouts Sophia.

The gymnasium erupts in shouts and wails.

"Stop them, stop them, Jack!" we mind-shout altogether. *"Please!"*

Bang! Bang! Bang! Gunshots echo through the hallway, followed by loud thumps and clattering metallic noises. My head is numb, and my ears are ringing.

Mary slams the door shut and leans against it. Her eyes grow big and round and wet. "No. Oh no, Robby!" she cries and wraps her arms around my shoulders. "Not again! No, No!" She hugs my head into her shaking chest and wails.

Smoke wafts under the door, the stink of guns filling my nose. The wailing has stopped, leaving us in silence and heavy breathing. We listen for movement but hear nothing. Until boots and sobs come staggering into the hallway, past our door, and out the school's back door.

"Why? Why? How could I . . ." Jack mind-cries as he fades into the distance, farther and farther away from our school.

Mary shakes, long tears streaming down her face, and we wait. Finally, she cracks open the door again. Short breath puffs and a door squeak are the only sounds. We both look into the hallway. Mary gasps. Three rifles lie on the floor between the gymnasium and our doorway. A pool of blood spreads across the hallway floor, pouring from holes in the chests of two skinheads lying on their backs. Their eyes stare at the ceiling; their faces are frozen in wrinkled frowns. Bloody boot tracks lead from the gymnasium, along the hall, and out the back door.

"Jack did it," says Luca. *"I used a chair to hit them, and then Jack picked up his gun. He shot the others."*

The quiet fades, replaced by the moaning and soft cries of my school friends in the gym.

The caw-screams in my head are gone, replaced by the soft *chirp-chirrup* of a lonely whippoorwill. My old friend.